DAYS OF SUN AND GLORY

Also by Anna Belfrage

Praise for The Graham Saga

"A brilliantly enjoyable read" *HNS Reviews*

"This is a series that will take both your heart and your head to places both light and dark, disheartening and uplifting, fantastic and frightening, but all utterly unforgettable"
WTF are you reading

"Anna writes deep, emotional historical novels, adding the fantastical element of the time slip and a "what if?" scenario, and creates for us a world in which to be lost in on rainy days and weekend reading fests."
Oh for the Hook of a Book

"It seems Belfrage cannot put a foot wrong. Long may she continue to give us installments in this truly wonderful series." *Kincavel's Korner*

"An admirably ambitious series" *The Bookseller*

Further to excellent reviews, The Graham Saga has been awarded multiple B.R.A.G. Medallions, five HNS Editor's Choice, has been shortlisted for the HNS Indie Book of the Year in 2014, and the sixth book in the series won the HNS Indie Book of the Year in 2015.

Praise for *In the Shadow of the Storm*
(first book in The King's Greatest Enemy)

ANNA
BELFRAGE

DAYS
of SUN &
GLORY

Matador
9 Priory Business Park,
Wistow Road, Kibworth Beauchamp,
Leicestershire. LE8 0RX
Tel: (+44) 116 279 2299
Email: books@troubador.co.uk
Web: www.troubador.co.uk/matador

ISBN 978 1785893 513 (pb)
ISBN 978 9198324 518 (eb)

British Library Cataloguing in Publication Data.
A catalogue record for this book is available from the British Library.

Typeset in 11pt Bembo by Troubador Publishing Ltd, Leicester, UK

Matador is an imprint of Troubador Publishing Ltd

This book is dedicated to my very own
honourable knight in armour, my Johan

England in the early fourteenth century was not a happy realm...

In 1321, the barons of England decided they'd had enough and rose in rebellion against their king, Edward II. They were sick of the king's rapacious favourites – the Lords Despenser, father and son – and this time they prevailed on the king to exile them, forever. For a short while it seemed the barons, led by Lord Roger Mortimer and Earl Thomas of Lancaster, had won. But fate is fickle and Edward II was not about to take this recent humiliation lying down. By late autumn of 1321, the king had assembled an army and rode west to punish his rebellious barons. Thomas of Lancaster retired north, leaving Lord Mortimer to face the king alone.

Against the full might of the king, Mortimer was helpless, and in January 1322 he submitted to his king, was struck in irons and transported to the Tower. Edward then turned his attention north, and by March Lancaster was dead. Everyone supposed it was but a matter of time before Mortimer was hanged, drawn and quartered, but for some reason, Edward stayed his hand.

In August of 1323, Roger Mortimer escaped the Tower and fled to France.

In England, an enraged and fearful Edward regretted not having killed his greatest enemy while he still had the chance...

Chapter 1

God forgive her, but Kit de Guirande had every intention of disliking Queen Isabella on sight. After months of listening to her husband's voice growing warm with adoration whenever he spoke of the queen, Kit felt entitled to hate this woman, who, apparently, was the equivalent of a heavenly angel come to earth.

She hurried after her limping husband as best as she could, too tired and confused to do more than glance at the magnificence of the royal Palace of Westminster – not that much of its splendour was visible in the flaring light of the few torches still burning in the sconces. If anything, this hasty trot in the early hours of the morning increased her resentment towards the unknown queen. Why send for them at this Godforsaken hour, why did the queen require that Sir Adam and his wife attend on her before dawn had properly broken? Kit said as much to Adam, but all she got for her trouble was a reproving look and an exasperated shake of his head.

"Better she sees us now, before anyone else is up and about," he said.

Kit rolled her eyes – discreetly. Of course; the queen had summoned Adam this early to discuss their favourite subject, that of Lord Roger Mortimer, at present in exile in France. If Kit was tired of listening to descriptions of Queen Isabella, that was nothing compared to the mental exhaustion she experienced whenever Adam spoke of his beloved Lord Mortimer.

Four months and counting since Lord Mortimer's spectacular escape from the Tower, four months in which Adam had been hounded by Lord Despenser, the only thing keeping Kit's husband safe from Mortimer's mortal enemy being the fact that Adam had pledged himself to Prince Edward of Windsor, heir to the throne. Kit glanced at her man, sending a fervent prayer to God that He would continue protecting him, keeping him far away from Despenser's grasping hands. She repeated this prayer on a daily basis, and had done so ever since Lord Mortimer fled for France.

As per Lord Despenser, royal chancellor and de facto ruler of England – what with King Edward giving his favourite anything his favourite desired – Adam was a traitor. Despenser insisted that Adam had helped Lord Mortimer escape, which was true, but fortunately there was no proof, and Despenser's attempts to have Adam arrested and turned over into his own tender care for further interrogation had been foiled, twice by the Earl of Pembroke and once by the queen herself. And thank the Lord for that: Kit had no illusions as to how her husband would fare in Despenser's hands.

Ever since Roger Mortimer's escape, the kingdom of England had sunk into a state of terror. The king – and Lord Despenser – lashed out viciously against anyone potentially involved in Mortimer's escape, and over the last few months countless men had been dragged before assizes, attainted and gruesomely executed, based on the fact that they had once served Roger Mortimer. Rotting corpses adorned gibbets all over the southwest of the country, and destitute widows and orphans were evicted from their homes, left to starve and die during the approaching winter.

The king's rage spilled over onto others as well: London merchants known to be Mortimer supporters had been severely punished, and recently the Bishops of Hereford and Lincoln had been accused and found guilty of helping Mortimer. Kit shook her head: so many men whose lives were permanently impaired on behalf of Roger Mortimer. And Hugh Despenser was not done – he intended to use Mortimer's escape to rid himself of every enemy he had in England.

Kit suppressed a little shiver and threw a hasty look over her shoulder. Lord Despenser was here, in residence with the king, and even if she had so far not encountered him, she knew it was but a matter of time before she'd be confronted by his dark eyes, his wet mouth and his wandering hands. Kit clasped her hands together, remembering all too well

2

just how violent Lord Despenser could become should he be sufficiently riled.

"Watch out!"

Kit stumbled; Adam's hand flew out, gripping her by the elbow and thereby stopping her from overbalancing down the short flight of stairs.

"Use your eyes, sweeting," he said with a little smile, sliding his hold down from her elbow to clasp her hand instead. She pressed herself against him, an affectionate gesture that had him tightening his hold on her hand, his lips brushing briefly at her brow.

They hastened on. Kit had a stitch up her side, and at one point she had to stop, clutching at her rounded belly. Her hand smoothed the cloth that covered their growing child – an inactive babe that gave her very little trouble beyond the odd pang of pain in her lower back. Adam gave her a concerned look.

"You should not have come," he said. "A woman great with child does best staying at home."

She gave him a level look. "I wanted to." Kit straightened up and hurried on.

Twice this autumn, Adam had been called to court at the behest of his lord, the young Edward of Windsor. Twice, Kit had spent her days in constant anxiety, fearing the summons was only intended to lure Adam into Despenser's waiting hands. So when the royal messenger had come riding down their lane some weeks back, demanding that Adam de Guirande attend his lord over Christmastide, Kit had insisted on coming along, no matter how great with child she might be. After all, she'd told him, he had promised her that he would never leave her behind again – a futile promise, she knew, as Adam had little say in how his life was ordered, but he had promised.

At present, she harboured certain regrets: she would have preferred spending the middle of winter at Tresaints, in the comfort of their own manor and surrounded by their loyal household. But Adam had no choice, so here they were.

"Here." The pageboy leading the way came to a halt, gesturing at a small door set discreetly into the wall.

"Very much subterfuge," Kit murmured.

"It is best that way," Adam replied, just as low, before stepping aside to allow her to enter first.

After the dark of the passage, the room Kit entered was surprisingly bright. The windows that gave to the east were unshuttered and set with precious glass, allowing the soft light of the impending dawn to spill into the room. There were lit candles everywhere, the fire in the hearth had recently been rekindled into crackling life, and standing in the centre of the room was the queen herself.

She was just as beautiful as people said she was. A spurt of dark green jealousy surged through Kit as she took in the elegant figure of the queen, dressed in silk that shimmered somewhere in between lavender and pink. In the privacy of her chambers, the queen's hair had been left to float loose around her head, soft, dark curls caressing the white skin of her neck. A veil so sheer it was ludicrous was held in place by a circlet of sweet water pearls, and beneath elegant brows eyes as green as emeralds regarded Kit with mild curiosity, a smile tugging at her perfect mouth.

The queen moved towards them, all elegant, willowy grace – a far cry from Kit's rounded state. Kit placed a hand on her belly and dipped into a reverence, dropping her gaze to the floor.

"Rise," the queen said. Even her voice was perfect, melodious and low. With Adam's support, Kit straightened up. "Here." The queen gestured at the window seat. "Please sit, Lady de Guirande. That child of yours seems heavy." She smiled at Adam. "Big men make big children, do they not?"

To Kit's annoyance, Adam gave the queen a brilliant smile, for all the world looking like a lovesick whelp, before raising her hand to his mouth and placing a reverential kiss on it. Kit frowned and concentrated her attention on her girdle. The queen laughed.

"Contrary to what people may say, I am not in the habit of consuming handsome men for breakfast."

Kit's cheeks heated.

"In fact," the queen continued, "I stay clear of all men, so your husband's virtue is safe with me, Lady de Guirande."

"My lady," Adam said, shaking his head. "My wife would never—"

"Wouldn't she?" the queen interrupted.

Adam turned to look at Kit, who did her best to avoid his eyes.

"Kit," he groaned, "how can you think—"

"Think what? That you hold our queen in much affection?" Kit almost bit her tongue off. Now why would she be so foolish as to say that out loud? Adam gave her a reproving look.

The queen laughed again. "You are quite the dim-witted creature, aren't you?"

Queen or not, that remark had Kit considering raking her nails over Queen Isabella's complacent face.

"I am not...my lady," Kit replied.

"No? And yet you don't see what I see? It has been made abundantly clear to me, Lady Katherine, that as far as your husband is concerned there is only one sun in his sky, and that sun is his beloved wife."

Kit looked at her husband, who had gone an interesting hue of bright pink. "He said that?"

"More or less," the queen said. "Maybe not quite as poetically, but I am right, am I not, Sir Adam?"

In reply, Adam set his hand to Kit's face, his thumb stroking gently over the ugly scar that marred her left cheek, courtesy of a far-too-close encounter with Lord Despenser some eighteen months ago. "Yes, my lady queen. This is my sun, my moon – my everything."

Kit's vision blurred. She leaned into his touch, covering his hand with her own. He had never said anything like that in front of other people before. Her Adam preferred his declarations of love to be in private – and in bed. Kit drew in a shaky breath and decided that Queen Isabella deserved a second chance.

"And now to the matters at hand," the queen said, her voice brisk. She clapped her hands, and a page brought in spiced wine, lacing the air with the distinctive scents of nutmeg and cloves. More clapped hands, and another page appeared with miniature wafers, bread and cheese, before scurrying off to leave them alone.

Kit settled back in the window seat, a goblet of wine in her hand, and took in her surroundings. The room not only bathed in light, it was also ablaze with brilliant colour, from the royal blue walls with miniature fleur-de-lis strewn over them, to the bedstead painted white and red, with gold inlays. The floorboards were covered by Turkish carpets, little squares of crimson and blue that Kit would never dream setting a foot upon, so beautiful were they. Adam came to sit beside her, while the queen paced like a caged leopard as she spoke.

"I'm under constant surveillance," she said. "Despenser weaves his web of whispered half-truths tighter round my husband's head and heart, and with every day, my lord king distances himself from me, regarding me as a roe deer would a wolf." She laughed harshly. "Despenser insists I was involved in Lord Mortimer's escape, and I dare say my husband is inclined to believe him."

Given that the queen *had* been involved – albeit indirectly – Kit could not dredge up much indignation on her behalf. But as Queen Isabella went on with her descriptions of how her life was being curtailed, Kit felt a twinge of pity – and fear – on behalf of this magnificent woman who was more or less held a prisoner in her own court.

"And this situation in Gascony doesn't help," the queen finished. "I dare say the king holds me personally responsible for every reprehensible act a Frenchman may commit, starting with the actions of my dear, royal brother." She grimaced. "Charles will never back down regarding Gascony, and Edward is as stubborn as my brother, so God alone knows how this will end." She broke off, muttered a prayer, and crossed herself.

"But my lady, this may work in your favour." Adam leapt to his feet to replenish the queen's empty goblet. Kit gave her husband an annoyed look. Did he need to be quite so attentive?

"How?" Queen Isabella sank down on the window seat beside Kit.

"Who is better placed than you to negotiate a truce?" Adam asked.

The queen sipped at her wine. "Maybe you're right," she said after some moments of silence. "I could write to Charles and—"

The door banged open and the room was filled with ladies in wimples and veils, surcoats of embroidered silk and velvet, and girdles that glittered with jewels and gold thread. Kit retreated into her corner and fiddled with the sheer length of silk that covered her head, fully aware of just how inconspicuous she was in comparison.

"What is the meaning of this?" The tallest of the ladies addressed the queen sharply. A sequence of unicorns embroidered in gold and silver pranced along the hem of her light-blue surcoat, her kirtle a darker shade of blue.

"The meaning of what?" Queen Isabella rose, her chin lifted demandingly as she stared down the ladies, standing as immobile as a statue until they all sank down into deep reverences.

"My queen," the first lady mumbled.

"And good morning to you too, Lady Eleanor," the queen replied.

Kit studied the lady with increased curiosity. So this was the famous Eleanor de Clare, niece to the king and Hugh Despenser's wife. Eleanor straightened up and glanced at Kit. Sharp blue eyes assessed and discarded her as uninteresting before darting over to Adam, where they lingered for substantially longer.

Adam bowed, and Lady Eleanor inclined her head and rounded on the queen.

"This is not seemly, my lady," she scolded. "A man in your chambers!" From under Lady Eleanor's loosely draped veil peeked a strand of red-gold hair, and for all that she had given that serpent Despenser numerous children, she retained a slim figure, adequately curved over her hips and bosom. All in all, Eleanor de Clare was an attractive woman – maybe not as beautiful as the queen, but still.

"With his wife," the queen retorted. "And what is it to you, Lady Eleanor? Are you perchance my gaoler, put in place to restrict access to my person?"

The lady flushed. "Your gaoler? Of course not, my lady. But I am—"

"My chief lady-in-waiting," the queen interrupted. "Chosen for me by my husband, not by me." Yet again, she gave Eleanor a mild smile, while her eyes shot darts. "And as my lady-in-waiting, you should do precisely that: wait on me. Not interrupt my discussions with my visitors, nor eavesdrop outside my door, or attempt to coerce my pages and maids to spy on me."

Lady Eleanor looked as if she wanted the floor to swallow her whole.

"So," the queen continued, "as I do not require your services at present, I suggest that you retire to my solar and wait for me. I am sure there is some sewing you can do to keep yourself occupied."

She raised her brows, crossed her arms over her chest and waited until the women had left the room before sweeping her arm over the table, sending the pitcher and the goblets to fly through the air, landing with loud clatters on the floor. "She used to be my friend and now she is my guard dog. I hate that woman!"

"As I hate her husband," Adam muttered.

Amen to that, Kit thought, suppressing yet another shiver.

As luck would have it, they ran into Lord Despenser on their way back to their allotted chamber. Kit didn't see him at first; she simply felt the muscles in Adam's arm tense.

"If it isn't my favourite traitor," Despenser said with a smirk, stepping out to block their path. Adam bowed, as did Kit – protocol required that they do so, even if Kit would have preferred to spit Despenser in the face. This was the man who had threatened her and abused her, who had tortured her Adam, leaving him permanently crippled.

"No traitor, my lord," Adam replied in a calm voice.

"Despite your repeated attempts to smear me as such, I remain a loyal servant of my master, Edward of Windsor."

Despenser's mouth curled into a sneer. "You may fool all others, de Guirande, but you do not fool me. You are Mortimer's man through and through, have been since he picked you out of the dirty squalor you grew up in." He moved closer, close enough that his heavy robes brushed Kit's skirts. "One day, Adam de Guirande, I will have the pleasure of housing you in my dungeons. All it takes is one false step, and then you will be at my mercy until you die."

Adam took a step back, dragging Kit with him. His hand was clenched round the hilt of his dagger, and under Kit's hand his muscles quivered. With rage? Fear? Both, Kit assumed, her knees weakening at the thought of her Adam in Despenser's custody.

Despenser came after, eyes bright. "You fettered and in chains – I rather like that image, dear Adam. Imagine yourself so helpless, incapable of stopping me from doing whatever it pleases me to do to you." He chuckled. "Pleases *me*, de Guirande." With that he was off, hurrying down the passage with his men at his heels.

Kit leaned back against the nearby wall, trying to calm her racing heart. Beside her, Adam slumped, sliding down to crouch with his face hid in his hands. Carefully, Kit lowered herself to his level.

"It won't happen," she said.

"No," he agreed in a shaky voice. "I'll leap off a cliff rather than end up in his hands."

Kit got down on her knees before him and prised his fingers off his face, cupping it and lifting it so that she could see his eyes. "It won't," she repeated. "I won't let it happen."

That made him smile. "My protective wife." Adam stroked her cheek.

Kit had risked her life to save him from Despenser once, and she'd do so again if she had to. She crossed herself, feeling vulnerable and defenceless. In this the year of Our Lord 1323, Despenser made a dangerous enemy, and Kit fervently wished she had skills with sharpened metal implements other than her embroidery needle.

Adam got to his feet and helped her to rise. "We are not over yet, Despenser and I," he said in a low voice.

"You can't touch him." Kit brushed at her dusty skirts.

"Not yet. But one day…"

"You will have to form a queue," Kit said. "There are many people who want to make Despenser pay, and first in line are your beloved queen and your equally beloved baron."

"My beloved queen?" He slid an arm round her waist and drew her as close as was possible with a rounded belly between them. "I only have one beloved, my lady." Adam took hold of her hand and raised it to his mouth, kissing each finger in turn. It made Kit's heart somersault, even more when he leaned towards her, his mouth pressing gently against hers. Warm lips, an insistent tongue, and Kit opened to him, her arms wound round his neck as he kissed her until she was breathless and flushed. She tightened her hold on him and heard the rumble of his responding laughter.

"Later, sweeting," he promised as he released her. He gave her cheek a little tweak. "In the privacy of our bed."

Chapter 2

The Christmas festivities at court were not turning out to be the glamorous event Kit had imagined, firstly because the king had chosen to celebrate the holiday season in Kenilworth, a not-so-subtle reminder that his cousin, Thomas of Lancaster, was now dead, and his favourite castle in the king's possession.

It had been a harrowing trip from Westminster to Kenilworth. Kit had insisted on riding, refusing the litter that held her elderly maid, Mabel, and young master de Guirande, Tom, but by the time Kenilworth's russet ramparts rose out of the misty December day, she'd been tired to the bone, the long days of travelling having left her with a chill and an irritating soreness all the way from her left hip to her foot. Not something she said much about, as Mabel and Adam would have insisted she travel in the litter.

The royal castle was an impressive sight. Set atop a knoll, it dominated the surrounding landscape, protected not only by its curtain wall but also by the large expanse of water that lay before it – a manmade mere, traversed by a causeway.

In some ways, Kenilworth reminded Kit of Wigmore. An enclosed castle, it consisted of a large outer bailey, a sizeable inner bailey and a number of buildings containing everything from a forge to an infirmary, as well as a buttery, pantries, chapels, stables, mews and kennels. But where Wigmore under Lady Joan had been efficiently run, with lavish meals appearing with a minimum of fuss no matter the constant chaos that characterised a large castle, Kenilworth was like a dog with fleas, always itching, always restless.

Instead of joyful spirits, the court of Edward II was filled with broody rumours, all of them centred round the evil intentions of Lord Mortimer. Not that Kit agreed with this description of Roger Mortimer. He was no saint, but from her limited interaction with him, she perceived him to be a fair if somewhat harsh man, and at present that would be a substantial improvement on affairs, as Despenser could be called many things, but none of those was 'fair'.

Surrounded by the king's barons and earls, and by men and women who wore fortunes in jewels round their necks and on their hands, Kit felt dowdy and bleached of colour, intimidated by people who spoke of landholdings in France, of new hawks and hunting steeds. Rarely did any of these high-bred creatures as much as bestow a look on her, but if they did, the men would often look twice, which caused Adam to glower and their lady wives to cast withering looks Kit's way.

"It's not my fault if they look," Kit said in an undertone when her husband's face set in yet another scowl. "Besides, it's probably my scar that catches their interest." Self-consciously, she patted at her cheek.

Adam's features softened. "That scar is your own badge of honour, sweeting – but we both know it's your other attributes that draw their attention."

"Hmm," Kit replied, more than pleased by how her pregnancy had rounded her breasts and left her with a permanent soft flush. "Who's that?" she asked to direct her husband's attention elsewhere. She nodded discreetly at a man in splendid attire who was presently fawning on the king. Slim and erect, with pleasing proportions and reddish-gold hair, the man was laughing at something the king had said.

"That is the king's half-brother, Edmund of Woodstock, the Earl of Kent," Adam said. "Lord of Gloucester Castle, recently invested with sizeable quantities of Mortimer land – well, what was left once Despenser claimed his rewards for his loyal service to his royal liege." He sounded bitter.

Kit regarded the young man with heightened interest. Edmund had to be some years younger than Adam, close to two decades younger than the king, and was brimming with energy. The king's half-brother was lithe and as bright as sunbeam – and devastatingly handsome, attracting almost every female eye in the hall. Something the young man well knew, Kit concluded, watching just how casually he twirled, his blue and silver robes lifting to allow a glimpse of long legs clad in black hose.

"As I hear it, he's quite capable," she said. Kent had distinguished himself in the recent strife that had torn – was tearing – the kingdom apart.

Adam snorted. "Good enough," he muttered, "but there was not much opposition to squash, was there?" He leaned closer. "The man is all surface, no depth, they say. And his royal half-brother keeps him on a very short leash." He chuckled. "One day, our Edmund will tire of scraps." He nodded at the dark-haired young man who was standing to the side, watching Edmund and the king with an inscrutable expression on his face. "And that is Edmund's brother." Adam lowered his voice. "Not a happy man, is Thomas – not when the king did not stop the Despensers from appropriating some of the earl's properties."

"Always the Despensers," Kit murmured, studying the silent statue that was Thomas of Brotherton, Earl of Norfolk. Yet another handsome man, although his features were of a sterner mould, sharp eyes studying his surroundings with keen interest. His gaze met Kit's, went on to study Adam before returning to her. He inclined his head in the slightest of greetings before returning his attention to the king.

"Where is Pembroke?" Kit liked Aymer de Valence, a man much marked by years of loyal service to the crown.

In response, Adam inclined his head to where the aging earl was sitting, quite isolated, at one end of the table. "New times, new men," he sighed. "And rumour has it that de Valence is deeply in debt."

Kit studied Lord Aymer, sitting slumped and alone with only his wife by his side. She didn't like the countess, but the lady was being a most dutiful wife, keeping up a one-sided conversation with her husband, who stared straight ahead and ate whatever she placed on his trencher.

"He's ailing." Kit wanted to approach Earl Aymer and say something, but to do so in front of the king might be doing him a disfavour – he did not need to be tarred with the suspicion of consorting further with men like her Adam. As it was, Kit suspected the earl was paying a heavy price for having saved Adam from Despenser on several occasions.

"He's old," Adam said brutally. "Well past it and wallowing in regrets. His heart was with the Mortimers, but his oath and arm belonged to the king. Such conflicts can tear even the strongest man to shreds."

On Twelfth Night, Kit was sitting beside her husband at one of the lower tables in the hall, watching the king and Despenser interact at the high table. While there were a lot of rumours about Edward and his favourite, Kit could not understand how their king could prefer Despenser to his wife. On the other hand, she knew for a fact that the king never visited his queen at night anymore, while it was common knowledge that Despenser and the king spent entire nights closeted together in the royal chambers.

Kit pursed her mouth, uncomfortable with the images these thoughts evoked. Two men in bed, taking pleasure from each other... No, it was wrong, a grievous sin, and surely no king would lower himself to such base pleasures. Except that when she shared her thoughts with Adam, he laughed and called her a right innocent – men enjoying the bodies of other men was not as uncommon as she might think.

The hall was ablaze with candles. If Kit craned her head back she could just make out the colours of the painted ceiling, here and there decorated with the royal arms. An occasional draught made the tapestries hung on the far wall lift and billow, causing the depicted wildlife to suddenly spring into life before it returned to immobility. The hall reverberated with noise; laughter, impromptu song that ended in a loud burp, and at the high table, the king threw his head back and guffawed.

To the far right of the king sat his eldest son, a boy of eleven or so. Prince Edward looked a lot like his father, with the same fair hair, the same eyes. The boy showed promise of becoming as tall as his father, and already there was an impressive width to his shoulders for one so young, the result, according to Adam, of many hours spent perfecting his fighting skills.

Beside the prince sat his mother, and often the queen's veiled head and that of Prince Edward leaned close together as they talked. Gallantly, the boy acted his mother's page, ensuring her goblet was always kept filled and her trencher laden with the choicest of morsels.

"He seems very close to his mother." Kit had met Prince Edward once, and had found him an engaging lad, possessed of the most mesmerising deep blue eyes she had ever encountered.

"Prince Edward is very fond of her." Adam wiped his hands on the cloth provided and sat back, goblet in hand. "Too fond, some would say." He cast a dark look at Despenser, who was presently entertaining the king, at least to judge from the king's grin.

Kit studied the two men, sitting side by side. Where the king was tall, fair and big-boned, Despenser was dark and slender, a few inches shorter. On the other side of the king sat Despenser's wife, and the king seemed as attentive to his niece as to his royal chancellor. Lady Eleanor basked in her uncle's admiring looks, her cheeks flushed a most becoming pink as she leaned towards their liege to whisper something. The king nodded, then turned the other way to say something to Lord Despenser.

"They truly care for each other, don't they?" Kit said, studying Despenser's hand, which was resting on the king's sleeve.

In reply, Adam muttered something very rude.

"Adam!" Kit threw their neighbours a nervous glance.

"Aye?" He leaned towards her and speared a slice of honey-glazed ham on the trencher. Kit was about to respond when there was a loud clatter behind her.

Three men hurried in, trailing gravel and ice behind them. Heavily bearded, wrapped in wet cloaks spattered with mud, they marched towards the dais. Despenser rose. The king rose. Everyone rose, thereby making it impossible for Kit to see anything beyond the madder rose tunic of the man in front of her.

"What?" The king's voice carried like a whiplash. "What are you? Incompetents? I want his head, damn you, not contradicting information about his whereabouts!" Something was slammed down on a table – the king's goblet, Kit guessed. Irritated at not seeing anything, she took hold of Adam's arm and stood on the bench.

On the dais, the king was walking back and forth, hands clenched into fists by his sides. The three men were kneeling before him, one of them saying something in a hushed voice.

"Well, unless he's sprouted wings, it can't be, can it? No mortal man can be in Flanders on the morrow and in Rouen by noon! Not even that accursed Mortimer!" The king's voice rose to a yell. He swivelled, glaring at Despenser. "Why haven't you rid me of him yet? You promised you would!"

"My liege, calm down." Despenser spoke softly but clearly. "It is but a matter of time, sire. Mortimer cannot cower forever behind the skirts of the French king."

This statement had the king turning to glower at his wife, who calmly looked back at him.

"We will catch him soon," Despenser continued, "and then…" He made a slicing movement across his throat. Out of the corner of her eye, Kit saw Adam smile.

The king was not appeased. He cursed, kicked at one of the unfortunate messengers and stood on his toes, glaring at the people in the hall. Kit saw his eyes narrow as they locked on Adam.

"You!" The king snarled. "Adam de Guirande, no less. How dare you show your traitorous face in my hall? I will not have it, you hear?" He snapped his fingers and two men-at-arms started towards Adam. Behind the king, Despenser grinned.

Adam had nowhere to go. The men-at-arms were only yards away, and even if he could have made it out of the hall, what then? He heard Kit exclaim, her hands on his arm. One of the men-at-arms caught hold of his other arm and yanked. Adam wrenched himself free.

"I walk on my own." Very slowly, he approached the king, exaggerating his limp. Beside him walked Kit, gripping his sleeve with both her hands. "Let me go, sweeting," he murmured as they approached. She shook her head, her blue eyes wide. "Kit," he said, covering her hands with his. "Stand aside. I'll not have you humiliated with me." Or killed. Adam didn't like the look on the king's face, nor on Despenser's.

"I can't," she whispered back. "If I let go of you, I'll fall."

And then they were standing before the king. Adam was forced to his knees, and as Kit still refused to let go, she kneeled beside him. She was trembling, her fingers clawed into the green wool of his tunic.

"Take the woman away," the king commanded. Two men moved forward and took hold of Kit, but she wouldn't let go, screaming like a wounded horse when they tried to separate her from Adam.

"Sweeting," Adam tried, "it will be all right."

"All right?" she groaned, the sound converting to a gasp when one of the men wrenched her hand off him. Moments later, she was dragged away and Adam struggled against the hands holding him when his wife was roughly manhandled to the side.

"She's with child," he growled.

"A traitor's whelp!" the king spat, but ordered his men to step away from Kit. She straightened up, eyes blue fire. Despite being with child, Adam's wife retained her willowy grace, and now, standing close enough that he could hear her every breath, she resembled a protective lioness, ready to spring.

"No traitor, my lord. I am your son's liegeman."

"Now you are! But you used to serve Roger Mortimer." Wild eyes glared at him, the normally so handsome royal features contorted into a scowl.

Adam raised his chin. "I did. I served him loyally for many years. I bled for him, I fought for him, I would have laid down my life for him. I follow my lord, sire – to Hell and beyond if required. But my lord is no longer Lord Mortimer. It is your son." It woke a hollow ache in him to repudiate his lord.

Lord Roger was the closest thing Adam had to a father, and not a day went by without Adam praying for his former lord's continued health.

"So you admit it, do you?" The king was barely coherent. Spittle flew from his mouth as he spoke, those large hands of his clenched into formidable fists. "You admit being a traitor? You rode with Mortimer against me, against your king!" He crashed his fist down on the table, causing everyone to jump.

"I followed my lord. I could do no other." Adam closed his eyes against the memories of the rebellion. Months of freezing in the winter cold, day after day of skirmishes, and all the while the king's army had slowly closed the noose around Mortimer's troops, forcing the capitulation which resulted in Mortimer's incarceration in the Tower, while most of Adam's companions were hanged in Shrewsbury. But not Adam: no, Adam had lain helpless as Despenser tortured him.

"You could do no other?" The king kicked Adam – hard. "I'll not tolerate a traitor at my court. Take him away and hang him! Now!"

"No!" Kit threw herself forward, covering Adam with her bulk. "He already paid."

"Get out of the way, woman!" The king bent as if to take hold of Kit and throw her to the side. She hung on, emitting one wordless scream after the other. The king roared; guards came rushing from all over, their booted feet and loud commands adding to the clamour.

"My lord! This is unseemly." The queen's voice rose above the din. "Besides, you have signed his pardon, my lord husband." Queen Isabella glided towards them. "Do you truly think your son would have accepted his pledge otherwise?"

"My son does as you ask him, my lady," the king replied in a voice so cold the queen recoiled.

"I do as you tell me too, Father." Prince Edward helped Kit to stand, placing himself between Adam and the king. "You've told me to surround myself with men I trust, have you not?"

The king nodded.

"I trust Adam de Guirande. He saved my life once." The

prince shared a quick look with Adam, his mouth quivering with a suppressed smile. Adam smiled back, briefly. The lad had been most irate at having been saved by Adam, insisting he was fully capable of swimming on his own.

"Son." The king cleared his throat. "I cannot have a man suspected of traitorous activities in your household." He gestured at the men-at-arms "Take de Guirande away."

"No, Father, please don't do this to me," Edward said, kneeling down beside Adam.

"To you?" The king ruffled his son's hair. "I'm doing this to protect you."

"You're shaming me," Prince Edward said.

"Shaming you?" The king looked at Adam, then at his son.

"Sir Adam is my liegeman. He has pledged himself to me, and I, in return, have pledged to protect him – isn't that what liege lords do?" The prince turned wide eyes on his father.

"My lord, don't listen to him. Our young prince is a gallant lad, but he is yet a child, incapable of fully comprehending the world of men," Despenser said.

"And which world is that, Lord Despenser?" the prince asked, getting to his feet. "Is that the world where some men ram a red-hot stake through the foot of a helpless man – just for sport?"

To Adam's grim amusement, Despenser blanched.

The king frowned. "That was badly done. To maim a belted knight…"

Despenser licked his lips. "I did it to incapacitate him, my dearest lord." He scowled at Adam. "But it would be best for all if he was hanged."

"No," Prince Edward said. "I will not allow it." He placed his hand on the hilt of his dagger.

"You will not allow it?" The king laughed. "Quite the fiery pup, aren't you?" He regarded his son in silence for some moments. "Very well, this time I will not harm your man. But if I pick up as much as a whiff of deceit, I'll have him hanged, drawn and disembowelled – and that is a promise, lad."

"If he betrays me, I will condemn him myself," the prince

replied, and Adam shivered at the steely edge to his voice. Prince Edward might as yet be a lad, but the lion cub was well on the way to becoming a lion, and woe betide the man who riled him.

"My liege," Despenser protested. "Surely you will not heed the voice of a child in this matter?"

"Your prince," Prince Edward bit off. "And one day I will be your king. Best keep that in mind, Lord Despenser."

Despenser spluttered, and the king laughed and whacked him hard. "You hear that, Hugh? Your future king demands your obedience." He laughed some more, his previously dark mood evaporating, and returned to the table, one arm affectionately draped round Despenser's shoulders.

Adam sagged in relief, placing his hands on the floor to support himself. His neck itched, his innards cramped. This had been uncomfortably close.

Prince Edward crouched down beside him. "Are you all right?"

"All right? I owe you my life, my lord."

"Yes, you do, don't you?" The lad regarded him with some amusement. "It seems we are even, Sir Adam."

Adam shook his head. "No, my lord. You could have saved yourself that day by the Tower. I would not have survived tonight without your help." He got to his feet, looking for Kit. "My wife?"

"Here. I'm here."

Adam turned in time to catch her as she fell into his arms. "Shhh," he crooned, running his hands up and down her back. He rested his cheek against her head and held her close, drawing in the scent of her, his woman.

"Your wife is upset," the queen said. "It would be best if you escort her to your rooms."

Adam bowed, relieved at being dismissed. With one more bow in the direction of the prince, he left, leading Kit by the hand.

Mabel couldn't stop fussing. When Kit and Adam appeared in the doorway, she had taken one look at them and sent

Adam's new squire, a lanky fourteen-year-old named Gavin, to fetch mulled wine and honey. Ignoring both Kit's and Adam's protests, she proceeded to help Kit out of her clothes, replacing the deep green surcoat lined with squirrel fur and the matching woollen kirtle with a long-sleeved robe in dove blue. Adam was instructed to take off his boots and sit down by the fire, a sleeping Tom placed in his arms.

Kit smiled weakly; to hand a man reprieved from imminent death his sleeping child had to count as one of Mabel's more inspired notions, at least to judge by how Adam buried his nose in Tom's hair, eyes closed as he inhaled their son's scent.

"And Lord Mortimer remains safe and sound?" Mabel asked once she'd handed Kit and Adam a posset each.

"To judge from the king's reaction I'd say Roger Mortimer is in the best of health," Kit replied.

"As I hear it, he remains in France." Adam sounded casual.

"As you hear it?" Kit pounced. "Are you in contact with him?"

Adam sighed. "No, I am not. But others are."

Like the queen, Kit thought snidely.

"William, not the queen." Adam said, and she felt caught out.

"Is William here?" she asked instead, smiling at the thought of Adam's priest-turned-spy brother.

"Here?" Adam shook his head. "No, sweeting, that would be too dangerous. But he's in London, so once we're back in Westminster we can meet with him – he's staying with a vintner up by Aldgate Street."

Kit shrugged. She did not know London well enough to be able to place the street. Twice, she'd accompanied Adam to the city, finding the entire experience more than daunting. It was an assault on the senses – and especially that of smell – to visit the city. Dark, narrow streets, large, looming buildings, too many people, too many unwashed urchins, too many beggars, too much filth, too much abject misery – no, all in all, Kit preferred to stay clear of London.

"Why didn't you tell me?" she asked instead.

"I got his message moments before we were due at the

hall. I was going to tell you, but other things happened." Adam kissed his son's head.

"When can we see him?" Kit had not laid eyes on William for over a year.

"Well, not tonight, sweeting. It is a long ride from here to London."

"M'lady is not going anywhere until she is somewhat recovered," Mabel interrupted.

"I wasn't planning on a midnight departure," Adam replied with a smile. His features tightened. "The king would probably take it as an attempted flight, an admission of my guilt, and kill me on the spot."

"The king is a fool," Mabel stated. "So yes, he might do just that."

Kit clasped her hands together to stop them from trembling.

"But as you'll not be traipsing off in the dark, he'll have no reason to, will he?" Mabel continued. In passing, she patted Kit on the back. "Nothing happened, m'lady."

"Nothing." Kit stretched her mouth into a smile, while tears ran down her cheeks.

Once Kit had stopped crying and Mabel had decided they had recovered, she took Tom with her, shooed Gavin before her and left them alone in the small chamber. The only source of light was the fire, by now reduced to a heap of glowing embers. Adam moved close enough to take Kit's hand, and sat toying with her fingers.

"Bed?" he asked, breaking the silence. He kissed her wrist, and at her nod, helped her to stand. He undressed them both before the fire, smoothing his fingers over her skin. Kit shivered under his touch and rested her head against his chest. The golden fuzz that decorated most of his body tickled her nose, and she rubbed her cheek against him, relishing the sensation of his skin against hers. Had the prince not spoken up… Kit shoved the thoughts away from her. Adam was here, he was warm and alive.

"We should not be doing this," Adam murmured, but his hands contradicted his words, gliding over her rounded belly, her heavy breasts. "It is a sin."

"How can it be a sin?" She fondled him. "Why would God frown when we, his creatures, take pleasure from each other?"

Adam groaned, tensing his buttocks when she closed her hand around him. "Man should only lie with woman for procreation," he said breathlessly.

"Not my man." She tightened her hold.

"No, not your man." Adam cupped her bottom and gathered her as close as possible. "Your man is in your thrall, my lady, willing to risk his immortal soul for you."

"What? Your immortal soul for a slice of Heaven? Not a bad trade, my lord."

Adam laughed, his breath tickling her neck. "I'm not complaining, sweeting."

He guided her backwards towards the bed, and helped her down before lighting the candle on the nearby table. The comforting scent of beeswax filled the room, a circle of light in the gloom. Sufficient light to see each other by, enough that she could see how his pupils dilated when he lay down beside her, a heavy hand moving up her thigh, over the slope of her hip, up to caress her breasts, before tracing leisurely circles over the taut skin of her belly in the direction of her pubic mound. A finger, two fingers sliding through her folds, teasing, touching. His mouth whispering her name, kissing her neck, her ear.

Kit closed her eyes, submerged in a sea of tactile sensations. She almost smiled when his fingers stopped moving, and she knew what he was going to say before his nose brushed against hers.

"Open your eyes," he whispered, nipping her earlobe. "My wife loves me with her eyes open. You know that by now, sweeting."

So she did, staring up at him as he entered her carefully with most of his weight on his braced arms.

"I love you," she told him, trying to envelop as much of him as she could with her legs and her arms.

"I know." Adam smiled down at her, flexing his hips in slow, measured movements that stoked the heat inside of her, a concentrated point of pleasure that craved his proximity, his strength and virility. Kit heard her breathing, loud and ragged in the quiet of their room. She hooked a leg round his hips, using her heel to spur him deeper, faster, harder. Adam increased his pace, the muscles of his arms quivered under her hands and Kit could no longer form any coherent thoughts beyond his name, one long, extended 'Adam' ringing in her head.

With a soft exclamation, Adam reached his release. His head dipped, his breathing slowed and he pulled out to lie beside her. "I love you too," he murmured, clasping her hand and placing it atop his beating heart.

Chapter 3

"I will not ride in a litter." Kit gave Adam an exasperated look. They had gone by boat from Westminster to Byling's Gate, and Kit had not regained her composure after the choppy ride, very much aggravated by the rising wind and churning tides. She glanced at the bridge, now to her left, and suppressed a shiver. Shooting under those dank, dark arches was an experience she could gladly have done without. To ride a litter after her recent encounter with the river would only increase her queasiness – besides, she'd spent too much time in litters recently and wanted to see something of the crowded and dirty streets that surrounded her, curious despite the stench and the squalor.

"If you're walking, then so am I." She stretched. She might be carrying, but she wasn't weak, and the occasional discomfort that flowered up her back was nothing but a consequence of her being tired.

They'd been back in Westminster no more than three days, this after trailing the king and his retinue as he first rode west, then turned back east. This time, Kit had acquiesced to travelling part of the way in one of the litters, mostly because the queen had insisted, saying a woman so swollen with child should not expose herself to the strains of riding. It had been on the tip of Kit's tongue to remind her of the old king's second wife, by all accounts a most dignified and cultured lady, who all the same was out hunting when afflicted by labour pains.

Adam adopted a stern look, but she could see he wasn't about to insist, so she slipped her arm into his, lifted her skirts as high as she could do with decency, and followed him up through Watergate to Thames Street where they turned left before turning right again, this time up a crooked street Adam told her was Harp Lane.

It was like walking through a crowded, unkempt farmyard. Hens, the odd pig, far too many dogs, soiled straw and offal in the gutters – Kit's nostril's widened, incapable of closing out the disagreeable odour of very many people living in far too much proximity. She clutched at Adam's arm as she slipped on the wet cobbles, and for an instant she regretted having insisted on walking. No matter her care, the dark blue wool of her kirtle was already splattered with mud, and had it not been for her pattens, her shoes would have been covered with filth.

As they proceeded up the street, Kit was afflicted by the sensation of being trapped. The streets were dark and narrow; the houses stood cheek to jowl, the upper storeys straining towards each other at the expense of the light, casting the ground below into a constant dusk. Add to this a multitude of people, most of them hastening by with a determined look on their faces that spoke of important matters to handle, and Kit almost regretted having insisted on accompanying Adam.

She shuddered at the state of some of the people they passed. Crippled children sat in the filth, hands extended mutely. Bare-headed women far younger than her leaned provocatively against walls, necklines gaping open over breasts that pimpled in the cold. Old hags teetered along, bent double under loads of kindling or rags, and here and there they came across men, already so drunk at this hour of the day to be incapable of anything more than bleary looks and staggers.

"London's underbelly. Not a pretty sight, is it?" Adam twitched his shoulders, keeping his free hand on the hilt of his dagger.

"Terrible." A band of children in rags rushed by, yelling loudly. "But some are trying to help." She inclined her head in the direction of several black-clad men, their habits swishing round their legs as they made their way down the wet street. Behind them came other men, carrying baskets of bread.

"The friars do a good job, bless them all." Adam came to a halt. "William?"

In response, one of the friars straightened up and pulled back his cowl. "Brother!"

Adam released Kit, took three strides and crashed into his brother.

They were very much alike, Adam and his younger brother. Both of them over six feet tall, both of them fair, but where Adam had grey eyes that shifted from darkest pewter to brightest silver depending on the light and his mood, William's eyes were a light blue, fringed with fair lashes as thick and straight as those of his brother.

"William!" Kit hugged her brother-in-law, ignoring the disapproving look that flitted over Adam's features. Her man didn't like it when she was too familiar with other men, even his own brother.

"Kit." William disengaged himself and winked at her. "It is not seemly for a woman to embrace a friar."

"So you're a friar now?" she asked. "No more the queen's man?"

William grinned. "Most definitely the queen's man – but as of last night I am also a friar, travelling extensively through France and England as per my abbot's orders." He glanced furtively over his shoulder. "I couldn't stay with Robert – in the present climate it would place him and his family at risk," he continued, his voice lowered to a rumble. "I have news," he added with a smile.

Kit didn't need to ask what his news related to. She could see it in William's bright expression, mirrored in Adam's.

"Lord Roger sends his regards," William said, and Adam shone like a beacon. Kit retreated a couple of steps. Always Lord Roger Mortimer, who took up far too much space in Adam's life – and heart. She threw a concerned look down the street, fearing that at any moment they'd be surrounded by the king's men-at arms loudly proclaiming them to be plotting against the king.

Adam was too intent on his hushed conversation with William to notice when she took yet more steps away from him. She heard him mutter, "Lord Roger" a couple of times, and William nodded and said something that made Adam grin. It riled her that one moment he would refuse even considering allowing her to walk without his support, while

27

the next he had forgotten her presence, so focused was he on hearing news of Lord Mortimer, the king's greatest traitor. So Kit turned on her heel, disregarded the little voice inside of her that was telling her she was being foolish, and walked up towards Cheapside and the beckoning market stalls.

In a matter of moments, she was accosted by urchins, children who gripped at her skirts and begged for pennies, for bread. She walked on, ignoring their entreating eyes. They grew insistent, latching on to her and shoving her with them.

"Let me go," she demanded of one of the boys, cuffing him over the head. The child ducked, let go, and was immediately replaced by another, pushing her with determination towards a nearby alley. Kit dug in her heels and yelled for help. A quick glance over her shoulder indicated she'd left Adam further behind than intended, but when she attempted to call his name a shove sent her further into the gloom of the narrow passage. Kit slipped in the mud underfoot, righted herself, and swung madly, sending at least one of the children flying. More hands, many, many hands, and out of the shadows the lanky shape of a man appeared, knife in hand.

If anything, the appearance of the man had her increasing her efforts to fight free. The man laughed, saying something she couldn't quite interpret. There was an odd, stinging sensation down her arm. She was pushed back, her head hitting a nearby wall. The man's acrid breath was far too close, his hands on her cloak. There was the sound of something tearing. Her brooch. Kit tried to wrest herself free, but there were too many hands on her. The man pinched her breast and grinned, making yet another unintelligible comment, even if Kit recognised the word 'whore'.

When he pawed her again, Kit succeeded in pulling a hand free and punched him straight in the mouth. The man snarled. Kit shoved at him, almost collapsing under what seemed like a thousand small bodies. There was a roar, children were flung this way and that, there were squeals and screams of pain. The man landed face first on the ground and emitted a howl when a booted foot came down on his hand clutching the knife. Just like that it was over, Adam heaving the man to stand while William reclaimed Kit's brooch and helped her adjust her clothes.

William stayed with her while Adam dragged the man off, calling for the constables.

"He didn't hurt you?" William led her over to a nearby stall, digging into his pouch to produce the groat required to buy her a mug of hot cider.

Kit shook her head, not trusting herself to speak. When yet another band of children passed by, she backed into William in her haste to maintain her distance from these potential miniature abductors.

"What…" She coughed. "They only meant to rob me, I assume."

William didn't reply. Instead he steered the subject over to his nephew and the people of Tresaints.

After several minutes discussing old John and Mabel, Kit's pulse had returned to normal. When Adam reappeared, minus the man, she gave him a tremulous smile. He spoke over her head to his brother, deciding to meet up again in a week's time. With one last hug, the brothers parted. William gave Kit a little smile before melting back into the crowd, his black habit visible only for some instants.

Adam didn't speak to her at all on their way back to the wharf. His hand was a clamp on her wrist, and he walked with such haste that she had to trot, one hand clutching at her belly. Only when they were on the docks did he turn to face her, eyes narrowed into slits.

"You could have been harmed! Killed, even."

"I—"

"I've told you, have I not? London is not safe for a woman on her own – and especially not for a woman like you."

"A woman like me?"

Adam blew out his cheeks. "Look at you! You're well-dressed and healthy, you have rings on your fingers and baubles in your ears." He took hold of an escaped tendril of her hair and yanked – a tad too hard. "And you're lovely," he added, sounding as if this was an unfortunate fact. "Women like you disappear all the time."

"Disappear? Don't be silly. Besides, look at me – I'm huge."

"A temporary condition," Adam reminded her. "And there are many men who'd find you tempting anyway."

"You think?" She hoped for a compliment or a smile. All she got was a glower.

"Why did you walk off like that?"

"Why didn't you notice I did?" she snapped back. "One moment you're like a protective wolfhound, the next you forget I'm there at all."

"He's my brother," Adam protested. "I haven't seen him that much lately."

"We both know it wasn't William who distracted you." She turned her back on him. Behind her, she heard him sigh.

"Are you all right?" he asked instead. She just nodded. The cut to her arm was shallow, and other than that she was more frightened than hurt. "Kit," he murmured, wrapping his arms round her and pulling her close enough that he could rest his hands on her belly. "I'm sorry," he said simply. "I should not have left you unguarded like that. I got carried away."

"And I'm sorry too. I shouldn't have walked off."

"No, you shouldn't." His teeth nipped gently at her ear. "A woman as enticing as you must never walk without her husband."

"Enticing?" She softened against him.

His soft chuckle tickled her skin. "Enticing, tempting, enthralling...all of them suit." The bristles on his jaw scrubbed against her cheek, sending all sorts of sensations rushing through her.

"I like them all." She turned in his arms and lifted herself on her toes to give him a kiss.

"Please don't punish me by risking yourself," he said once they broke apart. "I couldn't bear it if—"

A quick brush of her lips on his silenced him. "I know." Which was why it was such a good way to punish him, but she didn't say that. "So what news of Lord Mortimer?"

"Do you care?"

"Of course I care – if nothing else because you do." She gnawed at her lip. "I like him too, you know."

"Do you now?" there was a slight edge to his voice that made Kit laugh.

"Not like that – which you well know, Adam de Guirande."

"He's a handsome man. And rich."

"He isn't you." She cupped his cheek, smiling at the pleased look on Adam's face. "And he is married – something the queen should keep in mind." She sighed at the thought of Lady Joan, Lord Mortimer's wife, who would soon enter her third year of captivity.

"Kit!"

"Oh, come! Every time Queen Isabella speaks of Roger Mortimer, her features soften."

"Lord Roger is a man of honour," Adam reproved. "And the queen is a faithful wife – and devout."

"I didn't say they'd acted on it," Kit told him. "I'm just saying that she would very much want to."

"Wanting and acting are two very different things." Adam sounded very serious.

"A narrow precipice that separates the thought of sin from actual sin," Kit said. "So, is he faring well?"

Adam nodded, going on to regale her with a detailed description of Mortimer's recent months of freedom. After almost two years in the Tower, Kit supposed the man needed to savour life at its fullest, which was probably why he seemed to invest most of his time in pleasurable pastimes. On the other hand, what could he do? It wasn't as if he could return home and pick up the pieces of his previous life. But she felt a sting of ire at the fact that Roger Mortimer was feasting with the French nobility while his wife and most of his children languished in captivity here in England – a captivity that had grown that much harsher after Mortimer escaped back in August.

"Any news of Lady Joan?" she interrupted Adam. He grimaced and dragged a hand through his thick thatch of hair. She needed to cut it, she noted, smiling at how it stood every which way.

"The lady suffers under the king's new measures." Briefly, he told her how Lady Joan lived under constant supervision, prohibited from communicating with her children. The Mortimer daughters were sequestered in nunneries, the sons were locked up – with the exception of Geoffrey, who was with his father in France. "In difference to her husband, she fares badly," he finished. "I hope Lord Roger's letter will bring her some hope."

"A letter?"

"William has been entrusted with it. He will make sure she gets it. I am tasked with getting Mortimer's other letter to the queen." He patted himself at heart level. "Will you accompany me to see her later?"

Kit had no intention of letting him talk to the beautiful queen alone. Besides, she might be able to help. Smuggling a letter to the queen under the watchful eyes of Eleanor de Clare was the equivalent of entering the lion's den – with a hungry and wide-awake lion in it.

Later that day, Adam and Kit exited the queen's chambers after an uncomfortable hour in the presence of the queen and her ladies. Adam frowned; the queen lived in a gilded cage, her every step monitored by Despenser's wife. Only through Kit's clumsy spilling of wine on Lady Eleanor's skirts, causing all eyes to fly to her, had Adam succeeded in slipping the queen the missive. A fleeting smile was his reward, those luminous green eyes glittering in his direction.

When they left, the queen's hand had, as per chance, brushed at Adam's wrist, long fingers caressing his skin. The imprint of her touch still tingled. The queen was an attractive woman, and it would take a man of rock – or a eunuch – to be impervious to her. Beside him, Kit walked in stony silence, and a glance in her direction confirmed that she had seen the queen touching him – and did not like it.

"Shall we walk outside?" he asked, gesturing at the surprising brightness of the January day. His lord and master was supposedly still at his Latin lessons, so Adam had some time on his hands prior to the hard riding he had promised

Prince Edward later on. In silence, she followed him outside, keeping her hands very much to herself.

With the king in residence, Westminster became a hub of activity, men-at-arms jostling with clerks and accountants, with priests and tradesmen. From the smithy came the incessant sound of hammering, through the gate rolled cart after cart piled high with victuals of all kinds, from wine to be stored in the darker cellars to salted fish and waddling ducks. Courtiers bedecked in velvet and silk hastened across the muddy yard, from chapel to hall, from hall to private chambers, flocking round their handsome king like starlings round a bushel. Not that the king was anywhere in sight at present – their liege preferred to take counsel with his closest circle, and would at this moment be closeted in the Painted Chamber with Despenser and Stapleton, no doubt with flagons of good wine at hand.

Yet another look in Kit's direction, and Adam had to quell the urge to grin. He enjoyed seeing her jealous, chin up, bosom pushed forward and those blue eyes glittering with anger.

"If she touches you like that again, I'll be tempted to claw her face, queen or no queen," Kit said.

"She brushed my hand by mistake." Not true – Queen Isabella rarely did anything by mistake, and these last few months living under constant supervision had, if anything, reinforced that trait in her.

In response, Kit snorted. "Did you enjoy it?"

"Enjoy what precisely? That a beautiful woman touched my hand in gratitude?" He drew her to a halt. "You've said it yourself: if the queen has a fondness for anyone but her husband, it is for Lord Roger." Adam frowned. "And let us hope the poor woman has little fondness for her lord husband. Otherwise, his present behaviour would break her heart."

"Hmm," Kit replied, but her mouth softened somewhat. "Does the king visit her at all?" She pressed back against him as a group of men hurried past.

"Not recently. Despenser and his wife are driving a wedge between them. It suits Despenser's purposes to isolate the king, so their communication is restricted to the words they exchange when they preside over the festivities in the great hall – or when they discuss their children." Recently, the king was rarely seen without either Lord Despenser or Lady Eleanor by his side. The king was inordinately – at times inappropriately – fond of his niece, and there were some that whispered it was Lady Eleanor, not Lord Despenser, who kept the king company at night. Or both.

"Poor children," Kit said, slipping her hand into Adam's.

"Aye. Prince Edward in particular. The poor lad is being torn apart by his parents. It is fortunate, I think, that he has his own household to grant him some stability." Prince Edward was rarely at court, but when he was, he stayed with his mother as did all the royal children, a handsome brood consisting of Edward, his younger brother John, the pretty little Eleanor and the baby Joan, a plump toddler who had the most contagious laugh. "The prince has made it clear that I am required to stay with him for some time. I presume that includes you as well." Adam hoped it would.

Kit did not look happy. "Live with him? I want to go back to Tresaints."

Adam lifted her hand to his mouth and gave it a brief kiss. "So do I, sweeting. But my life is not mine to order – you know that." He braided his fingers with hers. "But if you want to return to Tresaints, I'd understand. I wouldn't like it, but I'd understand."

"You wouldn't like it?" She sounded pleased.

"No. I want you here, with me." Adam quietly congratulated himself. His wife's cheeks had gone a pleasing pink, and her grip on his hand tightened. She was about to say something, when a distant shout had them both focusing on the gatehouse – or more specifically on the person dangling from a rope affixed to the roof.

"What…" Kit never got to finish. With all the speed he could muster, Adam made for the building. Long before he'd reached the base of the tower, he heard the mewling sounds coming from the young person tangled in the ropes – and he had already recognised that head of bright hair, the tunic in cornflower blue wool hemmed with green and red.

"Hang still!" he called up. The rope was attached to grappling hooks, and too much movement could easily dislodge the hooks and send the prince down to land on the stones below. Adam swallowed. The lad was hanging upside down, and well over fifteen feet from the ground.

There was a gargle from Edward.

"The rope!" Kit's voice came in gasps. "It's round his neck!" Fortunately, the prince's arm was also caught in the makeshift noose.

"A rope!" Adam yelled, making a quick assessment of the situation. Reaching the lad from the battlements would take too much time, and to pull him up with the rope round his neck…no, that would not work. One of the hooks screeched over the stone and gave way. The prince whimpered as he dropped yet another foot.

A guard came running with rope and grapples. Adam steadied himself, drew in a deep breath and threw the rope. There was a satisfying clunk as the hooks caught on something.

"Talk to him," Adam said to Kit. "Keep him as still as possible."

"What are you doing?" She took hold of his cloak. "You can't climb!" She gestured at his foot.

"Aye, I can – I have to." He leaned towards her. "And I've done it before." With that, he was off, using his arms to heave himself upwards towards his young lord. From below came Kit's voice, low and reassuring as she spoke to the lad, telling him to look at her, only at her, and concentrate on his breathing.

Yet another of the hooks gave. The prince fell downwards a foot or so before being brought to a jarring halt by the rope. He was choking, his hand pressed against his windpipe. Eyes wide with fright, he stared at Adam.

"I'll be right there." Adam grunted, trying to find purchase for his good foot to push himself upwards. A crack in the mortar offered a foothold, and suddenly the prince was within reach, hanging like a helpless chrysalis.

"The hook!" Kit yelled from below. Adam threw out his free arm and caught hold of the lad just as the last grapple gave. The prince fell, brought up short by Adam's hold.

"Sweet Lord!" The tendons in Adam's shoulder shrieked in protest, but somehow he managed to hold on to the boy. With an effort, he succeeded in lifting Edward sufficiently to hold him clumsily against his chest while lowering himself to the ground.

By the time Adam's booted foot touched the stone flags, a large audience had collected. Standing in silence, they watched as he set Prince Edward down.

"Can you stand, my lordling?" he asked in an undertone. Edward nodded, holding on to Adam as he straightened up. A cheer went up from the crowd and the prince gave them a sheepish wave.

"What were you doing, my lord?" Kit chided, inspecting the lad for damage. "No more than a bad rope-burn, I think." A thick red abrasion decorated the prince's neck.

"I was learning how to climb walls," Prince Edward replied in a pinched voice.

"Climb walls?" Adam echoed.

The prince flashed him a look. "How else to enter a besieged castle?"

Adam could think of various other methods, but held his tongue.

"Well, don't do that again. You could have died!" Kit tweaked Edward's tunic into place before smoothing his hair, retracting her hand as if scalded when the king burst through the spectators, with Despenser at his heels.

"You saved my son." The king looked from Adam to Edward and back again.

"My liege." Adam bowed deeply, pulling Kit into a reverence with him.

"Thank you," the king said in a gravelly voice, hugging his son to him.

"My pleasure, my lord." When Adam raised his head, he met the jet-black gaze of Despenser, hovering behind the king. Adam couldn't help it; he grinned, causing Despenser's scowl to deepen into an expression resembling that of a disgruntled gargoyle.

Chapter 4

After the excitement of smuggling letters to the queen and saving the prince, life settled down into a predictable routine of meals and church services – either in St Stephen's Chapel or, occasionally, in the abbey church. Today was one of the abbey days, Kit standing among the women with Mabel while her husband stood close to his lord, their contact restricted to the odd shared look. Not at all the way it was back home. The chapel at Tresaints was a small stone structure, well over two centuries old, and although it had none of the grandeur of Westminster, it was suffused with peace, a far more intimate environment in which to speak with God.

Kit lingered in the abbey church after the service, enjoying the relative solitude and silence – a precious commodity at court. She wandered the large space, making huge eyes at the exquisitely painted stonework, the various sculptures and the portraits of saints on the walls. As always, there was an array of pilgrims come to kneel before the shrine of Edward the Confessor, but for Kit it was not the magnificent, gilded shrine that drew her eye – it was the altarpiece.

On one side stood St Peter with his keys, on the other St Paul with his sword, and in between was an explosion of gold and precious glass, of azure pieces Adam had told her were called lapis lazuli and came from so far away it would take a man on a good horse well over a year to ride that far. Kit genuflected before the altar, her gaze on the central panel, depicting Christ in all his glory, holding the world safe in his palm. Keep us all safe, she prayed, dearest Lord, keep me and mine safe. For good measure, she directed herself to the Holy Mother as well, depicted by her Son's side. After adding a prayer or two for Alaïs, her long-dead mother, she slipped through the heavy door, squinting in the harsh sunlight.

She took her time crossing the abbey yard, nodded

a greeting at the guard at the garden gate, and was pleased to discover the palace gardens were empty. The unseasonal warmth of the sun enticed her to sit for a while on a bench, nose in the air, eyes closed. She reclined against the backrest and ran a hand over her belly, prodding slightly in the hope of eliciting a reaction from within. A quiet child, she reflected, when the child kicked once in response. A daughter, she smiled, picturing a biddable little girl, quite the opposite of her overactive Tom.

Kit would have wanted to share these thoughts with Adam, but these days her private time with her husband was severely restricted. Ever since the incident at the gatehouse, the king insisted that wherever Edward went, there went Adam, even if the prince was anything but pleased at being saddled with a bodyguard. Kit kicked at a stone and got to her feet. With Adam always with Edward, it was either dance attendance on the queen or spend her days on the fringe of things. So far, Kit had opted for the fringe – and for time with Tom – but from the oblique comments the queen had made before mass, Kit knew it was but a matter of time before she would be required to serve her, a much-needed bulwark between Isabella and Lady Eleanor.

The queen detested Lady Despenser – although Lady Eleanor went by de Clare, proud as a peacock of her parentage – and at times Kit could but commiserate with Lady Eleanor, placed in an impossible position. No matter how correct the lady's behaviour, the queen found fault, treating Lady Eleanor with such disdain it bordered on rudeness.

Kit made a face. Cool and unfailingly polite, Lady Eleanor regarded Kit with mild contempt. On the single occasion when Kit had bumped into the lady together with her despicable husband, Lady Eleanor's gaze had flitted between her husband and Kit, brows pulled together in the slightest of frowns. It made Kit's skin crawl to be regarded so avidly by both the Despensers – one with eyes gleaming with maliciousness, the other looking as if she'd gladly crush Kit underfoot.

She skirted a yew, ducked under a denuded briar rose, and walked along the river wall. If the queen's allegations were correct, that Lady Eleanor was placed in her household to spy on her, it was an inefficient course of action. Queen Isabella was far too careful to let slip any indiscretions, and any missives were destroyed the moment they were read. Besides, in the queen's large household, Lady Eleanor commanded no loyalty, while the queen most certainly did.

Kit was halfway across the inner courtyard when her musings were interrupted by Lord Despenser himself, resplendent as always in a knee-length tunic of the softest wool, topped by an open, fur-lined surcoat in a deep burgundy red. Boots, a rakish hat, rings, a heavy gold chain on his chest, a tooled belt decorated with silver and gold stars – the man was a walking expression of wealth.

Hugh Despenser moved swiftly towards the great hall, accompanied by a motley collection of guards and acolytes. His hands rose and fell in time with whatever he was saying, and for all that Kit would gladly have nailed his intestines to a tree and have him walk around it until he'd disembowelled himself, she had to admit the man exuded some sort of magnetic allure, his sharp features enhanced by the neatly trimmed beard that clung to his cheeks and chin, his eyes glittering under dark, straight brows.

Unfortunately, he'd seen her. Kit wasn't quite sure what she'd done to deserve Despenser's attention – beyond hitting him over the head with a full chamber pot some time ago – but whenever he saw her, the man would leer, undressing her with his gaze. Not out of any desire to pleasure her, Kit assumed, more out of an urge to hurt and humiliate. It made her itch, to have him looking her over like an adder might study a succulent mouse, which was why she turned on her heel and made for the stables. Not to be. His voice called her back, and she had no choice but to obey, angered at being ordered to heel like one of Despenser's dogs.

"Ah, the fair Lady Katherine," he said, waving at her to indicate she could straighten up from her reverence. "And may I say you look deliciously pink and round at present – almost good enough to eat." He flashed his teeth at her and took a little stroll around her. She fixed her gaze on a cart trundling through the main gate. "Not your normal, witty self today?"

"I have nothing to say to you, my lord."

His brows rose. "No? And here I was, imagining myself to be quite the competent converser."

Kit shrugged. Maybe if she stayed silent, he'd grow bored.

Despenser took another turn around her, this time uncomfortably close, his fur-trimmed hem brushing against her skirts. "A competent climber, your man," he added when he was face to face with her again. "He scaled that wall as if he'd done so on various occasions in the past."

"He had no choice – but he paid for it later that night. His foot kept him awake." Not true, but it didn't hurt to remind Despenser that her husband was crippled – thanks to him.

He grinned. "I'm not sure I believe you, Lady Katherine. That foot of his is surely healed by now."

"He limps!"

"He walks," Despenser hissed. "The intention was that he wouldn't." Yet another turn around her, and this time his hand travelled over her back, her arm. "If he can walk – and climb – then he could very well have helped Mortimer escape."

"But he didn't," she lied, trying to sound exasperated.

"Of course he did." Despenser's exhalation tickled her ear. "And all I have to do is to find proof. I now have multiple witnesses to his climbing skills, and I'm sure if I look hard enough, I'll find someone to swear he was at the Tower on Lammas night."

"Perjury is a sin," she replied. "So whoever says Adam helped Lord Mortimer is a sinner, God save his soul."

"The things a man will do for gold, Lady Katherine." Despenser chuckled and leaned even closer. "And once I have dear Adam out of the way, who will stop me from having you? As I recall, you owe me for a cracked head."

"Fortunately, Adam is still here."

"Not for long, Lady Katherine." He laughed. "I'd wager he'll be gone by nightfall."

"By nightfall?" Kit didn't understand. Lord Despenser

didn't reply. He just smiled and sketched her a bow before taking his leave.

"Why are you packing?" Kit fell into their chamber, gasping for breath. She had been running, her cheeks flushed, her veil and wimple sufficiently askew to allow Adam a glimpse of her hair. Such beautiful hair, the colour of a fox-pelt, and where Kit would walk about with her hair uncovered at Tresaints – unless they had guests – here she conformed to expectations and covered her crowning glory.

"Why?" Adam threw a tunic at Gavin. "Because I am commanded to accompany Prince Edward."

"But…" Kit fell silent. She took a couple of deep breaths, hands clenching the dark blue of her skirts. "So when do we leave?"

Adam shook his head. "*I* leave, sweeting. You stay." He knew she wouldn't like it, but had not expected her reaction to be quite so strong. She paled and took hold of the nearest bedpost.

"You can't leave me here on my own!" Her pink tongue darted out to lick at her lips. "Who will…" She broke off, eyes flying to Gavin.

"Leave us," Adam told the lad. "Go and see to Goliath instead – and your rouncey."

The lad's grin was so wide, Adam couldn't help but smile back. From Kit came a low sound, and once Gavin was safely out of earshot, Adam went to her and took hold of her hands.

"You'll be safe here, and it is better that you remain in stillness, what with your condition."

"Safe?" She jerked her hands free. "Is Despenser going with you then?" She unclasped her cloak and draped it over a chair.

"No." He sat down on the bed, patting the counterpane to have her join him. "Just the prince and a selection of his men." He gave her a crooked smile. "The king is weaning his son from his mother, and what better way to woo a lad than to give him a palace of his own to refurbish? We leave for the Savoy within the hour to inspect the place, and then, as an additional boon, the king has given the prince permission to go on his very own hunt, accompanied by some of his friends and the men of his household."

Kit remained on her feet. "I can come with you."

"You have not been invited," Adam said. "And besides, we travel on horseback."

"I can ride!"

"You can't ride – not when you're heavy with child."

"I can!"

"I will not allow it." He stood. "I can't have you risking the well-being of our child – and yourself – by galloping about the wintry countryside. Besides, it is a moot point: my lord is taking a handful of men, no more." He went over to his chest and rooted about for a clean pair of hose.

"So you're leaving me at Despenser's disposal," she said.

"Don't be ridiculous! The man won't try anything here." He threw her a look over his shoulder.

"How do you know?" The bed creaked when she sat down. "He told me he would."

"What?" Adam crossed the floor in three strides. "What has he said to you?"

"That once you're out of the way, who is to stop him from…" She swallowed. "You know."

Adam cursed. No wonder his wife was shaking like an aspen leaf. "The queen will see you safe," he tried. "You can stay in her chambers."

"All the time?" she demanded. "Because the moment I step outside, he'll be there, won't he?"

"Sweeting, the man has other things to do than to plague us. He has a kingdom to run, a master who demands his attention, and more lurid schemes to hatch." He placed an arm round her shoulders. "He just wanted to frighten you."

"And he succeeded. I want you to stay. Please don't leave me, Adam."

"I have to."

"Then take me along!"

"I just said: I can't."

42

Kit shook off his arm and stood. "Then I'll go back home. I'm not staying here without you."

"No." He frowned. "You'll stay here – safe with the queen. A week on the road is too much of a strain in your present condition."

"Staying here is too much of a strain!" she yelled. "Please, Adam." Her voice broke and she swirled away from him.

"I'll speak to the queen. That is all I can do. Besides, you'll be going into confinement soon." Hesitantly, he touched her. She shrugged off his hand. "Kit," he groaned. "What can I do but obey the king?"

"How long?" she asked.

"Some weeks. And should you need me before, you can send me a message – we'll be at Windsor."

"Weeks?" Her voice shook. "And you're leaving today?"

"Yes."

"Well then, I'd best not hinder you, my lord." She grabbed at her cloak and rushed for the door.

He beat her to it. "Don't leave like this, Kit."

"I'm not the one leaving – you are." She shoved at him.

Adam was swept by a wave of irritation. What did the woman expect from him? He was duty-bound to accompany the prince, and while he had no doubts that her fear for Despenser was genuine, he also felt she was overreacting. Even Despenser would draw the line at harassing a woman heavy with child. Of course he would – at least here, at court.

"I can do no other. But I would have you kiss me before I go." He stroked her cheek, but she reared back.

"Kiss your precious lordling instead," she snapped, and just like that she was gone.

She stood to the side and watched them leave. Out of the corner of his eye, Adam studied his wife, standing very alone in the shade of the hall. He considered whether to go to her, try once more to bid her a proper farewell, but it should be her approaching him, not the other way around.

Her hands appeared from under her cloak, resting on the swell of their child, and he could feel her gaze burning into him, begging him to cross the yards that separated them. But he was too stubborn, too angry with her for not understanding that he had no choice, was as tethered to this new master of his as if he'd had a collar and leash attached to his neck.

Adam swung astride Goliath and spent some moments soothing his restless stallion. The horse pawed at the ground, dipping his head up and down in his eagerness to be off, and his excitement was contagious, sending a thrill through Adam's body. Once Goliath was under control, Adam rode over to where Kit was standing.

"I'll be back in a month at the latest." No endearment, no smile. She raised her face, her expression revealing how hurt and abandoned she felt.

"A month," she repeated hollowly. "Let's hope I'll still be here."

"Kit," he sighed. "You are to remain here, understood? I'll not—"

"Your master is calling for you," she interrupted. "Best make haste, my lord." Her lashes swept down, hiding her blue gaze.

"God keep you, my lady," he said to the top of her veiled head.

She didn't reply, and only when he turned the horse did he hear her whisper, "And you" to his back.

Chapter 5

As instructed by Adam, Mabel moved Kit and Tom into a small room within the queen's apartments. Kit protested, out of anger with her overbearing man at arranging things over her head, but when Mabel snapped and told her he wouldn't have had to do that if Kit had talked to him – properly – before he left, Kit subsided into a silent sulking.

"Stop this, m'lady," Mabel said, bending down to adjust Tom's coif. "You know well enough he has no choice. As his liege lord commands, so he must do."

Kit fiddled with her girdle. Yes, of course she knew just how insignificant Adam's wishes – or hers – were compared to the commands of his lord. And as a convicted traitor, Adam had much more to prove than any of his companions. But she couldn't suppress the sensation of having been abandoned, here in an environment that she found difficult to navigate, even more so when it contained the presence of Lord Despenser.

"He did not look overly dejected when he left," she said. "One could almost think he was looking forward to it."

Mabel rolled her eyes. "He's a man, my lady. Men have strange inclinations at times." She straightened up slowly and rubbed at her hip. "But to accuse him of wanting to leave you is unfair."

Kit knew the old woman was right, but that didn't help. These last few days, she had only ventured out of her room in the company of the queen and Lady Eleanor – where the queen went, Eleanor went, whether Isabella wanted her to or not – which meant her excursions were restricted to repeated visits to the chapel, the odd meal in the great hall, and languid strolls around the palace gardens.

The queen seemed to have no desire to see her husband. The king had not set foot in her chambers since the acrimonious exchange over Prince Edward's departure. As the other royal children had been returned to their country home, complete with nurses and a bevy of officers, the king no longer had any reason to visit the queen's apartments, so instead he filled his palace with the sound of laughter and merriment, pointedly ignoring his wife.

Now and then, Queen Isabella broke her self-imposed exile and swept into the hall at dinnertime. Impeccably dressed, the queen glided down the hall, stopping to exchange a gracious comment or two with one noble or the other. With a serene smile, she would then proceed to the high table, as a matter of course taking the seat beside the king's. As she was always late, this generally meant Despenser was forced to vacate his place, bowing his apologies. The king never said anything, but from the way his hand tightened round his eating knife, Kit suspected there were times when he was tempted to stab his wife.

"He can't very well protest," Mabel explained. Kit had slipped away from the queen's retinue to join Mabel right at the back of the hall, preferring to remain out of sight. "The court is filled with emissaries and spies from France, and it will not help the present situation with Gascony if King Charles were to hear his sister is badly treated."

"And you think she doesn't tell him?" Kit swept the hall, trying to guess who the spies might be.

"I think our lady queen is most circumspect." Mabel tapped her nose, hovering over Kit as she sat down at one of the tables. "She plans for the future, m'lady, and God help the king if that future doesn't include him."

"Shh!" Kit pulled Mabel down to sit beside her. "Talk like that can get you in trouble."

"Me?" Mabel laughed. "I'm an old nobody, m'lady. A witless crone with one foot in the grave." Kit laughed, despite herself. Mabel was old and wrinkled, her bosom sagged and her back had acquired a permanent curvature, but she was in the best of health, curious eyes registering everything around her.

"You don't fool everyone," she warned, but left it at that.

A week into Adam's absence, Kit woke to the sound of horses and loud male voices.

"The king is going to Dunstable, to hunt," Mabel informed her. "If you hurry, you can see them before they leave." Kit yawned. She wanted to sleep, not be dragged out of bed when it was still dark outside. She pressed the flat of her hand to her belly, trying to numb the sudden, mauling pain. An early contraction, she concluded, not something to share with Mabel or she'd find herself confined to her room within the hour.

"Despenser is going with him," Mabel continued, "as are most of the king's loyal nobles." She sniffed. "Off to hunt boar, I reckon. Pretend they're brave by taking on the cornered beast on foot."

"That does sounds brave," Kit said. "Or foolish."

"Mostly foolish. I've seen quite a few men carried home to die in agony after being gored by an enraged boar."

"Let's hope the boar takes a dislike to Despenser," Kit muttered before turning her back on Mabel and drifting back to sleep.

Westminster Palace without its king was a peaceful place. For the first time in days, Kit breathed freely. No Lord Despenser, no need to scurry along the passages like an elusive rat to avoid him. When she shared this with Mabel, the old woman burst out laughing.

"Is that why you've stayed in your room? Because you fear Lord Despenser?"

"Yes." Kit gave her a huffy look. This was not amusing.

"And you think he has nothing to do all day but to stalk you?"

"No. But I prefer not seeing him at all. He…" She plucked at her sleeve. "He intimidates me."

Mabel clucked. "Of course he does, m'lady. That man is the Devil come to earth." She crossed herself. "But from there to think the man may lie in wait for you – well, it's a stretch."

"Do you truly think so?" Adam had said the same thing, and since their encounter in the courtyard, Despenser had not as much as looked her way.

"I do." Mabel nodded repeatedly.

Kit was not the only one enjoying the king's absence. Some days after his departure, Queen Isabella took the opportunity to revolt against the constant presence of Lady Eleanor, ordering the lady out of her sight for having accidentally spilled wine on the queen's work in progress, an embroidered depiction of St Stephen meant for the royal chapel, complete with arrows in gold thread.

"I caused the stains myself," the queen confided to Kit. "She suspects as much, but can't very well accuse me of doing so." Queen Isabella grinned. "And I did sound most distressed, did I not?"

"Very, my lady."

The queen sighed and went back to unpicking the gold thread on the ruined panel. "A short-lived reprieve," she said. "Once my lord and king is back, Lady Eleanor will be back to spy on me."

"When will he be back?" Kit asked.

"God knows. In a week? Two?" The queen patted Kit's hand. "By then, you'll be in confinement. We can't have you walking about much longer – not with a belly the size of an ale keg."

"I don't want to be confined, my lady." Not here, so far from home.

The queen raised her brows. "All well-born ladies retire to their chambers when their time draws near."

"Yes, but I—"

"You will do so as well, Lady Katherine." The queen's tone brooked no discussion. Kit bowed her head submissively.

After vespers a week or so later, Kit was making for the kitchens, having offered to fetch some more marchpane for the queen. The recent altercation between the queen and Lady Eleanor had left her with a sour taste in the mouth, and a desire to escape the presence of the combatants – at least for a short while. She hastened by the various storages, passed the locked spiceries, and stepped aside when half-a-dozen pages came trotting by, carrying flagons of ale from the nearby brewery.

One of the lads could at most be seven, balancing a jug that was too heavy and too full, which resulted in ale spilling down his tunic. His companions laughed, but the lad seemed on the verge of tears, so Kit gave him an encouraging smile, thinking that could be her Tom in some years, sent away from home to serve a future lord and master. Not yet, she reminded herself, but her gaze lingered on the little page.

She was walking along one of the outer passages that connected one part of the sprawling palace buildings with another when she heard the sound of several men's voices from one of the adjoining rooms. Someone laughed, and for a moment Kit was convinced it was Adam. Without further thought, she entered the room.

"Adam? Are you…" She fell silent when two dozen men turned her way. Standing in the midst of them was Lord Despenser himself. Kit turned, making for the door, but someone banged it closed.

"Ah, the delightful Lady de Guirande!" Despenser clasped his hands together and bowed ever so slightly in Kit's direction, his eyes eating his way over her body. Her breasts, her rounded belly – Kit felt denuded by his gaze. His tongue flitted out, wetting his lips.

"My lord." Kit bowed.

"And where is your redoubtable husband, little Kate?" He studied her with bleary eyes, and from the way he swayed on his feet Kit deduced he was drunk.

"My husband is attending to his master's needs – as you well know, my lord."

Despenser chuckled. "Oh dear, and that leaves you all alone, does it not?"

"All alone?" Kit raised her brows and went on to look pointedly at the men that surrounded them.

"Most certainly all alone." Despenser was standing right in front of her. His breath tickled her ear, and she reared back from his unwelcome proximity. His hand closed on her arm, fingers sinking into her flesh with such force they immobilised her. "Have you missed me?" He tottered, crashed into her and squashed her against a nearby pillar.

"Take your hands off me!" Kit shoved at him – hard enough to send him staggering back a couple of paces. He lurched towards her and grabbed at her, fingers closing on the thick material of her sleeves.

"Why should I? There is no escaping me here, dearest Kate." He smelled of wine – far too much wine. He yanked, and she stumbled towards him.

"I'll scream!" She wrested herself free.

Despenser chuckled again, those avid eyes of his regarding her intently. "I like it when a woman screams." He brushed at her breasts, making her recoil. "So what will you do? Pull that dagger you carry and hope it will stop me from courting you?"

"Courting me?" Kit echoed. "You don't want to court me, Lord Despenser. You just want to humiliate me – and frighten me."

Despenser bowed. "You have me there, Lady Katherine. I am rather partial to redheads. It is rare that I get to frighten, humiliate *and* pander to my preferences in women at the same time."

"You're a repulsive man," she hissed, and made as if to walk away.

Once again, those fingers gripped her arm. "You do not have my leave to retire, Lady Katherine." Despenser's voice dripped ice. "And until I say you may, you will remain here."

"I'm going to bed," she told him.

"How delightful," Despenser smirked. "Now I have my head full of all these wonderful images of watching you disrobe." He tightened his hold. "But until I say so, you're not going anywhere. As the most senior noble present, I request your attendance." He steered her in the direction of a table and indicated she should sit.

Kit gave him a mulish look, upon which he increased the pressure on her arm to the point that she gasped.

"Sit."

So she did, and at Despenser's snapped fingers a knight she vaguely recognised came to sit on her further side, while Despenser sat to her right. A goblet was set before her.

"Drink."

She shook her head and concentrated on her breathing, willing away the memories the situation awoke of a previous evening in which she'd sat like this, trapped between Despenser and his henchman. That night, Despenser had attempted to rape her, and if it had not been for a brimming chamber pot he would likely have succeeded. The child inside her kicked, as if signalling she wasn't alone – but she was, terribly alone, surrounded by men wearing Despenser colours.

The knight to her left stank of wine and ale. On her right, Despenser placed his hand on her arm, gold rings glinting in the candlelight as he caressed her.

Kit snatched her arm away. "My lord!"

"Now, now," Despenser said. "We're among friends here, dear Kate. My friends." His mouth was uncomfortably close to her neck. "They will not crook a finger to help you," he told her, and suddenly his hand was on her breast.

"Let me go!" She twisted, but as if on cue, the man to her left leaned his weight against her, effectively immobilising her. Despenser laughed and stuck his finger down her neckline.

"Nowhere to go, little Kate. Nowhere to run, no one to help." He fondled her and she slapped his hand away. "Hold her still," Despenser commanded, and the knight rose, took hold of Kit's arms and pulled them behind her back, forcing her to arch her spine, her breasts rising up to meet Despenser's hands.

"Why are you doing this?" Kit struggled frantically to avoid his hands.

"Why?" Despenser tilted his head and regarded her. "Because I can. And because I can't stop dreaming of the look on Adam de Guirande's face when I tell him I've had his wife." His wine-laden breath was warm on her face. "I was cheated of my pleasures with Adam," he murmured. "I wanted him to die in pain and humiliation, but alas, that was not to be. So I intend to see myself compensated." He dragged a finger down her cheek, her neck, all the way to her cleavage.

"Please, my lord," she begged, hating it that her voice wobbled. "Don't do this. Please stop."

"Stop? I think not. This is but the beginning, Kate." His hands tore her neckline, her chemise, and his men cheered when Despenser uncovered first one, then the second breast. She wanted to disappear, tears of shame blurring her vision, even more so when he cupped her bosom.

"Ah!" she gasped when he squeezed. Despenser laughed, twisting one of her nipples until she cried out.

"Hugh?" A loud voice carried from further down the hall.

"Limping lepers, not now!" Despenser hastily rearranged Kit's clothing, ordered the knight to let go of her, and stood to greet the king, who came towards them.

"My liege!" Hugh hurried to meet him – somewhat unsteadily – and the two men embraced.

Kit's hands trembled wildly as she hid her disarray with her mantle. She stood, and when the knight tried to hinder her from leaving, she stomped on his foot. In response, he shoved her, and Kit stumbled, tried to right herself, but fell over a nearby bench. By sheer luck, she landed on her side rather than on her belly, sliding off the bench to end up on the floor. Agh! For some instances she couldn't breathe.

"My lady?" The king helped her to her feet. "Are you all right?"

Pain walked her side, and her belly, but she pasted a smile on her face and nodded. "Yes, my lord. I merely stumbled." Her eyes found the knight, and now she had a name for him as well. He was Godfrey, the knight sent by Despenser to arrest Adam in the aftermath of Mortimer's escape. The man sneered.

"I don't need another posset!" Kit hurled the mug to the floor. "I need Adam!" She'd written a message immediately upon reaching her room last night, and had spent all day pacing the courtyard, hoping for the distinctive shape of Adam on Goliath. But now the February day was gone, and Mabel had chided her inside, trying to calm her with sweetmeats and hot drinks.

Kit threw Mabel a look. "Sorry," she muttered. "It's not your fault." She scrubbed at her face. "Why hasn't he come?"

"The message might not have reached him yet."

"As I hear it he's at Windsor, not on the other side of the country." She took yet another turn round her room: six paces from the hearth to the window, ten back to the door. "Well, I can't stay here. If I haven't heard from him by tomorrow, we go home."

"My lady!" Mabel looked horrified. "You can't travel – not now."

"I am not staying here – not without Adam." Not after running into Godfrey today – albeit in the company of the queen – and having him mime palming her breasts before making an unequivocal gesture that had Kit pressing her thighs together. She glared at Mabel. "And don't you dare tell the queen I'm planning on going home."

Mabel pursed her mouth.

"Mabel! I'll have you promise you won't tell her."

After a couple of tense moments, Mabel finally nodded. "I promise."

"Good. Let's start packing."

Next morning, Kit had her head in one of her chests when there was a knock on the door. With a grunt, she got off her knees. Her hip and back were on fire after her fall, and the babe had scarcely moved these last few days – but then, she reminded herself, it had not moved much before either, so this was nothing to be overly concerned about. But she was, torn between telling Mabel and her desperate need to go home.

"My lady?" Kit bowed, backing away to allow the queen to enter.

"What is this I hear about you cavorting with Despenser?" the queen demanded.

"Cavorting?" Kit's mouth filled with bile. "Is that what he's saying?"

"It's what Lady Eleanor is saying." The queen peered at Kit. "You've been weeping."

"For two days," Mabel muttered. "Between throwing things and scrubbing at her face and chest."

Queen Isabella pulled her immaculate brows into a frown. "Am I to take it he took liberties?"

Kit looked away and nodded.

"Lady Eleanor tells a different story."

"Well, she would, wouldn't she?"

"But why?" Queen Isabella looked Kit up and down. "Our dear Hugh has other preferences."

Kit hitched her shoulders, uncertain as to how much to share of Adam's experiences at Despenser's hands.

"Ah," the queen said softly. "It's about Adam." She gave a dry chuckle. "That's why Eleanor de Clare is spreading all that gossip – she's making sure Adam will hear it."

"He won't believe it."

"No?" The queen looked sad. "It is my experience men can be made to believe anything."

"Not Adam. Not this."

"Hmm." The queen gave her an encouraging smile, which left her face when her gaze fell on the open chests. "What are you doing?"

"I'm leaving. I can't stay here." For the hundredth time since Despenser had pawed her, Kit scrubbed at her chest.

"You are in no condition to travel." The queen studied Kit's belly.

"You're talking to deaf ears, my lady," Mabel said. "Lady Kit has made up her mind."

"I can't…" Kit stopped, cleared her throat. "That man – I have to get away." And Godfrey, who yet again had appeared before her this morning when Kit returned from prime.

The queen looked anything but convinced. A heated discussion followed, with the queen threatening to confine Kit by force while Kit wept and begged that she be allowed to go home, because she would never feel safe here – not now. At long last, the queen relented.

"Go, then. But what about Adam, will he not fear for you?"

"I have sent him messages, my lady. He has, as yet, not replied."

Queen Isabella patted Kit's arm. "Not all messages reach their intended recipient. Trust me, I know."

Not much of a comfort, not when Kit couldn't quite

forgive Adam for abandoning her, for not sending her any word over the last few weeks. But she smiled and nodded all the same.

Once the queen had left, Kit went into a frenzy, ignoring just how much every movement hurt. All she could think of was getting out of here, of going back to Tresaints.

Hours later, they were finally on their way. After crossing the Thames, they'd transferred to a horse litter, and were now making their way southwest, accompanied by the four Tresaints men who had come with them to London back in December. For the first time in two days, Kit relaxed. The jerky movement of the litter made it difficult to enjoy the trip, but Kit didn't care, reclining against the pillows with a sleeping Tom beside her.

She stroked her son's hair, the exact same shade as Adam's, and for a moment she was suffused with longing for her man, for the look in his eyes when he loved her, the warmth of his hands on her skin. And then the anger came bubbling through, wiping the image of their lovemaking from her mind.

"You're doing this to punish him," Mabel voiced from the opposite side of the litter.

"I'm doing this because I cannot stay – not with Despenser in residence. Or that loathsome worm, Godfrey." Kit placed a hand on her belly, and a soft kick nudged at her palm. It made her smile, and reassured by this sign of life, she sank back against the pillows, calmly meeting Mabel's disapproving look.

Mabel gave a soft snort. "We both know the queen could have ensured he stayed away from you, had you but asked her. No, this is about you wanting Sir Adam to return and find you missing, to have him experience some of the fear you've experienced lately." She leaned forward and gripped Kit's hand. "This is a foolhardy thing to do, m'lady. That child of yours lies far too low, and all this jolting may harm it."

"I'm perfectly hale." Kit closed her eyes. Maybe Mabel was right and Kit should abort this adventure. No. After all,

Mabel *was* right when it came to Adam. Let him return to Westminster and find her gone, let him wonder what might have driven her to leave, let him hear the rumours and realise just what he'd left her to face on her own.

Chapter 6

"Your heart is not in this, Adam." Prince Edward upended the chessboard.

"No, my lord." Adam gave the lad a rueful grin. He missed his wife and at the back of his head was the gnawing guilt that he had left Kit without any attempt to reconcile. Not his fault, he reminded himself, it was Kit who had refused his kiss and embrace, but it didn't much help: he'd left his wife in what she perceived to be the equivalent of a lion's pit – no matter that he did not believe there was any real danger to her, because she did – and had not as much as caressed her face when he left.

He sighed. They'd returned to the Palace of Savoy some days ago, and where Adam had been hoping this signalled an imminent return to Westminster, instead they had been ordered to stay, the prince as irritated by this enforced exile as Adam was.

The prince leaned back in his chair. "I miss my lady mother," he said softly, sounding like the child he still was. He glanced warily at his companions sprawled about the room, not, Adam presumed, wanting them to hear such puling nonsense. Most of them were of an age with their young lord, noble brats who tended to treat Adam with disdain – or had done, until they'd seen him tutor the prince in sword fighting. Now all these fledgling lords begged to be taught as well, but Adam had little intention of doing so, and his prince seemed to be of the same opinion.

"And she misses you, my lord."

"Father…" Prince Edward frowned and corrected himself. "Our king says I am to remain here until he is back at Westminster." He gave his lavish surroundings an exasperated look. "He says a young prince must grow quickly into a man and refrain from taking counsel from weak and vapid women." The prince fiddled with a half-eaten fig. "My lady mother is neither weak nor vapid," he said, in a voice so low Adam had to lean forward to catch what he was saying.

"Queen Isabella is a magnificent lady," Adam said with a smile.

"So why not take her advice?" Prince Edward threw the fig into the blaze of the brazier. "He no longer cares for her. Ever since she told him Lord Despenser was a canker up the royal arse, he has stayed away from her." The boy squared his shoulders. "How can he prefer Lord Despenser to her?"

Adam shifted on his seat. "The king does as he pleases, my lord. And maybe this estrangement will pass. After all, your lady mother is the most beautiful woman in all of England."

"In the world," the prince corrected. "But things grow worse between them."

"Aye." Adam was not about to insult his young lord by lying.

"Maman said that all this…" Edward waved his hand, encompassing the new bed with its green bed-hangings, the sleeping alaunt, the silver candlesticks, the silk cushions, the fur-lined cloak, the exquisite prie-de-dieu in lacquered walnut – even the chamber pot, "…is a bribe from Father, to have me love him more and Maman less." He chewed his lip. "I love them both. Is that so wrong?"

Adam placed a hand on the lad's shoulder and squeezed. "No, my lord, that is not wrong."

"It's not easy being a man," Edward said. "I preferred it when I was a child."

At last came the messenger recalling them to court. A bevy of servants packed up the prince's apartments, loading carts with everything from chests of clothes to the precious featherbed. Prince Edward was astride his horse several hours before the planned departure, and amused himself by riding the poor creature in tight circles round the carts lined up in the lower ward, whooping whenever his antics caused one or other of the servants to drop whatever they were carrying.

"High spirits," Sir Henry commented, giving the prince a fond smile.

"Aye – and little regard for people serving him." It wasn't Adam's place to admonish his lord, but unless his guardian did so soon, he'd do it anyway. Sir Henry Beaumont sniffed, but called out sharply to the prince, reminding him that whatever got broken he would have to replace himself – not the hapless servants. To the lad's credit, he obeyed immediately, bringing his horse to a halt in front of Adam.

"Will you be giving your lady wife a gift?" he asked, a teasing note to his voice. "A little carved rose, perhaps?"

"Perhaps." Adam patted his pouch, in which he carried the labour of love he'd spent the better part of a week finishing.

"A gift for your wife?" Sir Henry snickered. "Don't you think she gets trinkets enough from Despenser?"

"Despenser?" The prince frowned. "Why would Lord Despenser give Lady Katherine gifts?"

In reply, Sir Henry laughed. "For services rendered, perhaps?"

In one smooth movement, Adam had the man by the scruff of his neck. "What are you talking about?"

"It's the talk of the court," Sir Henry replied. "How your wife and Despenser—"

"My wife hates Despenser!"

Sir Henry pulled free of Adam's hold. "And when has that ever stopped Despenser?"

"Damn!" Adam ran for his horse, mounted and yelled Goliath into motion.

"Adam!" Prince Edward spurred his horse. "Adam, wait." He caught up. "Just because people say something, it isn't true. My lady mother says Despenser causes more damage with his cleft tongue than he does with his actions."

Adam nodded, incapable of speech.

The prince leaned over, placing a gloved hand on Adam's sleeve. "God be with you. Go and find your wife."

Adam stormed into Westminster Palace less than half an hour later, leaving a winded Goliath in the care of one of the stable boys. He ran from the stables, cut across the courtyard and took the worn stone treads of the staircase leading up to the queen's apartments in twos.

"Looking for your wife, Sir Adam?" Eleanor de Clare gave him a sly look. "Well, she isn't here – couldn't show herself after the incident."

"What incident?"

"An incident involving my lord, your false wife and her bared breasts."

Adam closed his eyes. His Kit would rather fondle a serpent than willingly submit to Despenser's touch. He drew in a shuddering breath: this was his fault, for leaving her alone. He brushed by Lady Eleanor, hastening towards the queen's hall.

From behind him, he heard Lady Eleanor's mocking laugh. "And you thought her true, did you?"

Adam turned. "I know she is. This is your warped husband doing what he does best – frightening those weaker than him."

"How dare you?" Lady Eleanor's face contorted into a scowl.

"I am but stating the truth, my lady." He didn't even bow; he spun on his toes and hurried on.

Queen Isabella rose to her feet when Adam entered. He kneeled before her.

"My wife?"

"She isn't here," the queen said, gesturing for him to rise. She gave him a shrewd look. "I take it you've heard the malicious slander Eleanor de Clare has been spreading."

"Aye." Adam clenched his teeth.

"Jealous old hag," the queen said. "She doesn't like it that your wife is so attractive." Old? As far as Adam knew, the queen and Lady Eleanor were of an age – not that he much cared at present.

"What happened?"

"I don't know. All I know is that Despenser was drunk and that Kit went about for two days afterwards, shaking as if she had the ague. And then she left, stating it was impossible for her to remain here without you."

"Left for where?" But he knew, cursing his wife for being so foolish as to travel all the way back home.

"For that little manor she speaks so much about – Tresaints, is it?" She smiled. "But surely you know all this? She sent you messages."

"Messages?" Adam shook his head. "I never got any."

The queen pursed her mouth, scanning her assembled ladies. "As I thought. Someone intercepted them." She gave a dry laugh. "Well, we both know who, don't we? Lady Eleanor is quite the magpie when it comes to other people's missives."

"I must go to her." Adam strode towards the door.

"Must, Sir Adam?" The queen's voice had him coming to a halt. She waited until he turned to face her, then held his gaze until he bowed. He knotted his hands and concentrated on his breathing lest he do something utterly foolish like shaking the queen until her teeth rattled. She laughed. "That's better." She touched his arm. "You have my leave to go to her."

They'd ridden like the wind. For four days straight, they'd been in the saddle, and by the time Tresaints rose before them, nestled into its protective dale, Adam and Gavin were covered head to toe in mud and dust, Adam so tired he was finding it a trial to stay awake. As he turned down the lane, he held in Goliath, studying the view before him.

In the soft light of the March sunset, the whitewashed walls of his little manor shimmered in the palest of pinks, as did the folds of the distant Malvern Hills. The house, the chapel, the stable and the barn – they all looked the same as when last he saw them, solid buildings that together with a man-high wooden fence created an enclosure. To his left, his sheep were grazing; closer to the manor were the pastures for the horses, and behind the gables of the manor house he could make out the as yet denuded orchard trees.

"Home, lad," he said to Gavin as he nudged Goliath back into a slow walk.

"Yes, m'lord." At present, Gavin was all bloodshot eyes

and pale cheeks, but he grinned back, casting a longing look at the house.

"Bath and bed, hey, lad?"

"Bed, m'lord," Gavin mumbled. "And food."

Adam laughed. "Yes, food would be good."

The lane was bordered by a hornbeam hedge, old enough that John, Mabel's brother, would brag that it was his grandfather who had planted it. To Adam's right, the fields had been ploughed and planted, narrow strips of black earth that extended towards the horizon. It was good to be home, he reflected, feeling his shoulders relax.

The moment he entered the yard, he knew something was wrong. He could see it in the furtive glances, in how the household kept their distance rather than swarming forward to greet him. An icy fist tightened round his innards.

"Kit?" he asked John as he dismounted. "Where is my wife?"

"Abed, m'lord," the old man replied. "She is doing poorly."

Mabel met him at the door, watching him leap up the wooden stairs to the main hall.

"Kit?"

"She lost the baby, m'lord." For the first time ever, Mabel looked about to weep. "There was nothing to do, the babe was born flaccid and blue." She rubbed at her face. "She was too frail. Even had she been carried to full term, she would have died."

"A daughter?" Adam's throat clogged.

"A girl." Mabel smiled through her tears. "A pretty little creature, destined to be one of God's angels." She motioned up the stairs to the solar. "Go to her, m'lord. She needs you."

Adam hesitated by the door, took a couple of deep breaths and shoved it open, stepping quietly into the chamber. It was sunk in gloom, the shutters closed and only one candle left burning by the bed. Not the way it was supposed to be, this, their private space: it should be full of light and joy.

Kit was lying on her side, facing away from the door. When he sat down on the bed, she turned, startled, and at first he saw her eyes widen, her lips stretching into a tremulous smile, but moments later she buried her face in the pillows.

"Go away," she said tonelessly. "You came too late."

"Too late?" He placed a hand on her shoulder. "I came as fast as I could."

"You weren't here!" She slapped away his hand and sat up. "I needed you and you weren't here!"

"I didn't know," he tried.

"I told you! I begged you not to leave me behind, but you did anyway. You just…"

"I had no choice!" With an effort, Adam lowered his voice. "You know I had no choice, sweeting."

"And that doesn't help. Not this time."

"I am sworn to serve the prince." She knew that, didn't she? He had no say in how his life was ordered, a minor knight who depended on the continued goodwill of the prince so as to remain alive.

She just nodded, studying her hands that were tying and untying the laces of her chemise. "She needed you too. Our daughter should have been held by her father at least once before she died."

He tried to take her hand, but she shook herself free.

"Kit," he groaned, "please, Kit. I never got your message – if I had, I would have come sooner."

"Would you?"

"Aye." He would have moved Heaven and earth to get to her had he known she was hurting, she knew that, didn't she? Apparently not, because instead of turning to face him, she shifted further away from him.

"Best hurry back to your precious lord," she said quietly. "After all, he needs you, doesn't he? And his needs are so much more important than mine – or those of your children." After a number of rebuffed attempts at conversation, Adam left.

"Well, you can't let it lie without sorting it," Mabel told him when he took his problems to her.

"I know. But how do I sort it?"

Mabel sighed and patted him on the arm. "She kept on asking for you, m'lord. All through those hellish hours when the babe was struggling to come out, and your wife was fighting to get her out, all she did was ask for you."

Christ in his glory, but that hurt! "I—"

"I know, m'lord. You were doing your duty by your lord, but in doing so you left her at the mercy of Despenser – or that is what she feels. And when you didn't respond to her messages—"

"I didn't get them!"

"And because you didn't, she set off for home. And now she believes it was that decision that precipitated her labour, thereby killing the babe."

"And did it?"

Mabel hitched her shoulders. "I already told you: the babe was simply not for this world." She handed him a mug of hot ale, and gestured for him to sit by the hearth. The hall was almost deserted, except for a small group of young lads in the further corner, among which Adam could make out Gavin – still as dirty and dishevelled, but looking much happier with a bowl of stew before him.

"You need a bath, m'lord," Mabel said. "A bath and hot food, and then I suggest you go back upstairs to talk to your wife."

"What can I say to her? She seems to be blaming me as much as herself."

"She's hurting, m'lord. At present, she isn't thinking, she is feeling."

Adam groaned. "So what do I do?"

Mabel gave him a tired look. "I don't know, m'lord."

After a long bath, Adam returned to the solar, clad only in a clean shirt. Kit was still lying in the bed, but he could see in the way her back tensed that she heard him enter. Struck by inspiration, he slipped into bed beside her, wrapped his arms about her and pulled her close, spooning himself protectively around her. She struggled at first, but he insisted, uttering soothing noises until she relaxed against him. They didn't talk. She didn't turn in his arms to face him or kiss him. But at least she remained within his embrace, a quiet, warm weight that slipped into sleep long before he did.

Adam woke to a room bathed in light. The shutters had been thrown wide open, and an icy March wind had him shivering as he dressed. Someone had set out clothes for him. Clean braies, thick woollen hose and a heavy tunic in dark blue.

"My wife?" he demanded of Mabel, stooping to kiss Tom noisily. His son giggled and held out his arms. Adam obliged, hugging the warm little body close.

Tom patted at his face with a sticky hand, warbling, "Papa" over and over again.

"Outside." Mabel took Tom back. "She's probably down by the water."

Mabel was right. Adam found Kit by the stream, in the little hollow that was their miniature Garden of Eden. He smiled at the memories of his Kit naked in the summer grass, of the way she laughed when she splashed through the shallow waters of the pool. She wasn't laughing now, sitting huddled just by the water, her thick winter cloak draped like protective armour around her.

"Tell me about her," Adam said, sinking down to sit beside her.

She didn't reply at first. Instead she sat staring at the water, now and then sending a pebble flying to land with a soft plop.

"There is nothing to tell. She is dead."

"But she lived before she died, did she not?" Adam had seen dead infants before, but never one of his own, and grief rushed through him. He'd had a daughter, but she was dead and he had never seen her nor held her. Something of his pain must have coloured his voice, because Kit turned her head to look at him, her heavy hair lying like a mantle down her back.

"She was bald, but I could see she'd be fair – like you." She gnawed at her lip. "She never opened her eyes. She lived for one pitiful day, and not once did she open them. So I don't know if they were blue or green or brown or grey. All I know is that she had long, fair lashes, and that when I held her, her eyelids fluttered, as if she was trying to open them but couldn't quite find the strength to do so." Her voice broke. "I knew the moment I saw her that she wouldn't live."

"Oh, Kit," he said, taking her hand. "I am so sorry I wasn't here – for you and for her. And I swear that had I known, I would have come, no matter what the prince might have said." He tightened his hold on her fingers. "In my heart, you always come first. You know that, don't you?"

"Not always." She kept her gaze on her lap, her posture stiff and unyielding.

"I…" He cleared his throat. "I do not have the luxury to order my life. If I had, I'd never be parted from you, never spend a night without you in my arms." He caught a flash of blue from under her lashes, the only sign she was listening to him. "This is home," he said softly, "this place, this house, but most of all it is you. You are my home and my life, and every day I spend away from you is a wasted day, a day I pray will pass as quickly as possible, that I might return to you all the sooner."

She glanced at him. "Quite the troubadour."

"No." He tugged at her hand, and she shifted closer. "It is the truth." He reached out to smooth at her hair. "As the queen once said, you are the sun in my existence. What man prefers stumbling about in the dark to standing in the brightness of a sunbeam?"

There was a muffled sound he first assumed to be sobs.

"The brightness of a sunbeam?" Kit lifted her face, her mouth quivering – with laughter. It bubbled from her, and then she was no longer laughing, she was weeping, and Adam gathered her close, pressing his cheek to her head. Only when she had quieted did he rear back sufficiently to see her face.

"Tell me everything, sweeting."

"Everything about what?"

"Let's start with what happened with Despenser."

She paled.

Over the coming hour, he wheedled the entire story out of her. He was rigid with anger when she was done – unjustly angry at her for having walked into the situation, righteously enraged with Despenser for having submitted his wife to such humiliation, and furious with himself for having abandoned her.

It tore at him that another man had pawed at her breasts, that an entire room full of men had seen them, these shapely orbs meant for his pleasure only. But most of all, he hated Despenser for the fear that lingered in Kit's eyes as she spoke of the incident. And as to that malicious gossip Eleanor de Clare…well, she deserved to be belted.

She fell silent once she was done, fiddling with the leather laces of her cloak. Now and then, he caught her looking at him, but he had no idea what to say, not yet, so he pulled at a straw of yesteryear's grass and lost himself in the undulating horizon. He felt helpless; he wanted to promise her redress but knew he couldn't, because what could he do against a man as powerful as Despenser? Another debt to call in later, he thought darkly, wishing things had been different.

"You think it's my fault, don't you?" she said, breaking the silence.

"Your fault?" Adam regarded her cautiously.

"The baby," she whispered, tightening her hands so that the knuckles stood white against her skin.

"The babe?" He was confused by the sudden change in subject.

"If I hadn't fled from Westminster, I'd—"

"Sweeting," he interrupted. "It was not your fault. The babe was not meant for this world. Mabel said she was too frail, too unformed."

"And is that not my fault?" she groaned. "Is it not the mother's fault if her children are born weak and unfit for life?"

"Shush." He cupped her face in his hands and tilted it upwards. Tears leaked out from her eyes, and he kissed them away, one by one. "You and I will have many more children – sons and daughters as hale and hearty as our Tom. This little one, she was meant for God – our own little guardian angel, if you will."

She gave him a tremulous smile. "An angel?"

"Most certainly an angel." He sealed his lips to hers and closed off any further discussion.

Chapter 7

April disappeared in a haze of apple blossom. Not one word from the prince, and as long as no one summoned him, Adam was content to remain at home – that was what he said to Kit, and she had no reason to disbelieve him. Here, at Tresaints, their days were filled with work and laughter, and as the weeks passed, Kit's grief for the little life she would never see grow into a being of its own lost its sharp edges, becoming a sad memory rather than an unbearable burden.

There was a cross in the graveyard with the baby's name, and Adam and Kit had agreed to bury the rose he'd carved for Kit with their child, sending something with her into the afterlife. Quite often, Kit would detour to sit by the small mound, but where initially her thoughts were dark and restless, she soon began to find an element of peace while sitting by her daughter's grave, and more often than not she found herself thinking of other things – like when was Adam going to return to her bed in the proper sense of the word.

After waiting in vain, Kit decided to take things into her own hands. It was more than six weeks since little Matilda had been born, and she missed her man, a throbbing ache building inside of her as she watched him from afar, often in only his braies as he helped with the work on the manor.

So she packed a basket. Mabel grinned lewdly when Kit explained her ulterior motives, and produced cheese, bread, and an egg and curd pudding, waggling her rather hairless brows as she informed Kit that eggs were good for enhancing male performance. Kit merely smiled. From previous experience, this was not an issue for Adam.

If Mabel found the notion of a meal outdoors risible, Adam looked confused – until Kit took his hand and ran a light finger over his inner wrist.

They walked along the stream for some time, and by the

time it was narrow enough to leap across, Adam suggested they do so, pointing at a collection of large boulders some way off. The sun was warm enough to allow them to walk without cloaks, and they walked hand in hand over tussocks of grass and the odd muddy puddle.

This early in the year, the grass was still a bright, rich green, dotted by thousands upon thousands of yellow dandelions. A gnarled hawthorn was draped in white blossom, perfuming the air with its scent. And there, just under the hawthorn, Adam spread his cloak and invited her to sit.

Adam was not a man to allow others to lead when it came to lovemaking, and Kit had long ago learnt that her skilled lover knew her body better than she did, eliciting reactions she never quite expected to experience. He started by undressing her, and she alternated between shyness at being so exposed and triumph when he devoured her with his eyes. She was soon on her back, gazing at the cloud-dotted blue that spread above her, while he explored her inner thighs with fingers that left scorch marks in their wake – or so it felt.

But it was what followed that she loved the most: the way he entered her, inch by careful inch, his eyes never leaving hers. The way he slid his hands under her buttocks and lifted her towards him, pressing himself so deeply inside of her she could swear his balls were pressed against her privates. The way he told her that he loved her, the way he thrust into her, rotating his hips so that he left her gasping his name. How he groaned her name when he climaxed, the way he kissed her afterwards, how he enveloped her in his body and rocked them both to sleep, while way up high a kestrel stood sentinel. Yes, that was by far the best part, Kit thought drowsily, scrubbing her face against the golden fuzz that covered his chest. All of it.

"Why haven't you been summoned back?" she asked much later, lying with her head pillowed on his shoulder.

"I don't know." He raised his head to look at her. "Nor do I care."

"Will it last?"

His chest expanded, the following exhalation loud and

long. "Of course not." Adam toyed with her hair. "Maybe next time you should stay here."

In response, she dug her chin into his chest. "Where you go, I go. Always."

"Unless I tell you not to," he said with a smile.

She raised herself on her arms. "But you won't."

"No," he sighed. "I won't. I need you with me in that human cesspit that passes for the royal court."

Kit laughed. "It's not that bad."

"No?" It came out very bitter, his hold on her hair tightening. "It's like wading through a stinking marsh, dotted with sink-holes."

Some weeks later, Adam was standing up to his ankles in mud and pig shit inspecting the new piglets when a familiar figure came walking down the lane, dark robes flapping round his tall frame.

"It's William!" Kit called, already running to meet their guest.

Adam shook his head at her exuberance, not sure whether to reprimand her for throwing herself into his brother's arms, or be pleased that she so obviously loved William as much as he did. A slight twinge of jealousy rushed through him at how she hung on William's arm for the last few yards down the lane, her face open and bright. Such looks of adoration should be reserved for him.

"You look well," Adam said in lieu of greeting, clasping William's hand.

"And you stink," William replied with a grin. He turned to Kit. "So where is my new nephew? Or is it a niece?"

Kit's features froze. "She died." She tore herself away, running for the chapel. Adam was already hastening after her when William stooped him.

"I'll go," William said. "You go and wash those feet of yours."

Adam's feet were still damp when he entered the chapel. The three saints that gave the manor its name gazed at him from their niches: St Winefride, St Odo and St Wulfstan. He touched St Winefride in greeting and stood for a moment in the entrance, breathing in the silence.

The chapel was alive with the light that poured in from the narrow stained-glass window, reflecting off the walls and gilding the ancient tile floor. Four painted pillars rose towards the high ceiling, the entire space smelling of beeswax and dust, of starched linen and warm wood.

Stark and empty, the chapel contained nothing but a couple of benches against one of the walls and the altar, decorated with two heavy candlesticks in silver and the triptych one of Kit's ancestors had brought back from the Crusades. The Lord Resurrected was depicted on the central pane, its vivid colours contrasting with the otherwise unadorned interior. A place of peace and prayer, Adam reflected as he genuflected before the altar, a haven of tranquillity in a world full of turmoil.

On one of the benches, William and Kit were deep in conversation. William held both of Kit's hands in his, but when Adam approached, Kit disengaged her right hand and held it out to him, as if inviting him into their private conversation. He sat down and extended his bare legs before him. Streaks of dirt decorated his calf, testament to the haste with which he had washed himself.

"I will say mass for her," William said with a little smile. "Commend her safely to Our Lord."

"Thank you," Kit replied, clasping his hand before letting it go.

"So what brings you here?" Adam asked.

"This and that." William's brows pulled together. "I have been travelling up and down this country of ours for months, and a sad and exhausting experience that has been. I needed some respite, I think."

"Is it that bad?" Kit asked.

"Very," William replied. "Everywhere, Despenser's men rule with impunity, and no one goes safe from his – or his father's – roving eye."

Adam nodded. While it was the younger Hugh Despenser he considered his own personal nemesis, the father was of the same ilk – at least where grasping greed was concerned.

Between them, the Earl of Winchester and his royal chancellor of a son were appropriating an ever-increasing share of the kingdom as their own, and in the process people who had held the land for generations were brutally evicted, replaced by Despenser favourites. It was wrong, Adam reflected, throwing a look at the altar. How could God allow men like Despenser to thrive?

William cleared his throat. "I saw Lady Joan some weeks back."

Adam could hear in his brother's voice that the news was not good. "And?"

William shook his head. "Hers is a sad, restricted life. Skipton is not a pleasant abode – and especially not for the king's prisoner."

Adam looked away, recalling Lady Joan as he had last seen her, on a January day more than two years in the past. As always composed, as always seeing her husband off with a calm smile. Only her eyes had given her away – darker than usual, they'd clung to Lord Roger. And now the lady, accustomed to a life of ease and plenty, a life in which she lived surrounded by her many children, her loving husband and adoring household, was locked up in a damp and dark room somewhere, forbidden any contact with her family.

William sighed. "She has aged. These last few years have robbed her of the last of her bloom, and she is no longer the wife Lord Roger recalls. Her hair has gone grey, her gowns gape over her shrunken frame, but she has no money to buy new ones and must make do with what little she has." He glanced at Adam. "When her husband last saw her, she was in the prime of her life. Now she is old – and bitter."

"Because of Lord Mortimer," Kit said.

"No, Kit. Because of the king, oath-breaker that he is." Adam frowned down at his shins. "What can we do to help her?" Lady Joan was the closest thing he had to a mother – a woman who had taken in a badly bruised and bleeding lad and tended to him herself, soft hands and a soft voice soothing his pain and heartache.

William chuckled softly. "For now, the lady is not entirely

penniless. I had to bribe the guards to see her, but I was able to smuggle her coins and word from her lord. Speaking of which…" William rose. "I am called to Paris."

"To Lord Roger?" Adam couldn't keep the longing out of his voice.

"Yes. Lady Joan has entrusted me with messages for him – and then there is the matter of replenishing his coffers."

"Ah." Adam stood as well, limping over to the altar. "Close the door," he told Kit.

Only once she had complied did he lower himself to his knees and insert his hand into the narrow groove at the base of the altar. He found the lever, pressed, and the floor behind the altar fell away, revealing a large, man-high space. A most excellent hiding place – unless one was plagued by fear of confined spaces, which Adam was. And right at the back were several heavy linen sacks, containing the coin and treasures Lady Joan had entrusted to Kit.

William left on the first day of June, weighed down with multiple miniature pouches he hid under his robes. And four weeks later, the summons came, curtly recalling Adam de Guirande to court. They coincided with the arrival of a messenger from Bristol, carrying the sad news that the Aymer de Valence was dead, struck down while negotiating on the king's behalf in Picardy.

"God have mercy on his soul," Adam said, crossing himself. A great man was dead, just when his country needed men like him, men of honour and integrity. And God alone knew what would happen in France with the earl gone. Not that Pembroke had succeeded in brokering a treaty between the aggrieved French king and his equally aggrieved English royal vassal, but at least he had been trusted by both sides – and not many men were.

"God have mercy on all of us," Kit said. "With Aymer de Valence dies the last restraint on the king."

Chapter 8

The court was at Woodstock for the summer. After several days in the saddle, it was with relief that Kit saw the outer walls of the royal demesne loom before her, but once through the gate it was a long ride to the palace as such, the narrow track winding its way through the wooded landscape that had once housed a royal menagerie. No more, Adam assured her, laughing when Kit expressed concerns that there might be a lion or two about.

The first buildings they came upon were old, dilapidated structures in wood that leaned against their neighbours as if the timbers could no longer support the heavy thatched roofs. A furlong or so further along, and the walls of the royal abode had them drawing their mounts to a halt. There was a line at the gatehouse, and only after having been thoroughly scrutinised by the guards were they allowed entry, hoof-beats echoing on the packed earth of the outer bailey.

Construction was ongoing, scaffolds raised around one of the various buildings, while men and lads scurried back and forth with lengths of timber and buckets of mortar. To their far right were the stables, and if Kit rose in her stirrups she had an uninterrupted view of the entrance to the main house, a sturdy construction of stone topped by several half-timbered storeys. Like a collection of manor houses, Kit concluded, sitting back down with a thump, thinking that she liked Woodstock much more than Westminster, no matter that this royal palace had far less grandeur. Maybe that was why, she reflected, sliding off her horse into Adam's waiting arms.

Compared to the bustle of Westminster, Woodstock was a country retreat, although the press of the assembled nobles, summoned from all over the country so as to be adequately supervised by the king and Despenser, converted the peaceful tranquillity into a crowded hubbub of voices.

"If they're here, they cannot plot against him," Adam explained to Kit. "Or that is what Despenser thinks." He grinned. "I'd say this summer court is a hotbed of grievances – Despenser best beware that it does not swell into something uncontainable."

For the first week, incessant rain kept most of the court indoors, the great hall a thronged and noisy place. Every morning, fresh herbs were strewn atop the rush mats. By the evening meal, they had wilted, dried sprigs lying amidst dropped food and wine stains, now and then further decorated by a smear of blood. Several days indoors resulted in frayed tempers and the odd drunken squabble.

Kit was distracted from a heated argument between two young men, one of them wearing the Despenser colours, the other with a badge proclaiming him to be a member of the Earl of Norfolk's household, when an unknown man entered the hall.

For a moment, the man stood in the doorway, heavy-lidded eyes regarding the scene before him. With a nod to one of the guards, he began a slow and stately walk towards the dais and the king.

"Who is that?" Kit asked Adam, trying to place the man. With a nose like a beak, he reminded her of an effigy, all sharp planes and no softness.

"That," Adam said, tearing off yet another piece of bread, "is Henry of Lancaster, Earl of Leicester, cousin to the king and brother of the executed traitor Thomas of Lancaster, God curse his soul."

Ah. He'd been at Kenilworth, Kit recalled, walking about with the expression of a severely constipated man. Kit studied Earl Henry curiously, listening with half an ear as Adam went on to say something most uncomplimentary about the former Earl of Lancaster, muttering that had Thomas of Lancaster only been true to the alliance he had formed with Roger Mortimer, then it would not have been Despenser sitting at the king's right hand, it would have been Earl Thomas and Lord Mortimer.

Henry of Lancaster had by now reached the king, and bowed deeply. The king nodded, no more, dismissing him with a wave of his hand before going back to his conversation with Hugh Despenser – the two of them, as both father and son Despenser were presently attending the king.

Henry straightened up, face bright red. For an instant, his eyes blazed, mouth so compressed his lips were all but invisible. Moments later, the king's cousin had arranged his countenance in a bland smile, and turned his attention to greeting his peers.

"As difficult as his brother and as convinced of his own infallibility," Adam muttered, regarding the strutting popinjay that was the Earl of Leicester with a deep crease between his brows. "But any man who takes on the role of being a burr up Despenser's arse is my friend, and Henry of Lancaster would gladly slit Despenser's throat wide open if he got the chance."

"As would many others," Kit said.

"Aye." Adam fingered his dagger. "There are many men with grievances towards the Despensers. And one day they'll pay, son and father both." He cleared his throat, his gaze never leaving the spectacle of Hugh Despenser elder and younger fawning on the king. "It is wrong that they should thrive while men like de Bohun and Badlesmere are dead. But soon, it will all change."

"Shh," Kit admonished, casting a nervous look over her shoulder.

"I have to hold on to that hope," Adam murmured.

"And will the king's cousin help?" Kit asked, inclining her head in the direction of Henry of Lancaster.

"He will, I think. At present he is a most disgruntled cousin, as the king has refused to give him the Lancaster lands, which are his by right. Throwing him the sop of the earldom of Leicester won't go a long way."

"Once burnt, twice shy. I suppose the king prefers keeping his cousin on a short leash so as to avoid yet another rebellion."

"He should be concerned about more than Henry of Lancaster. I'd say half the men in this room have reached the point where they are considering drastic measures. The kingdom must be rid of the Despensers before they gobble it all up for themselves." Discreetly, Adam nodded in the direction of a knot of men, with the Earl of Norfolk in their midst. Earl Thomas looked their way, eyes briefly meeting Kit's.

Their conversation was interrupted by Henry of Lancaster himself. Adam bowed deeply, and Kit followed suit, her head lowered.

Legs clad in red silk hose ended in shoes of finest leather, and what little she could see of Lancaster's robes were as red as his hose, embroidered with yellow suns and trimmed with yellow velvet.

"My lord," Adam said.

"De Guirande, is it not?" Henry of Lancaster sounded mildly curious, glancing at Adam's right foot. Adam stiffened, shifting from foot to foot as if to show the Earl of Leicester that Adam de Guirande was not incapacitated. A shadow of a smile crossed Earl Henry's lips, then he inclined his head and glided off.

"Wasn't he married to Despenser's half-sister?" Kit asked, watching Earl Henry flit like a huge red and gold butterfly from one man to the other, stopping to exchange a few words with most of them.

"Lady Maud," Adam confirmed. "She died some years ago." He grinned. "Not much love lost between her and her half-sibling. Maud Chaworth grew up with Henry of Lancaster, and was first and foremost his wife."

There was a commotion at the door and Queen Isabella entered, followed by her two sons. She swept through the assembled people, looking straight ahead, but Prince Edward grinned at Adam as he passed, one hand on his younger brother's shoulder.

The king stood. The queen made a deep reverence, as did her sons. King Edward indicated his wife should sit beside him, but throughout the meal he concentrated his attentions on his sons, leaving the queen to sit in silence – unless she chose to converse with Despenser, seated on her other side.

The queen did not. She ate and drank, now and then she smiled fleetingly at someone, but not once did she as much as glance at the royal chancellor.

Lord Despenser did not seem perturbed. He lavished his attention on Edmund of Woodstock instead.

"Must he humiliate her so openly?" Kit asked, feeling sorry for the queen, so regal and yet so vulnerable, an island of isolation in the merry sea that was King Edward's court.

"What fun would there be in a private humiliation?" Adam replied. "He no longer trusts her and has no compunction in showing the world how he feels. Everything our lady queen does is monitored. The women that share her bedchamber have been chosen by the king, and Lady Eleanor has her long nose in every aspect of the queen's life." He sighed. "A caged hawk, our Queen Isabella."

A most irate hawk, as Kit discovered over the coming days. With more clement weather, the queen chose to take her ladies for extended walks through the palace grounds, at a pace that had most of the women flagging – even the redoubtable Eleanor de Clare. Queen Isabella took the opportunity to spew her bitterness over her situation to Kit, who almost had to run to keep up with her, splendid and forceful in her anger.

"They will pay," the queen vowed. "All of them, and that Eleanor de Clare most of all."

"She doesn't have much choice, my lady. The king has—"

"Much choice? She enjoys it!" The queen directed a furious look at Despenser's wife, now several yards behind them. Kit silently agreed, even if now and then she got the impression Lady Eleanor was uncomfortable with her role as head gaoler – and quite exhausted by it, what with having her own affairs to handle as well. This was probably why Lady Eleanor was not constantly by the queen's side, a relief not only for the two women involved, but also for Kit and the other of the queen's ladies.

"Will your daughters be coming to join us?" she asked to change the subject.

The queen slowed her pace. "For some weeks," she said

with a shrug. "Small children do best far away from the bustle of court." She studied Kit. "Even your Tom would be happier at home."

At two, Tom was an active little lad, and fretted at always being shadowed by Amy, his long-suffering nurse. But having lost the baby, Kit required the reassurance of her son's presence – even if at present it resulted in unbearable sleeping conditions. Adam had been allotted a small room in which they all had to sleep – including Gavin, Mabel, Amy and Tom – reducing her private space with Adam to the murky interior of the bed, once the hangings had been closed.

"You'll not be seeing much of him now," the queen commented, jarring Kit out of her contemplation of her bed and Adam. The queen pointed at Adam, standing some distance away with Prince Edward and some other men. Kit smiled at the sight of her husband, well over half a head taller than the men surrounding him. The sunlight glinted off his fair hair, caught on the metal buckle of his belt and transformed the dull grey of his fustian tunic into something akin to silver silk – until the sun entered yet another cloud bank.

"I haven't been seeing much of him since Prince Edward arrived," Kit corrected. The prince had ridden in the day after them, accompanied by his extensive retinue, complete with tutors, chaplains and men-at-arms. Ever since, her husband was at the beck and call of his master, so to the inconvenience of restricted private space, Kit also had to add the further complication of very little time alone with Adam. But he seemed happy with his young lord, admitting to Kit that the boy was easy to love – and respect.

After rain came heat – with a vengeance. The king and his selected companions would ride out at dawn, return dusty and sweaty around midday, and pass the afternoon in the coolness of the hall. Tensions were riding high, Adam reflected, noting with interest how the assembled men gravitated towards different groups. No one was fool enough to treat either of the Despensers with less than the respect they required, but behind their backs, faces settled into harsh masks of dislike.

Years of riding roughshod over their countrymen had made the Despensers the most hated men in the kingdom, and while the king was surely aware of this, he was incapable of denying himself the pleasure of their company – that was Adam's conclusion after hearing the king's hissed comment to the Earl of Norfolk, telling his half-brother to not meddle in matters that did not concern him.

"Their reputation besmirches yours, brother," Earl Thomas insisted.

"I am your king first, your brother second," King Edward retorted. "And I need men like Hugh, men I can trust with my life."

"Men that can cost you your life." Earl Thomas lowered his voice so that Adam had to strain to hear him.

"Men I cannot turn my back on," the king said, sounding bleak. "Because the moment I do, they will die."

For the first time in years, Adam felt some compassion for his king. Not entirely without honour, he reflected as he ducked behind a pillar. The king was caught between the Devil and a bottomless pit when it came to the Despensers, his own fate linked to that of his favourites. But then Adam remembered Lord Roger, at present in frustrated exile in France, and Lady Joan, locked away at Skipton, and whatever pity he had was submerged in bitter, impotent rage.

Adam maintained a neutral distance from the various political groupings, all too aware of how Despenser's gaze burnt into the back of his head. Instead, he concentrated his attentions on the prince, and spent the stillness of the afternoons perfecting his future king's archery skills – not that Prince Edward felt there was much to improve.

"I don't think I have the temperament for this," Edward complained one afternoon, flinging the bow away from him.

"It is not a matter of temperament, it is a matter of perseverance," Sir Henry piped up from where he was sitting in the shade.

"A king must be proficient with the sword," Edward said haughtily.

Sir Henry laughed. "A warrior king must be capable with

all weapons, my prince." He softened his voice. "You are destined to be a great king, my lord. Best you be prepared for the task that lies ahead of you."

Prince Edward mulled this over. "A great king leads, he doesn't fight."

"In which case we should resume your studies," Sir Henry said, getting to his feet. "Strategy is best learnt from ancient tracts – at least at your age." He dusted down his tunic. "Let us retire indoors, Lord Edward."

The prince made a face but followed obediently, dragging his feet in a way that made Adam chuckle.

"You like the lad." The voice came from Adam's left.

"I do." Adam bowed in greeting. Henry of Lancaster waved him to stand.

"Will he be the king we need?" Lancaster asked, studying the departing prince. "Will he restore the dignity of the monarchy to its former state?"

Adam was not about to answer – he didn't know Henry of Lancaster well enough to risk saying something that could be twisted into an admission of planned treason.

Henry gave him a little smile and tapped his nose. "One can never be too cautious, eh?"

"My lord?"

"We all know who put you in Edward's household," Henry went on, "and we all know why. Whoever controls the heir to the throne in the coming reckoning, controls the board."

Adam chose to remain silent. After some moments, Henry sighed.

"As you wish, Sir Adam," he said with a mocking grin before flitting off. Adam watched him out of sight, feeling an uncomfortable tightening in his gut. They aimed to use the prince – the queen aimed to use the prince – against the king. Adam clenched his fist. He was the prince's man now, he reminded himself, and he would do whatever it took to keep his lordling safe – even from the ambitious plans of the queen.

Chapter 9

Kit followed her son at a desultory pace along the narrow path that bordered a wheat field. Almost ripe, the wheat stood close to man-high, and Kit had but to crouch to be entirely invisible. Tom's bare legs flashed under his smock, hands held aloft as he attempted to capture a butterfly.

"Look, look, look," he sang, pointing at the butterfly, a heavy head of wheat, an inquisitive ant. Kit smiled at his childish enthusiasm, at the way even the smallest of creatures could be a miracle to a lad of just two.

Excursions such as these were rare, with Kit expected to be at the queen's beck and call, but today the queen was ailing, having retired to her bed, and Kit was free to spend the hot July day as she pleased – which was with her son.

"Little boys tire quickly," Kit said an hour or so later, passing a heavy and warm Tom over to Mabel. Her son looked like an angel, his long, fair hair lying in soft curls round his face, which was pink with sleep and heat. "Have you seen Adam?"

"With the prince," Mabel replied. "Yonder."

Adam was standing surrounded by lads, among whom Prince Edward stuck out on account of his fair hair. A makeshift target was standing fifty feet further away, bows and arrows littered the ground, and when Adam saw Kit he raised his hand in greeting before returning to his charges.

These last few days, he had been a constant protective presence round the prince – most understandable, given his recent conversation with Henry of Lancaster. She frowned: as a further consequence, Adam's admiration for Queen Isabella had cooled somewhat, and Kit was inclined to agree, although she had pointed out that the queen would never jeopardise her son – of that she was certain – and nor would she have resorted to planning to use him as a pawn had she not felt threatened herself.

"I'll take this little man indoors," Mabel said, interrupting Kit's reverie. She kissed Tom's sweaty brow. "Coming, m'lady?"

Kit shook her head. "I'll find some shade outside, I think."

Woodstock was more of a royal hunting lodge than a castle as such, and most of the royal demesne was either cultivated fields or woodlands. Just behind the king's apartments, a herbal garden perfumed the air with sun-warmed lavender, with the scents of drying mints and roses. Kit strolled along the neat paths, and stooped now and then to smell a rose or nip of a sprig of one herb or the other, thinking it would make a fragrant little posy for their room.

It was a relief to step into the shade of the trees, and Kit drifted further into the green shadows, looking for somewhere to sit. An old willow rustled invitingly, the ground below it striped with shadow and sun. Kit ducked under the trailing branches and sat down. She yawned and stretched out on her back, regarding what little she could see of the blue sky through the foliage of the tree. She yawned again.

Kit woke to the sound of voices. In the glade before her, the king was sprawled on the ground, with Despenser sitting beside him. Kit shrank further into the protective shadow of the willow, glad of her dark green skirts.

"Pembroke was old. It was time for him to go," Despenser said. "Hot, is it not?"

"Time?" The king found the weather uninteresting – at least to judge from the look he gave his favourite. "How can you say thus? Aymer de Valence was the single peer in this realm capable of uniting my squabbling barons."

"If so, he didn't do a good job, did he?" Despenser scratched himself over the chest. "The old man was past it."

"The old man was my loyal servant." King Edward frowned. "He never forgave me for what I did to him at Shrewsbury – allowing him to pledge his word as surety to lure the Mortimers to submit, and then refusing to bide by his promise of leniency."

"What were you to do? Pardon that accursed Mortimer? In my opinion, you should have killed him then and there – as you did with Thomas of Lancaster. The only good rebel baron is a dead one, my lord."

The king gave him a sour look. "There are many who would say Mortimer was justified in taking up arms – he was merely defending what was his, knowing full well that if I allowed you to return you would do everything in your power to destroy him."

Despenser snorted.

"And there are many more that remind me of just how ably Mortimer served the crown, before your presence alienated him from me, his royal master."

Despenser spluttered. "Serve the crown? Mortimer served himself! He—"

The king held up his hand. "The traitor Mortimer proved his worth more than once, dear Hugh. Let us keep that in mind." He chuckled drily. "And had it not been his grandfather that severed your grandfather's head all those years ago at Evesham, maybe I would have been spared all this turmoil. My two ablest barons, locked in a vicious circle of revenge and retribution." He tugged at the grass. "A waste, if you ask me. But we have come too far down this particular road for there to ever be a way back – and with Pembroke died any hope of reconciliation. He is sorely missed, a man of integrity and honour, respected by all." He sounded sad and tired, the impression further strengthened by how he dragged a hand across his face.

"So honourable he saved traitors from the gallows," Despenser said scathingly.

The king sighed deeply. "Adam de Guirande again? Really, Hugh, why are you so fixated on one lowly knight?"

A most relevant question, Kit thought.

"Adam de Guirande is one of Mortimer's most capable captains. The man grew up adoring that whoreson of a traitor, and he should have been hanged at Shrewsbury together with his comrades."

"As I recall, you reprieved him." The king extended his shapely legs before him and twitched the folds of his long tunic into place.

Despenser cursed. "I did. A moment of weakness when faced with his begging wife. But I only did so because I believed he would die anyway. Instead, the damned man slipped through my fingers, and I don't like it when men do that."

"Slipped through your fingers?" There was a long silence as the king studied Despenser. "Do you desire him?" He lowered his voice. "Do you want him under you in bed, Hugh, is that what this is all about?"

Despenser laughed. "No, my liege, I do not want him in my bed. I want him in chains and on his knees, with his bared arse at my disposal."

Kit clapped a hand to her mouth to suppress her shocked exclamation. Fortunately, neither the king nor Despenser seemed to have heard her.

"Ah. Sodomy as punishment." The king stood, staring down at Despenser. "Do I not give you what you need? Should I be jealous?"

"My liege," Despenser stammered, getting to his feet.

"Not my liege, Hugh. Not when we are alone – then it is simply Hugh and Edward." He cupped Despenser's face. "And I will not have it that you think of another while you're in my company."

Hugh Despenser groaned. "Edward, my dearest lord, I am incapable of thinking anything at all when I'm with you. You own me. My heart, my soul, my life and body – they are yours, only yours." His voice rang with sincerity, his hands trembling as he placed them on the king's chest.

"If so, it will be no great matter for you to stop pursuing de Guirande – and his wife." The king covered Despenser's hands with his own and squeezed.

Despenser gasped. "But—"

"No, Hugh. You will leave him alone. I never want to see your attention linger on him again, you hear? You will rip him from your mind and give me your undiluted and undivided attention – always. I am a jealous man, and I will not share."

Despenser licked his lips. "The man is a threat to your kingdom."

"Goddamn it, do you think me stupid? He is an itch in your balls, that's all. The single threat to my kingdom is that accursed Mortimer – and perhaps my wife." The king let go of Despenser's wrists and cupped his face instead, hands sliding upwards, into Despenser's dark hair. The royal fingers tightened, and Despenser rose on his toes, a whimper catching in his throat. "Do I have your word?" the king rasped, his nose brushing Despenser's.

"My word," Despenser replied. "You have it, my lord."

"Good." The king bent his head and kissed Despenser full on the mouth. With a responding moan, Despenser slipped his arms round the king's neck and kissed him back. For a moment, Kit no longer saw her hated enemy. She saw a man in love with his king, a man who quivered with passion and whispered endearments. A man who would do anything for his lover – anything at all. Unfortunately, it made Despenser far too human, and therefore harder to hate.

Adam had hoped to be able to escort his wife to supper, but an afternoon spent at the quintain ended with a hasty wash before entering the hall with his young lord, and all he could do was share a rueful smile with Kit as he followed the prince to his table. All through the meal, he kept on glancing at his wife, now and then earning a responding smile, but mostly covertly, thinking he was a fortunate man to have such a comely wife.

A strand or two of her dark red hair had escaped her heavy braid and veil, caressing her face. The recent days of sun had given her skin a golden glow and he knew that should he look closer, he would find her nose covered by a smattering of minute freckles. And then she turned the other way and he saw the jagged scar that ran across her cheekbone, and he fisted his hands under the table, hating Despenser, the man responsible for marking her thus.

The heat of the day still lingered when they stepped outside after the meal. Adam looked for his wife, but couldn't find her, not at first. A flicker of movement caught his eye, a veil fluttering in the evening breeze as she disappeared in the direction of the river. Adam frowned; he didn't like it that his wife went about unaccompanied. A quick look the other way, and there was Hugh Despenser himself, the king by his side. The queen had not left her sickbed to partake of supper, and however disloyal it made him feel, Adam had to admit her absence had been a relief rather than a disappointment, with the presiding king relaxed and merry.

"Ah, de Guirande," the king said when he was within hailing distance. He beckoned Adam towards him, and there was a gleam in his eyes Adam didn't quite understand.

"Sire." Adam made as if to kneel, but was arrested by the king's hand.

"Walk with us," the king commanded, and suddenly Adam was hedged in by the king and Despenser. The king's eyes glittered with suppressed amusement, while Despenser looked as if he'd been force-fed horse shit.

"No traitorous plans brewing in your head?" the king asked. Adam came to a halt, his skin prickling.

"My liege?" he said.

"Just asking, de Guirande." King Edward fixed him with an icy stare. "After all, your former lord is our greatest traitor, and who is to know what he may be up to?"

Despenser chortled, but a look from the king silenced him as effectively as if the king had sliced his throat.

"No traitorous plans, my liege – unless you count escaping from yet another of Prince Edward's chess challenges as one." Adam managed a smile. "It is embarrassing, to be repeatedly defeated by a lad less than half your age."

The king gave him a genuine smile. "Yes, he is good, is he not? That son of mine will make me proud."

"Assuredly," Adam replied. "You and his lady mother both."

A shadow crossed the king's face at the mention of his wife, just as Adam had intended.

"Watch your tongue!" Despenser snarled.

"My lord?" Adam gave him a vacant look. "I was merely expressing the hope that one day our prince may rule both England and France – assuming, of course, that an amicable relationship between our countries is established."

Adam laughed inside at the harried look on Despenser's face. It was no secret that it was Despenser who had advised King Edward to escalate the conflict in Gascony, and God alone knew what could be salvaged of that debacle, what with the French king having sent his formidable uncle to invade the English possessions. As Adam heard it, the young Earl of Kent had been thoroughly trounced by that wily warrior, Charles de Valois.

Adam continued, "It is therefore fortunate, is it not, sire, that the French king holds his sister in such high esteem – a bond of blood uniting our two kingdoms."

"A bond of blood?" King Edward scowled. Adam swallowed nervously. What was he playing at, baiting the king like this? "What sort of a bond is that when my brother-in-law welcomes Roger Mortimer in his kingdom – no, even worse, he entertains that traitorous bastard in his own palaces!"

"My liege, I was but making the point that King Charles has no male heir," Adam said.

The king shot him a look. "Were you? How kind of you to point out the obvious." He stroked his beard. "My son sings your praises," he said abruptly. "Well, not at chess," he continued with a little smile, "but when it comes to sword or mace, to bow or lance, it would appear Sir Adam has no competition, and will make my son a true champion of the lists."

"That is not true, my liege."

"No?" The king looked him up and down. "Then what purpose do you serve?"

"I teach him to survive," Adam replied. "Wars are rarely won by the dead, no matter how many tournaments they may have won."

"So who wins the war?" The king had come to a halt.

"Those that live, sire. Those that persevere and never give up."

"Like your precious baron?" Despenser said.

"Not my baron, not anymore. And Lord Mortimer lost, my lord – as you well know." For now, Adam added silently.

"And if it came to my son or Lord Mortimer, who would

you follow?" The king sounded only mildly curious. Adam raised his face.

"My prince," he replied emphatically. "I serve your son."

For a long time, the king held his gaze. Finally, he gave Adam a curt nod. "You may go."

"My liege." Adam bowed and went to look for his wife.

Kit had not intended to end up in the river – not when she set out. Instead, she had wandered along the narrow bridle path, stopping now and then to admire how the evening sun converted the ripening wheat fields into bands of bright white. But once she reached the bank of the Glyme, it was as if the water called to her, and Kit slipped off shoes and hose to paddle her feet in the dark coolness of the river. She exhaled and wiggled her toes.

Dipping her feet was not enough. Kit rose and walked along the river, hoping to find somewhere secluded enough for her to undress. A bend, a copse of trees, and Kit ducked into the inviting green. Sunbeams rippled through the foliage, speckling the ground below with a dancing pattern of sun and shade. The grass was damp underfoot, and Kit hastened down a slope to where the waters lapped at the shore.

The river was wider here, with stands of alders creating a screen of greenery to shield her from prying eyes. Off came her veil, floating down to join her hose and shoes. Kit twisted like an eel to undo the laces down her side, hoping she'd manage to lace them back up afterwards. She pulled the kirtle over her head, and approached the water in only her shift.

Further out from the bank, the river glittered in the sun, but where she was the water was dark, the bottom muddy and slippery. From somewhere to her left came the distinctive barking sound of a roebuck in heat, but other than that the woods were quiet. Kit kicked up a spray of water, did it again, and laughed out loud. She ran through the shallows and dived into the deeper water, swimming to the other bank and back again before turning on her back to float.

"You should not be wandering about alone." Adam's voice cut through the stillness of the evening.

Kit swam towards him. "I like being alone," she said. "All those people, all those assessing eyes – at times I need to get away."

"Don't we all?" Adam was standing in hose and braies, boots, shirt and tunic heaped on top of her clothes. "But you should still not walk about alone, and what if someone were to see you here?"

Kit laughed. "I'm wearing my shift."

"And? That doesn't help much, does it?" He frowned at her as he shed his braies. A blur of blue to her left caught Kit's attention. A man was standing behind an oak, almost hidden in the shadow. "I'll not have any man see what is only mine to see," Adam went on, wading naked through the shallows. "Come here."

"Why should I?" She glanced at the man just as a patch of sunlight caught him full in the face. Earl Thomas. How long had he been there, spying on her? And what would Adam do if he saw him? Best not find out. "Catch me instead!" She turned, swimming for the deeper end.

"Catch you?" Adam dived into the water and some moments later his arms were round her waist, holding her very close as he surfaced. He kissed her. Deeply. When Kit looked again, the earl was gone.

The next day, Earl Thomas appeared before her just as she left the chapel.

"A word, my lady?" he said, his tone conveying that this was not a request. She was sorely tempted to tell him no, but Adam's conversation with the king last night had her concerned, and it was unwise to antagonise the king's younger brother. So she acquiesced, indicating for Mabel to come along but keep her distance.

"Your wife is not here?" she asked mildly, mainly to unbalance him. Thomas of Brotherton had married well beneath him, a little nobody with no lands, no wealth. Why he had done so was an open question, although speculation ranged from extortion to momentary insanity. When Kit had suggested the earl might have married for love, Adam had laughed out loud, telling her the sons of kings rarely married for love – they kept mistresses for that.

"No – as you well know." Earl Thomas gave her a dark look. "She prefers it that way."

"Ah. And I prefer it if men don't spy on me."

He smiled, those hazel eyes of his contrasting with his sun-tanned face and dark hair. "Some women would consider it a compliment."

"Not me, my lord." She congratulated herself on sounding affronted – and she was, however flattering the admiring look in his eyes.

"No?" he chuckled. "You were quite irresistible, my lady. I had no intention of lingering, but when you pranced about in the shallows, I just had to stay."

Kit's face heated, recalling with some discomfort just how transparent wet linen was – and how short her shift was, exposing most of her calves. "It was wrong of you to do so."

"When you waded deeper, I had to stay. How was I to know you could swim? Besides, there's a current."

"In the Glyme?" Kit snorted.

"All rivers have a current. Some just run deeper than others." His brows pulled together. "Just like some men," he muttered.

"Men like yourself?"

"Like me – and your husband." He smirked. "We have some things in common, your husband and I. Well, not only us, but the queen and Henry of Lancaster, and the Bishops of Hereford and Lincoln, and—"

Kit held up her hand. "I can guess."

Earl Thomas nodded. "I hate Despenser," he said almost inaudibly. "I just thought you should know." He gave her a slight bow, clasped his hands behind his back and sauntered off. "Who taught you to swim?" he called over his shoulder.

"My father," she responded automatically, even if it was a lie. Her father had taught her absolutely nothing, and Kit knew how to swim only because her mother was the daughter of a Lymington salt maker who had no desire to see Kit drown as she'd watched her brother do.

"Really?" the earl threw back. "As I recall, Thomas de Monmouth was scared of water." He swivelled on his toes to face her, a smile tugging at his mouth. "You're a most enigmatic woman, my lady." Yet another bow and he was gone, dipping into the shade of the surrounding buildings.

"His way of letting us know he stands with the queen, I suppose," Adam said when Kit recounted the relevant bits of her meeting with the earl. "Things are starting to turn, Kit. The wheel of fortune is slowly beginning to revolve our way."

"Our way?" Kit frowned. "Is that Lord Mortimer's way or Prince Edward's way?"

"I hope to God there is no conflict," Adam replied fervently.

"And if there is?"

"Then I must stand with the prince – whatever it costs me."

Chapter 10

The court returned to London sometime after St Bartholomew, the queen and her household riding separately from the king's. Prince Edward rode for the Savoy, and at his request, Kit accompanied her husband, relieved to escape the constant, chilly battle of wills between the queen and the king.

Kit's only regret was having to ride without Tom, but Adam had insisted that their son and his nurse return home, saying he preferred it if his child spent his days far away from the infected situation at court.

"It's not as if he notices," Kit had protested, smoothing her son's hair into place before putting on his coif.

"Maybe not. But he is happier at home." Adam had kissed his son's cheek, hoisted him in the air a couple of times, and handed him over to Amy. And that was that, as far as Adam was concerned, so Kit had no choice but to send Tom off in a litter with Amy and Mabel, who refused to be separated from her little lamb.

"Someone must keep an eye on Amy," she confided to Kit. "That girl has the wits of a headless chicken."

So now Kit travelled without son or maid. "It's the first time since I met her that I am going somewhere without Mabel," she commented to Adam. Almost three years, she calculated, recalling that September day when she first met Mabel – under inauspicious circumstances.

"Hmm," he said, glancing at her in a way that made Kit's cheeks heat.

"I had no choice at the time," she told him. "You know that." Kit shifted in her saddle under Adam's level stare. It was the truth, after all. She'd been abducted from Tresaints by Lady Cecily, the mother from Hell. Fortunately, Lady Cecily was not Kit's mother – but she was the wife of Kit's father, Thomas de Monmouth, since some years rotting in his grave.

At the time, Lady Cecily had arranged a marriage for her daughter – Kit's half-sister – with Lord Mortimer's trusted captain, Adam de Guirande. Too low-born, Katherine de Monmouth had sniffed, and had therefore run away, leaving her mother with an unravelling alliance to save. Which was where Kit, Sir Thomas' bastard daughter, had come in useful, seeing as she not only shared her name with little Katherine, but also her looks. And so Kit had been extorted into marrying Adam under a name not her own.

"You should have told me," Adam said, sounding stern. Kit sighed – loudly. Yes, of course she should have told him, but she was forbidden to. With Katherine's marriage to Adam came a number of benefits for the de Monmouth family – and for Adam, as the intended bride was generously dowered by Lord Mortimer for certain services rendered. Kit grimaced, recalling just how angry and hurt Adam had been when he finally found out the truth.

"Would you have preferred it, to be married to her?" she asked. Not an option any longer, as Katherine de Monmouth was dead – but at Sir Thomas' insistence she'd been buried under Kit's name, thereby making Kit Sir Thomas' trueborn daughter – if only in name.

"You know I wouldn't," he replied. "She despised me and would have cuckolded me at the first opportunity." With Lord Mortimer, Kit thought – or with whichever other highborn man attracted her interest.

"Oh, so those are the only reasons why you prefer me to her?" She felt hurt, somehow. In reply, Adam rode Goliath close enough that his leg brushed against hers.

"Not the only reasons," he said, eyes glittering with laughter. "Not the main reason."

"So what is the main reason?"

"Fishing for compliments, Lady de Guirande?"

"Yes." She gave him an annoyed look.

He smiled down at her. "The main reason is that I have a wife who risked her life to save mine, and who loves me and desires me almost as much as I desire and love her."

"Almost as much?" She laughed. "I love you much, much more."

"No you don't – that would be quite impossible." With that he left her, spurring Goliath to catch up with Prince Edward.

The prince's household consisted mostly of men – and a handful of women who'd been with him since he was a child. They did not precisely resent Kit, but Edward's former nurse, a dimpled lady by the name of Margaret, made it very clear who was in charge of the practical arrangements of the prince's life, and so Kit wandered about at loose ends for some weeks until the messenger rode in from London, demanding that Prince Edward attend on his father.

"Why the haste?" Kit asked Adam.

"The king has received grave news," Adam replied, tightening Goliath's girth. "Lord Roger is apparently planning an invasion."

Kit lowered her voice. "Is he?"

Adam frowned, setting a finger to his lips. "No," he replied almost inaudibly. "Not yet."

The imminent invasion had resulted in the king increasing his security. The court had retired to the Tower, and Adam counted twice as many men as necessary manning the huge barbican gate. Good, capable men, he concluded after having watched the guards scrutinise the prince's entourage – including Kit. As they rode along the inner curtain wall, they encountered more men-at-arms than he had ever seen here before, all of them displaying the royal arms of England.

"Are we at war?" Prince Edward asked, keen eyes taking in every single guard.

"Not that I know, my lord," Adam replied.

The lad threw him a look. "Would Lord Mortimer truly come here?" he asked. "To the Tower?"

Adam laughed softly. Lord Roger was no fool, and should he ever invade, he'd land well away from London. Adam studied the walls that rose above him and shivered. If he were Mortimer, he would never return to the Tower – unless it was to free his ailing uncle, who still lingered behind bars.

Very cautiously, Adam had informed himself as to where old Lord Mortimer was being held, but beyond arranging for coin to reach the old warrior, he could do nothing to help him – as he heard it, Lord Mortimer was in no fit state to escape, and Adam was far too aware of the Despenser spies who always lurked at his back to even consider attempting a visit.

Beside him, Kit craned her neck back, studying the sheer height of the walls. Her gaze flew from the inner curtain wall to the outer before landing briefly on him. She placed a hand on his and squeezed, and he knew she was thinking of that August night a year in the past when he had scaled these walls together with Lord Roger to help him escape.

After stabling their horses and finding their accommodation, Adam escorted Kit to the hall, snugly positioned within the inner curtain wall. Behind them the white keep loomed, in the inner bailey a gaggle of small boys were playing a loud game with a ball, and in the hall itself the chill of winter reigned, with Queen Isabella speaking with so much ice in her voice it was a miracle the words did not fall to the floor and shatter into fragments.

"You are doing what?" Isabella stood so straight she resembled a lance.

"I have confiscated your dower estates – for now," the king replied offhandedly, his eyes on anything but his wife.

"You have no right! Those are my lands, mine, given to me by contract! How dare you?"

"I have every right!" The king rose from his chair. "Your lands are ultimately my lands – as all are lands in this, my kingdom!" He glared at the assembled barons, shoulders shoved forward in a menacing stance.

"But why? What have I done—"

"I have reason to suspect you may have consorted with traitors."

"Traitors?" Prince Edward gasped. "My lady mother?"

The king blinked, looking at his son as if he had just realised he was there. He beckoned him towards him, but instead the prince shifted closer to his mother, mouth setting in a straight gash.

"I have done nothing of the sort! Where is your proof? Your witnesses?" the queen demanded.

"I have no need for proof."

"So I am accused and judged guilty on what? On his say-so?" The queen spun around, pointing at Lord Despenser. "Is it his poisonous lies that you believe, my liege? His preposterous accusations that you act upon?"

Despenser almost tripped in his haste to distance himself from the angry queen.

"I follow my own counsel!" the king roared.

"Your own counsel?" The queen laughed out loud.

"Silence!" The king had gone the colour of a scalded ham. With an effort, he composed himself. "I have decided to relieve you of your dower lands. With the impending war with France, the kingdom needs the income, and surely you will not begrudge me the monies I need to build up a defensive army, will you?"

"And what of my expenses?" The queen demanded.

"Your expenses will be covered – at a level I find reasonable." King Edward inclined his head slightly. "My queen must live as her position requires."

"A level you find reasonable?" the queen echoed. "What precisely does that mean, husband?"

"It means I control the purse strings." The king smirked. "I dare say there will be some minor changes."

"What changes?" the prince demanded. At almost twelve, he was already as tall as his mother, and standing side by side with her, they looked remarkably alike – except in colouring.

"That is a matter between your mother and me," the king snapped, making the prince flush. The king relented. "We must all economise, my son. Arms and soldiers are expensive."

"Couldn't you have asked Maman to contribute instead of stealing her lands?" The prince's voice shook.

"Tread carefully, my son," the king warned.

Adam pressed his lips together. Now was not the moment for his lord to explode into the famed Angevin temper, however impressive his lordling looked. Apparently, the queen agreed, and she said something in a low and earnest voice that had Prince Edward at first shaking his head. Everyone heard him mutter, "But it isn't right, Maman!" and everyone saw him glare at Despenser, who quailed under the weight of his stare.

"Will he flee the country, do you think, once the prince becomes king?" Kit murmured in Adam's ear.

"He will try," Adam replied, just as low. But God would not be so unjust as to allow Despenser to flee, and Adam knotted his hands, thinking of alternative ways to make Despenser pay for everything he'd done.

By the dais, the prince knelt before his father and mumbled an apology. The king ruffled his hair, and the prince tensed, much like a cur expecting to be kicked.

"He won't forgive his father for this," Adam said, watching as Prince Edward regained his feet.

"I fear there is more to come," Kit whispered back, nodding in the direction of Despenser, now with his head very close to the king's. The king nodded and said something in a low voice to the queen.

"What?" The queen had no compunction about keeping her voice down. She looked from the king to Eleanor de Clare and back again. "You're putting her in charge of John's household? Why her?"

"Why not her?" the king asked.

"Because she's your lapdog's wife!" the queen screeched. "And he, Hugh Despenser, he wants to steal my children's affection from me." She hugged her eldest son close.

"You hear that, Hugh? My lapdog?" The king laughed. No one else did, least of all Despenser, who was looking at the queen as if he would gladly disembowel her there and then. "*Our* son is old enough to have his own household," the king continued calmly. "John must be brought up closer to court, while his sisters—"

"Yes, what about his sisters – my daughters?"

"*Our* daughters will be transferred into the care of Roger and Isabel Monthermer."

"His sister!" Yet again, the queen pointed at Hugh Despenser. "And you," Queen Isabella rounded on Eleanor de Clare, "do not believe I don't know that you're behind all this. I swear that one day I will do to you what is done to me today. I will take your precious children from you, and you will rue the day you took mine."

Lady Eleanor's face crumpled, her gaze darting to the king.

"What nonsense is this?" The king scowled at his wife. "Eleanor had nothing to do with this – and besides, you seem to forget, my lady, that it is I, not you, who has the ultimate say in our children's lives. All of our children," he added significantly, looking at his eldest son.

"Previously, you have always discussed these issues with me," the queen flared, "not with them." Queen Isabella looked at Eleanor de Clare as if the woman was a maggot-infested corpse. Under that bright green stare the lady shrank, pressing back against her husband, who looked as discomfited as his wife.

"I do as I please," the king retorted.

"You always do as you please, not as you must," the queen said. "And today, at your pleasure, you have deprived me of my income and my say in how our children's lives should be ordered." She bowed. "I have no option but to obey, being your loyal wife and subject, but I fear that for this, my lord husband, you will suffer the everlasting fires of Hell. God will punish you as I, weak woman that I am, cannot. This, my lord, will cost you everything. Everything."

The king paled visibly. "Are you then my enemy?"

"Your enemy? I am your wife, the mother of your children. Have I ever not done my duty by you? Is this how you repay me? By stealing everything away from me?"

"It is best this way," the king said.

"So says every thief!" The queen drew herself up to stand as straight as a lance before the king. "Tell me, my lord, was this your own little scheme? Or is it Despenser who thinks, while you merely obey?"

A hush followed these words.

"Maman," Prince Edward groaned, taking a step towards his mother.

"Do not move, son," the king snapped, his gaze never

leaving his queen. "You will do as I bid and go with Lady Eleanor – now!"

Lady Eleanor made as if to take the prince by the arm.

"Do not touch me!" The prince reared back. "I will do as my father commands, but I will not tolerate your hands on my body." Prince Edward looked at the king, and at Queen Isabella. "I excuse myself, my lord," he said, bowing to his father. "My lady mother." He knelt before her, and Isabella's eyes blazed in triumph. Before anyone could stop him, the prince got to his feet and left.

"I must go after him," Adam murmured to Kit.

"As I must go after her," Kit replied, nodding in the direction of the queen, already leaving the hall in a flurry of skirts.

Adam found the prince in the kennels, fondling a long-legged pup. The lad had been weeping, but Adam knew from personal experience just how prickly an adolescent's self-esteem could be, so he pretended not to notice the tear-streaked face and knelt down to tickle the pup behind its ear.

"Why?" Edward extended his legs before him, studying his shoes as if he had never seen them before.

"The king has his reasons," Adam replied.

"The king accuses my mother of dabbling in treason." Prince Edward shoved the pup off his lap. "How can he do that?"

Adam couldn't very well tell the lad that there was some merit to the king's accusations. Over the last few years, the king's open preference for Hugh Despenser's company – even over that of his wife – had killed whatever affection the queen might once have harboured for her handsome royal husband, and this, coupled with the king's inability – or unwillingness – to curb Despenser's greed and hunger for power, had effectively driven the queen into the rebels' camp. Plus, of course, there was the matter of the ongoing feud with France.

"Maybe he believes it to be true," Adam prevaricated.

"True?" Dark blue eyes glared at him. "What fool would

believe that of my mother? No, this is all Hugh Despenser and that lying, wicked tongue of his"

Adam was not about to dispute this description of Despenser. "You may be right, my lord."

"May be?" Prince Edward gave him a withering look. "I am no fool, Adam. I know you hate Despenser – would gladly kill him if you could." He gestured at Adam's foot. "For that, I suppose, but also for the grief he has indirectly caused the Mortimers and the other rebel barons." He chewed his lip. "I only saw Roger Mortimer once – at Shrewsbury. Is he truly as great a leader of men as they say?"

Adam gave him a wary look. "He is."

"And could he invade us? Could he defeat my father?"

Adam sighed. "He could – assuming he had the gold required to find an army, which he doesn't have."

"And is that good or bad?" the prince pushed.

"War is always an ugly thing." Adam gave the lad a serious look. "Whether Lord Mortimer invades or not, I fear that war will come upon us anyway, my lord. Despenser has collected an impressive array of enemies, and unless the king distances himself from him…"

"…We will be plunged into a yet another bout of internal strife." The prince closed his eyes.

"Yes."

"I love my father," Prince Edward whispered.

"As you should, my lord."

"I love my mother too." He groaned. "This will not end well, will it?"

"Things may yet change," Adam said gently. He touched the prince's cheek. "There is always hope, my lord." But not as long as Despenser sat by the king's side – of that Adam was sure.

Chapter 11

When Kit entered the queen's apartments, she found the queen on her knees in her little chapel. Her bloated face and red, swollen eyes were testament to recent weeping, but upon Kit's entry, the queen turned a composed face her way.

"Is Adam with my son?"

"Yes, my lady."

"Good. He needs someone he can trust." The queen got off her knees in one fluid moment. "He shouldn't have witnessed that, but maybe it was better he did. My son will never forgive his father for this."

No, because you will not let him do so, Kit thought. She helped the queen to stand.

"And now what, my lady?" she asked. It was close to supper time, but she assumed Queen Isabella would prefer eating here, in her chambers.

"Now, Kit, begins the battle." Isabella raised her chin, exposing her long, beautiful neck. "And I will not lose." She clapped her hands together. "We must dress for supper, my ladies." With that she stood, directing her ladies to fetch one garment after the other, while she herself stood quite still as she was disrobed and dressed anew, arms held out as her sleeves were sewed tightly into place.

The babble in the hall died away when Queen Isabella entered. In a kirtle of shimmering green silk, the narrow, close-fitting sleeves complemented by an open, sleeveless surcoat in madder rose and gold, a transparent veil affixed to her head by a golden circlet and her fingers covered in rings, she looked every inch the royal lady she was. She wafted down the hall, head held high, a soft smile pasted to her lips.

"My lord king," she said, sinking down into a graceful reverence before the king, who looked quite discomfited.

"My son," the queen went on, greeting the prince with a slight inclination of her head.

Prince Edward stood and bowed. "My lady mother. Will you not take your seat beside me?" He indicated the chair between him and his father, intended for Hugh Despenser. Kit had to stifle a nervous guffaw at the look of pure venom that passed between Lord Despenser and the queen. After today, there was no hope of the queen ever forgiving Despenser. Ever. Or the king.

For the coming days, the royal household was a hotbed of tension. People whispered and speculated, avid eyes studying the king, the royal chancellor, the ever-dazzling queen and the young prince. Wherever Queen Isabella went, she presented the same serene face to the world, smiling warmly at her son, less warmly at her husband. Not one single meal but the queen would make a late appearance, allowing her to yet again walk down the hall towards the high table in splendid isolation before bowing deeply to her lord and king. And the king could do nothing but invite her to sit beside him, always with her son on her other side.

During the days, poor Prince Edward was batted back and forth. Now the king requested his presence in his chambers, now the queen desired her son to accompany her to vespers. Suddenly, the king insisted his son should express an opinion on his new horses, while the queen said it was quite impossible for her to choose what tapestries with which to adorn her walls without her precious son's help.

The king held the upper hand in this silent contest of wills, and now and then he'd use it, like when he took the prince with him to Westminster Abbey, keeping his son by his side for the entire day. When they returned to the Tower, the king and his son were sitting side by side on the barge, and the prince was laughing at something the king was saying – until he saw his mother, standing silent by the Tower wharf.

"It's like navigating a battlefield," Kit said, turning so that Adam could help her with her laces. "And poor Edward is the contested prize."

"The lad doesn't know which way to turn: if he complies with his father's wishes, he is betraying his mother, and if he disobeys his father, he is betraying him." Adam lifted her kirtle over her head and let it drop to the floor. "New chemise?" he murmured, fingers tracing the narrow band of lace that decorated the high neckline.

"Yes. Do you like it?"

"I prefer you without," he said, already drawing the sheer linen over her head.

"It doesn't help that the king turned Prince John over to Eleanor de Clare. If there is one woman the queen really hates, it is she."

"Must we talk about this right now?" He propelled her backwards towards the bed, his hands running up her flanks to cup her breasts.

"You're still dressed," she reminded him.

"But you're not. That's the important thing." He lowered his head and nipped at her nipples. "Bed – now." Not a request, but a command, and Kit's insides tightened pleasantly. "On your front," he added.

"Like this?" She pressed herself flat to the bed.

"No, like this." A strong arm under her belly lifted her to her knees, while his other arm slid down her back to her nape, holding her shoulders and face pressed to the bed. "Don't move," he breathed in her ear, but that was an impossible command to obey when he began his slow, leisurely torture of her exposed privates. His fingers, his mouth – he ignited fires within, and she trembled and quivered, fisting her hands in the bedclothes.

When he entered her, she muffled her whimper into the pillow. Again, and she gasped, meeting his thrusts with her own in an attempt to bring him that much closer. His hands tightened on her hips, his breathing was as loud as her own, and she reached backwards to touch him, needing more than the pressure of his thighs against hers, his member inside of her.

Suddenly, she was on her back, her legs around his hips, her breasts pressed to his wide chest, and he kept on pounding into her, grunting her name in time with his thrusts. The bed shook; she gripped his arms and raised her head to kiss him. He growled into her mouth, sank a hand into her hair and climaxed.

"You're still dressed," she complained afterwards, tugging at his tunic. Adam smiled, sat up and undressed.

"Better?" he asked, turning to lie on his side. He ran a hand up and down her body, now and then tweaking at her breasts. "They seem heavier," he said in a casual tone that did not quite mask his question.

"They are," she replied, arching against his touch. "That's what happens when one makes love like rabbits."

"You're with child?" Joy leapt in his eyes, and his hand trembled slightly.

"I am." She basked in his gaze. "An April child, I think."

"A daughter," he whispered. "I hope for a girl."

"I hope for a healthy child."

Adam took hold of her chin. Very gently, he kissed first her eyes, then her nose, and finally her mouth.

"It will be," he promised. And he loved her again, but this time, he was gentle and slow, worshipping her body with his.

There was an incessant stream of rumours about Lord Roger Mortimer and his nefarious plans. Adam was of the opinion that most of these rumours came from the mouth of Hugh Despenser, or his trusted friend, that sad excuse for a man of the church Walter Stapledon, Bishop of Exeter and Royal Treasurer. From Lord Mortimer himself, neither Adam nor the queen had heard anything, and as September wore on, Adam grew restless, confiding to Kit that he'd have liked some sign of life from Lord Roger.

"Hmm," said Kit, stydying her husband as he sprawled on the window bench.

"And I haven't heard from William either," Adam continued. "What if he has been caught?"

"Wouldn't we have heard if he was?" Kit tried to sound unconcerned, all the while trying to assess just what the consequences might be for William – and for them – should he be captured carrying secret messages from Lord Roger.

"Not necessarily," Adam replied. "That Stapledon would be more than happy to tie a spy to a stake and leave him to drown in the tide."

"Oh." She swallowed. "But he has to prove he is a spy first, doesn't he?"

In reply, Adam just raised his brows.

Fortunately, William had not been caught. Two days later, he came through the gate to the inner bailey, but Kit didn't recognise him at first. No longer in friar's robes, William approached her in the guise of a servant, back bent obsequiously. Only when he was close enough for her to see his eyes did she know him, having to bite back on a pleased smile.

"It suits you," she said, pinching his leather jerkin. "Much better than those gloomy, dark robes."

"Makes it easier to slip around unnoticed," he replied, scratching at his bristling beard. He cast a cautious look at the people milling about in the courtyard and straightened up, standing with his back towards her. Kit stared off in the other direction, pretending great interest in a couple of chattering magpies.

"Is he well?" Kit asked.

"He took the news of Pembroke's passing hard," William replied with a sigh.

"Didn't we all?" Kit owed the earl for Adam's life, and she'd liked Aymer de Valence, a relic of honour and integrity in this new world where greed and self-interest seemed to have eclipsed such values.

"Lord Mortimer had hoped the earl would be able to negotiate some sort of truce," William went on, "but now there is no hope of a peaceful reconciliation."

Kit rolled her eyes. "Lord Mortimer is far too astute to have hoped for that. As long as dear Hugh Despenser – both of them, I might add – is alive and well, the king will never exchange the kiss of peace with Roger Mortimer."

"And yet he hoped."

"No he didn't. Aymer de Valence lost his mettle at the debacle of Shrewsbury. He would never have attempted to reconcile the king and Mortimer – not again."

"So you still haven't forgiven him for that?" William sounded censorious.

"Have you? Aymer pledged his word to Mortimer. He promised that if they laid down their swords at the feet of the king they'd be treated magnanimously, and instead they were put in irons – or killed." Like her father, Thomas de Monmouth, hanged like a criminal before they'd chopped off his head and sat it atop a spike.

"De Valence never forgave himself for that," William said softly.

"No, he didn't, did he? His honour in tatters and a man he respected dragged off to the Tower." Kit stooped and picked up a pebble. "So what are Lord Mortimer's plans?"

"At present to remain alive," William replied drily. "It is rumoured Despenser offers a lot of gold for Roger Mortimer's head." He hunched over and pretended great interest in his sack of oats as two guards hurried by. "His first priority is to bring Queen Isabella over to France."

Kit snorted with laughter. "And he plans on storming in here on a white horse to do so?"

"No." William gave her a brief smile. "He aims to have the queen's royal brother help him. Charles of France is not much pleased with Edward of England right now. If Edward wants to keep Gascony, he will need to send envoys to negotiate – and Lord Roger has suggested that Charles make it a demand that his sister be one of them."

Kit nodded at the wisdom in this. Once free of her present constraints, the queen could be a rallying point for all the discontent that brewed in the kingdom – but God help them all if that came to pass.

"I think she'd like that. At present, Queen Isabella is held in very restricted circumstances." She moved away, smiling vaguely at five young girls who strolled by. She returned to her previous position. "Anything else?"

"A little bird tells me the Earl of Norfolk is in contact with Lord Roger."

"Really? Earl Thomas is quite the busy bee. He has made his inclinations known to the queen as well." Kit kept a wary eye on the four guards standing by the hall. One of them was staring at her and William. Kit turned away, fiddling with her veil.

"Thomas of Brotherton has little reason to love Hugh Despenser," William mumbled. He lifted the burlap sack to his shoulder and bumped into her, one hand gripping at her sleeve.

"Hey!" One of the guards came striding across the yard. "Be off with you, you lout. If I see you anywhere close to one of our ladies again I'll have you whipped, y'hear?"

"Sorry m'lord, I'm so sorry, so sorry," William mumbled. "It's me poor feet, it is." With one last bow he was gone, limping exaggeratedly towards the kitchens. Kit closed her hands around the scrap of parchment he'd slipped her.

"He is well," was all Adam said once he had read the missive.

"Yes, William told me. What else?"

"Lord Roger counts many of England's peers among his allies, first and foremost Henry of Lancaster. And he has approached various parties regarding ships and soldiers." Adam sounded bleak. He gave Kit an anguished look. "What am I to do if he lands and threatens the prince? How am I to choose between my young lord and the man to whom I owe my entire life?"

"Lord Mortimer won't threaten Edward," Kit said. "The queen won't let him." No, the queen would never let anyone harm her son, a lad still young enough to take her advice on everything. Kit looked at her husband. "If Lord Mortimer threatens anyone, it will be the king."

Adam held the scrap of parchment over the glowing embers in the hearth, holding it until it had properly taken fire before letting it go. "For now, Lord Roger has no ships or men." He straightened up. "But that will change, I fear."

Some days later, Kit and Adam had just exited the chapel after mass and were halfway across the inner bailey, when Adam uttered an irritated expletive and came to a halt. The way he stiffened at the sight of the woman approaching could have been amusing – if he hadn't been Kit's man, clearly discomfited by the buxom lady in russet coming towards them. Small and dark, the lady in question had slanted brown eyes, a plump mouth and two deep dimples that appeared when she smiled at Adam. He bowed in return.

"Adam! How nice to see you again." The woman's smile broadened, her gaze flying up and down Adam's body in a way that had Kit wanting to slap her. "Still as big as ever, still as..." one long digit poked Adam in the belly, "...hard." She giggled.

"My lady!" Adam hissed, taking a step back.

This close, Kit could see the fine wrinkles at the corners of the woman's eyes, the thin lines along her upper lip and the flaky texture of her skin. More mutton than lamb, Kit concluded, but very attractive – and far too familiar with her husband.

"I do not believe we have met," Kit said. The woman glanced at her, brows rising as if to show just how insignificant she considered Kit to be. "I am Adam's wife."

"His wife?" The woman's eyes narrowed as she studied Kit. "Really, Adam? I always thought you liked your women well-endowed and curvy."

"Maybe he prefers women with wits and manners," Kit retorted, glaring at the woman. She tugged at her kirtle, arching her back so as to enhance her breasts, most definitely deficient compared with the chest of the small woman in front of her.

"He didn't care much about wits when I knew him," the woman replied. "As I recall, he did care a lot about..." She winked, using her hands to lift her breasts somewhat.

"Stop it, Cassandra!" Adam snapped. "I will not have you insulting or upsetting my wife." In a most uncharacteristic gesture – at least when in company – Adam took hold of Kit's hand and raised it to his mouth, kissing the palm ever so lightly before closing her fingers round the kiss. "My most beloved wife," he added in a sultry tone.

"I can see that." This unknown Cassandra sounded amused, in contrast to the fleeting look of hunger that flew over her face as she studied Adam. Kit moved that much closer to her man. "I am sure we will run into each other again," Cassandra went on. "Ample opportunity to reminisce about our common past, Adam – maybe even relive parts of it." With yet another giggle she left them, her hips swinging back and forth as she made for the courtyard.

"Who was that?" Kit couldn't tear her gaze away from the woman's round backside.

"That was Cassandra de Ley." Adam sounded as if he intended to say nothing more.

"And?"

He sighed. "She made that very clear, didn't she? At one point in time, I had the pleasure of sharing her bed."

"Pleasure?" Kit detached herself from him and crossed her arms over her chest.

"At the time. But I was a callow youth, inexperienced in the arts of love."

"And she wasn't."

Adam chuckled. "No, Cassandra was most experienced – and demanding."

Kit didn't want to hear more. Her head filled with images of Adam cavorting with a naked Cassandra, all swelling bosoms and a lot of dark hair. A young Adam with a sheen of perspiration on his skin, head thrown back as the woman below him urged him on with her hands and her legs. Ugh. She gave herself a little hug.

A big hand cupped her chin, lifting her face. Eyes the soft grey of a November day met hers. "She means nothing to me now."

"But once she did."

"Aye, she did. But that was long before I met you, sweeting." His thumb brushed over her cheek. "That was before I knew what it could truly be like with a woman – *my* woman. She never set my heart on fire like you do."

"But I gather she made the bedclothes singe."

"At times." He gave her a tender kiss. "But you and I, we burn our bed to ashes, do we not?"

Not always, they didn't. Sometimes they made love in

110

drowsy contentment, no more. But often they did, and Kit felt a tightening in her womb and loins, a sudden spike of desire, further fuelled by the touch of his fingers and the darkening of his eyes.

Chapter 12

Three days before Michaelmas, Kit was awakened by a series of shrill screams. The queen? She leapt out of bed, already empty of Adam, and pulled on her clothes, yelling at Hawise, her temporary maid, to come and help her.

"What is happening?" she asked, dragging a comb through her heavy hair.

"The king has chosen to evict the queen's French retainers, my lady," Hawise replied, tightening Kit's lacings with strong, nimble fingers. "I heard it from one of the cooks, how the king had the Bishop of Exeter informing the queen this morning."

"But why?" Kit had by now finished braiding her hair, and looked about for her veil.

"Why?" Hawise sniffed. "Well, because they're French, I reckon. One can't trust a Frenchman, my lady, everyone knows that – and especially not now, what with all that mess in Gascony."

"The queen is French," Kit said icily.

Hawise just shook her head, muttering that therein was the cause of all the recent trouble.

"All!" The queen paced back and forth. "My clerks, my physicians – even my chaplains! All are to leave the country on pain of death." She took yet another turn around her room. "My maids, my ladies – women who have been with me for close to two decades!"

An earthenware jug was sent flying across the room, and one of the pages squawked and ducked, covering his head with his arms as the projectile shattered against the wall above him.

"I hate him!" the queen hissed.

"My lady!" Kit warned, throwing a nervous look in the

direction of Eleanor de Clare, who was standing some distance away, gnawing at her lip.

"What?" The queen sent two silver candlesticks crashing to the floor. "Am I not allowed to feel? To rage at the humiliations he imposes on me?"

"This doesn't help, my lady," Kit said, making an attempt to grab the queen's arm.

"Help? Nothing helps!"

Kit was shoved backwards, slipped, and landed on her rump. Someone snickered, and Kit looked up to find Cassandra standing just behind Eleanor. The queen, however, was already bending down to help Kit up.

"My apologies." Queen Isabella cleared her throat and lifted her chin. "I am a daughter of France," she said as if to herself, before giving Kit a faint smile. "You are right, it doesn't help. I must handle this with fortitude and dignity." She turned to study the assembled women on the other side of the room. "My new household?" she asked, looking from one to the other.

"Not all of us are new, my lady," Eleanor de Clare said.

"Unfortunately," the queen muttered. She turned to Cassandra de Ley. "And you are...?"

"Cassandra de Ley, my lady, daughter to one of Queen Eleanor's—"

"Yes, yes – if I am interested in your ancestors, I will let you know. What skills do you have?" The queen studied Cassandra's full figure. "Well, beyond the obvious one of near on being able to smother a man with your breasts."

Kit gave the queen a stunned look. She'd never heard her be so coarse before.

"My lady!" Eleanor de Clare drew herself up straight, pale blue eyes drilling into the queen. "I'll not have you insult us. We are but following the king's orders – as all of us, including you, must do."

The queen raised her brows. "I was but stating a truth, Lady Eleanor." Her nostrils flared. "And now, ladies, I will retire to my chapel for my private devotions. Please have the king know I require a new chaplain immediately – and it best not be one of the Bishop of Exeter's clerks." With that she was gone, a whirlwind of pale blue silks and immaculate linens.

Michaelmas was one of Adam's favourite holidays, and had been so ever since he was a child and first heard of how St Michael defeated Satan and threw him out of Heaven. This year, however, Michaelmas was anything but festive, with the queen a brittle presence among her new ladies while the king presided over the midday feast with a scowl, spending most of the meal in hushed conversation with the men seated beside him at the high table. The queen had claimed illness and chosen not to attend, but had insisted her ladies stay with her in her chambers – out of spite, Adam assumed, wishing Kit had been here with him instead.

Even the weather was foul, and the short run to the hall had left people wet and irritated. Adam sighed and nodded for one of the pages to fill his cup, gnawing listlessly at what little meat was left on the goose-leg presently on his trencher. The men beside him were talking about dice and dogs, and now and then Adam would throw in a comment or two, but his mind was elsewhere, grappling with the problem of his conflicting loyalties.

He glanced at the prince, smiling slightly at how flushed the lad looked. Too much wine, Adam surmised – and a sense of relief when only one of his parents was present. The prince's fair hair was tousled and damp, and he was laughing at something Earl Thomas was saying, leaning towards his young uncle with a bright look in his eyes. As yet too young to rule a kingdom – far too young – but Adam studied Prince Edward's face and nodded to himself, thinking that the prince was more like his grandsire than his sire, and God be praised for that.

Adam sighed again, gesturing for a refill. On one side the prince, who awoke all of Adam's protective instincts, on the other Lord Roger, the man Adam had loved since he was a lad of ten.

"Dear God, spare me the choice," he muttered, but he knew that was a futile wish: at some point he would have to declare for either one or the other – and it would likely tear him apart.

"We'll cross that bridge when we get there," Kit had said last night when he shared all this with her. She'd snuggled closer, a warm, inviting presence by his side. And maybe she was right, his wife. Maybe. Adam drank deeply, and with an effort returned his attention to his companions, who were now arguing the merits of Spanish horses over Friesians.

After the meal, Adam retired to the chapel, considering whether he should lighten his heart through confession. But he distrusted the priests of the royal chapel, and after some time at prayer he retreated to sit behind one of the huge pillars, leaning his shoulder against the decorated stone.

He was deep in thought when he heard the door squeak open.

"Adam?" someone called, and he recognised his lord's voice. He made as if to stand, when he heard another voice.

"Son?"

The king. Adam sank back down.

"My liege," the prince said, and Adam heard the sound of cloth rustling as the lad bowed.

"Your father," the king said gently. "Come here, lad." There was the sound of muted footfall, and when Adam sneaked a look, he saw Prince Edward enfolded in his father's arms. Young shoulders were rigid, young arms hung passive, and after some moments the king released him.

"Are you that aggrieved with me?" he asked.

"It is not my place to be aggrieved, my lord." Edward took a step or two backwards.

"I am doing what I must to ensure the safety of my realm," the king said.

"So my mother's household was a threat?" the prince demanded. "Her chaplains spies, her physicians your mortal enemies?"

A deep red suffused the king's face. "You don't understand – how can you, mere stripling that you are?"

The prince bowed. "As I said, my lord: it is not my place to be aggrieved."

"But you are."

Prince Edward looked at his father. "I am. I love my lady mother and don't want any harm to come to her."

"Most commendable," the king said sarcastically. "A dutiful son to his mother – but what about your duties to me?"

"To you, my lord? I try to do my duty by you as well – I always do." The lad sounded on the verge of tears.

The king relented. "I know you do, Ned. And I understand how difficult all of this must be for you." He studied his son. "I do as I must. Your lady mother is not always the most dutiful of my subjects."

"She is my mother."

"And she may be plotting against me!"

"But you have no proof, do you, my liege? All you have are the whispered accusations of men like Lord Despenser, vile insinuations that my mother aims to betray you."

"And if she does? What then, son? What will you do if your mother harms me?"

"But she hasn't, has she? And it isn't you who has had your dower lands stripped away from you, it is not you who has been bereft the company of men and women you trust and love." The prince scuffed at the floor. "I love her, Father. And over the last few weeks you have repeatedly humiliated and hurt her."

"I have no choice," The king said.

His son gave him an anguished look. "I don't believe you, Father – no one does."

"No one?" The king almost growled. "What do you mean by that?"

Prince Edward backed away from his father. "It is not my mother's fault that you place higher value on Hugh Despenser than on her."

The slap sent Prince Edward reeling. His head struck the wall, and Adam was hard put not to emerge from his hiding place to rush to his lord's aid. The prince straightened up, wiped at his mouth and studied his bloody fingers. The king groaned out loud.

"Forgive me," he said. "I didn't mean to…"

"Maybe you had no choice, my lord," Prince Edward said before ducking under his father's arm and fleeing the chapel. Behind him, the king sank to his knees and covered his face with his hands. Adam fidgeted. Too much ale with the midday meal had left his bladder uncomfortably full, but at present he was trapped, incapable of leaving before the king did.

The door creaked open and Hugh Despenser entered, coming to a halt at the sight of his liege.

"Edward?" Hugh hurried down the aisle. "What is the matter, my dearest lord?"

"I hit him," the king mumbled. "I hit my own son. I fear he will never forgive me."

"For hitting him?" Hugh Despenser gave the king an awkward hug, stroking him gently over his head.

"For what I have done to his mother." The king reared back from Despenser. "I listened to you and Walter in this matter. But if it drives my son away from me, I will never forgive you. Never." He rose and left, his robes swishing round his legs. With a muttered curse, Hugh Despenser followed.

Over the following days, Adam's life became increasingly complicated by Cassandra de Ley – and his wife's reaction to this determined lady, who seemed to make it her purpose in life to run into Adam as often as possible. If he went to the stables, Cassandra would materialise out of nowhere, commenting on the size of his horse. If he were at the armoury, discussing the merits of broadheads over bodkins, sure enough, Cassandra would come wandering by in rose-coloured silks, and ask him if he had properly covered the issue of penetration – by an arrowhead, of course.

"Who invited her to court?" Kit complained, throwing eye-darts at the hastily departing Cassandra. She had come to find him in the bailey, where he was overseeing the prince's sword practice, and had been anything but pleased at finding Cassandra among the spectators.

"I have no idea," Adam said, wiping at his face. "But as I hear it, she has some distant association to the de Clares."

"Really?" Kit gave him a surprised look. "Eleanor de Clare may be many things, but she is nothing if not propriety itself, so what can she have in common with *her*?" She scowled. "It would help if you told her you have no interest in her."

"I already have. So what can I do but avoid her?"

"Tell her again? Loudly?" Kit moved away.

Adam caught up with her. "I've told you, she is nothing but a ghost from my past."

"Good. Keep it that way – unless you want me to deprive you of your balls."

Adam gave her an insulted look. "That was uncalled for."

Kit's shoulders sank from their rigid stance. "I know," she admitted. "It's just…" Her gaze met his. "I can't help it. Every time I see her, it's as if she is eating you with her eyes, and I…" She scuffed at the ground. "They say no one forgets their first lover."

"Maybe not." Adam tugged at an escaped tendril of her hair. "But that was a long time ago, sweeting, and whatever memories I may have of her are faded and dull compared to you." He kissed her brow. "And what would you know of first lovers? You have only had one lover – me."

"I know I wouldn't forget him – ever," she replied, placing her hand on his chest. "And my memories stand stark and bright – they always will."

"As will mine of you." Adam cleared his throat and lowered his voice. "Especially that time when you…" He went on to whisper the details in her ear, and his wife blushed – vividly.

"Adam!" she hissed.

Other than Cassandra's annoying presence, Adam was also concerned for his little lord. Since that discussion in the chapel, Prince Edward determinedly avoided his father as much as he could, the king as determinedly insisting his son spend time with him. Where Prince Edward went, there went Adam, and so it was that he was the reluctant witness to the king's clumsy attempts at rebuilding his relationship with his son, all of them politely rebuffed.

All in all, it was something of a relief when the prince was given permission to take his household with him to the Savoy – except that this time Kit was staying behind, at the express command of the queen.

"I don't want you to go," Kit said, but with little heat. She nodded for Hawise to light the candles and then dismissed the maid, lying back against the pillows to watch him pack. "And I'll still be uncomfortable, with you gone while Hugh Despenser is here."

Adam made a concurring sound, even if Despenser had not as much as glanced at his wife lately, so maybe the man intended to honour his promise to the king and leave both her and Adam alone. Kit stretched out her hand and patted his thigh – the only part she could reach without getting out of bed. In response, he gave her a brief smile.

"It will not be for long," Adam said. "The prince is uncomfortable leaving his mother."

"And she is devastated at him leaving." Kit frowned. "She told him so, as well." She fell silent, mouth pursed.

"What?" Adam asked. He strode over to the door, yanked it open and called for Gavin.

"I don't know. It's as if the queen has suddenly has developed very strong maternal instincts, previously quite well hidden." Kit fretted at the fringe on the counterpane. "She's a royal consort, and her life has been much more about court and king than about her sons and daughters, but now—" She broke off when Gavin more or less fell into the room.

Adam handed him his boots and winter cloak, told Gavin to treat the cloak to a fuller's brush and polish the boots, and sent him on his way.

"Now…" Adam prompted.

"Now she is the suffering mother and the cruelly spurned wife. It is a role she excels at."

"Ah." Adam came over to sit beside her. "She has the right to be upset."

Kit nodded. "Of course she does. But she puts her son in an untenable position – no mother should do that."

On the morrow of their intended departure, the prince woke to a headache, his eyes uncommonly bright.

"It will pass," Prince Edward insisted, stomping his feet into his boots. "By the time we reach the Savoy I will be fine – it is but a short ride."

"Or we wait," Adam suggested. "You're more comfortable here, my lord, than in that half-finished palace of yours."

"We do not wait." The prince buckled his belt.

It was cold outside, a heavy fog seeping straight through cloaks and tunics. Adam shivered in a gust of wind, patted Goliath on his neck and waited for Edward to mount. Other than the dozen or so of the prince's companions, the party also consisted of twenty men-at-arms, handpicked by Adam. Horses snorted, harnesses jangled, and finally they were off, trotting under the Byward Tower, over the moat, through the Middle Tower, past the reeking pit that held the king's collection of mangy lions, under the barbican and over the drawbridge into the city proper.

"It never sleeps, does it?" Sir Henry commented to Adam as they rode in tight formation up Thames Street. They rode side by side – they often did these days, Adam having taken quite a liking to the prince's guardian, for all that Sir Henry was a stickler for decorum and protocol. Adam nodded, taking in the bustling beehive of activity that surrounded them.

To their left, the wharves were already busy, cumbersome wooden cranes swinging back and forth to unload the contents of the cogs presently moored to the docks, several of them flying the distinctive red and silver banner of the Hanseatic League.

They left Byling's Gate behind, turned up Watling Street, and Adam rode that much closer to his young lord as they slowed their pace to a walk through the busy street, where people were already going about their business with only an irritated glance or two thrown in the direction of the prince's party.

Prince Edward coughed.

"Maybe we should turn back," Adam said, riding close enough to peer at the lad's face, half-hidden under his hood.

"I coughed," the prince said. "Once."

"You look ill, my lord," Adam told him.

The prince gave him an impatient look. "What are you, Sir Adam? My nursemaid?" He clapped spurs into his surprised mount, and any further conversation was put on hold as Adam concentrated on keeping up with his lord, who despite the throngs was trotting briskly in the direction of Ludgate.

They skirted St Paul's, had to stop when a contingent of black-clad friars crossed the street, and then at last they were at the gate. The prince swayed in his saddle.

"My lord," Sir Henry said. "Are you well?"

Two angry eyes glared at him. "I am."

"Hmm," Adam voiced, inspecting Prince Edward's flushed face. "You have a fever."

"I am not turning back," the prince said, and the moment they had passed the gate he set off at a gallop.

Adam caught up, leaned over and took hold of the reins. "I am sorry, my lord, but I must insist we return."

In response, the prince sneezed, twice. "I don't want to," he mumbled, shivering in his cloak. "It's unbearable there."

"But we must," Sir Henry said. "You are ailing – and the king's physicians are the best."

Some hours later, and the prince was shivering under a pile of bedclothes, his forehead hot to the touch. The king's physician sniffed at the lad's urine and pronounced that the prince needed to be bled, and just like that, Adam and Sir Henry were dismissed from the room. Adam sat down on the window ledge of the antechamber.

Instants later, the king burst through the door with Despenser at his heels. "My son?"

"In there, my liege," Sir Henry said.

The king made as if to enter.

"No, wait, my dearest lord." Lord Despenser blocked his way. "We must first know what ails him."

"What ails him? Get out of my way!" The king shoved Lord Despenser aside. Despenser raked his fingers through his hair.

"How ill is he?" he asked Sir Henry.

"Ill enough that we chose not to ride on, my lord," Adam replied from his perch. "But not—"

He was interrupted by the arrival of the queen, shadowed by Kit and one of her younger ladies-in-waiting. He bowed low; the queen gave him a distracted nod and walked straight into her son's room.

The fever continued to rise. By nightfall, the king threw the physician out, threatening him with dire death should the prince not survive. Instead, Lady Eleanor arrived, with basins of sweet-smelling waters, with bitter infusions made of willow-bark and feverfew. The queen came out, looking quite pale. Without a word she departed, Kit and the other lady hurrying after. The king came out, and Lord Despenser rushed to him.

"My liege, you must eat, have some rest."

The king shook his head. "I am staying with my son, but the rest of you may leave."

"I'm staying," Sir Henry said.

"As am I." Adam stood up.

Prince Edward was sunk somewhere in between sleep and delirium, and Lady Eleanor was sponging his heated skin. Adam went to help, and once they were done, he lifted the lad so that Lady Eleanor and the servants could remove the drenched sheets.

"I...I...mmmmm...soo...c-c-cold," Edward stuttered, fever-bright eyes burning into Adam's.

"Here." The king draped his arms in the heavy counterpane and held them out. Adam lifted the boy into the king's waiting arms, and wrapped the thick cloth around him. With a little sigh, the prince nestled close to his father, who held him as easily and as gently as if his son were a fragile egg.

Two never-ending days followed, days in which the queen and king took turns at their son's bedside, while Sir Henry and Adam remained with their lord all the time, catching what sleep they could leaning against the wall. Lady Eleanor came and went, chiding the prince into drinking one more aromatic concoction after the other.

It was close to dawn on the third night when the fever broke. Lord Edward sat up.

"I need to piss," he said in a gravelly voice. He blinked at his father, then at Lady Eleanor. "And I'm hungry."

The king swept his son to his chest. "Thank the Lord," he whispered.

The prince fidgeted. "The garderobe," he murmured. The king laughed, dashed at his eyes and helped his son to stand.

An hour or so later, the much-recovered prince was fast asleep.

"Find your beds," the king commanded, and Sir Henry and Adam got to their feet. They walked in silence through the deserted rooms and passages, and when they reached the inner ward, Adam turned off, making for his lodgings in the Flint Tower. Far too many treads, he reflected as he mounted the interminable stairs. He had to take them with his hale foot first, trying to ignore just how much his other foot throbbed. Three days more or less constantly on his feet had not done it any good.

Adam didn't bother undressing. He just pulled off his tunic, kicked off his boots and fell into bed beside Kit, who did no more than grunt and pat at him before falling back into her dreams. Come morning proper, Adam had the vaguest impression of soft lips being pressed to his cheek, and Kit's voice telling him to sleep on. So he did.

Chapter 13

Once her tasks were done, Kit begged the queen's leave to return to her husband. Queen Isabella waved her off with a weary smile, saying she herself planned to retire and sleep, now that her son was safely on the way to recovery.

Kit hastened along the passage, took the narrow, winding stairs two treads at a time, and burst through the door to their room, breathless and hot. She came to an abrupt halt.

On one side of the bed stood Adam, while Cassandra de Ley was kneeling on their mattress, hair tumbling lose around her shoulders. Kit's husband's shirt was unlaced, baring most of his chest, and his cheeks were an uncharacteristic pink.

"Oh dear," Cassandra said, dark, slanted eyes glittering maliciously.

Kit turned and fled, banging the door in her wake. How she made it down the stairs, she did not know, blinded with tears and rage.

"Kit! Stop!" He came pounding after her, in only his hose and shirt. "It is not what you think!" He cornered her.

"Really?" She hated it that she was crying, aware of just how red her nose must be.

Adam scrubbed at his hair. "How can you think I would…" He drew in breath. "I was asleep – you know I was, you left me to sleep."

"Alone! Not with her."

"I didn't invite her in! She sneaked in. And had you but come a minute later, you would have found her sprawled on the floor, so enraged was I by her behaviour."

"Hmm." Kit regarded him in silence. He looked exhausted, with a grey tinge to his skin that spoke of too many nights with too little sleep.

"She undid your shirt," she said. "She must have touched you."

Adam groaned. "I thought it was you, I was still half-asleep."

"And did you touch her back?"

"I might have, I don't know. But then I woke up, and—"

"I came in."

"I was already out of the bed by then." He licked his thumb and rubbed at a smudge on her cheek. "I think I've made it quite clear – to her and to you – that I don't want her." He smiled at her. "Cassandra de Ley may think herself a temptress, but I find her nothing but an old nuisance."

"Old?" Kit softened somewhat.

"And bawdy – quite the hussy." He kissed her nose. "Come to bed?"

"And what if she's still there?"

"If she is, I'll throw her out," Adam said, taking Kit's hand. "But I told Gavin to chase her out – and to use his feet if he had to."

"Ah." The queen raised her gaze from her embroidery to study Cassandra. "A harlot?" She'd sat silent as Kit recounted yesterday's events, now and then interjecting a little "hmm".

Kit squirmed. "At least where my husband is concerned."

"Cassandra de Ley is four times a widow," the queen said, "and rich, by all accounts." She ran a digit over the carefully executed embroidery depicting the lamb and the lion. "They've all died quite suddenly, those men of hers."

Kit gasped. "What is it you are saying, my lady?"

"I am saying nothing – yet. But I'd be wary of any sweetmeats she offers you – or me." The queen's mouth hardened. "She has not joined my household without some ulterior motive."

"She wants my husband?"

"Don't be ridiculous! Adam de Guirande may be an additional boon, but Lady Cassandra is here for other reasons." She lowered her voice. "Interestingly enough, I have heard that she has some connections with the Despensers – but Lady Eleanor does not seem to like her much, does she?"

"No," Kit agreed. Most of the time, Lady Eleanor ignored

Cassandra, but now and then she would study the dark, voluptuous lady as a pike might study a perch. Kit inched closer to the queen. "Maybe she doesn't want her too close to her own husband."

"Hugh?" The queen snorted softly. "The man is sickeningly fond of his wife – and my husband. Too fond for anyone else to stand a chance."

"And what about what he did to me?" Kit hissed.

"That had nothing to do with lust," the queen said. "That was dear Hugh playing mind-games with Adam."

"He almost raped me once," Kit protested.

"You were a challenge, a person to break – with the added benefit that if he breaks you, he breaks Adam." The queen smiled at Kit's open mouth. "Surely you know that, Kit? If Despenser hurts you, it will gut Adam."

"Oh." Kit set down her embroidery. "It doesn't make me feel better, my lady."

The queen shrugged. "Just stay away from him – and from her," she added, inclining her head in the direction of Cassandra. "That one has mischief on her mind."

As always, the queen assembled her ladies for mass, leading the way to the royal chapel with her new chaplain at her side. Kit enjoyed these hours spent in devotion and prayer, if nothing else because they left the queen calm and content – a state of mind that would last an hour or so, before she once again retired into silence, those magnificent eyes of hers darting from one lady-in-waiting to the other as if she were trying to decide who to trust.

Not only was mass mandatory, so was confession, the queen ensuring all her ladies went regularly to see Father Simon. Today it was Kit's turn, and she emerged from the chapel quite flustered after the priest's little talk about carnal sin. As she hurried towards the queen's apartments, Earl Thomas came striding towards her, his fur-trimmed surcoat lifting with the speed of his movement.

"Lady Kit!" He smiled and bowed deeply. "Imagine seeing you here."

Kit rolled her eyes. This was standard procedure for the earl, who seemed to enjoy pretending he came upon her by chance whenever they met – which was quite frequently of late. "Yes," she replied with an edge, "how strange that one of the queen's ladies should be at court."

The earl laughed. "I stand rebuked, my lady." His eyes twinkled as he leaned towards her. "But every time I see you, it brightens my day."

Kit's cheeks heated, and the earl's smile widened into a pleased grin.

"You're acting like your brother," she snapped. Earl Edmund was quite the ladies' man, setting innumerable female hearts on fire simply by strolling past, all that male beauty encased in velvets and silks that enhanced his slim build.

"I never act like my brother," Earl Thomas retorted, brows pulling together. No, Kit admitted to herself, Earl Thomas rarely did, preferring to stand on the outskirts and watch as his brother fawned all over the king.

"You're very different." And not only on the outside, with Earl Thomas being broader and taller than his younger brother. Where Earl Edmund was all scented golden hair and immaculate clothes, Earl Thomas was dark of hair and clothes, dressing in garments as rich as his brother's, but considerably less ostentatious. And where Edmund was all contagious, bubbling energy, Thomas was circumspect, silent unless asked to voice an opinion.

"Oh, yes." Earl Thomas gave her a wry smile. "Edmund, I am told, takes after our mother, a carefree soul who survives on his devastating charm and good looks. I, on the other hand, resemble our father – or so they say – which means I am gifted with brains rather than graces." He bowed slightly. "Nor am I as handsome as my brother, I fear."

"That would depend on the beholder." To Kit, Earl Thomas was by far the more attractive of the two – dangerously attractive, especially for a married woman such as herself. She put some distance between them, and yet again the earl grinned.

"Can I take that as a compliment?" he teased.

"I was merely stating a well-known truth." Kit shook her head at his offered arm. The earl looked offended, but shrugged and suggested they take a walk to the mews and back.

"Why?"

"Because it is better I pretend to woo you than speak directly to your husband."

"Oh." Kit felt diminished.

"I would be more than happy to woo you for real," the earl said, "but I fear I'd be making a fool of myself."

"Probably." Kit stared straight ahead. "So what is it you wish to share with my husband?"

The earl chuckled. "I've insulted you – and that was not my intention, Lady Kit. In fact, I was hoping to offer you the opportunity to make your husband experience those emotions Lady Cassandra makes you feel."

"I have no emotions for Cassandra." Kit sniffed loudly.

"No? You go green at the sight of her – and I dare say de Guirande enjoys seeing you so affected by jealousy. What man wouldn't?"

"I am not jealous! I have no reason to be."

"Yes, you are – but you're right: you have no reason to be. Your husband regards Lady Cassandra with as much affection as he would expend on a louse. But..." He moved closer to her, his arm brushing against hers, "...there's no harm in waking the green-eyed serpent in him as well."

"No." Kit stepped away from him. The earl looked disappointed. He shrugged, his face acquiring a distant look, and they walked in silence for a while.

"The rift between the queen and the king must be healed," Earl Thomas finally said. He glanced at Kit. "Your husband can help, by encouraging the prince to act as an intermediary."

"But why?"

"Why?" The earl laughed softly. "Unless the queen succeeds in winning back his trust, the king will never send her to France as his emissary. And we need the queen in France."

"We?" Kit's pulse picked up, an uncomfortably loud noise in her head.

"We, Lady Kit. Those of us who will not tolerate Lord Despenser for much longer."

Three days later, Lady Eleanor requested that Kit accompany her outside. It was not as if Kit had much choice in the matter, so she retrieved her cloak and followed the lady into the cold October day. The bailey lay deserted, there was a taste of frost in the air, and the cobbles underfoot were slippery after the recent rain. A gust of wind had Kit's cloak billowing like a sail, and she trudged along behind Lady Eleanor all the way to the wharf. The waters of the Thames slapped angrily against the quayside, one of the royal barges had just cast off and was making for the bridge, carried along by the forces of the incoming tide.

"The queen no longer requires your services," Lady Eleanor said, having to lean towards Kit to make herself heard in the wind.

"If that were the truth, she'd tell me herself," Kit replied.

Lady Eleanor shrugged. "Very well. The king no longer wants your services. You are ordered to leave court." She led the way to the further end of the quay. There were three men waiting, all of them in Despenser livery. Kit dragged her feet. Were they there to carry her off? Kit coughed to clear her throat of an uncomfortable congestion, her head filling with images of what they would do to her to make her talk. Ridiculous, she berated herself – but then she recalled her recent conversation with Earl Thomas, and it took considerable effort to return her attention to Lady Eleanor, presently regarding her with a frown on her face.

"Leave? But I have my husband here."

"Ah, yes, the redoubtable Adam de Guirande." Lady Eleanor made a face. "Well, he stays, unfortunately. The king is quite convinced the prince cannot survive a day without his stalwart knight by his side." She hailed the men, rattled out instructions, and to Kit's relief they bowed and made off towards the city.

"If Adam stays, I stay," Kit said.

Lady Eleanor shook her head. "The king does not wish

it so – it distracts your husband from his duties." A wisp of her hair whipped free from her braid and veil, floating like an aggravated snake back and forth across her face.

"The king or your husband?"

"Does it matter?" Lady Eleanor gave Kit a beady look. "Besides, the king wants people he trusts in his wife's household."

"And have I given him reason not to trust me?" Yet another gust of wind, and one of the moored boats groaned and squeaked against its ropes.

"Let me see: your father died a traitor's death, your brother is a convicted traitor, squire to Mortimer, your younger brother fought and died with de Bohun…"

"He was thirteen! A child – and he didn't die fighting, he was hanged! Hanged, I tell you!"

Lady Eleanor sighed. "I didn't know, and I am sorry to hear it. Boys that young should not die like that. But nevertheless, you come from a family of traitors, you are married to a traitor—"

"Who apparently is irreplaceable in the prince's household!"

"…And the king has decided that with all this in mind, he prefers it if you no longer serve the queen. Or stay at court." Lady Eleanor apparently considered the matter concluded, and made as if to turn away.

"I have a right to be with my husband."

Lady Eleanor laughed. "Your husband has duties to his lord. You are merely an encumbrance." She pulled her cloak tight around her shoulders. "The king expects you gone no later than tomorrow."

"And who takes over my duties to the queen?"

"Cassandra de Ley." Lady Eleanor wrinkled her nose. "*Not* my choice, I assure you."

"Or the queen's," Kit said bitterly. She straightened up. "I must say my farewells to the queen."

"No, you will not. I will inform her of the changes." Lady Eleanor sounded tired. "Yet another sin the queen will hold against me."

Kit was not about to commiserate.

She found Adam with Gavin in one of the rooms adjoining the stables, two heads bent over the saddle they were inspecting. At the sight of her, Adam stood, handed his rag to Gavin and followed her outside.

"They're sending me away," she said.

"Who?" Adam's eyes narrowed.

"Who do you think? The king and Despenser." She took his hand. "I don't want to go."

She'd hoped he'd say something to the effect that he wouldn't allow her to leave, but instead Adam dragged a hand through his hair, making it resemble a shaggy haystack.

"They isolate her further – and me. With you gone, I have no one to talk to, no one to trust – well, beyond my young lord, but I can't talk to him about everything." He gave her a little smile. "You are sent away and I am left to handle the quagmire of shifting loyalties all on my own – as is the queen. With you gone, they have effectively severed all possible contact between me and the queen."

"But that would mean they still suspect you of traitorous intents."

Adam tweaked her cheek. "Of course they do. And what better place to have a traitor than right under your eye – in this case in the prince's household?" He drew her into his arms. "We can't fight this, Kit."

"I know," she groaned. "But I wish we could."

Adam insisted on arranging everything. Horses, men and panniers – he oversaw it all, making Kit feel rather superfluous. By noon next day, everything was ready for her departure, and Kit stood in their little room, dressing as warmly as she could. Two pairs of hose, two shifts under her old green kirtle, her heavy cloak and her gloves – and yet she knew she'd be cold within the hour, and even colder before she arrived at Tresaints.

Once dressed, she went looking for Adam, hoping for some moments alone with him, but as he was nowhere to be found, she did some desultory pacing in the small herbal garden, up and down the narrow paths.

Any moment now, and she'd be on her way, and God alone knew when she'd next see her husband, but from the way he'd avoided answering that particular question, she had the distinct impression Adam feared it would be several months at least. Months...Her eyes brimmed.

Silly goose, she berated herself, this is nothing to weep for. But it was – she was feeling brittle and nauseous with the new babe, and she wanted Adam to hold her and cuddle her, keeping both her and their unformed child safe within his arms.

"My lady?"

Kit turned at the sound of the young voice, wiping at her face. "My lord," she said, bowing deeply.

"I..." Prince Edward stuttered, looking at face. "You are sad."

She gave him a watery smile. "I am. I don't like being separated from my husband. Foolish, I know, and yet..." She lifted her shoulders. And it wasn't only the babe, she admitted to herself, it was also the fact that she didn't want to leave Adam behind with a prowling Cassandra at large, but that was not something to be shared with a mere lad.

"I wish I could do something," the prince said, coming over to stand beside her. He offered her his arm, and Kit took it, allowing him to lead her yet another little turn around the deserted garden. "Maman does not like Cassandra de Ley."

"No, and I believe that is why she was chosen," Kit muttered.

The prince gave her a pained look. "Why is he doing this? How can he treat her thus? Her dower lands, her companions...I don't understand."

"Yes you do, my lord," Kit said.

The prince scuffed at the ground. "I do," he admitted. "He no longer trusts her – his wife! Instead he listens only to that snake Despenser." He looked away. "My mother would never betray her husband – or me."

Kit concentrated her attention on a nearby apple tree. After all her recent humiliations, Queen Isabella was fully capable of killing the king – with her own hands if needed.

But the lad was right in one aspect: the queen adored her son.

"I don't know what to do," Prince Edward continued.

Kit tightened her hold on his arm, noting strong muscle and sinew. "You must do as you've always done: you must love and respect them both. It is not your quarrel, my lord. It is a matter that the king and queen must sort themselves."

Prince Edward gnawed his lip. "And if they don't sort it? What then?"

Then they will tear you apart, she thought. But she didn't say that; instead she gave him a reassuring smile.

"Of course they will, my lord. Give them time."

"And hope that meanwhile Lord Despenser drowns in a moat somewhere," the prince muttered viciously. He glanced at Kit. "He is the festering boil in all this, is he not?"

Kit did not reply – there was no need to.

They finished their little walk in companionable silence, and once back at the garden gate, the prince bid her farewell.

"I will keep your husband safe from Lady Cassandra," he promised, smiling at her.

"That," Adam said from behind them, "is not something I need your help with, my lord."

The prince's smile widened. "No? As I hear it, Lady Cassandra is a veritable she-wolf when it comes to men."

"But I am no sheep, my lord," Adam replied. "Besides, I already have the woman I love and adore – as my wife." He set his hand over his heart and bowed, eyes never leaving Kit's. She reciprocated the gesture, making Adam smile. "I would require some moments alone, to bid my wife farewell," he went on.

"Oh." The prince blushed. "Of course." He departed at speed, and Adam took Kit's hand, leading her over to a nearby bench.

"Will you be all right?" he asked, brushing the backs of his fingers down her cheek.

"Will you?" she countered, leaning into his touch.

"No." He regarded her seriously. "I'll miss you too much."

"As will I." Kit cupped his face. "Keep yourself safe, my dearest lord." Not only from Despenser and his wiles, but also from Cassandra de Ley, she added silently.

He gave her the softest of smiles, nodded, and kissed her tenderly. "I will come back to you, sweeting. We have many moonlit nights before us, you and I." His recurring reassurance; words he'd first spoken as he departed to fight in Mortimer's rebellion, words he'd repeated when he was imprisoned.

"Many moonlit nights," she echoed, smiling at him through her tears.

Chapter 14

Adam resented being separated from his wife. It almost made him laugh that he should miss her as much as he did – most men spent long periods away from their wives and children, and he'd never expected it to be different for him. But that was before Kit, before coming to realise that there were instances when marriage and love could go hand in hand – as it had done for Lord Roger and Lady Joan, with the lady accompanying her husband all over the country, even when she was with child.

Should he have wanted to, Adam could easily have found himself a bedmate among the various women who were in some way connected to the court – were he to have a silver penny for every come-hither look he'd received in the fortnight since Kit left, he'd have had enough to buy himself a destrier – but he wasn't interested, preferring to think of Kit as he lay alone in his bed.

"She'd never find out," Sir Henry said, not quite keeping the laughter out of his voice when Adam yet again refused his offer to find him a female companion.

"Maybe not. But I would know – and besides, I don't want to."

Sir Henry clapped him on the shoulder. "Let me know when you change your mind."

"I won't."

"No?" Sir Henry dipped his head in the direction of Cassandra de Ley, who was making a beeline for them. "Maybe she will change your mind for you."

Adam scowled, grabbed his cloak and left the hall, ignoring Cassandra's voice asking him to wait.

Fortunately, Adam could escape into his duties, even more so when the king decided it was safe to return to Westminster in time for All Hallows'. Adam was put in charge of organising the prince's household, and in between packing up his lord's belongings and arranging for barges and carts, he was kept more than busy – so occupied he scarcely had time to eat or sleep.

Returning to Westminster was a relief. Living under the looming walls of the Tower had been a distinctly uncomfortable experience, reminding Adam far too often of the night in which he'd helped Lord Roger escape – and of old Lord Mortimer, slowly rotting to death in his cell. Here at Westminster, the court relaxed, helped along by the fact that the king and queen had established some sort of armistice, this very much due to their son's recent illness, but also because Queen Isabella played the role of devoted, obedient wife and mother to perfection.

"I'm no longer ill," Prince Edward protested, flapping his hands at his mother. "And I am too old to be treated like a cosset."

"There, there," the queen replied. "Indulge your concerned mother, my little princeling."

"I am not little!" But Edward ate the rice boiled with almonds and milk, he bit into the flaky pastry of the marrow pies, and obediently swallowed down the livers boiled in wine, the salmon cooked in cream, making both his royal parents beam at him.

"I have to leave," the prince confided to Adam one morning. "All this pampering is suffocating."

"You can't leave without the king's permission, my lord."

"I know." The lad sighed, kicked at the ground and looked utterly miserable.

"We could go riding," Adam suggested.

"Now?" Prince Edward brightened.

"Not now, I fear," Adam replied, hard put not to laugh. "Sir Henry awaits you with your tutor – Master Richard, is it not?"

The prince groaned. "How much more must I learn?" he whined.

"As much as Sir Henry deems necessary, my lord." Adam

grinned at Edward's crestfallen expression. "We can go riding this afternoon, but for now you must go to your lessons."

Adam set Gavin to archery practice and ambled over to the stables to see to Goliath. In difference to most knights, Adam preferred to curry his horse himself when he could, enjoying the silence and the warm, reassuring strength of his ill-tempered stallion. Goliath snorted and shifted in his stall, now and then he rolled a warning eye at Adam, but in general the stallion submitted to his master's ministrations with good grace.

"That's a magnificent horse."

Adam straightened up and studied Despenser over the broad expanse of Goliath's back. It was the first time in months the royal chancellor had as much as exchanged a word with him.

"My lord," Adam said with little warmth. Despenser placed a gloved hand on Goliath's neck, retracting it as if burnt when Goliath whipped his head around, teeth bared. "He bites," Adam told him. "A tad testy with strangers."

"As treacherous as his master?" Despenser retreated out of Goliath's range. "Such beasts are best put down, don't you think?"

"Are you talking about me or my horse?" Adam asked.

"You, of course. I remain of the opinion that it is most unfortunate that you remain alive – for me and for the king." Despenser leaned against the stall and crossed his arms over his chest. "But fortunately, dearest Adam, there are ways for me to rectify this." He flicked at something on his silk surcoat, for the day in a bright, eye-catching saffron that offset Despenser's dark looks to perfection.

"You wouldn't dare."

"No? Come, come, Adam, surely by now you know there is very little I wouldn't dare – or do – if I deem it necessary to keep the realm safe."

"Keep yourself safe, you mean."

"At present very much one and the same," Despenser replied with a grin. But it was a strained smile, and when Adam looked closer, he noted that the royal chancellor was tense, with eyes sunk into bruised hollows that spoke of many sleepless nights.

"For now," Adam muttered.

"What?" Despenser made as if to approach, but a warning snort from Goliath had him backing away. "What did you say?"

"Nothing, my lord."

"You're lying, dearest Adam." Despenser shook his head from side to side. "Liars must be punished – as must traitors." He chuckled. "Now I can think of several ways in which to punish you – all of them ending with you begging for death."

Adam swallowed. Once, twice. His hand tightened round the curry brush. "I serve the prince," he said.

"And I serve the king," Despenser hissed back.

"How? By killing me? You can try, my lord!"

"Me? Do I look like a fool to you? Besides, I don't sully my hands unnecessarily, but others might – especially if I dangle the prize of the fair Lady de Guirande and her lands in front of them." Despenser lowered his voice to a soft, sibilant whisper. "So beware, dear Adam: when least you expect it, the smiler with the knife may be waiting for you."

Like a ghost he flitted away, as soundlessly as he had appeared. Adam slid down to sit on the floor, trying to suppress the sickening, gut-cramping fear that flowed through him. Despenser was not making an idle threat.

"It appears you have an implacable enemy," someone said. Adam rose, and Earl Thomas nodded a greeting. Adam bowed before the king's half-brother, not certain if it was a good thing or a bad one that this man had eavesdropped on his altercation with Despenser.

"I do," Adam sighed. "And a powerful one at that." So far, Adam had contrived to keep a cautious distance from both Earl Thomas and Henry of Lancaster. But the message he had received through Kit had confirmed his suspicions that these kinsmen to the king were reaching the end of their tethers, however unctuously they behaved to Despenser's face.

Adam shifted on his feet – with some gentle prodding, the prince had in fact done his best to reconcile his parents, but

Adam was ashamed of having used the lad like that, and had promised himself he would not do it again.

Earl Thomas fiddled with his leather jerkin, a beautiful fur-trimmed garment that sat snugly round his broad shoulders and chest, tapering off to a slim waist. "Not as powerful as he thinks – or not for much longer."

Adam did not quite know what to say.

Earl Thomas chuckled. "You are not friendless, Adam de Guirande."

"The friends I have are either dead, in exile, or the sort that can see me hanged and disembowelled," Adam replied drily.

"Best you make some new friends then," Earl Thomas said. "Men like me – like Henry of Lancaster."

"My lord?" Adam licked his lips. This was dangerous talk. "I serve the prince. I will not do anything that puts my lord in danger."

"Nor will we," Earl Thomas assured him with an easy smile. "The prince is young."

And malleable, Adam thought wryly, but he didn't say so.

The earl gave him yet another winning smile. "New friends, Adam de Guirande. Just what you need to keep you safe." He slapped Goliath on his rump and sauntered off.

For days, Adam walked about on his toes, ever on guard, ever watchful. His nights were long vigils with snatches of sleep, eyes on the heavy door, and at mealtimes he made sure to always sit with his back to a wall, constantly scanning the people closest to him. He never ate anything unless it was from a shared trencher, he never drank unless he witnessed the serving lads pour the ale into his mug.

He became irascible and distracted, cuffed at Gavin for no reasons, scowled at the prince when he did less than well at sword practice. Eleven days into this, and Adam's nerves were so frayed he jumped at any sound, any movement, causing Sir Henry to take him aside.

"What is the matter?" Sir Henry asked. "These last few days, you're as skittish as a newborn foal – but with the temper of an aggravated lion."

Adam studied him in silence, uncertain as to how much he could confide in him. But he needed to speak to someone before he burst apart with all this tension, so he inhaled a couple of times for courage and told Sir Henry about his recent conversation with Despenser. He left out any mention of Earl Thomas – for the earl's sake. When he was done, Sir Henry shook his head, causing his long grey hair to bounce.

"He would be a fool to try anything here."

"Whatever else he may be, Hugh Despenser is not a fool. And he will try – or rather, he will put someone else up to trying."

Sir Henry pursed his lips, studying the two daggers at Adam's waist and his sword. "You're a hard man to beat, Adam."

"One on one, yes. Which Despenser knows." Adam shrugged. "And it doesn't help that I don't sleep – or eat – much."

"That I can help you with," Sir Henry said. "I'll have you moved into the prince's apartments." He smiled. "Less private, but safer."

That same evening, Adam was installed in a small hole of a room, with only an arrow-loop for a window. A narrow bed, a truckle for Gavin and a stool made up the entire furnishing, and once Adam's chest was in place there was just enough floor space available for him to walk from his bed to the door without stepping on Gavin. No matter: for the first time in over a week, Adam slept, the heavy, dreamless sleep of the truly exhausted.

On top of his constant fear of being assassinated, Adam had to deal with an increasingly more determined Cassandra.

"I don't understand," he groaned to Sir Henry. "Why is she pursuing me, when she could find a dozen of welcoming arms elsewhere? I don't want her!"

"Precisely because of that," Sir Henry said with a grin. "The lady feels insulted by your lack of interest, and so she will persevere until she wins."

"She won't," Adam told him.

"As I hear it, you've bedded with her before. Was it such a dreary experience that you don't want to relive it?"

"No." Adam smiled slightly. Cassandra de Ley had woken fires in him, had driven him to the extremes of passion and beyond – but all of that was before Kit. Where Cassandra had been the master and him the apprentice, with Kit it was he who led and instructed, she who followed and learnt, an eager disciple who trusted him implicitly, no matter how much he pushed her. He liked that, he admitted to himself, he enjoyed being the one in charge. It added a titillating whiff of power to his lovemaking, further enforced by the warmth in his heart that Kit's mere presence evoked.

"So why not partake of her pleasures again?" Sir Henry asked.

"Because I don't want to." Adam cast Cassandra a look, and she smiled, dimpling prettily as she made him a reverence. A lot of woman, he reflected, his gaze travelling over her ample chest, down her narrow waist to her wide hips. As if in response, the lady preened. Adam reverted to studying his goblet of wine.

That night, he dreamed of Kit – he often dreamed of Kit – and woke to a pounding member and fragmented images of his wife, head thrown back in abandon. He pleasured himself in concentrated silence, and somewhere midway through, his visions of his wife changed to those of Cassandra, as she'd been all those years ago. With a loud groan, Adam stopped what he was doing and rolled over on his side.

Next morning, Adam stayed behind after mass. He needed to confess, have the priest help him fortify his resolve to resist the constant temptation of Cassandra de Ley. He laughed softly, thinking it was a step in the right direction that he admitted to not being entirely unperturbed by the lady's flattering attention – even if he truly wanted nothing to do with her.

A strong, familiar grip on his shoulder had Adam spinning around.

"William!"

In priest robes, with his head severely tonsured and a wide grin on his face, William stood before him.

"A priest, brother?" Adam asked, lowering his voice. "Is that so wise, here in Westminster? What if someone recognises you?"

William made a dismissive gesture. "Recognise me? I was never more than one of Lord Roger's lowlier priests and clerks." He led the way towards the side-chapels, and Adam accompanied him, stopping for a moment at Aymer de Valence's tomb, as yet undecorated, even if Adam had heard the dowager countess had plans for a magnificent effigy. "It does give me an opportunity to see the queen," William added.

"See the queen? Are you out of your mind?" Adam studied the recently repainted doorway to St John's chapel: bold strokes of red, offset against borders of paler blues and whites, here and there dotted with gold. The paint still looked wet, so he swept his cloak tight around himself as he entered. He bowed before the statue of the saint and crossed himself.

"I have to, I am entrusted with messages for her." William grimaced. "I also have messages to Lord Roger, from the Bishops of Hereford and Lincoln, from Henry of Lancaster himself, and from one or two London Merchants. Lord Roger casts a wide net." He scratched at his neck and gave a hollow laugh. "All those missives – it's like carrying my own personal noose around."

There was a rumble of voices from the ambulatory, and Adam recognised the prior and some of the monks. They threw a beady look at William, and Adam clasped William's hand.

"Forgive me, Father, but I have sinned," he mumbled, sounding adequately penitent.

A soft chuckle emanated from William once the dark-clad men had moved away. "You want to confess to me?" He sat down on a bench and gestured for Adam to kneel in front of him.

"Of course I don't. You're my brother." Adam knelt all the same. "But it accords us some privacy."

"It does." William gave him a sharp look. "But something is preying on your conscience – why else would you have lingered after mass?" He settled back against the bench. "So why not kill two birds with one stone?"

Adam looked away from his penetrating light-blue eyes. "I have..." His cheeks heated, and he took a deep breath before spilling everything about Cassandra and his struggle with lust. William listened, scowled at the mention of Cassandra's wiles, and once Adam had finished, he patted him on his shoulder.

"You're a man," he said simply. "A man who misses his wife."

"I do," Adam admitted.

William grinned. "I'll not give you much penance – but you must promise to resist this sloe-eyed temptress. Kit deserves as much."

"She does," Adam agreed, smiling slightly at the thought of his wife. "Are you bound for Tresaints?" he asked, getting off his knees.

William nodded, extending his sandal-shod feet before him. "It is an expensive matter, being an exiled baron."

"I can imagine." Lord Mortimer was accustomed to an affluent lifestyle, with excellent horses, wines and clothes. It must be difficult for such a man to be dependent on the goodwill of others. "Will you carry a letter to Kit for me? I must warn her about Despenser's threat."

"His threat?" William sounded angry. "Now what?"

Once Adam had told him of his recent confrontation with Despenser, William rose.

"Damn the man!" He took a couple of deep breaths. "I'll tell John to keep an eye out, he'll see Kit safe." Old like the hills, with a face the texture of an old boot, John was the best shot Adam had ever met, and his two grandsons were almost as skilled with the bow as he was. "But now, if you excuse me, I have a queen to meet," William continued, leading the way into the nave.

"How?" Adam hissed. "She is watched day and night!"

"But not here – and not when she comes to light candles and pray." William dipped his head slightly in the direction of a woman, covered in a dark veil and accompanied by two other women.

"God keep you safe, brother," Adam whispered.

"And you," William whispered back. "I leave on the morrow," he added, "so any letter I must have by tonight."

Adam nodded. He'd send Gavin down with it after vespers.

The prince obtained his father's permission to retire from court, but was instructed to be back by Christmastide. On the Monday following the first Sunday of Advent, they rode off, making for Windsor, and Adam felt free for the first time in weeks. No assassin to watch for, no Cassandra to avoid, and instead the days were filled with hunting, the evenings with chess and dice games.

On St Lucy's Eve, Adam wandered out into the gardens, wishing he were home instead. He'd had a letter from his wife the day before, a vivid description of his home and son, of how much she missed him and prayed for him. Above him, the winter sky was ablaze with stars, below him the grass crackled with frost, and he shivered in his cloak as he prayed that Kit and the babe would be safe, and that he would soon be allowed to reunite with her.

"Go home?" Prince Edward looked at him. "But I need you here, Sir Adam."

The form of address told Adam his request would be denied – again. He suppressed an urge to curse at the lad who held his life in his hands, angered at this enforced separation from the people who truly mattered to him.

"My lord father insists that you attend on me," the prince went on in a pained voice.

"And he also insists that my wife be banished from court." Adam couldn't keep the harsh tone out of his voice. "Why am I the only man to be so deprived of his wife?"

"I don't know," the prince muttered. "And I wish I could help you – and Lady Kit."

"Then let me go home!"

"Not now," the prince replied. "We are ordered to join the court at Nottingham in ten days hence. You will accompany me there, and then we shall see." He sighed. "I

144

will talk to my father, Sir Adam. More than that, I cannot do."

It was a long, wet ride north, and when the castle of Nottingham finally loomed before them in the winter dusk, all Adam could think of was dry clothes and a warm bed. He barely glanced at his surroundings as they rode through the town, at this time of the day mostly a collection of solid houses and wet cobbled streets. Affluent, he noted, with a large friary halfway between the city gates and the castle itself, perched atop a height.

The castle was huge. The curtain wall surrounded a sizeable outer ward, and once through the second gatehouse they entered the upper bailey, dominated by an ancient keep.

"We are to be lodged there," Sir Henry said, waving at the buildings beyond the keep.

"With the prince?" Adam peered through the sleet. Not the most elegant of apartments.

"Our lord will stay in the royal apartments." Sir Henry pointed to yet another gatehouse and the bailey beyond. "With his mother, I believe."

Christmas Eve was a splendid affair, marred only by Kit's absence and Despenser's grinning presence. These last few weeks, Adam had almost forgotten his threats, but the avid look on Hugh Despenser's face had warning prickles travelling up and down Adam's spine, and so he spent most of the festivities on his guard, tasting little of the succulent dishes that graced the table. Roasted salmon, pickled eels, perch afloat in a sea of jellied gravy, looking eerily alive, and a massive subtlety representing St George and the dragon – Adam but glanced at them.

On the other side of the hall, Cassandra de Ley was making cow's eyes at him, that pretty mouth of hers now and then blowing him a kiss. Adam pretended not to notice. He sank his nose into his cup and inhaled the heady sweetness of the mulled wine, but what with Despenser's leering face and Cassandra's hungry eyes, he deemed it wise not to imbibe more than necessary, restricting himself to shallow sips.

He scratched at his legs, for the night encased in new green hose that matched the embroidered hems and cuffs of

145

his dark blue surcoat – in silk, no less, falling to his knees and with wide, sweeping sleeves that revealed the lighter blue of the tunic he wore below. He'd had a bath the night before, and at his insistence the barber had clean-shaved his bristling cheeks, making him something of an oddity in this room where almost all of the men had plenty of facial hair. Adam had never sported a beard – the bristles the barber had relieved him of earlier were merely the consequence of those weeks at Windsor. In this he had followed the lead of Lord Roger.

As soon as he could, Adam left the hall, preferring the company of his own bed to the inebriated people in the hall. At his side padded Gavin, looking flushed and humming something under his breath. They made their way across the middle bailey, through the dark gatehouse and hastened over the upper ward, their cloaks offering little protection against the icy rain.

Once inside, Adam exchanged a curt greeting with the guards, both of whom snickered behind his back as he passed them. Up the winding stairs, along a narrow, badly lit passage, and Adam opened the door to his room.

In his bed was Cassandra, in nothing but her shift and silk hose. A surge of lust rushed through Adam, hastily quelled by the simple expedient of bringing forth the image of Kit's face all those months ago when she'd found Cassandra in their room.

"Get out," he said, retreating towards the open door. Cassandra laughed, rising towards him so that her breasts nearly popped out from under her shift. Beautiful breasts, heavy and round, and Adam's member twitched in appreciation.

"Come here instead," she purred, extending her arm towards him. From behind him came an appreciative squeak. Adam glanced at Gavin, who was staring at Cassandra.

"You can have her," he said. "I don't bed with whores."

"How dare you!" Cassandra pulled the sheets up.

"I am but stating the truth." He gave her a weary look. "Give up, Cassandra. I am not interested – as I have tried to convey to you on various occasions."

"Your mouth says one thing, your eyes another," she countered.

Adam exhaled and pinched the bridge of his nose. "I am not made of stone, and yes, you are an attractive woman. But that doesn't change a thing. Now, if that itch of yours is so bad as to have you throw yourself at a man who doesn't want you, I am sure both Gavin and the men-at-arms outside would be happy to serve you."

With impressive dignity, Cassandra left the bed, ignoring Gavin's gawking. "I think not." She pulled on her kirtle. "Help me with my laces."

"Not me," Adam said. "Gavin here can do it." He was going nowhere close to her, suspecting that once he was within reach she would grab him, kiss him even, and God knew what stories would get back to Kit if that happened. He stepped outside into the passage and remained there until Cassandra left his room, all of her covered in a black hooded cloak.

"Don't come back," he called after her.

"Should I ever enter your room again it will be to kill you," she replied.

"As I said: don't come back."

"Don't count on it!" she snarled, before disappearing down the stairs.

One day after the other followed, a long progression of dark, wet days that only served to fray men's tempers. Twelfth Night came and went, and still Adam was not allowed to return home, the prince offering a weak, apologetic smile. Adam spent most of his time with his lord or in the stables, and he had just seen to the prince's new mare when four men stepped out to block his way. Adam recognised the knight leading them as Godfrey of Broseley, the bastard who had once told Kit that once Adam was out of the way, he'd be given the widow and her manors.

"Well, well, if it isn't Adam de Guirande," Godfrey said, effectively backing Adam further into the shadow afforded by the stables and the nearby storage sheds. Adam managed to get hold of a pitchfork, and pulled his dagger with his left hand. He licked his lips: not only was he unarmed, but

Godfrey had chosen his ground well – the cobbles beneath Adam's feet were slippery and uneven, a trial with his crippled foot.

When the first man attacked, Adam sidestepped and whacked the fool over his head, sending him sprawling to his knees. The sword clattered to the ground and Adam dove for it, coming back up on his feet to meet the onrush of the other three. Adam was suddenly fighting on all fronts, pressed further back towards the wall.

He slipped, his right foot screaming in protest when he put all his weight on it. Godfrey laughed, lunged, and when Adam parried his sword, Godfrey brought the small mace he was carrying in his other hand down on Adam's foot. Pain exploded up his leg, sizzled his toes. His knee buckled, and only through sheer instinct was he able to parry Godfrey's follow-up swipe.

In one desperate movement, Adam attacked, and his blade connected with something that gave, a low howl cutting through the January drizzle. The men fell back. One of them was cradling his arm, another was moaning and clutching at his thigh. Godfrey was bleeding profusely from his face, his intent gaze never leaving Adam – and his foot. Adam was bleeding inside his boot, he could feel the warm stickiness pooling inside the leather, and at present the agony of placing any weight at all on his foot had black spots rising before his eyes.

Godfrey removed his hand from his bleeding face. "Damn you, de Guirande, look what you've done, you bastard!"

"No matter. You're ugly as sin anyway," Adam snarled.

"And you're dead," Godfrey hissed. "How long can you hold out?" he jeered, dancing forward to swipe yet again at Adam's head.

Adam stumbled, went down on a knee, but managed to get his sword up, deflecting the other man's blow. He blinked to clear his eyes, and tightened his grip on his sword. If nothing else, he was going to kill Godfrey before he died.

"Long enough, I think." The voice came from behind Godfrey. Adam squinted through the rain, seeing only a hooded figure accompanied by two others. "Four against one, Broseley? Well, we can't have that, can we?" Steel glinted in the weak light of the stable lanterns.

"My lord," Godfrey stuttered, "this is a matter between de Guirande and me."

"Really? Not between de Guirande and your master?" A blade sliced through the air, and Godfrey cringed. "Leave while you can, Broseley. I will count to three, and if you're still here then…" The blade swooped down, arrested only an inch from Godfrey's arm. The man mewled, and just like that, he was off, his companions loping after him.

The man pulled back his hood and strode towards Adam. "Can you walk?"

"I think not," Adam said, before falling forward into Earl Thomas' arms.

He came to when they reached the stairs. Earl Thomas was standing over him, shaking him none too gently in his efforts to wake him up.

"You're a heavy man," Thomas panted. "It took two of us to get you this far, but you will need to help if we're to get you upstairs."

No matter how he tried, Adam could not avoid bumping his foot up the narrow staircase, and by the time they had reached his room, he was covered with cold sweat, teeth gritted in an effort not to cry out. The coming hour was one of the longest in his life, and by the time the physician was done, Adam was trembling all over, his jaws aching. But he hadn't uttered a sound, he thought fuzzily as he sank into sleep, not as much as a squeak.

The next day, Godfrey of Broseley and his three companions were not to be located anywhere, despite Sir Henry's and the earl's determined search.

"With Godfrey gone, we can't prove it was Despenser who did this." Earl Thomas sat down on Adam's bed. Adam winced at the resulting jolt to his foot.

"That's why he is gone," he said through tight lips. "Despenser has sent him off to skulk far away from court –

maybe he's even killed him. The price of failure is high if you're Despenser's man."

"I must tell my father," the prince said. He hadn't left Adam's bedside since the earl had carried him back last night.

"That won't help, Ned." Earl Thomas ruffled his nephew's hair. "Your father will not listen to anyone accusing his favourite. No, the best thing we can do is to give out that Adam was attacked by ruffians, and ended up so injured you've sent him home to recuperate."

"Home?" Adam sat up. He studied his bandaged extremity, trying to close out the memory of just how much it had hurt when the physician had cleaned it and treated it last night. The mace's spikes had left a series of deep puncture wounds, leaving the original injury irritated and raw.

"Home," the earl said firmly. "Don't you agree, Ned?"

"I do." The lad studied the bloodstains that decorated the linen bandages. "Best leave as soon as you can, Adam."

"Today," Adam replied, casting a look out the small window. "I leave today."

Chapter 15

Adam came home a week before Candlemas. The intervening time, Kit had filled with work – a lot of work – and accordingly there were new shirts and tunics for Adam, new smocks for Tom, a new kirtle in a bright blue for herself, and new bed-hangings in heavy, dark red fustian. And yet, she'd fretted, reading the few short missives from her husband over and over again in an attempt to create some insight in his life, which was more than difficult given that Adam's messages tended to be terse, along the lines of him being well and hoping she was too.

She was sitting in the solar when she heard the horses, and moments later she was flying down the stairs, rushing through the hall.

Adam was dismounting when she burst out of the door, and then she was enfolded in his arms, her cheek pressed to the itchy wool of his tunic. They stood like that, her ear to his heart, his cheek on her head, for a long time. She nestled even closer, drawing in the comforting and familiar scents of her man – damp wool, leather, and that salty tang that was all his own.

"Sweeting," he murmured, and she raised her face to his, kissing him until she was breathless and hot all over. Adam smiled, his grey eyes never leaving hers. "I take it you've missed me."

"Now and then," she replied.

"Now and then?" Mabel snorted loudly. "God help us, m'lord, but we are that happy to have you home. Your lady wife has been driving us to distraction these last few months."

"Ah." Adam's smile widened, and he released her from his arms, taking her hand instead. "And the babe?" he asked, his free hand stroking her belly.

"The babe does well," Mabel answered for Kit. "It is your wife that has suffered your absence, not the little mite within." She beamed at Adam. "I dare say your lady wife is quite besotted with you, my lord."

"Mabel!" Kit tried to scowl, but couldn't quite suppress her smile, thereby spoiling the effect.

"I am but telling the truth, m'lady," Mabel sniffed. "And unless your lord husband has the wits of a newt, he already knows."

"I do," Adam agreed. He tightened his hold on Kit's hand, and looked as if he were about to say something, but was interrupted by a loud "Papa!" followed by Tom himself, who threw his arms around his father's legs.

Kit stepped aside to allow father and son to properly greet each other.

"Gavin," she said, nodding in greeting. Adam's squire had shot up these last few months and was now taller than Kit – and substantially broader. "You look...big."

Gavin grinned, clearly pleased by her statement, and bowed.

"That's what you get when you eat like a horse," Adam put in, giving Tom one last kiss before setting him down.

"I do not, m'lord," Gavin protested.

"No, that's right – you eat like two horses," Adam retorted. He sniffed the air. "What's for dinner?"

"Another one that can eat like a horse." Kit grinned. "We'll have to ask Mall what she's planning."

Mall's broad face broke into a wide smile. "Baked onions, roasted pork with apples and pottage, m'lord. Will that suit?"

"It will suit just fine," Adam replied. He took a hesitant step towards the manor house, his face draining of colour.

"You're hurt!" Kit rushed to support him.

"It's not too bad," Adam replied.

"Not too bad?" Gavin muttered. "Not too bad, and he can barely stand on it."

"Who?" Kit asked in an undertone.

"You know who," Adam replied with a sigh. He scratched at his head. "I need a bath."

"Now?" She shivered in the January sun, thinking she might just as well join him.

"No," Adam replied. "Food first, then a bath." He drew her close. "The bath will take a very long time, my love," he whispered in her ear, and Kit's face heated with expectation.

The bath had to wait. No sooner were they alone in the solar, but Adam pulled the bolt, and guided her towards the bed, one slow limp at the time.

"Undress me," he commanded, and she did, clumsy in her haste. He fell to the bed, and she fell after, now clad in only her shift.

"Take it off," he said, and his hands were in her hair, undoing her braid. At his silent urgings, she straddled him, and so much had she wanted him, longed for him, that she was already wet and warm, emitting a soft gasp when his member impaled her. A waterfall of dark red hair covered them both when she leaned forward to kiss him. His hands in her hair, on her breast, on her swelling belly, and he bucked upwards, breath coming in short, loud gasps, while she pushed down, meeting him with a slap of damp skin against skin.

Afterwards, she lay beside him, and the little knot of fear she'd carried inside her heart since she'd left London in October finally dissipated. He was here, and she nestled as close as she could, pillowing her head on his shoulder.

Adam toyed with her hair as he recounted his recent adventures, but when she made as if to rise and inspect his foot, he tightened his hold on her.

"It will keep, sweeting. Right now, I just want to lie like this." He craned his head back. "New canopy?" he said, going on to inspect the matching bed-hangings. He rose on his elbow. "You've changed everything."

"Not quite," she protested. "I've just rehung the tapestries, and John has made us a new chest." She pushed him back down. "And I've moved Tom out." Their son now slept with Amy and Mabel in a newly constructed chamber – a nursery.

"Ah." He smiled. "So it's just us here now?"

"Yes. As it should be."

There was a knock on the door. Kit kissed his nose, pulled

on her shift and a mantle, and went over to open it, instructing the men to set the tub down as close as they could to the hearth.

"How is the queen?" Kit unwound the bandages round his foot, sniffing discreetly for any sign of rot. Nothing. The physician had done a good job, and what Adam needed was rest – an opportunity for lacerated skin and flesh to heal.

"Our lady queen is the perfect dutiful wife," Adam commented with a laugh. "She's not set one foot wrong since September, and last I heard the king is considering sending her to France as his envoy." He covered his crotch with his discarded shirt when a stream of men and boys filed in, carrying bucket after bucket of hot water. He flinched when she applied pressure to his foot, grimacing when she asked him to flex and bend his toes.

"It hurts?" she asked.

"Aye."

"So she makes her escape at last." Kit gestured for him to get into the bath.

"Escape? If the queen goes to France, she travels with companions picked for her by the king. She will be watched at all times, and one false move may mean she will never see her children again." He limped across the floor. "There will be no opportunity for her to see Lord Roger."

"But there will be ample opportunity for her to communicate with him," Kit countered. Adam nodded before sitting down in the bath with a contented sound.

He relaxed under her hands. Head thrown back, eyes closed, he was almost asleep as she washed him.

"And Cassandra?"

"Cassandra?" He opened one eye. "I haven't seen her much."

"I find that hard to believe." She scrubbed his back with excessive force, making him twist. "After all, you've been at court, she's been at court, and William told me you were vexed with her."

"Precisely. Vexed." His jaw clenched.

"Why?"

154

Adam inhaled, held his breath, and expelled it in a rush. "Because she has the irritating habit of placing herself before me whenever she can." He glanced at Kit. "I knew you wouldn't like to hear that."

"And what have you done, when confronted by her generous bosom and come-hither looks?" Kit asked.

"Nothing!" He glared at her. She glared back, and his mouth twitched. "Well, she might not agree," he added with a grin. "Her last attempt at seduction ended not at all as she wanted."

"Ah." She wasn't going to ask. No, she was not going to ask. "What happened?"

"I suggested she try her wiles on Gavin instead."

"Gavin?" Kit laughed. "And was Gavin willing?"

"If Gavin's member had stood higher, the lad would have been unconscious from blood loss," Adam commented drily. "She was lying near on naked in my bed."

"And how did she end up there?" Kit asked icily.

"Ask her," he snapped.

She cast her husband a long look. Adam was young and virile, a man who was accustomed to regular and enthusiastic bed-play with her. Such men tended to find other welcoming arms when separated from their wives, but just the thought of Adam seeking release with another woman had something green and vicious twisting through her innards. A strong hand gripped her chin, raised her face to meet smouldering grey eyes.

"No," he said.

"No what?"

"I can see what you're thinking, and I can assure you that whatever itch I may have suffered, I would never satisfy it with Cassandra de Ley – I would rather have visited the stews."

"And have you?" Her voice trembled.

"God's truth, woman, what makes you think that?"

"But you just said—"

"Any itch I have, I have for you," he interrupted.

"Truly?" She smiled at him.

"Come here and I'll show you," he growled, knotting his

hand into her hair and pulling her close enough to kiss her. A long, deep kiss. A kiss where he held her very still as his lips covered hers, his tongue demanding entry. A wonderful kiss, in truth, and Kit was leaning towards him, the fabric across her breasts already wet, when he gently pushed her away. "The water is getting cold – and it's dirty."

At present, Kit did not much care, arms reaching for him, heat rushing through her loins to gather as a throbbing ache between her legs. Adam chuckled and stood, water sluicing off him. He climbed out of the bath, and she was in his arms, clasping his hot, wet body to hers.

"Wanton," he said, brushing her damp hair off her brow. He relieved her of her garment and guided her to the floor, just by the hearth. The old, worn Moorish rug was neither particularly soft nor thick, but the fire was warm, and Adam was here, his fingers were everywhere, his mouth in her ear, on her jawline, sliding further down to cover her belly with a series of kisses. The baby kicked, and Adam laughed, scrubbing his unshaved cheeks against her belly.

His fingers inside of her, his mouth on hers, and she was burning up from within.

"Beautiful," he whispered, releasing her lips. "Look at you, pink and flushed, rounded with my child." She twisted under his expert touch. "Is it for me you burn, sweeting?"

"Only for you," she moaned. "Only ever for you, my dearest husband."

"Forever?" His eyes bored into hers.

"Forever and ever," she panted. "Take me, fill me – now, Adam, now, before…"

Before all of her fragmented, she tried to say, but the words escaped her, drowned in a sea of sensations, from the way her toes curled to how her hips rose. Her breathing hitched as wave after wave of multi-coloured, spinning heat rose and crested within her veins, flinging her spinning into a precipice where all she could do was hold on to him, her lifeline, her man.

He gave her a satisfied smile once she returned to herself. Very gently, he entered her, moving slowly until once again she heard herself begin to gasp, hands clutching at him. This time, his harsh breaths echoed hers, and with a guttural sound midway between a growl and her name, he climaxed. Not once did his eyes leave hers, pools of dark grey locked into hers.

Chapter 16

Six weeks later, Lent was firmly upon them. Kit scowled at the salted herring left to soak overnight in the kitchen, and went to find Mall – an easy enterprise, as either the cook was in the storage sheds or she was in the root cellar.

"More herring?" Kit asked, addressing Mall, who was presently inspecting the last of the parsnips, carefully dusting them free from soil and straw. The root cellar was cold – and almost empty, something that had Kit frowning as she mentally revised her other food stores. Well, at least they had plenty of cabbage, she thought, eyeing the sizeable heap in a wooden bin.

"I've got smoked trout for tomorrow," the cook offered as some sort of comfort, "and there will be eel pie on Sunday." She bundled the parsnips into her apron and suggested that they stop by the storage shed for some dried peas so she could make some nice pottage to go with the herring.

Kit trailed her out of the cellar. The March day was brisk and overcast, with a promise of rain before noon. The men were either in the fields or in the pastures, overseeing the last of the lambing. Most of the women were working the fields beside the men, and the enclosed space that went for their own little bailey – a somewhat ridiculous bailey, seeing as it was protected by a stout wooden fence rather than a stone wall – was unusually empty of people.

One of the dogs lumbered to its feet, snout raised. It was one of Adam's hounds, a large beast with a brindled coat and paws the size of a horse's hooves. It sniffed and moved towards the gate, accompanied by a couple of other dogs. Coming down the lane was a man on a galloping steed with another horse on a leading rein. Kit shaded her eyes. There was something lying atop the second horse, and she caught a glimpse of a hand clutching the pommel, and a shock of bright red hair spilling from the hood.

"William!" Adam exclaimed, having appeared from the stables.

"It is?" Kit squinted. The rider pulled his hood back, and yes, it was William, looking as if the hounds of Hell were snapping at his heels.

"Help!" he gasped, pulling his mount to a brutal halt. "He's injured, and they're after us, and—"

"Calm down." Adam's gaze flew over the wounded man.

"Calm down?" William shook his head. "I have the king's soldiers at my heels!"

"And you lead them here, to us?" Adam's mouth set in a displeased line.

"No choice," William said. "Richard will die otherwise." He threw a look over his shoulder. "Take him, and I'll ride on, lead them away."

"I'll go with you," Adam offered.

"What?" Kit looked at her husband, but he was already leading the second horse through the yard in the direction of the chapel. He moved with speed, despite his limp.

"They rode through the yard," he said to Kit. "Two unknown men came riding through the bailey, nearly trampled our hens to death and then rode off towards Wales." With a quick look at the bailey, still empty of people, Adam offloaded the man into the shade of the chapel, staggering under his weight. "The door," he grunted, and Kit held it open, before rushing past him to the altar where she bent and pushed the hidden lever, thereby causing the floor to yawn open behind her.

"I don't want you to go," she said, helping him lower the injured man to the floor in the hideaway.

"I must. I have to help my brother, just as you have to help yours."

"My brother?" Kit studied the unconscious man, her gaze lingering on his red hair. Dearest Lord, but he was right! This was Richard de Monmouth, Mortimer's trusted squire and Kit's half-brother.

"No time, not now!" Adam pulled her close and kissed her. With that he was gone, and moments later, Kit heard the sound of hooves, loud against the cobbles of the bailey, then quickly muffled into silence when the horses reached the grass.

There was no time to do anything more than pile what few blankets she had in the hiding place atop the man. Already she could hear the sounds of men and horses outside, calling for the master of the manor. Kit scrambled out of the hole with an effort, activated the mechanism and waited until the floor had closed before exiting the chapel. She clasped her heavy belly with both hands and hurried towards the men presently scowling at John and his grandsons.

"We are chasing two rebels," one of the mounted men was saying. "Get out of my way, you fool, before I ride your down!"

"They went that way," Kit said, pointing to the west. "They charged through my manor yard."

"When?" the leader of the men demanded. With a start, Kit recognised the king's younger half-brother. She bowed to allow herself some time in which to take control of her face. What had William and Richard been up to, that they were pursued by the Earl of Kent?

"Earl Edmund," she said. "I didn't recognise you at first."

The earl gave her a blank look. And then his face cleared – somewhat – and he offered Kit a slight nod.

"Lady de Guirande." His eyes sharpened. "And your husband?"

Kit exhaled. "Not here." She lowered her voice, as if sharing a confidence. "Ever since he got back, badly injured yet again, he escapes us all, preferring the wineskin to our company."

"Ah." A flash of contempt on Kent's face, a twitch to his lips, and Kit could see him dismissing her husband as a weakling. "So when…?"

"Just now. One of the horses was flagging." She gave him an encouraging smile. "As I said, they went yonder." Kit pointed towards the undulating hills. "Making for the safety of Wales, perhaps?"

"Making for a port, more likely," Kent muttered. "Spies, Lady de Guirande, dangerous men in the employ of that greatest traitor, Mortimer."

By now, the household had assembled in the yard, and a soft hiss rushed through them. This was Mortimer land, had been for years, and Edmund of Woodstock would find little support among these people when it came to apprehending Lord Mortimer's servants.

Fortunately, Kent did not seem to notice, even if one or two of his men did, scowling at the people of Tresaints. The earl was already moving out, urging the splendid black stallion he was riding towards the postern gate – as open as the main gate. His men fell in behind him, and in a cloud of dust they departed, headed due west.

"John." Kit beckoned the old man towards her. "I need your help. We have a wounded visitor in the chapel – and we have to get him inside with no one seeing us."

"No one?" John gestured at Mabel.

"Mabel doesn't count!" Kit took hold of Mabel. "Needles and gut strings, Mabel. Hot water, linen bands, yarrow and wormwood, meadowsweet and marigold." Kit ticked off the items on her fingers. "Honey," she added as an afterthought, watching John clear the yard of people by ordering them back to the fields.

Kit closed the door to her solar and leaned against it. Her knees trembled, and her belly was heaving wildly. Richard was still unconscious, dark red strands of hair plastered to his damp brow.

She tugged off his boots, his hose. The tunic was drenched with blood, and Mabel moaned and clucked, smoothing Richard over his head.

"My little laddie," she crooned, "my little man."

There was nothing little about their wounded guest. Kit grunted with effort as she cut off his tunic and shirt. Large bruises covered his left side, and a wound sliced through his flank, welling blood. Together, they washed him, and someway midway through, Richard regained consciousness, sitting up on the pallet bed with a hoarse yell. Bright blue eyes stared at them, so wide Kit could see the entire iris. He blinked.

"Kate?"

"Kit," Kit corrected. "Kate is dead, remember?" She shivered. Kate was dead because she'd eaten subtleties intended for Kit.

"Kit," Richard mumbled, falling back into Mabel's arms. He glanced down his naked torso. "Is it bad?"

"Yes." She threaded the curved needle. "What are you doing here?"

"Bleeding," he croaked. He closed his eyes. "Dying?"

"Not dying," Kit said firmly.

He clasped her free hand. "Promise? I don't want to die, not just yet." He drew in a shuddering breath when Mabel began washing the long, gaping wound.

"So why here?" Kit said, mostly to distract him as she heated the knife.

"Mere chance. I was making for Bristol. Agh!" Richard's body jerked, and the room filled with the stench of scorched flesh.

"I have to," Kit said. "You know I do."

He breathed through his nose, eyes wild. Kit applied the heated blade again and he bucked, teeth gritted.

"Once more." Kit gave him a weak smile.

She had finished sewing the gash together and was helping Mabel apply a thin layer of honey to her handiwork, when John erupted into the room, wheezing like a broken bellows.

"They're back!"

From the look on John's face, Kit surmised it was the earl that was back. "And Adam?" she asked, feeling her innards clench.

"Not back." John looked grim. "At present, not our greatest concern, m'lady."

From the yard came the sound of men dismounting, and Kent's voice calling for her.

"Go," John said. "Mabel and I will see young Richard safe." Kit vacillated, but John set his hands to her shoulders and shoved. "Go! Buy us time."

Time? Kit smoothed her veil into place, threw the bloodied apron into a corner and slipped on her new surcoat before descending to the hall. Just as she set foot on the rush mats, she discovered that her nails were rimmed with blood, and she discreetly tried to wipe her hands clean on the patterned red silk of her surcoat. Fortunately, Kent was in too much of a state to do more than glance at her.

"Are you sure?" Kent paced back and forth in the hall. "We could find no trace of them – none!"

"I saw what I saw, my lord," Kit replied. "They rode west."

"Or they didn't." Earl Edmund narrowed his eyes. "As I recall, you're kin to Mortimer's squire."

"Richard? Yes, he's my brother."

"And are you much alike?" The earl stood just in front of her, close enough that she could inhale his scent.

"I…" Kit was not sure what to do. Lie, and risk that the earl knew what Richard looked like? She opted for truth. "We share the same colouring, my lord."

"And would it surprise you to hear Richard de Monmouth is my quarry?"

"Richard here?" Kit's voice squeaked. "But he's in France!"

Kent studied her for a couple of heartbeats. "Search the place," he commanded his men. "Tear it apart if you must, but leave no stone unturned, y'hear? If Richard de Monmouth is here, I want him found!" When Kit made as if to sidle away, the earl grabbed her arm and gave her a little shake. "And you, Lady de Guirande, you'll stay here. I am very anxious to hear more about your husband's whereabouts."

"Unhand my wife, my lord." Adam's voice was low and laden with ice. "Now." He strode into the hall, exaggerating his limp. "What's this about escaped rebels?"

"Two," Kent replied curtly, releasing Kit. "And one of them is your lady wife's brother, squire to your first lord and master, that accursed Mortimer."

The men he had sent up the stairs to the solar came clattering back down, shaking their heads. Kit's shoulders relaxed.

"But now I serve another." Adam reached Kit and planted himself in front of her, shielding her with his bulk.

Kent's mouth thinned, the carefully barbered beard quivering. "So you say, de Guirande, but some are not convinced."

Adam shrugged. "I have pledged myself to the prince. I will not break that pledge."

From outside came loud barks, and voices raised in anger. Kent hastened to the door, throwing a triumphant look at Kit.

"William?" she asked Adam in an undertone as they followed the earl.

"Not here. Richard?"

"I don't know. I hope John got him out through the window." She gripped his hand. "What have they been doing?"

"Later," he murmured, giving her hand a warning squeeze.

Two hours later, the earl left, having offered a half-hearted apology for the havoc his men had caused. But not until sunset did John and his grandsons return, with Richard on a makeshift litter consisting of nothing but a length of cloth and two poles.

Adam refused to have him in the manor. "Kent may well return."

"He's ailing!"

"I can see that." He drew his wife close. "And so are you, sweeting. You're as pale as lard. All this upheaval is not good for you." She looked about to protest, but Adam brushed a finger over her mouth. "Shush, wife," he said gently. "I am ordering you to bed – now."

"But Richard—"

"We will see to him," Adam promised. "But you will do as I say." He watched her out of the hall, up the stairs, the heavy braid of dark red hair she shared with her brother swinging back and forth with every step. He could see from her posture that she was angry – hurt, even – but he was not about to risk yet another babe.

His brother-in-law he installed in a croft well away from the manor, with Harry, the eldest of John's grandsons, to guard him and Mabel to tend him.

"And m'lady?" Mabel asked as they trudged up a long

incline, following the swinging litter. Adam kept his gaze on the ground; precarious in the dark, no matter that he was holding a lantern.

"I'll take care of Kit," he said. "You take care of your lambkin."

Mabel sniffed. "My lambkin? Not since he was old enough to knot his hose."

"Ah. When he was twelve?"

Mabel swatted his arm. "You don't like him much, do you, m'lord?"

"Oh, I like Richard de Monmouth well enough. A steadfast and loyal squire, a good companion – but he was quite willing to sacrifice Kit to get what he wanted, even to the point of placing her in Lord Roger's bed, and standing by while his witch of a mother coerced her to wed me."

"But she never did end up in Lord Roger's bed, did she?" Mabel pointed out. "Lady Kit would have clawed his eyes out had he tried something like that. And as to that other matter, I dare say she is more than happy with how things played out."

"As am I," Adam replied with a smile.

He stayed long enough to help Mabel dress the wound with fresh poultices of marigold and St John's wort. Richard was shaken awake and Adam held him as Mabel coaxed several cups of heated ale fortified with honey down his gullet.

"Will he heal?" Adam asked, helping Richard back down. Mabel tsked, holding a hand to Richard's burning brow.

"It's in the Lord's hands," she said. "But it is best we pray."

When Adam returned home, he sank down in the hall, weary to the bones after this far too long day.

"Lady Kit?" he asked Gavin, flexing his toes gingerly.

"Here," she replied from behind him. "William is in the solar," she added. "Will you not join us there instead?"

"William?" That fool of a brother should have been long gone by now, making for the safety of France! Adam stomped up the stairs, ignoring just how much that made his foot hurt, and flung the door open. The room was suffused in a golden glow from several candles, there was a fire burning in the hearth and on the small table were the remains of a meal. Adam's stomach growled. William was sitting on a stool, newly shaved and tonsured.

"I found my old robes here," William said with a grin. "And no one will be looking for a priest, will they? After all—"

"Why are you here?" Adam cut him off.

"Too many pursuers, too lame a horse," William replied. "I had no choice but to turn back."

Adam gave him a grudging nod. "Who shaved you?"

"Kit."

"Ah." He looked at his wife, then at his brother, before sinking down to sit on the bed. Kit came to sit beside him.

"Richard?" she asked.

"Still alive," he replied, making William groan and scrub at his newly shaved face.

"A mess," William muttered. "All of it, ever since our attempt to visit Lady Joan."

"Why bring Richard?" Kit asked.

"He wanted to. Tired of kicking his heels at the French court, I reckon. Besides, he knows some of the men we were supposed to meet."

Adam sipped at his wine. "Is he coming?"

"Lord Roger?" William shook his head. "Not at the moment. At the moment he has been requested to leave the French court – in preparation for the arrival of Queen Isabella." He brightened like a newly lit torch. "She'll be leaving any day now."

"The trusted wife is sent off to negotiate on the king's behalf," Kit said, a cutting edge to her voice.

Adam regarded her over the rim of his cup. "You disapprove?" He twirled his wine around.

"Of her negotiating on his behalf? No. Of her considering betraying her husband – sometimes."

"Not much of a husband," Adam said harshly. "Not much of a king either."

"No." Kit slid closer to him. "But a wife should remain

true to her husband." Her hand was on his thigh, a light touch, no more.

"As should he to her," Adam said softly, covering her hand with his own. William cleared his throat, bringing Adam tumbling back to the reality of having to find a way of smuggling his brother – and Richard – to France. "You came here for funds, I assume."

William nodded. "Now that Lord Mortimer must leave France, he needs ready gold. But we also came to get a feel for how the wind blows."

"And how does it blow?" Kit asked.

William grinned. "It blows as it pleases Lord Roger. Rarely have I heard of men as skilled as the Despensers in making lifelong enemies."

"Greed," Adam said.

"And ambition," Kit put in.

Adam nodded. Hugh Despenser and Roger Mortimer were two very different men, but the one thing they had in common was ruthless ambition. He shifted on the bed and extended his right leg. His foot throbbed, and he needed Kit to help him soothe it.

"When must you return to the prince?" William asked, watching Adam pull off his boots.

"Once my foot is healed." Adam reclined with a pleased sigh, lifting his foot into Kit's lap.

"And when will that be?"

"When?" Adam shared a look with his wife. "Well, not before the babe is born."

William nodded. "Will you help us…" He left the rest unsaid, and Kit's hands tightened on Adam's foot.

"I have no choice, do I?" Adam said. "But first of all we have to ensure Richard lives."

Chapter 17

Next day, just after noon, Kent was back – accompanied by Earl Thomas and none less than Lord Despenser. Kit's knees dipped, and only when Adam quietly pointed out that Prince Edward's colours were also represented did she succeed in pasting a calm expression onto her face.

Adam limped out into the yard.

"The rebel spies," Lord Despenser said without any introduction.

"Gone," Adam replied.

"Oh, I think not." Despenser dismounted, an eager gleam in his eyes. "Edmund here says one of them was badly wounded – and yet they managed the incredible feat of disappearing into thin air."

"Edmund also says he searched the place yesterday," Earl Thomas drawled. "Isn't that so, brother? A most thorough search, as you told it."

"It was!" Edmund of Woodstock gave his older brother a belligerent glare.

"Well, then," Earl Thomas said, "so why are we here?"

"Because I wished it so, dear Thomas," Lord Despenser replied.

"Earl Thomas – or Norfolk – my lord, not dear Thomas." Thomas of Brotherton affixed light eyes on Hugh Despenser, his voice as chilly as a November hailstorm.

"Earl Thomas," Despenser said after a while, looking as if his mouth was full of worms.

"And so our Thomas has definitely crossed the line to the men Despenser dislikes," Kit murmured to Adam. She shifted on her feet. "What if they find William?"

"What are you whispering about?" Lord Despenser demanded.

"My wife is concerned that the food will not suffice," Adam lied smoothly.

"Food?" Despenser laughed. "We haven't come here to eat, have we?" He clapped his hands, and his men dismounted. "Find them," he said, and it was like unleashing a pack of hounds.

A very young man, attired in dark blue and astride a chestnut mare, came riding towards Kit and Adam.

"Lady Kit, I trust you are well?"

Kit didn't recognise the voice, and only when the young man drew back his hood did she see who it was.

"Lord Edward!" she exclaimed. "My, you've shot up like a leek in a dungheap!" She clapped a hand to her mouth, mortified, but the prince just laughed, leaping off his horse to land before them.

"Your foot?" he asked Adam, shaking his head when Adam made as if to kneel.

"Healing, my lord."

The prince nodded. "I will have you back the week after Easter." He smiled at Kit. "I trust that babe of yours will be safely in the world by then."

"So do I, my lord." She didn't smile. "But what if it isn't?" She threw a wary look in the direction of Despenser's men.

"Sir Adam returns to my service nonetheless." The prince's jaw set, and Adam gave Kit's hand a warning squeeze. Kit wanted to argue, to plead that he be allowed to remain with her, but knew it was futile. When the prince glanced her way, she looked away, angered that a half-grown pup should have a larger say in her husband's life than he himself did.

Three of Despenser's men came back herding a protesting William. There was a scuffle, there was a yelp, and William was on his knees in the yard, one arm twisted up behind his back.

"He's a priest!" Kit exclaimed.

"Any man can pretend to be a priest," Despenser sneered. "All it takes is a temporary loss of hair."

"I am a man of God," William wheezed, raising a bloodied face to Despenser.

"Really?" Despenser tapped his fingers together and did a little walk around William, graceful like a heron as he stepped around the kneeling man. "Can you prove it?"

"Can you prove you're Lord Despenser?" William retorted, and beside Kit Adam inhaled when one of the men-at-arms clouted William over the head.

"Oh, I think I can prove that," Despenser said with a snicker. "If nothing else the king will vouch for who I am." He jerked his head, and William was hauled to stand. "A priest, you say?" His gaze flickered from William to Adam and back again. "William de Guirande, is it?"

"It is." William straightened up.

"How fortuitous." Despenser ran a hand languidly down William's back, over his buttocks. Adam tensed, but Kit took a firm hold of his arm. "I have a liking for de Guirande men."

Despenser's hand went on with its exploration, following the contour of William's belt to his front before dropping lower. Despenser squeezed. William gasped and bent over.

"Such memories, Adam, don't you agree?" Despenser jeered, wiping his hand fastidiously on William's habit. Adam shifted on his feet, tremors rippling up and down his arms. But he didn't move or say anything, restricted by Kit on one side, and by the presence of Prince Edward on the other. Kit threw the prince a grateful look, receiving a shy smile in return.

Earl Thomas cleared his throat. "Is this one of the men you pursued yesterday?" he asked his brother. "A priest?" He sauntered over to study William.

"If so, he didn't look like a priest yesterday," Edmund retorted. "And did not our Lord Despenser just say he might not be a priest?"

"Oh, he is a priest," Despenser said. "William de Guirande is yet another of those religious fools attracted by Mortimer's false piety."

"There is nothing false about Lord Mortimer's piety." William gave Despenser a scathing look. "In difference to some, Lord Mortimer has ever suffered a prickly conscience."

"Dearest Lord," Adam groaned under his breath. "Why must he rile him so?"

"Because he's your brother?" Kit suggested, just as low, wincing when Despenser punched William full in the face.

"So, was it you our Edmund here pursued yesterday?"

Despenser asked. Kent gave him a displeased look, while his brother's mouth quirked into an amused smile.

"No." William's reply came out muffled, one hand to his nose.

"No what, priest?" Despenser leaned forward.

"No, my lord," William muttered. In response, Despenser patted his cheek, and William flinched, making Despenser laugh.

"And what say you, Edmund?" Despenser asked, twirling on his heel. "Was this one of the men you gave chase to?"

"If he was, I'd have found him yesterday," Edmund replied, looking down his nose at William. "He's too big to hide away."

Kit's shoulders softened in relief.

"Yes." Despenser tapped himself over the mouth with one long digit. His gaze flitted over to Adam. "When did your brother arrive?"

"Just before vespers yesterday – on foot." Adam sounded controlled.

"Did he?" Despenser took yet another turn around William. "And tell me, dear William, have you been to Yorkshire recently?"

William paled. "What if I have, my lord?"

"Have you or haven't you?" Despenser's hand was back, but now it was at William's nape, squeezing so hard William tumbled back down on his knees.

"I have," William gasped.

"And it is you, is it not, that has twice bribed the guards to visit Mortimer's wife?" The pressure increased, and William squirmed.

"It is," he managed to say. "But only to bring the lady food and comfort."

With a push, Despenser sent William flying. "Food your king doesn't want her to have. Comfort that your king has chosen to deny her." He grinned at Adam and kicked William, as if daring Adam to do something. Kit hung on for dear life to her husband, who stood like a quivering rock under her hands.

"Take him away," Despenser ordered. "Even traitorous priests must be punished. I dare say the Bishop of Exeter will take good care of him." He chuckled. "Once I have finished my interrogations, of course." He gripped William by what little hair he had and pulled. "And by the time I am done, I dare say I will know exactly everything you know, dear William. Everything – including where to find Richard de Monmouth." He bent down and whispered something in William's ear, and William's eyes grew round, his tongue darting out to lick his lips. Despenser smiled, dark eyes gleaming, before he turned to Kit.

"And now, Lady de Guirande, I would partake of whatever you can offer us."

Two hours on, and Tresaints' hall was still filled with far too many men and far too much noise. On the pretext of seeing to his wife, who had retired immediately after having arranged the meal, Adam made his way up to the solar, his head one constant ache as he attempted to find a solution to the present situation. William had been tied up and was presently under guard in the bailey, his face a collection of bruises and blood.

"I have to save him!" Adam was frantic, stalking back and forth in their solar.

"You can't," Kit said.

"He…" Adam broke off and took a series of deep breaths. "What do you think Despenser will do to him, to my brother?" He kicked at a stool, fighting the foolish urge to pull his sword and single-handedly free his brother. Sweet Jesu, but what would Despenser do to him? Adam's foot throbbed in response, and his balls shrivelled as he recalled far too many hours at Despenser's mercy.

"William is a priest. Surely that will count for something?" Kit was sitting on the bed, face drawn, hands clutching at her belly.

"I don't know." Adam sank down to sit beside her. "And what about Richard?" he muttered. "How are we to tend to him with all these men here?" He scowled. Despenser had announced that Earl Thomas was to remain at Tresaints and continue looking for the two escaped rebels – or at least one of them, as Despenser was quite certain they'd already apprehended the other. This said with a long look in the direction of Adam.

Adam gnawed at a nail. He didn't quite know how far he could trust Thomas, despite the relatively recent events in London. Aye, the man detested Despenser. But it was quite the stretch from hating Hugh Despenser to turning a blind eye while Adam and his household aided a wounded rebel. And what about William?

"How much does he know?" Thomas of Norfolk entered the room, apparently unaccustomed to knocking before entering.

"My lord?" Adam hedged.

In five strides, Earl Thomas was by the bed. "Don't give me that! How much does your brother know?"

"Everything." Adam scrubbed at his face.

"And how quickly will he break?" Thomas sat down and reclined against one of the bedposts.

"He won't break, my lord," Kit said staunchly. "William is a brave man."

The earl raised his brows and stroked his beard. "The man is a priest, unaccustomed to pain." He slapped his thighs. "We must free him – or kill him."

Adam choked. "Kill him?"

"He cannot remain in Despenser's custody. What if he starts naming men?" Norfolk's composure cracked. "What if he names me?" He rose and took a couple of paces. "Well, we can't do anything here, but it's a long ride to Tewkesbury. We must make sure he never arrives."

"How?"

"How? We must ride like the wind, de Guirande, and hope Despenser's company is slowed down by his retinue, by his pipers and clerks." He grinned. "And by the prince's lame horse." He tapped his nose. "Ned is very fond of his new mare, and will insist the pace be adapted to suit her. What a pity she's just trod on a caltrop, eh?"

"They are two score strong – at least," Adam pointed

out. But his mind was already mapping the best place for an ambush and the best way to cover their retreat.

"But they will not expect an attack, will they?" Earl Thomas said.

"This is foolish!" Kit struggled to her feet. "They will return here immediately."

"So we must return faster," Earl Thomas said with a shrug.

"It can't be done!" Kit's voice was uncommonly high. "Adam, please!" She spread her hands over her belly. "They will kill you," she moaned.

"He's my brother," Adam said. "I must try, Kit."

Kit shook her head, eyes huge in entreaty.

"I must," he repeated, and hurried out of the solar before she could say anything.

Despenser exited the hall in high spirits and ordered his men to sit up. William was hoisted up to sit with one of the men-at arms, and all the while his eyes clung to Adam's. Kit swallowed down a sob. Her brother-in-law was terrified, and with good reason: he knew as well as she did what Despenser had put Adam through.

She tried to edge closer to her husband, but he slipped away, maintaining sufficient distance that she couldn't get hold of him and talk him out of his plans. She scowled at Earl Thomas, got nothing but a bland smile back, and went back to massaging her belly. Tight as a drum, it was – had been ever since Despenser rode into their yard.

There was a loud, angry eruption. Despenser glared at the prince, who glared back, before dismounting his horse to inspect his mare's hoof. Adam and Earl Thomas exchanged a look.

Kit held her breath. If the prince insisted he had to stay on account of his horse, any attempts to free William had to be aborted – the prince could not be made party to such. Kit prayed. For the horse to be too lame, for it not to be, for a heavenly angel to sweep down and smite Despenser to dust, for William to suddenly burst his fetters, leap off the horse and run like the wind for the hills.

None of that happened. The prince called for a new horse, sat up, and took his mare on a leading rein – but Earl Thomas was right, this was going to slow them down substantially.

Finally, the bailey was empty. The banners were still visible at the top of the lane, but neither Adam nor the earl wasted any time. Already the horses were being saddled, and when Adam disappeared into the stables, Kit followed.

He kept his back to her, but she knew he knew she was there; she could see it in how stiffly he held his shoulders.

"How?" she asked.

"One quick attack," he said, saddling up one of their sturdy rounceys. In his stall, Goliath snorted, but for Adam to ride his distinctive stallion would be suicidal – both Despenser and the prince would recognise it.

"And then what?"

"William goes north. That they will not expect."

"And you?" She set a hand to the wooden wall, took a couple of steadying breaths. A far too familiar pain was spreading from her back through her womb.

"Kit?" Adam crouched beside her. "What is it?"

"The babe," she said.

"Now?" He helped her up. In reply, she doubled over, her waters cascading down her legs. "Holy Mother and her angels, not now!" Adam exclaimed. "Sweeting, I have to…" He more or less carried her out of the stables.

Thomas and his men were mounted. "We have to go – now!" The earl gave Kit's wet skirts a cursory glance.

"Kit?" Adam brushed at her face. "I have to do this."

She averted her face. He gripped her chin and forced her to face him. "I must. I can't leave William to suffer." He lowered his voice. "And if I don't ride with them, I fear they will simply kill him."

Kit wanted to scream at him. What about me, she wailed inside, why is everyone else so much more important than me?

"And if I die?" she asked, making him wince.

"You won't."

"But you don't know that," she whispered. "And still you

will ride off – and if I die, you won't even be here to hold my hand."

"Hush, sweeting!" He gripped her shoulders roughly. "Don't, please don't." He gave her an anguished look. She moaned, trying to breathe normally as yet another contraction swept through her. Mabel. Her arm came round Kit's waist, her voice crooned Kit's name, and slowly the contraction faded and Kit could straighten up, taking a tentative step towards the manor.

"Richard?" she whispered.

"Harry is with him," Mabel whispered back. "At present, you need me more."

Kit was not about to argue – to face a birthing without Mabel was quite inconceivable.

Adam was already on his horse, hand raised in farewell.

Kit turned away, her throat clogging with tears and reprimands. "Inside," she said to Mabel. "I must go inside."

Feet landed on the cobbles. She heard him limping towards her in haste, and here came his arms, crushing her to him, his mouth covering hers. Kit clung to him, inhaling his scent, his warmth.

"Be safe," she whispered. "Come home this time as well."

"I will." One last kiss and he was gone.

"We must get you inside, m'lady," Mabel said. "This baby isn't waiting."

"But it must! It must wait until Adam is back and—"

Mabel snorted. "That will be hours from now – at best." She patted Kit's hand. "He'll be back, m'lady."

Kit gave her a wild look. How did she know? But she followed Mabel inside, and was grateful for her help in making it up the stairs to the solar, where she supported herself against the wall when the next contraction struck. Kit clasped Mabel's hand, counting in her head as the pain peaked and then relented, leaving her sagging against Mabel's stout frame.

"Will he be all right?" she asked, some hours later.

"Assuredly," Mabel replied in a soothing tone that did nothing to relieve the pressure around Kit's heart.

Yet another tightening band of pain, and Kit breathed through her nose, all thoughts of Adam forgotten.

"This will be quick," Mabel said.

"Is that good?" Kit asked, closing out the memories of last year's labour and the sad, frail little child that was the result of all those hours of pain. Mabel didn't reply, but Kit didn't quite register that, as one contraction after the other rolled in, leaving her gasping for breath and with quivering legs. With sudden clarity, she recalled just how much it was going to hurt to birth the child, and she was overcome with the urge to flee, to run away from it all. It made her laugh: run where? A woman's lot in life was to bear new life and suffer the pains of birth – this was her punishment for the fall from grace.

"Sit!" Mabel shoved Kit down on the birthing chair, lifted her chemise and uttered a series of pleased sounds. "It is crowning." Kit didn't need Mabel to tell her that. The next contraction had her gritting her teeth, fighting the overwhelming urge to push. "That's a good girl," Mabel crooned, "not yet, m'lady." At the next contraction Kit gave in, pushing with all her might. Something heavy and slippery slid from between her thighs.

"Is it…" No, she did not dare to finalise her question.

"A girl," Mabel replied, "A healthy, strong girl." As if on cue, the baby wailed.

Chapter 18

They rode in parallel to the narrow track that went for a road, meandering its way in a southerly direction. Adam took the lead, Earl Thomas at his right, and it wasn't long before they could see the telltale cloud of dust raised by Despenser's colonnade.

"We wait until dusk," Adam said, assuming command without as much as considering what the earl might think. To his credit, the earl nodded, no more, urging his ragged mount on. They rode in silence, Adam attempting to concentrate on the task at hand when all of him twitched with the need to turn his horse and ride back home. Kit's face, her pleas, the way her eyes had darkened with fear – for him, but also for her – all of it plagued him, and for the hundredth time this day he cursed his brother for being a fool. Why had he not ridden on yesterday?

The closer they got, the slower the approach, Adam having them riding in a wide circle so as to avoid discovery. To their right, the hills rose, the lower slopes dotted with copses of stunted trees and stands of gorse. They rode in single file, far enough apart that should one be sighted the others would not necessarily be discovered, and as the sun began its descent, the shadows lengthened, offering them further protection.

They were huddled behind some outcrops of rock on a height when below them Despenser called a halt. Men dropped off their horses and made for the trees and bordering bushes, Despenser himself disappeared behind a boulder, and with the approaching night, various men busied themselves with the torches. William was still astride, but his guard had dismounted, and when Adam looked closer, he could see that William's hands were tied to the pommel.

This was it: they'd get one opportunity to do this. Adam swallowed in an attempt to lubricate a throat as dry as cinders.

"We scare off as many of the horses as possible," the earl murmured beside him.

Adam nodded, not quite sure he could talk. If this failed, if they were caught…a royal brother could hope for a reprieve, but Adam de Guirande would be screaming for the release of death before Despenser was done with him. And as to Kit and his children…Adam wiped his hands on his tunic. He wrapped a length of cloth around his face and head.

"Now," the earl hissed.

Adam spurred his mount and charged, sword in hand. His task was to get to William. Earl Thomas made for the horses, yelling like a tormented soul, and with the earl went his men. John rode beside Adam, silent as the grave. Their descent had men raising their faces, someone yelled a warning, and from behind the boulder came Despenser, fumbling with his clothes.

Adam estimated it took Despenser at most a heartbeat to grasp the situation. With a series of loud curses, Despenser leapt towards William, who was staring at the men riding towards him with a gaping mouth. Out of the corner of his eye, Adam saw a distinctive mop of bright hair, the dark blue velvet shimmering in what remained of daylight. The prince was also running for William, long legs pumping at speed as he rushed through the disordered lines of men.

Adam yelled his horse on. May the prince stumble and fall, he prayed, may he…And then his horse near on crashed into William's mount, and Adam leaned over, took hold of the reins and shrieked the horse into motion. For good measure, John slapped the surprised animal over its rump with the flat of his sword, and just like that they were through, racing for the woodlands beyond.

From behind came Despenser's howl of rage, and Adam had to suppress the desire to yell in triumph. Instead, he clapped heels to his mount and galloped on.

Earl Thomas was grinning from ear to ear. His right arm was bloodied up to his elbow, as was his sword, and one of his men was bleeding from a cut to his arm, but other than that their little group had emerged unscathed.

"No time to lose," Adam said when they drew their horses to a halt. They could still hear the distant sounds of men yelling, of horses neighing. It would take Despenser some time to bring order to his troops, but once he did, they'd be riding back the way they'd come – fast.

"Here." Thomas handed William a pouch. "Go," he said, pointing to the north.

William nodded, clutching the bundle of clothes John had given him to his chest. He extended his hand to Adam, who clasped it hard.

"Ride for home, brother," William said hoarsely. He turned his horse and set off, with John at his side.

They rode back in silence, pushing their horses well beyond what the poor beasts were used to. The moment they arrived at Tresaints, Gavin and the stable boys rushed for the animals. They had to be dried and watered before Despenser arrived.

"Will he come, do you think?" Earl Thomas tore off his tunic as they crossed the bailey and threw it at one of his men.

"Don't you?" Adam was itching to run for the solar.

"I do. Whatever his faults, Despenser is no fool." Thomas chuckled. "He will be most enraged." He waved Adam off, saying he needed to find a clean tunic.

Adam took the stairs two treads at a time. The door to the solar was closed, and he stood outside, not quite sure what to expect on the other side. A deep breath, and he opened the door, causing a number of indignant female voices to tell him to step outside – immediately.

"Kit?" he asked, looking towards the bed.

"Here," she replied, and in her arms was a bundle. She gave him a tired smile.

"Out." Mabel shoved at Adam. "Once m'lady has been properly washed and dressed, I will call for you."

"The babe?"

"A daughter, m'lord, a lusty little girl."

And with that he would have to make do for now, the door closing firmly in his face.

Adam had as yet not been allowed in to see Kit when a commotion in the yard indicated Despenser was here. He set down his cup of wine and followed Earl Thomas outside. Only a handful of men had accompanied Despenser – tired, dirty men who dropped off their equally weary horses. Adam sighed, resigning himself to having unwelcome houseguests overnight, and was considering where exactly to house them when Despenser exploded, accusing everyone – including the earl – of having participated in the ambush.

The earl took it badly. He demanded an apology – immediately.

"Apologise?" Despenser stomped into the hall, calling for wine as if he were the master of the manor, not Adam. "I find it mightily strange that the only thing those ruffians carried off was the priest – his brother!" He stabbed his finger in the direction of Adam.

"I can assure you de Guirande has not been out of my sight," Thomas retorted. "I will swear to it on everything holy." He moved with the languid ease of a large cat as he approached Despenser. "And I'll not have you accuse me of this foul deed." He bared his teeth in a dangerous smile. "The king will not be pleased by your incompetence, will he? And even less if you try and blame me for your own inadequacy. After all, I am his brother – we share blood, he and I, royal blood."

"Someone knew where we were. Someone knew who the priest was." Despenser drank and slammed the goblet down, gesturing for more wine.

"The rebels my brother failed to apprehend yesterday, perhaps?" Earl Thomas shrugged.

"One of them was wounded, badly so," Despenser replied. "And it wasn't two men who rode us down earlier this evening – it was at least ten."

"And what makes you assume there are only two rebels in this fair land of ours?" The earl chuckled. "I'd say they'll be crawling out of every fissure we have – soon."

Despenser made a choking sound. "That's treason!"

"Is it treason to speak the truth?" Thomas flung himself

into Adam's chair, sprawling elegantly with a teasing smile on his lips. "I think not."

"The prince, is he well?" Adam interrupted, angry with the earl for baiting Despenser. Thomas of Norfolk was no more than four years or so Adam's junior, but at present Adam felt as old as the rocks in comparison. To show one's hand too soon with Despenser was to invite death and ruin.

"The prince is tending to his mare, safe in the company of his uncle." Despenser grimaced, muttering under his breath that the damned horse had cost him his golden opportunity to once and for all reveal Mortimer's accomplices. He slapped his gloves against his leg. "We'll be staying the night," he announced. "I'll have the solar."

"No," Earl Thomas said, "that will not be possible. Lady de Guirande is just delivered of a child. You'll have to bed down with the rest of us, in the hall."

If at all possible, that statement further deteriorated Despenser's black mood. After yet another long diatribe regarding the loss of his prisoner, he retired to the further corner of the hall, loudly demanding pillows and bedding – clean bedding, if you please!

And then, at last, Adam was free to visit his wife. Kit was fast asleep, the room smelled of herbs and of sweetened wine, and in the cradle beside the bed slept his daughter, at present no more than a rosebud mouth and two closed eyelids, delicately framed by the longest lashes Adam had ever seen. A dusting of light hair indicated future eyebrows, a wisp of dark hair peeked out from under the embroidered little coif, and Adam's heart expanded to fit this newborn little creature beside his beloved wife and son.

"Can one, do you think?" he asked Kit much later, sitting with his daughter in his arms. He traced the little mouth, at present blistered after having nursed.

"Love them all as much?" Kit nestled close and kissed his cheek. "I think one simply does. The moment you hold them, they have taken your heart hostage – forever."

"Little Margaret," Adam crooned. "Our little Meg." He

glanced at Kit. "After my mother," he mumbled, and she just nodded, her eyelids drooping. "Tired?" Adam shifted the babe so that he could use one arm to hold his wife close.

"Very. It has been a long, long day." Kit yawned, and just like that she was asleep, and Adam did not have the heart to wake her – or his daughter.

Come morning, Adam woke to the sounds of someone in the solar. He had a crick in his neck, one arm was uncomfortably numb, and there was an instant of panic when he realised Meg was no longer on his chest – until he saw Mabel beaming down at him, the infant in her arms.

"They're leaving," Mabel informed him.

"All of them?" Adam yawned and slid his arm out from under Kit.

"All." Mabel's face clouded. "About time, if you ask me. Lord Richard is not doing well."

"In God's hands," Adam replied, crossing himself hastily. He frowned: an element of caution would be required in going back and forth to the croft – Despenser was wily enough to have left a man or two to spy on them.

"And in ours. God helps those that help themselves, my lord," Mabel said.

Adam nodded, distracted by the voices from outside, calling his name. "It seems I must bid our guests farewell." He found his tunic on the stool, decided to forego the hose, and pulled on his boots.

"And may they never return," Mabel muttered

"Amen to that." Adam tightened his belt. "Let her sleep," he threw over his shoulder. "She needs it."

In response, Mabel sniffed. "I dare say I have more experience of recently delivered women than you do, m'lord." She shooed him out of the room.

"A daughter, I heard," Despenser said when Adam stepped outside. He was already astride his Spanish stallion, an exquisite animal that had Adam salivating with envy.

"And is she hale?" Earl Thomas asked.

"Both she and her mother thrive." Adam smiled up at the earl. "Will you not be staying then, my lord?"

"No – matters recall us to London," Despenser answered in the earl's stead. He raised his hand and waved at his men to ride out. "Prince Edward expects you to attend Easter mass with him," he added, grinning down at Adam.

"Easter Mass?" That would mean leaving in less than a week. "The prince said the week after Easter."

"I dare say he changed his mind. Besides, your wife has already whelped."

Adam stiffened at the offensive wording. Despenser smirked and leaned towards him.

"And do not fear for your brother, dearest Adam. I have men riding east, west, north and south in search of him. We will find him – and when we do, rest assured I will take very personal care of him."

With that parting shot he was off, his horse cantering up the lane.

Earl Thomas regarded Adam from under dark brows. "Let's hope he never catches your brother. But if he does, I will have no choice but to have him killed." A nod and he was charging after Despenser. Adam wanted very much to kick someone – hard.

Chapter 19

Adam blinked. It was an effort to keep awake, and repeatedly the prince jabbed at him with an elbow. Adam swallowed back on a yawn, on another, and fell in with the others as they chanted along with the priest. The abbey church was packed with courtiers, with the king and the Despensers right at the front, a couple of yards from the altar.

Yet another yawn, and the prince glared at him. Adam was tempted to glare back; it was the prince who had recalled him to court, thereby subjecting him to hours of interrogation at the hands of the king's officers.

Over and over again, they had thrown the same questions at him: was his brother a traitor? If not, why had he fled during the ambush? Where was he now? Who had ambushed Despenser's party? Was Adam a traitor? And Adam repeated that no, he was not a traitor, and no, he didn't think William was one either, but his brother had always been inordinately fond of Lady Joan, which was why he had taken it upon himself to visit her. And as to the ambush, how could it possibly be him? Had not Earl Thomas himself vouched for his whereabouts?

This last stumped them. To accuse the king's brother of having participated in the ambush was going a step too far, leading Adam to conclude that so far the king harboured no suspicions as to his half-brother.

Earlier on Easter Sunday, when they finally released Adam from the dark room in which he had been held, it had been Earl Thomas and the prince who came to fetch him, his young lord more than angered at Adam's disoriented state.

"You haven't fed him?" he'd yelled at the interrogators. "Given him water?"

No, the Bishop of Exeter had informed the prince – rather haughtily, in Adam's opinion – the entire purpose of holding a man in the dark without food or sleep was to weaken his resolve, thereby making it easier to catch any lies. "There are other methods one could use," the bishop continued. "The application of pain loosens most men's tongues."

"Hurt a man sufficiently and he will say anything to stop the pain," Earl Thomas pointed out. "And I am sure you are aware, the king does not approve of torture."

"Unfortunately," the bishop said, and Prince Edward looked as if he wanted to spit him in the face, before curtly ordering Adam to accompany him to his chambers where there was food waiting.

"I'm sorry," the prince had muttered later, watching Adam eat.

"It's not your fault, my lord," Adam replied, looking with longing at the bed. Not to be, as the church bells were already ringing for mass.

"Is he a traitor?" the prince asked as they crossed the abbey yard together.

"William?" Adam shook his head. "My brother is a priest, my lord."

"Priests can be as treacherous as any other man," the prince said.

"My brother stands with the weak and oppressed, my lord."

"Standing with the weak and oppressed could be considered treason." Prince Edward pursed his mouth. "At least at present."

Adam chose not to reply.

Now, standing in the abbey church, all Adam could think of was his brother. Was he safe? He hoped so, closing his eyes as he commended the safekeeping of his brother to God, to the Holy Virgin, and to each and every one of the saints he could remember by name.

Adam had hoped to escape to his bed after the service, but from the look on the prince's face, this was not to be.

"First we eat, then you sleep," the prince said as he hastened to catch up with his father, for the day resplendent in white and green. Adam had no desire to meet the king

– not at present – but he was beckoned forward and had no choice but to obey. Adam knelt before the king, who studied him in silence for such a long time that Adam had to force himself to remain still, focussing on the cobbles. An embroidered shoe nudged at him, and Adam raised his face, meeting eyes as inscrutable as the jewels that decorated the king's gold collar.

"Treason seems to run in your family," the king said.

"I disagree, my liege."

"So your brother is not a Mortimer spy?" The shoe was back, this time nudging with such force Adam had to suppress a gasp.

"Not as far as I know." Adam licked his lips. "But he loves Lady Joan dearly – as do I."

"And she owes her loyalty to her husband," the king said, "which makes her a traitor by definition."

"It makes her an unhappy woman, my lord. She is not to blame."

"Quiet!" That shoe again, now hard enough that Adam grunted. "And what will you do, when we bring this priest brother of yours back here, to question him and maybe even hang him?"

A black pit yawned before Adam. Had they captured William? He didn't dare to ask. Out of the corner of his eye, he saw Earl Thomas. A barely perceptible shake of his head, and Adam's heart sang with relief. The king was still waiting for his reply. Adam cleared his throat.

"Should it be proven that my brother is a traitor, I will gladly see him hang. But I know no such proof exists, as my brother is first and foremost a priest. All he wants to do is help those who need him – like Lady Joan."

"I say he's a traitor!" Despenser snarled. "A spy, my dearest lord, using his priestly garb to travel unhindered through your kingdom."

"If you say so, you must have proof," Earl Thomas put in, sauntering over to join them. "Your word is not enough, Lord Despenser – or is it, my liege?"

"Of course not," the king snapped. "But Hugh here has a

fine nose for treachery, so if he believes the priest guilty, then he probably is."

"Lord Despenser has a tendency to accuse wildly – without a shred of proof." Earl Thomas stared at Despenser. "I myself would not place my faith in a man that accuses your own brother of treachery."

Adam frowned at the cobbles. What was Thomas playing at?

"He did?" The king looked at his brother, then at Despenser.

"Most certainly: he accused me and Adam here of having ridden like madmen to free this priest, and all the while we were in Adam's hall."

"I was upset," Despenser muttered. "And I have begged your pardon."

"Yes," the earl drawled, "but my point is rather that when you are upset you throw out the most ludicrous accusations. And lately, Sir Hugh, you have been more upset than not."

Someone chuckled. Adam held his breath, waiting for an explosion of royal ire.

"Enough of this," the king said, frowning at his favourite. "Our food awaits us." He gestured for Adam to regain his feet. "Just so you know, I will be keeping a close watch on you, Sir Adam. And should my nose twitch with the scent of deceit…" He left the rest of the sentence unsaid, drawing his finger over his throat instead.

It was only once he was seated at one of the tables in the hall that Adam at last had the opportunity to catch up on what had happened at court during his absence. He already knew that the queen had left for France in March, accompanied by a household befitting her state. According to Sir Henry, very few of the people who went with her had been chosen by the queen. Instead, Lord Despenser and his wife had carefully selected an adequate entourage.

"Peppered with Despenser spies, of course," Sir Henry commented drily.

"Of course," Adam agreed.

He grimaced as Sir Henry described the touching reconciliation tableau played out before Queen Isabella left. It had been a royal command that the king's wife and favourites exchange the kiss of peace before she left, and the queen had obediently done so, even if, according to Sir Henry, there was not a man present who did not see just how much she hated being obliged to do this.

"She's happier there than she was here," Sir Henry concluded. He sighed. "Methinks she won't be coming back."

"Not while they're still here." Adam nodded in the direction of Lady Eleanor and her husband.

"No." Sir Henry gave him a bleak look. "But with her gone, they rule unhindered, don't they? Not a day since she left, but that Lord and Lady Despenser have feasted with the king, as happy as gambolling lambs now that the she-wolf has finally gone."

"The she-wolf?" Adam gave Sir Henry an incredulous look. "They call her that?"

"Not to her son's face." Sir Henry broke off yet another piece of bread, and tore at his chicken leg with his teeth. He chewed for a while, wiped his hands fastidiously, and reached for the wine. "A she-wolf is not necessarily a bad thing," he said with a grin. "Had there not been a she-wolf, there would not have been a Rome."

Adam didn't quite follow, but was reluctant to say so, being tired of having more holes poked through his rudimentary education. So he nodded and concentrated on his food.

With the exception of a short visit back home in June, Adam remained at his lord's side for the entire summer. When he requested permission to go home for the harvest, Prince Edward shook his head, saying it was the king's command that Adam de Guirande remain at court. The lad blushed, squirming as he admitted that his royal father still harboured doubts about Adam.

"I know that isn't true," the prince hastened to add, "but my father—"

"My lord, you do not need to make excuses for the king,"

Adam interrupted. "He is the king, after all, and I am his lowly subject, here to serve his pleasure." He congratulated himself on sounding so unruffled, while inside he seethed at not being allowed to return home to his wife and children.

"There's nothing you can do," Sir Henry said when Adam shared his frustration with him. "Without the king's permission, you can't leave."

"I know that." Adam swept his too-long hair off his face and studied the almost abandoned courtyard. The king and his closest companions had departed for Kent for what remained of August, and so Westminster was eerily deserted. At present, only Prince Edward and his younger brother remained in residence, supervised by a harried Lady Eleanor, who had her own sizeable brood to care for as well.

It irked Adam to see his lord and the two younger Despenser lads spend so much time together, but the prince seemed to enjoy the company of his second cousins, especially that of his namesake, a couple of years his senior and quite the daredevil. At present, the lads were riding at the quintain, supervised by one of the men-at-arms, and Adam had to smile as Prince John whooped when he hit the target.

"Any news of the queen?" he asked, without taking his eyes off the lads.

"Eh?" Sir Henry set down his goblet.

"The she-wolf," Adam clarified, and they shared a little smile.

"Not really. I heard one of the clerks comment that her latest letter indicated a truce was in the making," Sir Henry said with a shrug. He gave Adam a guarded look. "And I heard something else this morning."

"You did?"

"They say they've apprehended your brother." Sir Henry sounded apologetic. "I'm so sorry, Adam. Word is, Despenser is already riding north to take custody of him."

Adam concentrated on his breathing. Should William break, it would be a matter of days before Despenser's troops descended on Tresaints to look for Richard – long gone, thank heavens – and claim the treasure under the altar, which in itself would suffice to brand Adam a traitor. And this time, there would be no reprieve. Adam clenched his hands to stop them from shaking. He had to get a message to Kit, but how on earth was he to do that?

"Are you all right?" Sir Henry's voice came as if from a distance. Adam made an effort and composed himself.

"Why wouldn't I be?" he asked. "Even if they have found William, he is innocent of anything but aiding Lady Joan."

"Hmm," said Sir Henry, and poured them both some more wine.

It was not until after compline that Adam got an opportunity to draft a message to his wife. It had to be short, ambiguous, and still clear enough that Kit should understand what he needed her to do – hide the treasure. After several attempts, he finally had a finished missive and was considering just which one of the men-at-arms he could trust sufficiently to give it to, when from outside came the sound of horses – many horses.

Dear God, this was it, Adam thought, even if the saner part of him protested that it was impossible – unless, of course, William had been arrested well before Sir Henry heard of it. He held his carefully worded letter in his hand, but at the sound of booted feet on the stairs outside, he threw it into the fire and rose, trying to stiffen his spine with the resolve required of a man who was to die the most horrible of deaths.

The door burst open and Earl Thomas strode in, covered in dust. Had the earl come to tell him he had murdered William? Adam was torn between hope and despair, and he had to grip the table to remain upright. If William had died before Despenser had claimed him, chances were their secrets were still safe. But his brother, dead! Adam's chest tightened with so many emotions he was incapable of speech. He just stood there, like a dumb beast awaiting the knacker's blow.

"It wasn't your brother," was all Earl Thomas said, and Adam's knees gave way.

"Thank you, Merciful Father," he whispered. "Dear God, thank you!"

Chapter 20

Kit stretched and fell back against the pillows, trying to assess just how cold it would be outside the protective warmth of the bed. September so far had been cold and wet, and the room they'd been assigned here at Westminster had the drawback of being a corner room, with one window facing north, the other east. As a consequence, a constant, chilling draught swept through the room.

A mewling sound from the cradle had Kit smiling, but she remained where she was, as little Meg no longer suckled at her breasts. Three months, no more, and then her daughter had been transferred over to Amy's care – coincidentally, when Adam returned home for a brief visit in June.

Kit sighed, thinking that this year she'd seen far too little of her husband, and the recent summons to court had come as a Godsend – albeit that Kit was happier in the tranquillity of her home than in the bustle of the court. Not that the spring had been all that peaceful, what with her injured brother and the frequent, unannounced visits by Despenser men, who conducted thorough searches of her home, looking for William.

As she heard it, they were still looking, which meant that they'd not apprehended him – and Kit fervently wished things would remain that way, but six months without word from William led her to fear he was dead. Adam agreed, but became tight-lipped whenever she tried to bring up the subject, so Kit no longer did – beyond slipping her hand into his when they visited the abbey church together to pray for William.

Richard, however, was safely back in France, this passed on to her not by any secret message, but by the king's white-hot rage at hearing that Mortimer's squire had appeared at the royal palace in Paris – rage he had directed at his younger half-brother, verbally lashing the Earl of Kent before the entire assembled court. Most humiliating for the poor earl, and to the side his older brother had stood silent, an inscrutable expression on his face as Earl Edmund repeated that he had done everything he could to apprehend the fugitives.

"Not enough!" the king had roared. "If you'd done enough, Richard de Monmouth would have been dead!"

Well, that had been a close shave, Kit reflected. The young man who rode for Bristol in late May was nothing but skin and bones, and Kit had feared incessantly for him, even after Harry came back to inform her he'd seen the young lord aboard a cog destined for Honfleur. With Richard had gone sizeable quantities of gold destined for Lord Mortimer – and a carefully embroidered shirt that Kit had made for her brother, a gesture that had made him beam at her.

After several weeks tending to him, she had developed a liking for Richard, a man who was as honourable as her Adam – and as besotted with his precious lord as Adam had been when she first met him.

"He will return," he'd told Kit one day, lying very still as she inspected his healing wound. "Maybe not this year, or the next, but one day my lord will have his day in the sun." He'd chuckled, the sound converting into a gasp when Kit prodded a tad too hard. "My lord has the virtue of patience. He will sit and wait, planning his revenge until the time is right."

"Vengeance is something best left to God," Kit had remonstrated.

"Tell that to Lord Roger. Oh no, Kit, he means to have his revenge – and the colder the dish, the better it will taste."

From Richard, Kit had also learnt that Lord Roger was busy forging the alliances he needed to create an army. One such potential ally was the Count of Hainaut, and according to Richard the man was rich enough to finance the invasion more or less on his own.

"Why would he do that?" Kit asked, head reeling as Richard described the complicated network that allied the royal French house of Capet with almost everyone of importance – or so it seemed – on the continent. The Count of Hainaut, as an example, was wed to Jeanne of Valois, cousin to the French king – and to Queen Isabella – but that did not seem a good enough reason for the man to support a convicted traitor against an anointed king.

Richard had smiled, saying that counts were rarely happy to be mere counts, and that Lord Mortimer had dangled quite the appetising little morsel before Hainaut's nose.

"Our prince," Adam had told her brusquely when she'd shared all this with him. "If the count aids Lord Mortimer, he'll have the pleasure of seeing one of his daughters as Queen of England."

"Ah." Kit gnawed her lip. "What will Edward say?"

Adam just shook his head. "He will have little say in this matter, sweeting – just as he has little say in anything."

At present, though, Prince Edward was unaware of any wedding plans involving him – and as Kit heard it, the king had reached out to his distant cousins in Castile, suggesting a marital union. Instead, the prince expended his considerable energy in improving his martial skills, and at times Adam returned exhausted to their little room, complaining that what Edward lacked in skills, he more than made up for in perseverance and energy.

Once Kit had braved the chill of the floors, she dressed quickly, smiling with pleasure as she stood with her arms high to allow Mabel to reach the side lacings of her new kirtle. In a vibrant green velvet, the kirtle was the prettiest garment Kit had ever owned, and the matching surcoat, in saffron and green, made her feel as regal as a queen – even if her veil was held in place by a braided coronet, not a circlet of gold or pearls.

"I should get one of those crespines," she said to Mabel, tweaking her veil into place.

Mabel sniffed. "Ugly things. Makes your face look wide."

Kit didn't agree, and ever since she'd seen Eleanor de Clare in a creation of gilded net and jewelled headband, she'd desired one of those headdresses. Mabel gestured for Kit to hold out her arms and quickly laced her sleeves tight around her wrists and forearms.

"There." Mabel studied her. "Very pretty, if I may say so myself."

The morning passed as it was wont to do – seeing to the children, and now and then catching a glimpse of her husband. A few hours of embroidery, and it was time for dinner, and while Mabel and Amy remained behind in the chamber with the children, Kit made her way to the hall.

The moment she entered the huge, vaulted room, Kit could sense something was afoot. On the dais, the king and Despenser were conducting an intense discussion, and from what Kit had gathered over the last few days, she supposed they were back to arguing over whether or not the king should depart for France to do homage, or send his son.

"Our queen has been successful," Adam had explained some nights back. "Together with her uncle, Charles of Valois, she has convinced King Charles to offer terms of peace, and now all our liege has to do is to travel to Paris and there do homage for Gascony and Aquitaine. There is, however, a but." Adam grinned. "The king wishes for Despenser to remain behind to rule the country, but Despenser is fearful of what might happen to him should the king not be at his side."

"Would anyone dare?" Kit had asked.

"With the king away? Oh yes, sweeting, I think so. Too many men have a bone to pick with our dear Hugh." Which was why, he explained, the king had sent to the French court to hear if King Charles would accept homage from his son instead of the king.

Being no fool, King Edward remained doubtful as to the wisdom of allowing his son and heir to travel to France and into the welcoming arms of his French kin – and had said so, a number of times, over the last few days. But every time he did, Despenser would argue that the kingdom needed its king much more than the heir.

Today, the king was standing in a little group consisting of the French emissary, Bishop Stapledon and Despenser. Beside them stood a clerk, carefully rolling together the parchment he had just read to them, the broken seal dangling from its cord.

"Sire, send your son!" Despenser's voice carried over the hall, causing more than one face to turn in his direction.

"Please, my liege," he added, falling to his knees. "Do not rob me of your presence."

"Of his protection, he means," someone muttered in Kit's ear, and she didn't need to turn around to know it was Earl Thomas.

"Will the French king accept homage from the prince?" She kept her eyes on the touching scene before her, where the king seemed most affected by Despenser's behaviour.

"As per the recently arrived emissary, he will. But our liege is as yet undecided: does he dare send his son into the arms of the queen? He holds little hope that she has truly forgiven him for the humiliations he has put her through of late. One of his more perceptive conclusions, if you ask me." Earl Thomas moved even closer. "You are looking quite radiant, Lady Kit." His breath tickled her skin.

"Gallant!" She sidled away. "But thank you all the same, my lord." Kit fiddled with one of her sleeves. "My husband is partial to me in green."

The earl laughed softly. "I wonder why, my lady. Might it be because it brings out your eyes?"

"My lord!"

Earl Thomas took her hand and raised it to his mouth, placing a soft but intimate kiss on it. Kit jerked it away.

"I personally would not mind if you wore sacking – or nothing," he grinned. "I rather liked what I saw at Woodstock." A bow and he was gone, leaving Kit flustered – even more so when she saw her husband staring at her from the opposite side of the room.

Adam was rigid with anger. The temerity of Norfolk, to press his suit on his wife! And Kit, why had she not moved away from the man immediately? Her eyes met his, her mouth wobbled into a smile, and Adam turned his back on her, concentrating instead on what was happening at the dais. He was close enough that he could hear most of what was being said, standing only some yards away from the prince, who was listening in silence.

"I think it's an excellent idea, my liege," Walter Stapledon was saying. "I can accompany your son, and I'll ensure the queen returns with me." He smirked. "What can she do but obey, when faced with your instructions?"

"So far, she has not obeyed," the king muttered. "She has prevaricated and delayed."

"So far, you have not sent me." Stapledon lifted himself up and down on his toes a couple of times. Pompous oaf! The queen would no more listen to the Bishop of Exeter than she would to a whore.

"Hmm." The king looked at the bishop, at his son, then glanced at Adam. "Very well, I'll send my son, but I'll have de Guirande go with him."

"De Guirande?" Despenser spluttered. "He's one of Mortimer's most trusted captains!"

"He *was* one of Mortimer's captains, but now he's my son's man – and I owe him Edward's life."

Despenser snorted. "One act of heroism does not erase years of treachery." He knelt before the king again, a supplicant. "At least take some precautions, my beloved lord."

The king smiled down at him, running light fingers over Despenser's face. "Oh, I will, Hugh. Trust me, I will." He beckoned for Adam to come forward. "You and your wife are to accompany my son to France."

"My liege." Adam bowed deeply, still trying to envision just what precautions the king was considering.

"Is she here, your wife?" The king scanned the crowds. "Ah yes, there she is." He beckoned for Kit to approach, and Adam took pride in how she walked, head held high, skirts swirling. Beautiful – and his, which she had best remember.

The king held a hushed conference with the bishop, who nodded repeatedly. Beside them, Despenser listened, a satisfied expression spreading over his features. He whispered something in the king's ear and the king laughed, and Adam did not like the look in Despenser's eyes.

"Kneel," the king commanded, and Kit and Adam obeyed.

"Son?" The king had Edward stand before them, his hands clasping Adam's and Kit's. Adam frowned. What was this?

"And now, repeat after me," the bishop said. "I swear, on

my immortal soul, on the lives of my children, that I will hold myself to Edward of Windsor and only to him, until the day either he or death releases me. And should I break my word, my lands and all my worldly possessions will be attainted, and I myself will be forever expelled from the church and from England."

Kit's fingers tightened like a vice round Adam's at the mention of their children.

The prince looked at the bishop, then at Adam and Kit, and frowned. "Father?" His hands loosened their grip. "What sort of an oath is this?"

"A binding one," the king replied. "Go on," he told Adam and Kit. "I am waiting."

Kit licked her lips and gave Adam a look. He cleared his throat, and slowly, word by word, he repeated the oath, Kit's voice shadowing his.

"There, that wasn't too bad, was it?" The king clapped his son on the shoulder. "A man for life, Edward. Make sure you use him well."

"Is that all?" Kit whispered as she and Adam got to their feet.

"I'm not sure," he murmured back. He shook himself. "But it suffices, don't you think? We've been fettered by our words and our immortal souls."

"And Tom? Meg?" she said in an undertone.

"They're with us, sweeting. We go to France, so do they." He squeezed her hand in reassurance.

"Tomorrow," the king said, directing himself to the prince, "we set out for Dover at dawn." He nodded to Kit. "Best start packing, my lady." He grinned. "How does it feel, to be my son's sworn woman for life? God alone knows what services he may require of you."

Despenser laughed, as did Stapledon. No one else did. Prince Edward's cheeks suffused with blood, the blush spreading down his throat as well. The king turned his back and called for wine.

Adam had lost his appetite. Taking his wife by the hand, he left the hall, more or less dragging Kit along. He ducked into one of the covered archways, pulled her close and kissed her, roughly.

"I will not have you ogled by other men," he said when he released her. "You're mine, y'hear? Only mine." And God help the man who laid as much as a finger on her, be he a prince or an earl or even a king. He kissed her again, a forceful, possessive kiss that left her gasping for breath, her lips swollen and red.

"I didn't invite his attentions," Kit protested weakly.

"I know. But I don't like it, what he did." Or what the king had just done.

"Why not punish him then?"

"I can't very well go kissing Thomas of Norfolk, can I?" He nuzzled her neck. "And you didn't mind much, did you?" Yet another kiss, but this one soft and gentle, his hands cupping her face. When he finally let her go, she was smiling, her skin a promising pink hue that had Adam regretting the constricted circumstances of their lodgings. On the other hand...

She had to half-run to keep up with him, her veil fluttering behind her. Up the winding staircase, and on the next floor he pressed her against the wall, his hands following the contours of her legs as he explored her mouth. Yet another set of stairs, narrow and dark, and they emerged in the passage leading to their room. He kissed her hand, her wrist, her throat, and led her to their door.

"Out," he said to Mabel. "My lady and I require privacy."

"Now?" Mabel threw a look at Kit and chortled. Adam couldn't help but smile at the picture his wife presented, skin flushed, eyes dark and lustrous.

"Now."

Amy and Mabel scuttled off with Tom and Meg. Alone. He took off her veil and undid her hair.

"Don't move," he said, doing a slow turn round her. The surcoat came off next, and then her kirtle, and she tried to touch him, to undress him, but he batted away her hands. Her shift – he tugged at the pleated neckline, and by the time he was done her garment gaped open, revealing her breasts and her pink nipples.

There, she was naked, except for her gartered hose, and he had no intention of relieving her of them.

"Here." He lifted her atop the table, urging her backwards until her back was flat against the tabletop. He suckled her breasts and dropped a line of kisses down her belly all the way to her privates. He inhaled. His woman, a rich, heavy scent that belonged only to him. She squirmed under his mouth; she arched her back and called his name, hands tugging at his hair.

Her legs in the air, leaning against his shoulders, and he entered her slowly, sinking himself into her welcoming warmth. She was helpless, unable to move when he pushed forward, pinning her in place. Slowly. Oh, so slowly, and he flexed his hips in long, leisurely movements, his gaze locked on the place of their joining. Dark red curls glistened with her arousal, his own pubic hair just as damp.

"Mine," he hissed as he increased the pace. "Only mine."

"Yours," she replied, and her eyes were pools of midnight blue.

The stay in Dover was short – only five nights, thank the Lord, as the king travelled with a retinue so large it resulted in far too many people for the available beds. Accordingly, Kit and her children had to bed down on one side of the hall with the women, while Adam slept with the knights. Even so, Kit had never had to sleep in such close proximity to so many unknown people, and was uncomfortable with having veritable strangers press their backs or limbs against hers.

Kit was still bleary with lack of sleep when they made their way down to the harbour, and from the silence of the men accompanying them, she suspected they were all nursing a headache or two – a consequence of the feast in honour of the new Duke of Aquitaine last night. The duke himself was riding side by side with the king, a bright, eager look on his face.

"So young and already a duke," Kit said to Adam with a smile.

"You forget he's been an earl since he was a puling babe,"

Adam replied, smiling at his lord. "Besides, the king had to invest him with the duchy – how else can our young prince do homage for it?"

Kit nodded, somewhat distracted by the two creaking cogs that were to transport them over to France. She'd never been on a ship before, and one part of her was thrilled, the other terrified. What if there was a storm and they sank?

"We're just going across to France," Adam laughed. "At most two days, depending on the winds."

It had taken far too long to load the cog. The captain of the *Urchin* was pacing his deck, one eye on the tide, one on the overcast skies. Kit was standing by the mast, mainly to stop Tom from climbing it. Her three-year-old had a stubborn set to his mouth that reminded her very much of his father, but the determination shining out of his eyes was no match for hers. Yet.

"You may not," she repeated yet again.

"Why not?" Tom whined. "I can climb, Mama, I..." The rest of his little speech was drowned by the captain's colourful exclamations, along the lines that some men were destined to be lowered head first into the sea. Kit took hold of Tom and dragged him over to where Adam was standing by the railing.

"What now?" she asked.

"I don't rightly know," he said bleakly, "but those are the Despenser colours." He pointed at the approaching boat and the banner flying above it, proudly displaying the red, gold and black of the Despenser arms.

"Is he coming too?" Mabel spat over the railing, jiggling a fretting Meg in her arms. "If so, I'll be staying behind."

"As will I," Kit said, staring at the familiar figure of Despenser, standing in the prow of his boat. With the grace of a cat, Despenser boarded the ship, followed by four of his men, all of them heavily armed.

"My lord." The captain bowed.

Despenser responded by patting him on the back and saying something in a low tone that had the captain straightening up to look at Adam and Kit.

"Now?" he groaned. "I will miss the tide if—"

"This will not take long," Despenser said, moving agilely towards where Adam and Kit were standing.

"My lord." Adam bowed, as did Kit.

"Yes, yes," Despenser said, and just like that he snatched Tom.

"What are you doing?" Kit lunged, but Despenser tossed her son into the arms of one of his men.

"A surety," Despenser said with a grin, "and we're taking the babe too."

"No!" Kit shrieked. Adam actually growled. His hand closed on the hilt of his sword, but at Despenser's snapped fingers, a knife appeared at Tom's throat. Their son wailed and kicked.

"Pull the sword, dear Adam," Despenser taunted. "Pull it, and we'll see if you come out of this alive. And even if you do, your son most certainly will not."

This couldn't be happening. "You can't take my children!" Kit threw herself at Despenser, pummelling him with her fists. Hands like iron vices came down on her wrists.

"Oh, but I can, Lady Katherine. The king requires hostages – just to ensure your husband does not return to the fold of the traitor Mortimer." He jerked his head towards Meg, and one of his men approached Mabel, who backed away until she slammed into the captain. Mabel protested loudly when the captain pinned her to the spot. Adam made as if to attack, but the two remaining men crowded him back against the railing.

"But he gave you his oath." Kit was crying by now. "So did I." Not her babies, please, not this. Tom was still wailing, still screaming for her, while Mabel was being dragged forward, with Meg cradled protectively against her chest.

Despenser laughed. "And we are but taking further precaution. As long as you do your duty by the prince, your children remain safe."

Kit fell to her knees. "Not my children! I'll do anything, my lord, anything!"

Despenser tweaked his robes free of her hands. "An intriguing offer, Lady Katherine, but not one I am in a position to accept."

"I'll go with you," Kit said, getting to her feet. "Adam, I must—"

"You're not coming." Despenser cut her off. "What better surety for Adam's pledge than to have the despairing mother at his side, begging him not to risk the children?" He snickered. "One of my more brilliant ideas, if I may say so myself."

"Bastard!" Adam snarled, and was rewarded by a whack to his head that had him staggering back.

"Careful, de Guirande," Despenser said. "You might fall overboard."

"My babies." Kit was on her knees again. "Please, my lord, don't take my babies!" Her voice broke, and she moaned out loud.

Something akin to compassion drifted fleetingly over Despenser's face. "They will be well cared for. Whatever you may think of me, I do not make war on children." Despenser glanced at Mabel. "The old hag can come along if she wants."

"Oh, I will. No one takes my lambs from me," Mabel said. "I'll see them safe, m'lady."

"My children!" Kit stretched out her arms towards Tom, but Despenser shook his head.

"No time for farewells, my lady."

"Tom!" Kit shrieked.

"Mama!" He son struggled and kicked as he was carried away; he screamed for her as he was lowered into the waiting boat. "Mama!" he yelled. "Mama!"

Kit rushed to the railing. "Tom!" She stretched out her hand towards him. "Tom, I'm coming..." She made as if to clamber atop the railing, but was pulled back by Adam, his arms tight around her waist.

"Tom!" she shrieked. "God curse you for this, Hugh Despenser!"

In response, Despenser doffed his hat. A curt order, and the rowers threw themselves on the oars. And just like that, they were gone: Mabel, the wet nurse, and her children.

Chapter 21

Adam had never felt so helpless. No matter how he wheedled, how he begged, Kit spent the crossing in her berth, her back to the world.

When they disembarked in Wissant, Kit was a shadow of her normal self, but at least the autumn wind painted roses on her cheeks.

"We will stay here overnight," the bishop informed them. "Our prince requires his rest."

"Our Edward?" Sir Henry snorted softly. "More likely the bishop himself. The man is no sailor."

That comment elicited a ghost of a smile from Kit, and Adam squeezed her hand, trying to catch her eyes. She returned the pressure, and for the first time since their children had been ripped from them she met his gaze, those blue eyes of hers fringed with lashes as dark as those of little Meg.

Meg. He inhaled. A babe, torn from her mother's arms; from his. With an effort, he banished these dark musings and turned his attention to squabbling with Sir Henry, insisting he and his wife needed a room of their own.

Adam won, and he led Kit across the main room, through the back door, over the small cobbled yard and up the outside stairs that led to the room over the stables. Not the best room he had ever slept in, but it was moderately clean and the bed was wide enough to accommodate them both.

There was a fire in the hearth, a tallow candle sent up more soot than light, and on the table someone had placed a pitcher of water – hot enough to steam. With a little grunt, Kit took off her veil, scratching at her head.

"I have to change my clothes," she said, rubbing at her arm. Something caught her attention, and her movement stilled. "I have lice!" Kit's face scrunched up, her hands scratching at her hair, her clothes. "I have them everywhere!" She batted wildly at herself.

Adam took hold of her hands. "We all have lice. It's what you get after sleeping like herrings in a barrel in a hall."

"But I've never had lice before – not like this!" She began to cry, loud sobs Adam surmised had more to do with the loss of their children than the vermin – especially given how she kept on blubbering that all of this was too much, first her babies, then the lice. His heart ached for her, but there was nothing to do about Tom and wee Meg – except to pray for their health. As to the lice, those he could sort.

An hour or so later, Kit was sitting as naked as the day she was born at his feet. The water in the tub had cooled, the surface dotted with dead lice, and Kit smelled of soap and lavender – as did he. Adam unwound the towel round her head and started unravelling the oily hair, using his fingers to slide the odd dead louse off.

"Oil always helps. That's one of the few memories I have of my mother: how she would douse us in oil when we had lice." He smiled, recalling soft hands and a plump face. "She would sing as she combed us." He picked up the narrow-toothed comb he had borrowed from the innkeeper's wife and began tugging through her dark red tresses.

"You're not singing." She reclined against his legs.

"We both know why," he laughed. "I can't." Once he was done, he poured more oil into his hands and took his time massaging it into her scalp and hair, before winding a long length of linen round it all. "My turn," he said.

They exchanged places. The comb tugged through his hair, a soothing motion that had him closing his eyes, transported to the few moments of contentment he had known in his childhood.

"You've never told me about her," Kit said.

"My mother? I don't remember much about her. I was too young when she died, so she's just a vague, warm shape."

"Was she fair or dark?"

"Fair – like me." He furrowed his brow. "Light eyes, I

think, and she had a laugh that sort of gurgled out of her – like William's." He fell silent.

She leaned forward, resting her cheek against his head. "We would have heard if he was dead," she said. He nodded, and Kit went back to her combing.

"They say she was pretty," he said.

"Mmm?"

"My mother." He laughed. "My father most definitely wasn't."

"Pretty?" She chuckled. "I didn't know men could be pretty."

"Handsome, then. Big ugly brute…" His voice tailed off. A mean bastard of a man who took his rage out on his eldest son, and to this day Adam could not think of his father without causing the thin white scar that decorated his face, all the way from brow to chin, to itch.

"So you look like her, then."

He tilted his head back. "Are you saying I am pretty?"

"Very."

"You said men couldn't be pretty." He gripped her by the nape, pulling her head down so that he could kiss her – softly.

"Will they be all right?" she asked when he released her.

"They have Mabel and Amy to care for them." He rose. "Despenser is no match for Mabel if he threatens her little lambs."

Kit gnawed at her lip. "Will they miss me?"

"Every day, sweeting – but hopefully not too much." Children as small as theirs were easily distracted, and Adam did not think Meg would miss them at all – but that was not what Kit needed to hear. "Let's go to bed," he suggested. "You, me and our oily, bandaged heads." That made Kit laugh, and for the first time in a week she slept in his arms, her head a welcome weight upon his chest.

The ride from Wissant to Paris took well over a week – more due to the bishop's insistence on plodding along at a stately pace than the distance as such. At the procession's head rode the prince, in garments of velvet and silk, his hair brushed to a shine, his velvet hat at a rakish angle. His banners fluttered in the wind, his men rode in close formation around him, and closest of all rode Adam, one hand always on his sword.

Not that they had anything to fear, because the people they passed would glance up, straighten up to gawk, and wave and cheer, welcoming the handsome grandson of Philippe le Bel to France. At every such accolade, Prince Edward grew, sitting that bit straighter in the saddle until the bishop drily commented that one could think the lad had a spit up his arse.

Adam had only been to France twice before, once to Bordeaux and once to Picardy, and he studied the landscape with interest, finding the fields fertile and well tended, the cattle fat and the houses sturdy. More cows than sheep – not at all like in his corner of the world, where cows were rare creatures, while sheep were as plentiful as fleas on a rat. The prince studied their surroundings avidly, a keen expression on his face as he took in hills and folds, waterways and meadows.

"Are you planning a campaign, my lord?" Adam teased.

"A campaign?" Prince Edward laughed. "I am merely looking at what could be mine one day."

"Yours?" Sir Henry gave him a sharp look. "The House of Capet has heirs aplenty, my lord."

"Not in the direct line," Edward countered.

Adam pursed his lips. "Your royal uncle may yet leave an heir."

"Yes." Edward urged his horse into a trot. "But so far, he has had little success."

"Which is why he has recently wed again," Sir Henry muttered to his back.

In the evenings, Adam would retire to sit beside Kit, singularly alone in this retinue that consisted only of men. Now and then during the day, she'd urge her horse forward to ride beside him for a while, and at times it was to him she spoke, just as often it was to the prince, who had offered a mumbled apology as to the fate of their children and had won Kit's heart when he told her he'd already written to his royal father to ask him to be gentle with the babes.

The bishop did not like it that Edward spent time with

Kit, and would discourage any lengthier conversations by the simple means of commanding the prince to ride beside him instead. Obediently, he would do so, but generally not without a wild rolling of his eyes or any other such grimace, causing Adam and Kit to laugh.

"He's almost a man, isn't he?" Kit commented to Adam, watching the prince take his place by the bishop. "Look at him – already as tall as I am, and filling out at the shoulders." She sighed. "And yet, he is still mostly a boy, so eager to see his mother again." She took hold of her fluttering veil and fastened it. "Does he understand, do you think, that the queen may not allow him to return home?"

"Allow him to?" Adam threw a cautious look at the prince. "And how can she stop him, if his father demands it?"

"And how is he to leave her, if she weeps and clings to him, reminding him of every perfidy his father has done to her?" Kit looked at Edward. "Queen Isabella will use every single female wile in her considerable arsenal to guilt her son into staying with her. Poor boy – he will walk confused from now on."

"The king has commanded the queen to return home," Adam reminded her, in a voice that carried all the way to the bishop. "The bishop has instructions to ensure she complies, so we will be back in England within the month." Out of the corner of his eye, he saw Stapledon's satisfied smirk.

Kit shook her head. "I wish it were so," she murmured, and her mouth trembled. "But I think you are wrong."

"So do I," he replied in an undertone. "God help us all, but so do I."

"Paris." The prince stood in his stirrups, awestruck. "It's huge!"

"And that's the Palais de la Cité," their French companion said, pointing at the collection of turrets and roofs in the far distance that loomed over the other buildings. He looked fit to burst with pride, young Louis Valois. "Have you anything this big, this grand in England?"

Prince Edward merely shook his head, making the sixteen-year-old cousin of the French king grin like a merry gargoyle.

"The city walls are those built by Philippe Augustus," Louis continued with a sly look at Edward. "You know, your French ancestor who defeated the Lionheart."

"He wasn't defeated!" Prince Edward rose to the bait, causing Louis to laugh. "He was the greatest general alive, and then he was tricked and deceived by men like Philippe Augustus."

"Ah. So more brawn than brains, eh?" Louis said, laughing even more when Edward launched himself into an impassionate defence of the Lionheart.

Louis Valois had ridden out to meet them two days ago, accompanied by a retinue of young men as pretty as he himself was. Adam bit back a smile: Count Louis proved once and for all that men could be pretty, because this slight young man with perfumed locks and clothes of precious silk reminded him of Queen Isabella, with a soft, plump mouth and delicate features.

No matter his feminine looks, Count Louis was a merry and energetic companion, and that slight frame of his was stronger than it seemed, the dark grey stallion he was riding held in total control. Adam had caught Prince Edward casting more than one covetous look at the horse – and it was a magnificent horse, spirited and agile. Thunder, his name was, and Adam found the name more than apt, even if he had been hard put not to burst out laughing when the young imp of a Frenchman had leaned over to confide that what Thunder could do to a mare, he, Louis, could do twice as well to a woman.

"Oh," Edward had replied, looking somewhat lost. Louis had laughed and promised his English *p'tit cousin* he would explain exactly what he meant once they were in Paris.

And now Paris lay before them, a myriad of streets and buildings, with an endless number of church towers dotting the sprawling city. To Adam's regret, they did not ride towards the city. Instead Count Louis turned east, explaining that the king was in residence at Vincennes, his favourite royal palace.

"And my mother?"

"She awaits you there, cousin." Louis grinned. "Likely she'll smother you in embraces and kisses."

"Likely," Prince Edward agreed morosely, his cheeks a dusky red.

The bishop decided he'd been ignored for too long, and rode up to join the two cousins. Adam chose to fall back, holding in his horse until Kit caught up with him. His wife was an excellent rider and had fretted somewhat at being set astride a placid rouncey with little temperament and no energy, but eight days on she had the horse firmly in hand, making it fall into a sharp trot when she saw him waiting for her.

She looked more herself today, all the new sights offering a welcome distraction from her constant concern for their children. Adam sighed: first thing in the morning and last thing at night, he prayed for them, hoping they were safe in Mabel's competent care.

"Kennel food," she told the horse once she'd reached Adam. "That's what you're good for, lazy beast that you are." She regarded Adam's horse with open envy. "Why didn't I get a Friesian horse?"

"Because this is a man's horse," he replied, "not at all a suitable ride for a weak and demure lady."

"And since when am I weak and demure?" She rode closer. "I'd have this one bending his neck to my will in no time."

"Aye, he's right docile, for all his size and colour." Adam stroked the black mane. A princely gift; a gift that left the bishop's face the colour of day-old pottage as he berated Prince Edward for his excessively generous gesture. A gift made out of guilt, Adam reflected, the prince stammering that he hoped the horse would somewhat soothe Adam's heartache.

"Well, he's not Goliath," Kit said.

"No horse is like Goliath," Adam answered with a laugh. His evil-tempered stallion remained at Tresaints. "Even the mares find him obnoxious."

"Have you named him yet?"

"Raven." He tightened his thighs, and the black stallion responded immediately, breaking into a flowing trot that quickly left Kit on her rouncey far behind. Adam turned the horse, set him to a canter, and returned to his wife. "If you're good, I might let you ride him."

"Unless you let me ride him, I won't be good," she retorted.

"Won't you now?" He leaned over and brushed a finger down her nose. "We'll see about that, shall we?" That was his other method for distracting her: every night he loved her, ensuring she fell asleep safe in his arms.

Vincennes was like Woodstock, but loftier, more elegant, more spacious, more…French, Adam decided, quite in awe as they rode in through the arch that gave onto the large, cobbled bailey. Even the cobbling was elegant, arranged in patterns so as to create squares of darker and lighter stones. The royal demesne was encircled by a low wall – very much like Woodstock, but within it was less woodland and more orchards and meadows, expanses of gardens and clambering roses that scented the air as daintily as the showering rose petals covered the ground.

Where Woodstock was heavy stone with several timbered upper floors, this was a creation in golden stone, window arches soaring upwards and doorways leading to covered walks. Not the most defensible of royal palaces, Adam concluded as he dismounted Raven, handing Gavin the reins, but all the same a wonderful place, drowsy in the golden warmth of the September afternoon.

Standing in the middle of the courtyard was a man Adam immediately deduced to be King Charles. Nicknamed *le Bel*, just like his father, the French king was indeed most handsome – if somewhat plump. Clean-shaven, with thick, fair hair that fell in soft locks round his face, a cleft chin and eyes as bright as those of his sister, Charles was an imposing figure – even more so due to his magnificent clothes, the heavy robe in dark green velvet falling to well below his knees. A belt with silver inlays, a heavy collar set with jewels across his chest, gloves of burgundy red that matched his boots and cap – all in all, Adam was hard put not to gawk. He collected himself and bent knee, as did all of the English party.

"Edward!" Queen Isabella's voice was loud with joy, and here she came, running in her haste to greet her son.

"Maman!" The young almost-man was gone, replaced by a boy, a lad with wet eyes and a wavering smile who ran towards his mother.

They met just in front of King Charles, two bodies that slammed into each other with far less decorum than was appropriate, and yet the French king did nothing but smile, head tilted to the side as he watched his sister and nephew embrace.

Queen Isabella released Edward, hands skimming down his arms to grip his hands instead. "You've grown! Look at you, a man!"

At this Count Louis snorted – loudly – and several of the assembled Frenchmen laughed. And then the king moved forward to greet the prince, and there were more embraces, more welcoming exclamations. To the side throughout all this stood the young woman Adam assumed to be the new French queen, a young woman who clasped her hands nervously in front of her, white, dainty teeth gnawing at her lower lip.

"Will she give him the sons he requires?" Sir Henry murmured in Adam's ear.

"It's in God's hands," Adam replied, and then he was being beckoned forward to greet Queen Isabella.

The next morning, Prince Edward gave homage to the French king. In a magnificent red robe decorated with the three English lions, he knelt before the feet of his uncle, for the day wearing blue with embroidered fleur-de-lis. At the prince's side stood his proud mother, while some steps further away was Stapledon, regarding the entire ceremony with the face of a man struggling very hard not to open his mouth and spew bitter bile over the table.

"Has the king considered that Lord Edward now has substantial means of his own?" Sir Henry whispered to Adam. "Enough to finance an invasion, almost."

"Shhh!" Adam glared at his friend. "He is his father's dutiful son."

"Ah, yes: but where is the father now? And who stands close enough to control whatever the prince does?" Sir Henry sighed. "It has begun, Adam, mark my words. And I fear it will cost our dear young lord more than his fair share of anguish." He nodded discreetly in the direction of a collection of English nobles, standing very much to the back. "And look who is here, if not the prince's royal uncle, the Earl of Kent. It is rumoured he is to wed Mortimer's cousin, Margaret Wake. I tell you, Adam, the rats have begun abandoning the ship, and God knows how this will end."

"And do you think it so strange, that people have had enough of the Despensers?"

"Of the Despensers? No. But it would break my heart if ridding England of the Despensers also entails crushing the king."

Adam was quite aghast. "The king?" He coughed, to clear his voice of the croak. "No one wants to harm the king," he continued in a lower voice.

"At a minimum, they want him on a leash. Is that not to harm him?" Sir Henry stood when the people around them rose. "Well, it is in God's hands, my friend."

It is in Lord Mortimer's and the queen's hands, Adam thought, but found it wise not say as much.

It was at the following dinner that the Bishop of Exeter decided it was time to show who exactly was in charge of the English party. Adam had just bit into a most delicious concoction consisting of apples, cinnamon and something Kit said was called *mazapán* – a Spanish invention, she believed, having heard this from one of the queen's ladies – when Stapledon rose from his chair. For all that he was a florid man, Stapledon was light on his feet, moving with purpose until he was standing directly in front of Queen Isabella.

"King Charles," the bishop said, bowing to the French king. "My lady queen," he continued, inclining his head in the direction of Queen Isabella, who looked straight through him. No wonder: it was Stapledon who had masterminded the plan that had relieved the queen of her dower lands, it was he who had reduced her monies to a pittance, who had urged the expulsion of her French companions. The bishop cleared his throat.

"It is my obligation to inform you, my lady, that your husband and liege lord demands that you return home immediately – with me." The bishop looked expectantly at the queen, who continued to stare straight ahead. "I have instructions from my dear lord to personally ensure your return, my lady. It is your moral and legal obligation to obey your husband and king, and as you well understand you have neither choice nor word in this matter. The king, your husband, has spoken, and you can but comply – as must any obedient and dutiful wife."

"Dearest Lord!" Kit whispered, gripping Adam's arm with both her hands. Other than his wife's whispered words and the odd mumbled exclamation, the grand hall of Vincennes was as silent as the grave, all eyes on the bishop, who looked quite pleased with himself.

"Well, my lady?" he demanded.

Slowly, Queen Isabella rose to her feet, dabbing her mouth on her linen napkin. She placed a hand on her son's shoulder, as if to support herself, and looked at the bishop. Silence. From somewhere came a gust of nervous laughter, quickly suppressed. Silence. The bishop shifted on his feet. The queen inhaled.

"It is my understanding that matrimony is a joining together of man and woman, two bodies made one, two hearts beating as one." She raised a brow, and the bishop nodded that yes, this was so. "And yet, Lord Bishop, in my matrimony there is an intruder, a third person claiming my husband's affection and care, a person, moreover, who has for years attempted to break the natural bond between man and wife." She held up her hand when the bishop seemed on the verge of interrupting.

"You say my lord husband demands my return to his side. I say I will gladly do so, once he has cast the intruder out and promises to hold himself only to me, his wife. Until then, I will don the robes of widowhood, weep and wail for the loss of my dearest husband – for as long as that Pharisee Despenser rules my husband's heart, he is dead to me."

The bishop gaped. Prince Edward was staring at his mother as if he'd never seen her before.

The French king merely smiled, an avid look on his face as he leaned towards Stapledon. "Well, Lord Bishop, what say you to that?" he demanded.

"What I say?" The bishop's voice soared. "I say this is wrong! A woman speaking out against her husband – her royal husband! Sire, I beg of you to help me lead your deranged sister up the right path. Exile her from your country, oblige her to return to her husband, to do her duty as mother and wife."

"Deranged, you say?" The king sounded amused, but his hand had tightened round the handle of his eating knife. Queen Isabella made as if to speak, but King Charles raised his hand. "I do not think it deranged that she demands the king be true to her. Nor do I think it deranged that she no longer trusts her husband – or his counsellors. Why should she, when she has been deprived of the lands and incomes settled on her as part of the marriage contract? Why should she when you – yes, you…" and now the king was shouting, pointing at the bishop, "separated her from her trusted officers and friends? Would you trust such a person, Lord Bishop? Would you?"

Stapledon chose not to reply, his tongue flitting out to lick his lips.

"So," the king went on, in his normal voice, "I will not command my sister to return to her husband. Whether she chooses to stay or leave is up to her, but as long as she wishes it, she has a home at my court, here in the land of her birth."

The hall erupted: whistles and catcalls, men stamping their feet, clapping their hands. Adam cheered with the others, but by his side Kit stood silent, still clutching his arm.

"What, sweeting?" he asked. In reply, she just shook her head, her eyes brimming with tears. "What?" he repeated.

"I fear it will be a very long time before we see our babies again," she replied hoarsely. "A very long time indeed."

Chapter 22

To her chagrin, Kit discovered that Cassandra de Ley was in residence at Vincennes, ostensibly as one of Queen Isabella's ladies, even if the queen expressed doubts as to Cassandra's usefulness.

"She has an irritating habit of retiring to her room for days on end, complaining of megrims or seizures. That's why she wasn't present at the ceremony," the queen said, smiling at the young girl who set down a goblet before her. "Thank you, Maud." The girl made a courtesy and retired to join her companions.

"So what ails her?" Kit sneaked Cassandra a look, thinking the lady looked the epitome of health.

"I don't know. Personally, I much prefer it when she isn't in attendance, so I don't ask. In fact, Maud here told me the other day that she thinks Lady Cassandra slips out to meet someone." The queen waggled her brows. "A lover perhaps? Several lovers?" She frowned. "In any of my other ladies, I would not condone such behaviour, but Lady Cassandra's reputation is as it is, and she gives me the shivers, the way she sits in a corner and regards me as if she were a cat and I a mouse."

"So why don't you dismiss her?" Kit asked.

The queen suppressed a little smile. "Another thing Maud told me is that Cassandra sends messages – to Despenser. It suits me to know who the spy is – that way I can ensure the right information reaches Despenser's ears."

"Ah."

"In fact, most of these ladies are spies – but I don't have to tolerate their presence any longer, do I?" Queen Isabella smiled coldly. "And what with Stapledon running like a rabbit for the safety of England, why not have more people accompany him across the narrow sea?"

After the incident in the hall, Stapledon had walked about looking permanently constipated, saying it was utterly unacceptable that he, King Edward's valued counsellor, should be treated with such contempt by the King of France and his wilful, disobedient sister. This had not endeared him to the French court and two days previously, the bishop had fled Vincennes, bleating that he feared for his life.

"Assassination!" he had yelled. "The Mortimer intends to kill me!" Rather amusing, Kit had thought at the time. After all, Lord Mortimer was nowhere close.

"The only thing that can get you killed here is your own big mouth," the Earl of Kent had retorted. "Coming here and humiliating the queen like that in front of her own brother and countrymen. *My* countrymen," he had added, giving the bishop a wolfish grin. "The French love you not, my lord bishop. Best flee while you can."

The bishop had taken the royal earl at his word and left that same day, having first tried to coerce the prince to accompany him. Edward had refused, saying it would be an insult to his uncle to sneak off in disguise, and he held no fear for his own life. Besides, as Adam had commented to Kit, their young lord was enamoured not only of the French court, but also of Paris – and his energetic new best friend, Count Louis.

And as to Earl Edmund, as far as Kit could understand he was not here at the behest of his royal brother, but rather to openly proclaim his change of loyalty from the king to the queen. Kit smiled crookedly: the king's most loyal brother had become his most flamboyant enemy, and Kit could only imagine how hurt the king must be by his defection. Now and then, she wondered how Earl Thomas fared, left in England to bear the brunt of the king's anger. Well, she hoped, smiling slightly at the thought of the quiet, if determined, earl.

Queen Isabella was not one to prevaricate, and immediately after mass she called her household together and dismissed everyone she suspected of being loyal to her husband rather than herself – with the exception of Cassandra de Ley, who grinned like a smug cat, no doubt quite confident that the queen did not suspect her.

Women wept, men protested, but the queen was adamant, and over the following week a steady stream of her former officials and ladies left Vincennes, making for Calais.

"And we had better pack as well," the queen informed Kit. "We are going to Paris." She gave Kit a happy smile. "My father enjoyed Vincennes, but he loved the Palais de la Cité the most magnificent royal residence in the world.

"Really?" Kit struggled to see how anything could overshadow the golden haze of Vincennes, but took the queen at her word and retired to pack.

They shared a horse for the short ride into Paris. Adam hoisted Kit up to sit before him, and Raven did no more than dip his head a couple of times at the extra weight, before setting off at a stately walk.

The French king travelled in splendour, and the cavalcade extended well over a quarter of a mile, from the men-at-arms that rode at its head, to the two score men who marched at its end. Carts, litters for the ladies, baldachins over the king, banners flying in the wind, proudly displaying the fleur-de-lis, and all of this accompanied by well over fifty noblemen on horseback, all of them as richly dressed as the king. Kit had never seen quite so much wealth on display – even Prince Edward in his finest dark blue velvet looked drab in comparison to the multi-coloured French.

"Peacocks," Adam muttered, tugging at his best tunic, a rather dull light blue. He tightened his hold on Kit. "I'll not have you gawking at them, y'hear?"

"I look, Adam." She turned towards him and slid a hand in through the neckline of his tunic, wiggling it under his shirt to stroke his chest. "And they don't compare."

"No?" He sounded pleased.

"Only my man is dipped in gold," she replied. "Only my man stands half a head taller than most. Only my man has the ladies of the court ogling him on the sly." She tugged at his chest hair. "Except, of course, that you knew they were there when you stripped down to your braies and hose to wash in the stable yard the other evening."

"I did not!"

Kit snorted. "Yes you did. And Cassandra de Ley had her tongue hanging out." She made a face; the lady in question kept her distance from Kit, but contrived to be very close at hand whenever Adam was near.

"Let's hope she remembers to pull it in before it dries out," Adam commented, making Kit laugh before turning her attention to the city before them.

The gates to the city stood wide open to welcome the king and his party. Fore riders had gone ahead, ensuring the streets were passable, the people pressed up to the sides to allow the cavalcade passage. They passed through the gate, and a mighty cheer rose from the assembled populace, loud cries welcoming the king and his queen to the city of Paris.

Kit had never seen so many houses. Or people. Or churches. She had never heard so many bells ring out the hours, nor seen quite as many young men in priestly garb.

"Students," Adam explained. "It's the university." He leaned forward. "And just because they're tonsured and in clerical robes, don't make the mistake of taking them for men of God. They are young and wild, expending as much energy on finding their pleasures as on their studies. Come to think of it, they probably expend more energy on their pleasures."

Kit nodded, gawking at the shops that lined the streets, the large lateral shutters opened to display everything from bolts of silk and velvet to earthenware and honey cakes. People stopped to stare as they passed, and Kit shifted further into the protective warmth of Adam's arms, intimidated by the sounds and the smells, by the merchants calling out their wares, by the dogs and the urchins.

Like London, but on a bigger scale, and just like London, Paris had a river, but in this case the river hid a further treasure, the Île de la Cité, a small island on which stood the royal palace at one end, and that marvel of Christendom, the cathedral of Notre Dame at the other, its imposing towers looming over the Seine and dwarfing the few trees that grew in the gardens at its feet.

They clattered over a stone bridge, wide enough to allow the men-at-arms to ride four abreast, and then they were riding through the gate to the palace, a long, dark archway with double portcullises and massive doors.

"Magnificent, isn't it?" Prince Edward said, craning his head back to study the surrounding buildings.

"Very." So much glass! All the windows in the royal palace had been glazed, a not-so-subtle show of wealth.

"How provincial we must seem to the French," the prince continued. "How Maman must have missed the splendour of her early life while living in the dreary damp that is our England."

"It isn't that bad," Kit protested. Westminster might not be comparable to this, but the Tower was just as imposing, and Woodstock might be smaller than Vincennes, but...

Prince Edward laughed. "No, it isn't, Lady Kit. After all, it is home."

Unfortunately, Kit and Adam were allotted a room just beside that of Cassandra de Ley. Where Kit sulked, Adam shrugged, and as to Cassandra, she positively beamed.

"What difference does it make where she sleeps?" Adam said, inspecting their room with a slight furrow between his brows. A bed with dark green hangings, a pallet bed by the door for Gavin, another by the window for Aline, Kit's allotted maid, a stool, a sooty hearth and a chair by the table – all in all quite small, and for all that the walls were covered by tapestries, the floor by a threadbare Moorish carpet, the room lacked in comfort, probably due to the constant draught. "I'll have Gavin and Aline sleep in the passage."

"Is that wise?" Aline alternated between simpering at Adam and winking at Gavin.

"Gavin will not do anything improper – not if he wants to remain in my service." He'd pitched his voice loud enough that Gavin could hear him, and Kit suppressed a chuckle at how mortified the young man looked. All the same, she shook her head.

"If they're not sleeping with us, they'll bed down in the lower hall." If nothing else, it would be far too cold out in the passage.

Next day, the prince and Adam familiarised themselves with the tiltyard. Count Louis came along to lounge and watch, and soon enough they'd collected quite the little audience, most of the youngsters living in the palace yelling encouragements as Adam took his lord through the basic sword routines they were perfecting.

To one side stood a dark-haired lad Adam recognised from Vincennes, a serious child who seemed out of place among the gaudy younger members of the Valois and Capet families.

"Can I try?" the lad piped up when Edward motioned to Adam to indicate that they would take a break.

"You?" Count Louis drawled. "Really, Wenceslaus—"

"Charles," the boy bit off. "My name is Charles."

"No it isn't," Prince Edward said, wiping his brow. "You just want it to be Charles. But your dear Mama named you Wenceslaus, probably to spite your poor father."

"My name is Charles!" the lad insisted.

"Wenceslaus," Louis cooed. "Little Wenceslaus, have you heard from your mother lately?" He laughed. "No, that's right: you're not allowed to, are you? The madwoman tried to make you king instead of your father, and that didn't sit well with him, did it?"

"Shut up!" the dark-haired lad said, taking a step towards Louis.

"The truth," Louis said, waving a hand at him. "After all, why else would he have imprisoned you – his own son?"

Prince Edward blanched. "He did?" he asked the boy. "Your own father?"

Wenceslaus – or Charles – nodded. "For my own safety. I had to be removed from the corr…corr…corruptive influence of my…" He cleared his throat. "…mother." He looked away, and Adam's heart went out to him, this little boy who had been caught between his feuding parents.

"And now, here you are," Louis continued, quite oblivious to Prince Edward's white face, "betrothed to my baby sister and being raised in the most cultured court in Europe." He slid off his perch and sauntered over to Edward. "Done yet? I have plans for us, cousin."

Prince Edward gave Adam a questioning look.

"Go, my lord. We can work more on this some other day." He set a light hand on his lord's arm and switched to English. "And if anyone attempts to imprison you it will be over my dead body."

Edward's response was a wobbly smile and a curt nod and then Adam's princeling was gone, yelling at Louis to wait. With the lads went the spectators – except for Charles.

"Everyone says she's mad," he said in a low voice. "But she isn't. She just hates my father."

"Ah."

The boy shuffled on his feet. "I miss her." His eyes filled with tears. "My father says I'll never see her again."

Adam crouched in front of him. "I'm sorry to hear that, lad."

Charles wiped his face with his sleeve. "My father says it doesn't help to cry." He stiffened his spine. "He also says a son must always obey his father, not his mother." He glanced at Adam. "But Edward obeys his mother, doesn't he? Will that not displease his father?"

Out of the mouth of babes, Adam thought wryly.

That same afternoon, Adam and Kit were requested to attend on the queen – alone. The prince was off riding with Count Louis and the count's two younger sisters, and the queen had dismissed most of her attendants and invited them to sit, sweeping her hand over an assortment of fruit and wine.

"No Earl Edmund, my lady?" Adam asked in a teasing tone. Recently, wherever the queen went, there went Edmund of Woodstock.

Queen Isabella smiled. "A somewhat tedious young man, for all his exuberance. No, I sent him along with Edward." She reclined in the window seat, adjusted a cushion or two behind her back, and smiled at Adam. "Lord Mortimer will be back soon. It is finally time," she continued. "We will have our vengeance, and I will exact a heavy price for every humiliation, every slur. Despenser will rue the day he made an enemy of me – and of Lord Mortimer."

Kit studied the contents of her cup. Lord Mortimer and Despenser had been born enemies, yet another generation caught up in an infected blood feud that harked back over sixty years.

"You will ride with us, of course," the queen went on, directing herself to Adam. "We need captains like you at our side."

"Adam is sworn to the prince, my lady," Kit interrupted, ignoring Adam's dark look. "And besides, Despenser has our children."

"I heard." Queen Isabella lifted her goblet and regarded Kit over the rim as she drank. "But sometimes, one must rise above the fear of what may be done to your children."

"I'll not do anything that risks my son or daughter," Adam replied.

"Risks? At worst, your daughter will end up a nun, your son a monk." She looked Kit up and down. "And you will have more children." She ignored Kit's responding gasp. "It is time to act, Adam de Guirande."

"He can't! The king has our children," Kit protested.

"As he has mine!" The queen rose. "As he has Mortimer's!" She slammed the goblet down on the table. "Do you think you are the only one with fears for your children? Roger's – Lord Mortimer's – children have been held in captivity for close to four years. Four years!" She glared at Kit. "His daughters shut up alone in nunneries, his sons held at Windsor – young men old enough to drag out and behead, should the king so wish it."

"The king…" He would never harm the queen's children, Kit intended to say.

"Enough!" The queen's eyes spat fire. "You will do what is required of you, Lady Kit, as will you, Adam."

"I serve your son, my lady," Adam said calmly. "I shall do as he commands."

"My son is a boy not quite thirteen. He does not command – I do. Best remember that, Sir Adam."

Adam bowed low – very low. "I serve Prince Edward. I will not do anything that may cause him harm."

223

The queen pursed her mouth. "And if so, Sir Adam, we will do right well together. If anyone attempts to harm my son, I will personally tear them asunder – on that you have my word."

"Except, of course, that she is speaking in physical terms," Adam said to Kit once they were alone. The queen had dismissed them brusquely, saying she needed to pray. "She does not see how placing her son between her and his father may cause him grief and pain." They were in the palace gardens, making their way to the little turret that sat right at the uppermost tip of the triangular gardens, giving an excellent view of the waters of the Seine below, and the city of Paris on the opposite shore. The real Paris, as per that youthful fount of knowledge, Count Louis – the streets so old the Romans had marched their hobnailed sandals over them.

"No," Kit agreed. "But that's because she assumes Edward loves her the best." She plucked a couple of Michaelmas daisies and followed him into the turret.

"And does he?" He led the way up the narrow stairs, his words bouncing against the enclosing walls.

"He loves them both – but he is incensed on her behalf, and he is old enough to see for himself how inept his father is at being king." Kit paused. "Our young prince will strive to be everything his father is not – as a king. But as a man and as a father, King Edward is not all bad, is he?" She took Adam's offered hand and allowed him to pull her out onto the turret's roof.

"Maybe not. But we must judge him as a king – not as a father. And as a king, he has wreaked havoc on his kingdom." Adam's jaw tightened, his eyes glittering like old ice in a sudden burst of sun. "For that he must pay – him and Despenser both."

"So then what? You lock him up and throw away the key?"

"Lock him up?" Adam stared down at her. "The king is the king, Kit. No, his punishment will be to witness the deaths of his favourites – and to allow himself to be counselled by the peers of his realm."

"Ah." Kit hoped he was right – for the sake of Prince Edward. But she feared he was wrong.

The court of Charles Capet was a sophisticated place – at least according to the French, who took all opportunities to remind their English guests of how much more cultivated and elegant things were in Paris than in London. Adam was tired of sly comments as to the superiority of the French, but he kept his thoughts to himself and endeavoured to be polite in the company of his hosts.

One long, mind-numbing hour with two monks from St Denis had Adam in dire need of a drink, and it was with some relief he found a seat in the bottom end of the hall, there to nurse a goblet or two of fine Bordeaux.

"Hiding from the monks?" Cassandra de Ley slid down to sit beside him.

"Spare me their sermons," Adam muttered, shifting away from her.

Cassandra laughed. "I do not bite. Nor do I intend to continue pursuing a man so smitten with his wife." She wrinkled her nose. "It's a bit sickening to watch, how the two of you make eyes at each other, and I dare say you'll grow out of it soon enough." She lowered her voice. "Men need variation in their bed. Men as virile and…err…powerful as you, need it more than most. So," she said, sitting back, "once you decide you're up to a true bout in bed, a long, passionate session that will leave you truly spent, I'll be here. Maybe." She smiled and batted her lashes at him. "That's the risk you are taking, Adam dear – that I will have moved on to greener, younger pastures."

"A risk I gladly take," Adam retorted. "And do not sit around and wait for me to come to you, Cassandra. It will never happen."

"No?" She pouted, pressing her arms against her bosom so that her breasts rose towards him. "Let's say I have more faith in my attractions than you do." As if by chance, she raised one hand to brush at her bosom, the fine wool of her kirtle moulded to her generous breasts.

Adam burst out in laughter. "You are a persevering woman, Cassandra de Ley." He finished his wine and stood. "But as I already told you, I'm not interested."

"Not now, you're not." Cassandra stood up as well and before he knew what she was doing, she'd grabbed hold of his tunic, lifted herself up on her toes and kissed him. Adam used more force than necessary to pull himself free, causing Cassandra to stumble and crash against his wife.

"Kit!" He held out his hand.

She just looked at him, turned and walked away.

"Kit, wait." Behind him, Adam could hear Cassandra laugh. He faced her with a snarl. "Curse you, lewd whore that you are!" Cassandra swung at him. Adam deflected her blow and hastened after his wife.

She was entering their room before he caught up. The door slammed shut, and only by throwing himself at it did he hinder her from bolting it. When he entered, she was standing midway to the bed, veil askew, chest heaving after her run up the stairs. He rammed the bolt into place, the rusty iron squealing in protest as it hit the groove in the stone.

"Come here," he said, and moments later he was thrown against the wall, an angry, cursing woman in his arms, a woman who clawed at him, sank her fingers into his hair, tore at his tunic and shirt. She kissed him, kissed him again and bit his lip – hard enough to draw blood – and Adam's heart began to race. Heat surged through his veins as she disrobed him, he disrobed her.

When she kissed him again, he could taste his blood, and with a groan he fisted his hands in her hair, kissing her until his head spun with lack of air. Again, and he was half-carrying, half-dragging her towards the bed, one leg still encased in hose.

She gestured for him to lie down. It was not in his nature to be passive in bed. He disliked relinquishing control, and with sudden insight he understood this was because of his experiences at the hands of Cassandra: she the mistress, he the apprentice. But Kit was looking at him with an expression he could not quite decipher, so he was willing to accommodate her and do as she wished – for now.

The bed rustled and sank when she joined him, kneeling beside him. There was nothing she subsequently did to him that he hadn't taught her. The way her hands caused his breath to hitch, how her mouth and tongue had him arching upwards, away from the bed – over the years he had showed her just how he liked to be touched and pleasured. But he hadn't quite taught her to do it like this, not with this fiery, burning passion that demanded as much as it gave, not the way she alternated between kisses and nibbles – and at times a painful bite. And her hands, her hair, the softness of her breasts as she pressed them against his chest – no, he had no recollection of ever teaching her to tease him so, to drive him to the brink and then hold back, making him groan and fidget on the bed.

A punishment – a reward? Agh! Her teeth on his member, just enough to make him tense, not enough to truly hurt, but it made him throb and call her name, and Kit sat back on her heels and smiled. He pounced. Enough of her teasing; enough of her driving him close to insane. One swift movement, and it was her who was lying on her back, her body at his mercy. His turn. In a burst of inspiration, he undid the cords that held the hangings in place, and before Kit could protest, she was tied to the bed, her arms extended above her. And then Adam began his own, slow exploration, relishing the fact that she lay helpless as he kissed and fondled.

He had never had a woman like this before, never felt quite as powerful as he did when his wife was incapable of doing anything but taking what he gave her – and he gave her plenty, making that beautiful body of hers twist like a captive eel, her voice growing hoarse as she pleaded with him to stop, to not stop, to do it again, to not do it again.

Long before he entered her, she was reduced to a quivering warmth, mouth half-open, eyes burning into his – as he wanted it, because every time she made as if to close them, he stopped what he was doing, insisting she bare her very soul to him through her eyes.

As he thrust into her, she moaned. And when he finally allowed her to climax, she uttered a series of incoherent sounds among which the only thing he could truly make out was his name.

Afterwards, she pillowed her head against his shoulder.

"Next time she touches what is mine, I'll rake my nails across her face." It made him smile, the possessive note to her voice. Kit rose on her elbows. "You're my man, Adam de Guirande. Mine, and best you never forget it."

As if he possibly could, he thought drowsily. As if he would ever want to, he added with a little smile, pressing her down to rest her ear over his heart.

Chapter 23

"I could do no other," Prince Edward said, looking down at the letter in his hands. "How was I to leave my mother, when she begged me to stay?"

The letter from the king had arrived that same morning, a short, thrifty missive berating his son for not having returned to England with Stapledon.

"Besides, the man slunk away like a fox from a henhouse!" Edward crumpled the parchment and lobbed it into the hearth. "Was I to know our lord bishop had chosen that precise moment in time to spirit himself away disguised as a pilgrim?"

Sir Henry snickered. "A most God-fearing pilgrim, what with his haste." He patted Edward on his shoulder. "We shall write a reply to your father, my lord, explaining the details of this whole mess."

"The details?" Edward bent down to tug at the ear of his new hound, a gift from the little French queen, who was much taken with her husband's dashing young nephew. "My father does not care about the details. All he wants is for me to return home." He sucked in his lip. "It would be foolish to brave the journey at present, wouldn't it?"

The November day was bright and sunny, with nary a breeze to lift the king's banner to fly above the main gatehouse to the palace. But Adam saw no reason not to allow the lad this justification for remaining here, with his mother.

"Crossing the seas can be dangerous this time of the year, my lord," he therefore said, receiving an approving nod from Sir Henry. "Best you remind your father of the *White Ship*."

"Ah, yes." Sir Henry smiled at the prince. "He would not want to lose his heir to the depths of the seas like poor King Henry, the first of his name, did."

"Except that Father has a second son." Prince Edward scowled at the smoking heap of ashes that was all that remained of his father's letter. "And why does he keep on reminding me that I must not marry without his approval? I know my duty to him and to England – he has told me often enough how a king must marry as it helps his kingdom, not as his heart desires." He sighed. "He never loved Maman, did he?" Yet another scowl. "Why is it that troubadours and romances speak so much of love, of fair maidens that set their beloved's heart ablaze, when it seems love does not exist?"

"It does exist," Adam said.

"For you, maybe. Not for me – not for the son of a king who must wed as his father commands, no matter if the lady in question is ugly as sin and has the disposition of a rabid boar." The prince picked up his cloak. "I'm going out."

"Out?" Adam made as if to follow, but the prince shook his head.

"I ride with Louis and his guards. He has promised me a night in Paris to drown all my sorrows." With that, he stomped out.

"All his sorrows?" Sir Henry chuckled, but sounded sad all the same. "The lad has no idea of just how much grief all of this may cost him."

"Let's keep it that way – for now." Adam suggested. He opened the shutters wide enough that he could follow the prince's progress towards the waiting horses, now with Louis at his side. Already taller than his French cousin, definitely broader, Edward reminded Adam of an oversized butterfly trapped in its cocoon, about to burst its bindings.

"Thirteen." Adam smiled. "Quite the lad, eh?" He gestured to where their lord was already astride, dark blue cloak over a sea-green tunic that was his mother's gift on this, his birthday. Among his companions, Adam could make out Edmund of Kent, at present a constant shadow at his royal nephew's heels. Well, Kent had the capacity of making the prince laugh, and seemed to be able to keep even the boisterous Count Louis somewhat in check.

"A most handsome prince – let us hope he makes as handsome a king someday." Sir Henry sent one of the pages off for new quills. "And now for some writing."

It was very late when Prince Edward came back, grinning rather sheepishly as he was escorted to his mother's chambers. The bells had rung for curfew long ago, and the palace was sunk in sleep – except for here, where the irate queen paced like a caged lioness as she awaited the return of her son.

"Maman." The prince bowed, stumbled, and steadied himself against Adam.

"You're drunk," Queen Isabella concluded, approaching her son to sniff at him.

"I am," he replied, nodding several times. "So very, very, very…" His voice tailed off, and he blinked, giving the queen a bemused look. His clothes were in disarray, one leg of hose twisting up his leg in a crooked fashion that indicated the points had been cross-tied.

"And where have you been?" The queen rounded on Count Louis, as drunk as Edward, if somewhat more in control of himself.

"Ah!" Louis tapped his nose. "We have gone to places you, fair cousin, don't even know exist."

"A brothel," the queen said drily.

"A brothel, she says," Louis muttered. "A brothel, when it is a doorway to Heaven, a road to wonderful, carnal oblivion."

"He's thirteen!" The queen sounded exasperated, looking from her son to Count Louis.

"And now he is a man," Count Louis said, jabbing Edward with an elbow. The prince tried to jab back and stumbled. "He acquitted himself well, dear cousin, and—"

"I do not want to hear this!" The queen scowled, the impression somewhat undermined by the smile that tugged at her mouth. "My son a man, eh? Well, dear Edward, it takes more than swiving a whore or two to make a boy into a man."

"Four actually," Count Louis interrupted. "My birthday gift to him."

"You, Louis Valois, are incorrigible!"

Louis grinned and tossed his head, making all those curls bounce. "But quite the charmer, am I not?"

"I'll not have my son frequenting whores," the queen snapped.

"Not whores," Edward mumbled, "little angels, rosy things with round titties and—"

"Edward!" The queen shook him, her son gave her a wide smile and fell backwards, his fall broken by Adam's arms. She sighed. "Take him to bed. And I want him at his prayers by prime. I'll join him."

Adam suppressed a grin. Poor lad – knowing the queen, she'd keep him on his knees through most of tomorrow.

It had to be the most beautiful room in all of Christendom. While Notre Dame filled Kit with awe, the Sainte-Chapelle filled her with delight, a sensation of her spirit breaking free to soar upwards, ever upwards, towards the elegantly vaulted and painted ceiling and the light that streamed in through the huge windows. Even now, after well over a month in residence, with daily visits, Kit couldn't quite stop the smile that broke forth on her face when she entered the chapel.

While in here, she could believe things would end well, that her children were safe and sound, and that the infected situation between the king, his queen, his most traitorous baron and his equally treacherous favourite, could somehow be resolved without resorting to war. Outside of this peaceful place, she held little hope.

On this very early November morning, the chapel was lit by the soft glow of candles. As yet, night held the world in its grip, but the eastern windows were rimmed at the edges with the promise of dawn. Kit followed the queen down the central aisle, but when Isabella disappeared into Queen Blanche's chantry for her private devotions, Kit remained in the nave where she knelt and prayed for Tom and for Meg, and for Mabel to be hale enough to keep them safe. Behind her, the queen's ladies filed in, and after the ladies came the ladies' maids, among them Aline, looking as if she'd leapt directly from bed to the chapel.

Voices rose and fell, the Latin plain chant echoing under the vaults. On the other side of the aisle knelt Edward, the men of his household around him. Kit shifted. The floor was cold, and the thin cushion under her knees did little to relieve the chill – or the discomfort. The eastern windows brightened, light seeping in to illuminate the gilded woodwork and the lifelike statues of the apostles. Burning incense tickled her nose, and then the bells began to ring for prime, welcoming a new day here in the most gorgeous chapel of the world.

It was just as she was leaving that Kit saw him. There, among the monks, stood a familiar figure, taller than his brethren and with eyes the blue of a summer sky. Kit's hand flew to her mouth. She wanted to call out his name, pick up her skirts and run towards him, but such lack of decorum would be frowned upon, and for now she would have to make do with the way his eyes crinkled as he smiled at her. William! Her gaze flew to Adam, she gestured with her head, saw him follow the direction and come to an abrupt halt.

And then William was moving towards his brother, Adam was hurrying to meet him, and Kit chose to ignore the queen's hissed admonition, hastening to join them.

"So tell us – everything," Kit said some while later. The queen had relented when she recognised William, and Kit had been graciously given leave to catch up with her brother-in-law.

Prince Edward had been more difficult. Kit had seen him study William, glance at Adam and then back at William, and she could swear the lad was adding two and two together. But he was too tired, too affected by yesterday's escapades, to do more than wave Adam off, saying he would talk to Sir Adam later.

"That would take too long," William said, bracing his hands against the parapet of the low wall that separated the herbal garden from the kitchen garden. He had his back to them. "And it is not a particularly interesting tale – it was more a question of living like a rat, skulking from one haystack to the other." He shivered, and Kit had the distinct impression that it had been more complicated than he let on. "They almost caught me once, up in Yorkshire. Evaded them by going into the Ouse." He smiled at Kit, no doubt recalling the time they had both leapt into the Severn to save Adam.

"But you are safe now," Adam said.

"Safe?" William turned to face them. "Safe enough – unless those assassins Despenser has promised a barrel or two of silver for Mortimer's head kill me as well."

"Assassins?" Kit looked over her shoulder. "Here?"

"Assuredly here – somewhere. Despenser is counting on Mortimer showing his face here at the French court." William laughed. "But Mortimer is far too canny, and I'm far too unimportant. I hope, at least."

"Does the queen know?" Adam asked.

"That there is a threat to Lord Roger? Of course she does. What does that woman not know?" William shared a smile with his brother. "Queen Isabella has her own little spies at work. I would not want to end up in her net."

Despite the chilly wind, they found a bench and sat down, Adam draping an arm round Kit's shoulders to pull her close. She told William about their children, and about her mounting concern as to their well-being.

"We've only had the one message," she said, and Adam tightened his hold on her. "Mabel had one of the clerks write and inform us that the children thrive, but Amy is poorly." She shifted on the cold stone. "What if Amy dies? Who will nurse our baby?"

"Mabel will keep them safe," William said, "and Amy is robust, is she not?" He patted Kit's knee. "Do you know where they are?"

"To the west somewhere," Adam replied. "Mabel said they were within riding distance of Tewkesbury Abbey, at one of Despenser's minor manors."

"Ah." William smiled at Kit. "Close to home, then, aren't they?"

"But not at home," she replied harshly.

"I have a friend at the abbey," William said. "Would you want me to send word to him?"

"What good would that do? The abbey's single most generous patron is Lady Eleanor. Those monks would not do anything to risk her displeasure." Adam crossed his legs at the ankles and frowned down at his boots.

"And why would it displease her to have a monk send

you word about your children?" William asked. "Is she not a mother too?"

They left the subject of Tom and Meg and moved on to William's latest news about Lord Mortimer. The man had spent an inordinate amount of time lately with Guillaume of Hainaut, and as William understood things, the queen and Mortimer had been in direct correspondence with each other since Queen Isabella had landed in France back in March.

"He writes to her himself," William added with a little smile. "And she does him the honour of replying in her own hand."

"The fewer who read their letters, the better, I presume," Adam said. "And what has Lord Roger been doing in Hainaut?"

"You know well enough, brother. Hainaut has men and ships aplenty."

"And Lord Roger has..." Adam prompted.

"He has a prince – a young, comely, unwed prince." William slapped Adam on his back. "Why that disapproving face? A prince never gets to choose his bride, does he?"

"No, but rarely is a prince bartered as a fatted calf to purchase the arms and ships required to make war on his royal father."

"Not the king, Adam: Despenser."

Adam gave him a bleak look. "We both know the king and Despenser are joined at the hip."

William raised his shoulders. "The king made his choice years ago. A king who is in breach of his coronation oaths is as foresworn as any other man."

"Has he?" Kit asked as she and Adam made their way back to the queen's apartments. "Broken his coronation oaths, I mean."

"Repeatedly." Adam sighed. "And he has broken so many oaths over the years that no one trusts him."

"Oaths he made under duress," Kit said.

"An oath is an oath, sweeting. And had he but kept to his word back in 1321, we would not be in this situation, would we?" His face clouded at the sight of the prince, standing just outside the door to his mother's apartments, arms crossed over his chest. "And now, it seems, I have an irate lord to pacify." He groaned under his breath as the Earl of Kent came out to join his nephew, two startlingly similar pairs of eyes boring into him.

"Just because William is here does not mean you had anything to do with freeing him."

"And pigs fly too, do they? Edward is no fool, Kit. Best tell him the truth, or I risk him never trusting me again." He released her hand, straightened up and went to face his lord.

In the event, the prince did not berate him much, muttering that he knew Adam had anything but fond recollections of his own treatment at Despenser's hands, and so, the prince supposed, he was reluctant to have his priest brother suffer a similar fate.

"He would have driven him to despair and beyond, my lord," Adam agreed.

"Hmm, yes." Prince Edward studied Adam with a pursed mouth. "In the future, Sir Adam, you will not take it upon you to act in any way without my direct orders." His eyes hardened. "And should you disobey, you will find me a harsh master."

Adam did not doubt that for a moment. For the first time since he'd met him, the boy prince was showing him his claws, and Adam knew first-hand just how lethal royal claws could be. So he bowed and gave the lad his word that any future actions would be at his lord's command. Edward looked somewhat mollified.

"Good," was all he said, before ordering Adam to see to his horses. Kent snickered, and Adam's cheeks stung at being treated like a stable boy. But he didn't say anything; he simply made a reverence and moved as if to leave.

"Oh, Sir Adam?" the prince said, causing Adam to come to a halt. "The next time someone sets a caltrop to my horse, I'll have one shoved into your boot and have you walk on it a day."

"That wasn't me, my lord," Adam protested.

"I don't care. I hold you responsible." Edward advanced, straightening up so that his head was at Adam's shoulder level. "You hold yourself to me, Sir Adam. Only to me."

Adam swallowed, unnerved by the chill in those blue eyes. No longer a lad – and not because of last night's adventures among the whores – this was his future king staring at him, demanding his submission and loyalty. Adam's skin itched; Edward of Windsor would not be denied. Slowly, Adam fell to his knees before him.

"I am your man, sire," he said, hearing the prince's surprised intake of breath. "As I swore before the king, my life is pledged to you." This time, the prince smiled, and it was like seeing the sun break through a singularly dark patch of cloud.

"Get up, Adam." Edward set his hand under Adam's elbow. "Have Gavin see to the horses. You, on the other hand, will have the pleasure of playing me a game of chess."

Chapter 24

Lord Roger Mortimer returned to Paris in December. It was probably nothing more than a coincidence that he should ride into the palace as the bells of all the churches rang for vespers, but all the same, all that noise was an adequate complement when the man King Edward spoke of as The Mortimer, his greatest traitor, came clattering through the gatehouse.

Kit had not seen Lord Mortimer since January 1322 – at the time a man with a haunted expression and a severe set to his mouth that told of many sleepless nights as he attempted to find a way out of the conundrum posed by the king's increasing military strength, and his own restricted room for manoeuvring.

The man who rode into the royal palace was a man who had lost whatever softness had remained in him, a man of hard eyes and harsh features, dressed in saffron and black, with the handful of men at his heels in surcoats displaying the Mortimer arms. A powerful man, some years shy of his fortieth birthday, but agile and strong, leaping off his horse with the grace of a much younger man. Most of all, this was a determined man, as evidenced by the way he moved, striding purposefully to greet first the French king, who to Kit's surprise enfolded Lord Mortimer in an embrace, then to kneel at the feet of his queen.

The last time Kit had seen Lord Mortimer, he'd been sitting side by side with his wife. At the time, Kit had never before seen a man who so openly demonstrated his affection for his wife, and all through that last meal Lady Joan and her husband had shared, Lord Mortimer had offered his lady wife morsels of food, sharing his wine cup with her, his eyes never leaving hers. But what Kit had witnessed then was nothing to what she witnessed now, for the moment the queen's eyes met Mortimer's, it was as if a bolt of lightning surged between them, and Mortimer's posture faltered. The queen's mouth fell open, the tip of her tongue touching her upper lip.

Queen Isabella extended her hand. Lord Mortimer clasped it and kissed it. A murmur swept through the crowd when he kissed it again. The queen closed her eyes, lashes fluttering like dark butterflies against her pale cheeks. And then Mortimer was back on his feet, still holding on to the queen's hand. From where she was standing, Kit could see his fingers tighten round hers, could see how the queen responded in kind, before letting him go.

It was as if there were invisible threads attaching them to each other. Lord Mortimer raised his hand to brush at his hair; the queen raised hers to her veil, and from the way Mortimer's eyes grew dark and lustrous, one could think the queen's narrow, long-fingered hand was touching his brow, not hers. The queen turned slightly towards King Charles, and Mortimer did the same. At the king's invitation, Lord Mortimer moved forward to walk with him, and the queen was at Mortimer's other side, mirroring his movements.

Mortimer's hand brushed the queen's skirts. Her hand returned the gesture, lingering a tad too long on the heavy folds of his robe. As they reached the door, Mortimer stopped, bowing as he stepped back to allow the king to enter first. His head turned towards the queen's, and she turned towards him, having to tip her chin up to meet his gaze. They didn't touch. They didn't breathe. At long last, she took a step towards the door.

She stumbled – on purpose? Kit couldn't tell, but Mortimer's arm flew out to steady her. She straightened up, and his hand slid from her elbow to her wrist, then to her hand. This time, he didn't let her go. Instead, their fingers braided together, and Kit knew it was but a matter of hours before the queen and her baron would mate – and once they did, nothing would tear them apart. Nothing but death.

"Sister," someone said, causing Kit to tear her gaze away from Lord Mortimer and the queen.

"Richard!" She threw herself around his neck and he

staggered back some paces, complaining that she was far too heavy to launch herself like that at an unsuspecting man.

"Are you well?" she asked once she was back on her feet. An unnecessary question, in truth, what with how hale he looked.

Richard assured her that he was. "I owe you my life," he added seriously, but Kit waved him quiet.

"We're family," she said, and then someone was calling for him, making him groan and promise they'd find time to talk later.

Dinner was a lavish affair. The king had Mortimer on one side, his sister on the other, and he had placed Prince Edward on Mortimer's other side. Lord Mortimer conversed with the king; he leaned his dark head close to the prince's fair one and whispered something that had Edward first rearing back, then beaming and nodding eagerly.

"Yet another Mortimer acolyte?" Kit murmured to Adam, smiling at how eagerly the prince was talking, hands gesturing wildly as he explained something to Mortimer.

Adam merely grunted. He had so far not exchanged more than six words with his former lord, a stilted greeting, no more.

"What is the matter?" Kit asked, even if she knew exactly why Adam was as irascible as a wounded boar. She'd caught him staring at Mortimer's and the queen's interlaced hands earlier, brows pulled together in a ferocious scowl.

"He has a wife waiting for him," Adam replied in an undertone. "A wife who has suffered years of deprivation and shame, and what does he do? In front of the entire French court he makes love to the queen, never considering that every gesture, every tender word and caress will be making its way to his wife by the morrow."

"And will Lady Joan be surprised?" Kit had heard rumours of Lord Mortimer and the queen since well before he was imprisoned, but according to Adam they had been precisely that – rumours. Surely, if Kit had heard them, Lady Joan must have heard them, and two people better suited to each other

240

than the dark, harshly handsome baron with his chiselled features, and the queen, equally elegant of feature, equally fiercely beautiful, were difficult to find. Not that this would offer Lady Joan any comfort – rather the reverse.

"I think she will. My lady will have her heart broken, I fear."

"It may not be what you think," Kit tried. Adam laughed softly and took her hand in his, insistently working at it until she widened her fingers round his. He raised their braided hands to his lips and brushed a kiss over them.

"What man holds a woman's hand like this, if not a lover?" he said. "What man regards a woman with eyes hot enough to burn holes in her skin without being irrevocably in love? Lord Roger is a private man, sweeting. Rare are the occasions when I have seen him hold his wife or kiss her hand. But today I saw a man so smitten he could scarcely get to his feet – and a woman as helplessly drawn to him as he is to her."

"Like us?" she asked.

Adam shook his head. "Ours is a pretty fire, sweeting, a hot blaze to warm us through many a night. But it isn't a furnace, it doesn't consume us and leave us charred and smouldering."

"Oh." She was strangely disappointed. Was he not as drawn to her as Mortimer was to the queen? Her thoughts must have stood visible on her face, because moments later he nuzzled her neck.

"I burn, my lady wife. I burn for you, love you, desire you. But—"

"Not like that," she cut him off.

"No, not like that."

Kit tried to pull her hand free from his grip, but all he did was tighten his hold. "You misconstrue – or maybe I do not explain myself as I should." He cleared his throat. "What we have is a gift, Kit. What they have is a curse, because when passion rules, very little else survives."

"Passion?" Kit returned her attention to the high table, where Mortimer was still talking to the prince, while the queen was in a quiet conversation with her brother. And yet now and then she would look at Mortimer – or he at her – and whenever they did, the other would look back, eyes meeting for a fleeting moment.

"Passion for life, for each other – for revenge. And should one of them die, the other is left mortally wounded, near on incapable of continuing to breathe or live."

"Maybe you're right," she said. "But just so you know, I would not be able to breathe if you were not in my life to breathe with me." Kit lowered her lashes, feeling ridiculous.

"Ah, sweeting." His hold on her hand tightened, his voice suddenly very hoarse. "Neither would I, I think. Not like I do today."

It was not until four days later that Lord Roger came to find Adam. Newly shaved, in deep red silk with a matching velvet surcoat and one of those hats Count Louis was so fond of, Lord Roger looked every inch the rich nobleman he was – or should have been, had not the king attainted him.

"Appearances are important," he said with a laugh. "Do you want to inspect my braies and hose as well?"

"No, my lord," Adam muttered, suddenly very aware of the fact that he had not shaved, and that his hair could do with a wash, as could the rest of him. But his tunic was clean, recently returned from the fuller's, and his hose was new, of the finest dark green wool.

"Shall we walk?" Lord Roger asked, sweeping with his arm towards the gardens.

"The prince—"

"…Is with his mother," Lord Roger said. "I left them together." He threw Adam an oblique glance, as if daring him to comment on the fact that he was spending most of his days – and nights – with the queen. Adam held his tongue, and Lord Roger made an amused sound and led the way, ducking under the trailing branches of a climbing rose, at present denuded of anything but thorns.

"You look well, my lord," Adam said once they were abreast.

Lord Roger chuckled. "Compared with when you saw

me last, you mean?" His eyes tightened. "Almost two years as the king's reluctant guest did not do wonders for my physique, did it?"

"No, my lord." On that August day in 1323, Lord Roger had been dirty and underweight, dressed in the same tunic he'd worn when he was imprisoned, well over eighteen months earlier. Now he was back to being the powerful man Adam recalled from before, the hero of his youth, the man Adam would have gladly died for once.

Not as tall as Adam, Lord Roger was all the same broad over shoulders and chest, testament to his excellent jousting skills. Strong hands, forearms banded with muscle, and he walked like a cat: light on his feet, ever ready to pounce. But there was a shadow to his eyes that had not been there before the day he was imprisoned, and a tautness to his stance that revealed he had not gone unscathed through his experience. Come to think of it, Richard de Monmouth had that same set to him, as if constantly on his guard, and at times Adam suspected he had too, courtesy of those long months as the king's prisoner.

As they walked, they talked, and the initial stiffness melted away as Lord Roger spoke about Ireland and England, asking concerned question about those of his retainers who had survived the king's revenge. But he didn't mention his wife – nor his children – and Adam was not sure whether to raise the subject or hold his tongue.

"Do you think less of me, then?" Lord Roger asked as they returned to the stable yard.

"My lord?"

"You have eyes in your head, Adam – you know where I've been spending my time lately."

"It is not for me to judge, my lord."

"No, it most certainly isn't. But I asked you a question and would have an answer."

Adam was not quite sure what to say.

"Damn it, man! Answer me! Is it so strange that I should woo the most beautiful woman in Christendom? Do you think me too old, too decrepit?"

Adam raised his brows. Lord Roger was only nine years older than him, and was nowhere near to being either decrepit or old. "You're a married man, my lord," he said, and he couldn't keep the censure out of his voice – truth be told, he didn't try to.

"And she's a married lady," Lord Roger retorted with a grin – but the smile did not touch his eyes.

Adam sighed. "It isn't fair on Lady Joan. Or do you mean to put the queen aside once this venture is over and return to live by your wife's side?"

Lord Roger ran his hand through his hair, the jewels in his various rings glinting in the sun. "I don't know." He bent and picked up a discarded horseshoe. "Do you think this venture of ours will be successful?"

"I do – now that you have the prince in your hands."

"You sound disapproving." Lord Roger frowned.

"About the venture as such? No, my lord. You know I have reasons of my own to want to see Despenser and his followers swing by the neck until they're dead and more. But of your methods? I do not like it that Prince Edward is suddenly reduced to being your pawn."

"My pawn?" Lord Roger echoed. "His mother's pawn, not mine. Or do you think she is but a quiet, obedient partner in all this?"

Adam had to laugh. "No, probably not." He sobered up. "I have sworn to serve the prince, my lord. Please don't do something that will force me to choose between him and you."

"And if I did? What would you do?" Lord Roger sounded distant.

"I would go with the prince, my lord. It would tear the heart out of my body to do so, but I will not fail the prince."

Lord Roger studied the horseshoe in silence for some moments before letting it fall to the ground. "Tear the heart out of your body, eh?" He pulled Adam close and ruffled his hair, in a gesture that threw Adam back fifteen years and more, to when Lord Roger saved him from his father and took him in. "We can't have that, Adam, can we?" he continued in a softer voice. "I can't have a man I've raised and love die such a dire death."

"Love?" Adam asked.

"Like a son, Adam." Lord Roger grinned. "Well, the son I might have had had I lain with a huge, fair giantess in my distant youth."

Adam burst out laughing.

Someone called for Lord Roger. It was Richard, coming at a trot towards them, holding aloft what looked like a letter.

"I must go," Lord Roger said.

Adam just nodded. "And Lady Joan, my lord?" he asked as Lord Roger turned away. "What will you do?"

"God knows," Lord Roger replied without turning around. "But I think the queen will make her opinion in the matter count, don't you?"

Aye, Adam sighed. And from the look of things, the queen had set her heart on Mortimer.

"Do you think it's out of spite?" Adam asked Kit later that day. "Is it precisely because he is who he is that the queen has so openly shown the world her affection?"

"Hmm?" Kit frowned down at her sewing, squinting in the poor light.

"Lord Roger and the queen," he explained. "Is it the fact that she knows just how much the king will rage when he hears she's taken his greatest traitor as her lover that fuels her fire?"

"Oh." She lowered her work to her lap. "Maybe. But I think it's the man she's in love with, not the traitor. And the one playing with fire is Lord Mortimer."

"They both are! Adultery is a grievous sin."

"It is, but that is between them and God. I was thinking rather of our prince. One day, he'll be old enough – and man enough – to want to punish them for making his father a cuckold. He'll forgive his mother, but Lord Mortimer?" She shook her head.

Chapter 25

"Just leave me alone." Kit sidestepped, but Cassandra moved with her, effectively blocking the doorway – again. Kit was tempted to shove her. These last few days, Cassandra had become a constant, ingratiating presence, and Kit was of the opinion that she much preferred her as she was before.

"I'm trying to make amends." Cassandra opened her brown eyes wide. "It is my penance," she went on. "My confessor says I must repent and make amends before it is too late."

"Too late?" Kit looked her up and down. Cassandra looked to be in the best of health.

Cassandra grinned. "My sins are manifold. My penance is long." She sounded unperturbed.

"Your penance should not be my penance," Kit replied stiffly. "I have no reason to like you – or trust you."

Cassandra laughed, a low, throaty sound that Kit imagined most men found delightful. In fact, all of Lady Cassandra had to be tempting for a man, from the roundness of her bosom, to her dark hair, often artfully arranged so as to be visible in several long curls under her veils, and her curvy hips. For a woman bent on doing penance, she was dressed in surprisingly exposing kirtles, cut low over the chest and tight over the waist and hips before flaring out into skirts that billowed round her when she walked.

"How refreshing to meet someone as honest as you are," Cassandra said. "And I know you don't like me – nor have I gone out of my way to make a friend out of you – but could we perhaps start anew?" She tilted her head and gave Kit yet another smile.

"I don't know." No, Kit did not believe in a reformed Cassandra, but at least the woman no longer hovered around her man, so she supposed the lady had set her eyes elsewhere.

Some mornings later, and Kit had come to the conclusion that Cassandra's new male interest was Lord Mortimer's faithful shadow, Richard. No longer a mere squire, Richard was now a belted knight, but as Mortimer had as yet not found a new squire, things remained as they'd been for years, with Richard always in Mortimer's presence – or in an antechamber beyond.

On several occasions, she'd come upon Cassandra staring at her brother, and from the way her gaze travelled up her brother's body, Kit deduced the lady was smitten with Richard. It made her laugh – albeit quietly – because no matter how often Cassandra placed herself in Richard's way, she was studiously avoided, his focus never wavering from his lord and his lady queen.

One afternoon, Cassandra cornered her just as she was leaving the garderobe. "You have to help me." She looked uncharacteristically distraught, her dark eyes shimmering as if she was about to weep.

"Help you?"

Cassandra lifted her veil to wipe at her eyes. "For the first time in my life, I am struck with love, but he ignores me, doesn't even see me."

"Who?" Kit asked, even if she had her suspicions.

"Your brother! I see him, and my mouth dries up, my heart races and I…well, I feel as if I'll die if he doesn't smile at me."

Kit was torn between amusement and disgust. "He's young enough to be your son."

"What can I say? Love is blind." Cassandra gave Kit a tremulous smile. "Besides, I don't think I look like his mother, do I?"

Kit couldn't stop herself from laughing at the ridiculous image of Lady Cecily simpering at a man. Cassandra winked and preened, making Kit laugh even harder. "No," she said once she'd stopped laughing. "You most certainly don't." Lady Cecily was all narrow angles and emanated as much warmth as a block of ice, while Cassandra was nothing if not warm and welcoming.

"Well, then," Cassandra said with a little shrug. "So, will you help me?"

"With what, precisely?"

"Introduce us. I will manage it from there." Cassandra looked quite smug, reminding Kit of an overfed and pampered cat. Kit hesitated, but was subjected to such a torrent of pleading she finally gave up and promised Cassandra she would do what she could.

Once the introductions were made, Richard was lost. His blue eyes clung to Cassandra's ample curves, they lingered on her neckline, on her mouth, and with a little sigh Kit concluded it had taken Cassandra all of two nights to have totally enthralled her brother. Well, better Cassandra exercise her wiles on Richard than on Adam, but just in case, Kit decided to have a separate discussion with her brother.

Richard listened to her, but waved away her warnings as to predatory women. "I can handle myself in bed," he assured her. "Cassandra de Ley best hope she can handle the dragon she has ignited."

"The dragon?" Only through conscious effort did Kit stop herself from laughing outright.

"Contrary to what you may think, dear sister, I am quite experienced in these matters."

"Really?" Kit grinned, making Richard scowl before pointedly moving over to join Cassandra on a nearby window seat.

Kit returned to her stool and picked up her embroidery.

"I don't like her, my lady," Aline confided with a little sniff, gesturing in the direction of Cassandra. No, Kit thought, because you have eyes only for the dashing Richard de Monmouth, and he does not even see you, so bedazzled is he by the voluptuous Cassandra de Ley.

Kit gave Aline an encouraging smile. "I don't like her much either. Most women don't."

"It's wrong that she flaunts herself like that!" Aline stabbed the needle through the linen of her new shift.

"Flaunts herself? Come, come – Lady Cassandra has turned a new leaf and is now most demure." Kit chuckled at her own jest.

"Turned a new leaf?" Aline's voice squeaked. "She has her eyes set on your brother, m'lady! Look at him: young and handsome, high in Lord Mortimer's favour, ever in his presence. Mark my words, she wants Sir Richard as her husband."

"That will not happen," Kit told her drily. Cassandra had borne no children to any of her husbands, and Richard would look for a fertile wife – and a young one. Kit studied Aline thoughtfully. The girl was pretty enough, but poor as a pauper.

"The maids in the kitchen call her the spider," Aline muttered. "She devours men and spits them out." She gave Kit a sly look. "Your man too, as I hear it, m'lady."

"That was a long time ago."

"Really? And yet I saw her walking with him in the gardens yesterday."

"Did you?" Kit managed to sound only mildly interested, but the moment she was excused, she set off in search of her husband.

"I did no such thing!" Adam glared at her. "I was in the gardens with the prince and that confounded new pup of his, when out of nowhere she appeared. And when Edward was called away by his uncle, there I was with the fair Cassandra."

"But why didn't you tell me?"

"Because I knew you would react like this," he growled.

"Like what, exactly?"

"Like a jealous fishwife!"

Kit marched out of their room, took the steps in twos, and made for the tranquillity of the chapel. Bastard! She was never going to speak to him again, and as far as she was concerned, he could swive himself silly with Cassandra, because she no longer wanted anything to do with him. Jealous fishwife indeed! If she found him in bed with Cassandra, she'd stick his lying eyes out, and as to Cassandra… All of her was heaving with rage.

"Kit!"

She jumped at the sound of his voice, but when he took hold of her arm, she wrenched herself free.

"Let me go!" she snarled. "And, dear husband, just so you know, I do not care one whit – one whit, y'hear? – if you choose to pay court to Cassandra. But if you do, I will kill you!" That shut him up, she thought, entering the chapel with such speed she stumbled for a couple of paces. Infernal man, he was still at her side.

"Kit." His voice was soft, and when she slid him a look, she could see he was struggling not to laugh, which only incensed her further. But she couldn't quarrel with him here, in the silent peace of the royal chapel, so instead she ignored him and sank down to pray, hoping he would leave her to her anger.

He didn't, of course. Instead, he kneeled down beside her.

"I'm sorry," he murmured, interrupting her halfway through her Pater Noster. "For what I said, and for not telling you."

Kit gave him a haughty look, and met eyes that regarded her with so much tenderness all of her anger evaporated. She sighed and got to her feet, catching sight of a lonely figure kneeling just before the altar. It was the queen, unattended and with her face raised to the light spilling in from the windows. She was weeping, hands clasped round the heavy cross she always carried at her waist.

"Come," Adam whispered in her ear. "We are intruding."

Once outside, Adam suggested they go to the stables.

"I just don't understand," Kit said. "One moment she acts as if I'm her friend, entirely besotted with my brother, the next she is back to prowling round you like a hungry wolf."

"She wasn't prowling. She was sniffing."

"Sniffing?"

Adam just shook his head. "The lady has another quarry. Not your brother, I think – he is merely a way to pass time while she plans her next few moves."

"Richard won't like that," Kit replied distractedly. "Why was she weeping?"

"Cassandra?"

"No, the queen. She looked...I don't know, vulnerable and sad."

"Maybe she is." Adam slapped Raven on his rump. "A ride?" he suggested, calling for a stable boy to fetch the saddle.

"But why would she be sad?" Kit stood to the side and watched the stable boy hoist the saddle into place, giving the lad a brief smile when Adam dismissed him.

"Our queen is most devout," Adam said. "Living in sin must cause her much spiritual agony."

"In sin? She loves him!" Five weeks Lord Mortimer had been back, weeks in which he was rarely far from the queen's side – or she from his. There were a lot of mutterings at court, as yet held in check by the queen's brother, but of late King Charles looked somewhat displeased, and from what Kit had overheard some days ago this was not due to any moral objections, but rather to the fact that he felt the queen was being indiscreet.

Adam threw the reins over Raven's neck. "But she is wed elsewhere, bound by vows to be faithful until death. Remember what happened to her sisters-in-law and their lovers in the aftermath of the Tour de Nesle scandal."

Kit nodded. A most lurid tale involving King Charles' first wife, as well as his brothers' wives – a sordid story of debauchery and sin that had only come to light through Queen Isabella's accusations. The lovers had been brutally executed, the adulterous wives thrown into the darkest dungeon at Chateau de Gaillard, and only one of the three ladies ever succeeded in making it back to court.

"It's not the same. Our queen repudiated those vows back in September." Kit backed away as Adam led the horse out, following him out into the yard. In response, Adam grunted. He tightened the girth, adjusted the stirrups, and sat up, beckoning for her to come to him. Moments later, they were riding out of the castle and over the bridge, making for the closest gate out from the city.

"Do you truly think Cassandra has her eye set on Richard?" Adam asked, urging Raven into a slow trot. The streets were thronged with people, from a butcher's yard came the sound of an animal squealing in agony, and all along the street vendors were hawking everything from tallow candles to carp.

"Is that so strange?" Kit smiled at a child, genderless in a dirty smock, and was assailed with images of her Tom. Him she could at least envision – sturdy and fair – but Meg was nothing but a collection of haphazard details: long, dark lashes, wispy hair and ears with no earlobes to speak of.

"Cassandra doesn't need a boy in her bed." It came out in a tone that had Kit craning her head back, all thoughts of her children forgotten.

"A boy? Richard isn't an untried lad."

"Compared to some of us he is," Adam replied. "More to the point, he is at present as poor as a pauper, all his possessions attainted."

"So why all this interest in him?"

"I don't know, but I'm starting to wonder if it's Lord Roger she wants." Adam nodded a greeting to one of the guards at the city gate, received a raised hand in return, and then they were outside the walls.

"Mortimer?" Kit laughed. "As if he would even look her way when he has the queen by his side." Before her stretched an expanse of open land, the fields covered in the rotting stubble from last year's harvest, the road bordered by stands of trees, their branches bare and dark against the pale January sky.

"Not like that, Kit." Adam urged Raven into a canter, and the winter wind chilled her nose and cheeks in a matter of heartbeats.

"Then how?" she asked, once he'd brought Raven back down to a trot.

"You heard William: Despenser will pay a fortune for Lord Roger's head. Maybe she is here to pave the way for the assassin."

"What?" Kit almost fell off the horse in her efforts to turn to see his face. "No, Cassandra is too fond of her pretty neck to risk being involved in something that dangerous."

"And who is to say there isn't already a noose round her neck? Despenser is good at collaring people he might find useful in the future."

No sooner did they get back than Adam set off in search of the prince, having sworn Kit to secrecy regarding their suspicions about Cassandra.

"I will speak to Lord Roger," he said, "and you have the far more difficult task of pretending things are as they have always been." He grinned and tweaked her cheek. "Maybe you should throw a tantrum or two, yell at the lady to keep her hands off me. That will reassure her that no one has quite understood what she's up to."

"If she's up to something," Kit said.

"We both know she's up to something. The question is if it is merely the seduction of your brother, or if we are talking murder."

Or maybe Cassandra enjoyed causing havoc, Kit reflected, scowling when the lady in question, as if by chance, intercepted her husband halfway across the bailey. That low, gurgling laugh, a hand extended as if to touch him, but Adam gave her no opportunity to do so, exchanging but the curtest of greetings before moving on.

"You said you were a reformed character," Kit hissed when she caught up with Cassandra.

"A momentary lapse, no more," Cassandra said with a shrug. "He's a fine man, your husband – a man I know for a fact leaves a woman sated and happy. After all, I taught him how."

Kit did not have to pretend. Cassandra reeled back, clutching at her cheek, and Kit shook her stinging hand.

"You lay as much as a finger on my husband, and I'll break it."

In response, Cassandra laughed, tossed her head, and left.

Over the coming weeks, Kit kept a close watch over Cassandra de Ley, who had become a ubiquitous presence in the queen's room, a small smile on her mouth whenever Lord Mortimer – or Richard – chanced to look her way. Should Richard approach Kit for conversation, it took but moments before they were joined by Cassandra, all of her attention and tangible allure directed at Richard.

To Kit's vexation, her brother preened like a lovesick puppy under Cassandra's advances — a most nauseating spectacle, which was why Kit was more than happy on those occasions when the queen dismissed her household for the day, saying she needed to time to rest and reflect.

On this particular day, Kit had followed her mistress to the chapel, stayed with her throughout the queen's long, silent prayers, and when Queen Isabella was joined by Queen Jeanne, Kit had taken that as her cue to leave and went to find William instead.

Her brother-in-law gave her a harried look before going back to what he was writing. His fingers were stained, an array of broken quills lay at his feet, and to the side was a stack of neatly folded squares of parchment, awaiting only the wax and the imprint of Mortimer's seal.

"One hundred messages," William groaned, "and how to get them into England I have no idea, not now that King Edward has ordered that every ship that lands at any of his ports be thoroughly searched."

"So don't make for one of the ports," Kit said, peering over his shoulder to read the message. "September?" It made her innards clench: it was happening — not yet, but very soon Lord Mortimer and the queen were going to invade.

William covered the missive with his hand. "You're not supposed to see that." He smiled. "I may have to slit your throat for being privy to Lord Roger's secret plans."

"Does Edward know?"

"The prince?" William shook his head. "I imagine not. The queen speaks for her son, and he will be informed as she sees fit." He gave her a warning look. "It is not for you to tell him."

"I wouldn't want to." Kit adjusted the cloak around her shoulders. "He will not be pleased."

William rubbed at his cheek, leaving a smudge of ink behind. "It is for the best, Kit."

Despite her wheedling, William refused to accompany her for a stroll in the garden, saying he had several more copies to make before vespers. Kit pouted but left, stepping outside to stand for some moments in a bleak ray of February sun.

She was still standing there, nose to the sun, when the prince's voice interrupted her little reverie of sun-drenched meadows back home, with Tom and Meg running through the grass.

"My lady?" He gave her a concerned look. "Are you well?"

"Just enjoying the sun, my lord. We've seen precious little of it lately, haven't we?"

"We have?" The prince shrugged. "I haven't noticed, but then lately I spend little time outdoors." He scuffed at the ground. "Sir Henry has me working at my lessons from prime until mass, and then my lady mother insists I accompany her and Lord Mortimer for some hours." He grinned. "They don't want me spending too much time with Louis, I think."

"But you do anyway." Kit laughed, shaking her head. The prince and his cousin were more or less inseparable, two youths hell-bent on discovering all the pleasures Paris could offer. It made Adam groan at times, falling into bed well after midnight after yet another night of following his lord through the taverns and brothels of Paris. After curfew, only those with writs – and guards – moved through the darkened city, and to Adam's chagrin, Louis had the writs while Edward gladly supplied the guards, namely Adam and some of his other men.

"Less and less. And now Lord Mortimer has offered to teach me about warfare and strategy." Edward sounded eager, a light in his eyes as he went on to tell her just what an excellent military leader Mortimer was. "The best in England, they say," he finished. He looked down at his belt and fingered the hilt of the dagger he was carrying – a gift from Lord Mortimer. "One day, I aim to be the best," he said softly. "I shall be the perfect king – or try to be, at least." Prince Edward scrubbed at his chin, as yet as downy as that of a child, and gave her a long look. "A better king than a son, I hope. I can't be the perfect son. Not to both of them."

"But you do your best, my lord," Kit said with a little smile, feeling sorry for this very young man who was trying so hard to be a good son in both directions.

"I've left my father."

"You were sent here by him. And since then, you've been detained." Kit gave him a crooked smile. Neither Queen Isabella nor Mortimer would ever allow this precious pawn to slip through their fingers – not now, when they'd succeeded in bartering his hand in marriage for the military support of the Count of Hainaut.

In an effort to lighten his mood, she accompanied the prince to the mews, listening patiently as the boy extolled the virtues of his new peregrine falcon, a gift from his royal uncle.

"I've never hunted with a hawk," she said.

"You haven't?" Edward looked at her as if she'd just told him she was from the moon. "Maybe I can teach you," he suggested shyly, peeking at her from under his lashes.

"I'd be honoured, my lord." She smiled, and the boy grinned back.

After an hour of hawks, hounds and horses, they were strolling along in the general direction of the main hall when the sound of murmuring voices from behind a tangle of vines drew them to a stop. Kit recognised Queen Isabella's hair immediately – she herself had helped the queen braid it with silk ribbons earlier this morning. Her veil lay discarded on the ground, and the queen was plastered to Roger Mortimer's broad chest. If it hadn't been for how the gangly youth beside her tensed, Kit would have smiled at the scene: two lovers kissing each other ardently, his hand tangled in her hair, hers cupping his cheek.

"What are they doing?" Edward shifted on his feet. Kit supposed it was a rhetorical question. After his recent escapades in Paris, the prince was well acquainted with what happened between man and woman.

"They're expressing their affection for each other," she said.

"Affection?" Edward took hold of her and dragged her along until the vegetation hid his mother and her lover from their sight. "She's my father's wife!" He sounded devastated, and in that instant Kit realised he had not understood just how close the queen and Mortimer were. No doubt Adam and Sir

Henry had protected him from seeing what everyone else at court could see.

"Your father has spurned her, stolen her dower lands, taken away her income and thrown out her household staff, showing the entire world he no longer trusts her. Do you truly think she can ever forgive him for that?"

"He's her king! She shouldn't..." He fell silent.

"She's a woman. A beautiful, passionate woman who has been relegated to live the life of a nun for years, while your father has been cavorting with others." She regretted the words the moment they were out of her mouth. Prince Edward retreated a couple of paces, breathing heavily through his nose.

"Do you think it's true?" he demanded. "All that gossip about my father and Despenser – is it the truth?"

Kit shrugged. "I don't know for sure – no one knows."

"But what do you think?"

She was tempted to lie to him, but the boy deserved answers, and besides, this future King of England did not take kindly to sycophants.

"I think your father loves Hugh Despenser. And I believe Hugh Despenser loves him back."

The prince made a low, guttural sound and turned his back on her. "It's a sin."

"To love is not a sin, my lord." Kit put a hand on his shoulder. "What has been done in the name of that love might be a sin, but the love itself can never be a sin."

"Two men!" He gave her an anguished look. "If what they say is true, my father is a sodomite – and my mother is a whore."

"A whore?" Kit shook her head. "She is a woman utterly and completely in love with a man – a man who adores her in return, who sings her praises and admires her just as she is."

"A man who has rebelled against my father, and who is as married elsewhere as she is. Where is the honour in that, Lady Kit?"

"Honour?" Kit disregarded protocol and stepped close enough to embrace him. "This has nothing to do with honour, my dearest lord. This is love, an affliction almost, a power so potent it is impossible to fight."

"It is wrong," he moaned, standing as stiff as a poker in her arms.

"Yes it is," she agreed, rubbing her hands up and down his back. "But they can't help it, my lord. So don't judge them, see them for what they are: weak mortals, as fallible as all of us are."

Chapter 26

"You're growing whiskers!" Count Louis made a great show of clutching at his heart and stumbling backwards a couple of paces. "A man! Our prince is truly a man."

"Stop it," Prince Edward mumbled, but could not quite stop himself from brushing a finger over the coarser fair hairs that adorned his upper lip. Adam grinned, recalling with some clarity just how proud he'd been the day when he'd had to ask someone to loan him a sharp blade.

"And will you allow it to grow into a beard, dearest cousin? Cover your face like your countrymen do with all that smelly, unkempt hair?"

Sir Henry gave the count an irritated look, smoothing his hand over his very neat beard.

"It's not something the prince has to decide just yet," Adam put in. "And some Englishmen sport beards, other do not." He patted his own clean-shaven face.

"Your king does," Louis prattled on, oblivious to how the mention of the king had his cousin stiffening. "I recall quite clearly I was mesmerised by it – me a laddie still in smocks, and he this giant with a beautiful golden beard."

Prince Edward smiled – slightly. "A giant?"

"Your lord father is a big man," Sir Henry said. "A strong, powerful man with the grace of a lion."

"And the sense of a donkey," Louis muttered, but only Adam seemed to have heard him.

"My lord father is an aggrieved father," the prince said bitterly, indicating the letter he had received only yesterday. "Yet again, he commands me to return home, and not to marry without his consent." His blue eyes darkened, and Adam assumed he was recalling the rest of the letter's content, effectively branding Queen Isabella a whore for accompanying Mortimer at all times, and accusing his son of potential treason, given that he was openly consorting with that foul Mortimer.

"My mother has told him I am free to return to him, should I wish it," Prince Edward continued. "At times, I am right minded to try." He looked from Adam to Sir Henry, and onwards to his uncle, Edmund of Kent, slouching rather elegantly in the window seat.

Kent made a deprecating sound. "And then what, Ned? Would you prefer to live under the thumb of Despenser to that of your fair mother?"

"It's not my mother's thumb," the prince replied. "It is Mortimer's." There was a drop of venom in his tone, a set to his jaw that had a tingle rushing up Adam's spine.

Kent laughed out loud. "You may be growing whiskers, but you have a long way to go before you truly comprehend the wiles of women." He rose and sauntered over to his nephew. "Mortimer does as your lady mother tells him. Should she ask it of him, he would throw himself off a cliff."

"He does?" The prince sounded quite astounded. "But he—"

"…Is a man. A man captivated by the most beautiful woman of our time." Kent chuckled and cuffed the prince playfully on his shoulder. "Women, eh? We may think we rule the roost and still they have us by our balls."

Adam laughed softly. In his particular hen house, he most certainly ruled the roost – but then he wasn't wed to a lady as fiery or independent as the queen. The thought of Kit having him by the balls – in the literal sense – filled his mind with the most delicious erotic images, and it was with an effort that he returned to the conversation at hand.

"England must be rid of the Despensers," Sir Henry was saying, turning intent eyes on the prince. "Whatever must be done to achieve that must be done, or else you may find yourself heir to an illusion, to a kingdom pawned to the hilt."

The prince mulled this over. "We exile them?"

Kent shook his head. "That doesn't work. As long as they're alive, your father will yearn for them and contrive a way to have them returned to him. The Despensers must die, Ned. With them dies everything that is foul and rotten in England."

Count Louis rolled his eyes. "What is foul and rotten in England is its weak king." He ignored Prince Edward's scowl. "Cousin, look at your grandfathers – both of them. Did Edward, the first of his name, have others rule in his name? And as to my uncle and your grandsire, no one can accuse Philippe le Bel of ever heeding any counsel but his own." He shook out the skirts of his new robe – lined with purple silk, the same colour recurring in the embroidered stars that decorated the black velvet – and sat down in the seat vacated by the earl. "A king, Edward, is a lonely man. A king must be strong enough and wise enough to take decisions that don't please him personally – for the good of his realm."

Adam gave the count an admiring look. Apparently, young Louis was not quite the airhead he pretended to be.

"So what do I do?" Edward asked the room at large.

"Do?" Louis stretched, admiring his new shoes. "You stay here, of course." He flashed Edward a grin. "Your *maman* might spank you otherwise." He howled with laughter when Edward threw himself at him.

"…But by now, they're fast friends again," Adam finished, having recounted the conversation for his wife. Well, not all of it – certain aspects regarding women and their power over their men he had left out. He smiled in the direction of the high table, where the cousins were seated side by side.

"No matter what she wrote to the king, the queen would never allow him to leave," Kit commented, shoving the stewed eels to the side.

No, Adam sighed, of course not. The queen and Lord Roger had concluded their negotiations with the Count of Hainaut, and in some months they'd take Prince Edward to Valenciennes, there to meet his prospective bride, no matter that at present he refused to countenance such an arrangement without his father's approval. Poor lad; the queen would take whatever measures required to bend her son to her will, and come autumn the prince would be tied by vows to the Hainaut wench. Autumn… Adam slid Kit a look, wondering if she knew just how advanced the plans for the invasion were. The Earl of Norfolk had sent word, recommending they land on his shores, and Thomas had added that throughout the country the disenchanted barons were preparing to do battle.

"I already know," she told him when he shared this with her. "The queen was most pleased to hear from Earl Thomas – and from Henry of Lancaster." She lowered her voice. "I was more interested in the message Cassandra de Ley received. It came yesterday, and the lady went quite still upon reading it."

"What did it say?" Adam gestured for one of the serving wenches to pour him some more wine.

Kit snorted. "How would I know? She fed it to the fire immediately."

"Ah." Adam speared a slice of mackerel and offered it to her. With all the fish they were eating, he feared he might soon grow gills instead of lungs, but so far he had survived twenty-nine periods of Lent without that happening. "I shall warn Lord Roger."

"It would be a foolish assassin who attacks him here," Kit said. "If I were them, I'd do it when he rides through Paris. Trap him in in a dark alley and kill him and his companions."

Adam smiled. "Not an easy proposition. Our Lord Mortimer knows how to defend himself – as do his men." He returned his attention to his food, but now and then he looked at Lord Roger and the queen, for the day sitting side by side.

"They are too alike," Adam blurted, nodding at Lord Roger and his lady queen. "Both of them far too bright, far too ambitious. Who will be their voice of reason, when they both think so alike?" He studied his trencher, but did no more than shove the stewed onions back and forth. "Who will stop them, when their campaign to restore order and peace to a sundered kingdom becomes nothing but a bloody retribution?"

"He will," Kit said, indicating the prince.

"Edward? He is but an untried lad – no match at all for either the queen or Lord Roger."

"Untried lads grow into men, Adam." Kit placed a soft kiss on his cheek. "Best Lord Mortimer and his lady love keep that in mind."

After dinner, Kit did some sleuthing of her own, discreetly following Cassandra de Ley as she moved about the castle. There was a long, amorous encounter with Richard that had Kit pulling a face, and with the exception of a lengthy conversation with the castle's apothecary, Cassandra did little to excite Kit's interest. As Kit had need of herbs for her own personal reasons, she trailed Cassandra to the queen's apartments before returning to the apothecary, a wizened old man who constantly chewed his lip. He grunted at the herbs she requested, asked some pointed questions that had Kit's cheeks heating uncomfortably, and told her to sit down while he found them for her.

As she waited, she perused the earthenware jars on the shelves.

"Monkshood?" she asked, tapping at the jar in question. "That's poisonous."

"Very. As are nightshade and foxglove, and henbane and…" The old man waved his hands about. "Poison can be used as medicine – if one is careful with the dosage."

"But monkshood?" She had never heard of anyone using it as other than a poison.

"That is for the rats – and wolves, should we have any." The apothecary grinned. "A nicely sweetened wine – very sweet – and you add some monkshood to it and place it in the cellars. Come morning, there are dead rats everywhere." He shuddered. "It's a terrible, lingering death, causing the victim to vomit and void their bowels before the numbness sets in, making it difficult to breathe. At the end, they die of asphyxiation." He lifted the jar to the top shelf. "I always keep it up here," he grumbled. "One of my idiot apprentices must have moved it down."

"Or maybe one of your previous customers helped herself," Kit said.

"Helped herself?" The apothecary looked down his nose at her. "Ah, you mean the fair Cassandra. No, I can assure you she came for other reasons." He winked. "A love potion, no less."

"She doesn't need potions – all she has to do is to wiggle her hips."

The apothecary laughed. "You mistake lust with love, my lady." He stooped and produced a little bundle of herbs. "But if she places this under his pillow, the young man will be forever smitten with whoever he first lays eyes on when he wakes."

Poor Richard, Kit reflected as she left the apothecary's. Maybe she should warn him to check for bundles of herbs in his bedding.

It was after compline that Kit had time to steep her herbs. She'd sent Aline to bed and supposed Adam would not be back for some while yet, having seen him follow his lord to his chambers. She poured some water from the pitcher into an earthenware pot and set it down on the embers of the fire, tilting it slightly to the side. Once the water boiled, she added rue and tansy, dried raspberry leaves and a pinch of peppermint and stirred, wrapping her hand in her skirts before she lifted the pot to the side.

She had just poured herself a mug when Adam entered the room, bringing with him the smell of spring rains.

"It's raining," he said, shaking his cloak before hanging it up. He crossed over to the window and fastened the shutter before turning to look at her. Kit shifted on her stool and gave him a bland smile, hands clenched around the mug.

"What is it you're drinking?" Adam kneeled before her, a concerned expression on his face. "Are you poorly?"

Kit couldn't reply. She kept her gaze on the earthenware mug, the delicate scents of the infusion tickling her nose.

"Sweeting?" Adam sniffed at the cup. "What is this? Do your…" He cleared his throat. "…Monthlies trouble you?"

"In a manner of speaking," Kit replied, still looking at her cup.

"In a manner of speaking?" Absolute silence for some

moments, and then his hand was under her chin, forcing her face up to meet his eyes. "Is this what I think it is?" He sounded stern. "Are you meddling with life?"

"With life?" Kit twisted free. "I am merely making sure that—"

"There is no new life," he interrupted. "Am I right?"

She hung her head and whispered a yes. A sin, a terrible, terrible sin, and when he took the mug from her and poured its contents into the chamber pot, she did not object, waiting for his anger, his reprimands.

"Why?" was all he said.

Kit chewed her lip, searching for the right words to explain. "I..." She took a deep breath. "I couldn't stand the thought of being left behind when we go back, because you'd not allow me to travel were I big with child." She scuffed at the floor, studying the worn leather of her everyday shoe. "I want to be the first to embrace Tom and Meg again," she mumbled. She drew in a long, shaky breath. "I miss them. Every day I miss them so much."

He was on his knees before her again, cupping her face as gently as if he were cradling an egg. "We will see them soon enough."

"How do you know?" Kit fisted her hands in her kirtle. "They might die, and me not there to hold them, they might be cloistered, or be sent off to other lands, and we will never find them. They might—"

"No," he broke in. "None of that will happen. Our children await us in England, and no matter what else he may do or not do, the king will not allow Despenser to harm them – we have held to our oath, have we not?"

"Have we?" Kit took a shaky breath. "Will the king agree that we have, when we stand to the side and allow Lord Mortimer access to the prince?"

"And how are we to hinder it? The queen wills it so, and she's his mother. Besides, he does not seem to mind, does he? If anything our Edward regards Lord Roger with open admiration." He stroked her cheek. "Our children will be fine, sweeting."

"And when will I see them again?" she groaned.

"I don't know. But I'd hazard this autumn, when we accompany Lord Roger and the queen back to England." Adam brushed his lips over her brow. "As to this other matter, I will not have you drinking such potions. It is a grave sin, to tamper with God's will. What children He gives us, we will gladly receive and cherish." He leaned back to see her face. "Do I have your promise that you will not do such again?"

She could see it in his eyes that he would not accept anything but her acquiescence. Kit nodded once. In matter such as these, she could do nothing but obey – he was her husband, after all.

"Good," he said, kissing her brow again. "And now, let's get to bed before I freeze my balls off."

Come dawn, Kit woke up feeling sore but content. Her husband had chosen to ignore that it was Lent and had loved her repeatedly through the night, and even if she supposed part of his ardour arose from his need to show her that in certain matters he would not be questioned or denied, her Adam was a skilled and tender lover, driving her to repeated climaxes before he finally allowed himself release.

And then there'd been the long whispered conversations, him holding her to his chest as they spoke of their children, rolling her over to kiss her mouth when he told her how much he loved her. She'd needed that, she reflected – more than his loving she'd needed his words, assuring her that she came first in his heart.

She rose on her elbow and smiled down at him, still sunk in sleep. Sprawled on his back, he looked innocent and young, his mouth so much softer in sleep than it was during the day. She needed the chamber pot, and once she slid out of bed she heard the distinctive creaking sound of Cassandra's door opening. Cassandra was rarely up and about before Terce, so maybe she was returning to her room after a secret assignation, but in view of that recent message Cassandra had received, Kit padded to the door and opened it, seeing a glimpse of Cassandra as she made her way down the passage.

Kit followed. Down the stairs Cassandra went. She was carrying a candle, and when she turned a corner, Kit had a fleeting impression of a woman exposing very much skin, hair a cloud of dark brown that framed her head. Where was she going, dressed like that? Belatedly, Kit realised her own state of undress, but Cassandra was walking fast, so Kit hurried on, hoping to God no one would come upon her in only her shift.

It was obvious Cassandra knew exactly where she was going. Kit followed her down to the cellars, shrinking back somewhat at the damp darkness of the large, vaulted space. On tiptoe Kit slid after Cassandra, and was more than relieved when they reached a door that led onto a new set of stairs. She could hear Cassandra's footsteps on the treads, and Kit sneaked after, trying to get her bearings.

A small landing, and with a gasp Kit realised where they were: Mortimer's rooms, and there was Richard, fast asleep on a pallet. No wonder Cassandra had moved with such familiarity through the cellars; she must have been using them frequently to visit Kit's brother, thereby evading the guards at the foot of the stairs. After all, Richard could not leave his post outside Lord Mortimer's door, and so Cassandra had no option but to go to him. Did Cassandra intend to surprise him, slip in below the coverlets? Or maybe she was here to ensure she was the first thing Richard saw upon waking, what with that little posy of dried herbs the apothecary had shown Kit. Somehow, Cassandra did not strike her as a person who placed much trust in silly little bouquets.

There was a clatter, a murmured curse, and on the pallet bed Richard shifted a couple of times before rolling over on his side, eyes still firmly closed. What was Cassandra doing? Kit peeked round the corner. And then she understood, watching with horror as Cassandra produced a small stone flask and with a trembling hand poured careful measures from it into the two pitchers of wine that stood upon the table.

Kit took a careful step backwards, another. All she needed to do was to hide, and once Cassandra was gone, she'd wake Richard and warn him not to drink the wine. She caught her foot on something and stumbled, incapable of suppressing her exclamation.

"Who goes there?" Cassandra hissed. On the bed, Richard shifted restlessly. Kit opened her mouth to scream his name, but she never got the chance, because Cassandra pounced. Moments later, there was a knife at her throat and she was being manhandled down the stairs.

"Spying on me, were you?" Cassandra increased the pressure on the knife, causing Kit to whimper. "How unfortunate for you – and your man – that you should choose today to follow me." Cassandra cackled in her ear. "Very unfortunate indeed."

Adam woke to the sound of their door being banged closed. He sat up in bed, not quite understanding why Cassandra was in their room, and why she was holding a blade to Kit's throat. His jaw tensed as he saw the blood, thin rivulets that decorated Kit's skin.

"What is this?" he snapped, leaping out of bed.

"Don't!" Cassandra yanked Kit's head back. "Stay where you are – don't move until I tell you to."

Adam crossed his arms over his chest. "Is this about me again?" he asked – not because he thought so, but because he needed to win time.

"You? What do I care about you? Do you truly think you were that unforgettable? An enthusiastic pup with more cock than skill, that was what you were – a plaything." Her dark eyes glittered. "But without your dear wife and her brother, I would never have gained access to Mortimer, and by noon he'll be dead – as will you." She laughed. "It was Richard who indirectly showed me how to do it, telling me that every night he brought up wine from the cellars so as to have it on hand to serve Mortimer mulled and sweetened wine in the morning."

Cassandra released her hold on Kit's hair and tossed him a small bottle. "Pour yourself a cup of wine," she instructed, "and then add that. Do it!" Yet another line of bright red appeared on Kit's throat.

Adam did as he was told.

"Good. Now drink it. Monkshood makes for a painful death, but at least you'll be sharing in your beloved baron's fate."

"You think me a fool?" Adam shoved the cup away. "I have no desire to die."

Cassandra forced Kit to her knees, the blade of her knife sinking into Kit's skin. "Drink!" she hissed. "Drink or I will slit her throat."

"No," Kit gargled. "She'll kill me anyway." Her blue eyes met his, her inhalations accompanied with a whistling sound when Cassandra increased the pressure.

Adam agreed; Cassandra would never let Kit live – how could she? He tightened his hold on the heavy cup. If only... He calculated the distance, dropped his eyes to the cup, raised them to Kit's. Did she understand what he intended to do? He hefted the goblet a couple of times. She blinked once. Adam's guts tightened. He would be gambling his wife's life on Cassandra's reluctance to kill her before he himself was safely dead.

One last look at Kit, and his breath hitched. God, she was beautiful, kneeling in her bloodied shift, her dark red hair tumbling down her back. God, how he loved her, this woman who looked at him with so much trust shining out of her eyes.

"Do it!" Cassandra's voice cracked through the quiet of the room. "Do it now, or else..."

Adam rounded his shoulders. "I can't let her kill you," he said, raising the cup.

"No!" Kit extended her arms towards him. "No, don't!" She screamed, a sound of pure fear.

"Be quiet!" Cassandra lifted the knife off Kit's throat and struck her over the head with the hilt.

That was all the opportunity Adam needed. The goblet flew through the air, hitting Cassandra full in the face, and moments later she was flat on her back, Adam's hands at her throat.

Cassandra sputtered and squirmed like a viper in his hold, attempting to stab him with her dagger. Enough. Adam had a wife to see to. He lifted Cassandra's head off the floor and brought it down with a loud thump. Again, and she went limp, her head lolling to the side when he released his hold.

"Kit?" He cradled her to him. She was alive, she was warm and soft, blood oozing from the shallow gash circling her throat. "Kit?"

No words, just her hands on his cheeks, his hair, that beautiful mouth of hers trembling as she continued her tactile inspection. With a little moan, she pressed her face against his chest, and he held her to his heart and rocked her, silent tears trickling down his cheeks.

"Mortimer," she croaked. "We must warn him. If he drinks the doctored wine..." She shivered, looking with loathing at the unconscious Cassandra. She sat up, looking unusually pale in the silvered light of the returning dawn. "Go!" she urged him. "Run!"

"But what about her?" Adam gestured at Cassandra, whose limbs were beginning to twitch.

"Her?" Kit rose. "I'll manage, but you must make haste."

Without another word, Adam left the room.

Chapter 27

They hanged Cassandra de Ley on a Monday morning. And once she was properly dead, King Charles ordered her taken down and buried in unconsecrated ground. She died defiant, screaming curses at the assembled people while the noose was fastened around her neck.

"A close shave," Richard said to Adam, shivering despite the March sun. "Had you come but a moment later, it would have been too late – for me at least."

Adam nodded, recollecting Richard's shocked expression when he had thrown himself at him and knocked the goblet with its steaming wine to the floor.

"Well, you're still here," William said from Richard's other side. "That's twice our Kit has saved you from death."

"Our Kit?" Richard sounded amused, looking from Adam to William. "Surely you're not sharing her?"

He doubled over when Adam punched him in the gut. "That was not funny," Adam said. "And you'd best think twice about how you refer to *my* wife in the future, dear brother."

"I didn't mean it like that!" William helped Richard straighten up. "You know I didn't. Kit is my beloved sister, nothing more, nothing less."

"Tell him that," Adam snarled, pointing at Richard, who was still struggling for breath.

"My apologies," Richard wheezed. "Sweetest mother of God, but you pack a good punch, Adam." He wiped at his face.

"Next time it won't be my fist!" Adam turned, shouldered his way through the people surrounding the gallows, and ducked into one of the crooked streets that criss-crossed the Ile-de-la-Cité.

"What's the matter with you?" William caught up with him.

"Leave me alone." Adam threw him a surly look.

"Ever since that morning, you've been like an irascible bear where Kit is concerned, and—"

"Does that surprise you? *My* wife, *my* Kit, she nearly died!" Adam fisted his hand and studied his sore knuckles. "How would I have gone on without her?"

"A question you don't need to think about at present." William draped his arm around Adam's shoulder and gave him a hard, one-armed hug.

"A question I would have preferred never to start pondering," Adam retorted, half-closing his eyes at the memory of his wife, the blood on her throat and Cassandra's fingers whitening on the hilt of the knife. Had his aim been off, had she not raised her arm, had…He swallowed, coughed, and swallowed again. "It makes me feel vulnerable."

"Love does that to you," William replied with a smile in his voice. He gave Adam yet another squeeze. "But it also gives you strength and resilience – there's very little you wouldn't do for her, is there?"

Adam laughed. "Best not tell her that."

"Fool – she already knows."

Before them loomed the main façade of Notre Dame, the open space in front crowded with market stands, with moneylenders and whores. Everything was for sale in the shadow of God's house, and the truly pious had to navigate through the flotsam of sin and perdition to make it to the heavy, open doors.

Inside, it was silent. After the brightness of the day outside, it was dark – a collection of shadows lit by the odd, flaring light of a candle. Adam followed William down the nave and accompanied his brother in his prayers, peace descending on him as he thanked the Lord for his wife's life.

He was still on his knees when his scalp began to prickle. Beside him, William was sunk in meditation, eyes closed, face raised towards the heavens. Adam held his breath, trying to isolate the sounds that had all of him tingling. A soft shuffle, the swish of cloth as someone approached them stealthily. A spy? An assassin? Adam whirled, launched himself to the side and came up with his dagger in his hand. Prince Edward gave a startled yelp, stumbled, caught his foot and went down on his rump.

"My lord?" Adam helped the prince to his feet. "What are you doing here? And where is your escort?"

"I slipped away from them." The lad managed a grin, and Adam cursed. Incompetent oafs. "I…" Edward licked his lips. "I saw you were upset," he said in a rush. "At the hanging."

"I was." Adam looked away. "She could have killed my wife."

"And Lord Mortimer." The prince looked away. "It would have grieved my mother to lose him."

Adam nodded, no more.

"It would have been a loss to England as well," Prince Edward went on, glancing at Adam. His voice hardened. "A man so without honour as to send out assassins to kill his rivals should not sit so close to the throne. And from what Sir Henry tells me, Despenser has promised barrels of silver to whomever brings him Mortimer's head."

"To be fair, Lord Despenser does it on behalf of the king," William put in. "They fear Mortimer's return."

"As they should." Prince Edward squared his shoulders. "The queen, I fear, is right. Unless she takes it upon herself to restore order to the kingdom, England will collapse under the double yoke of Despenser, father and son." He crossed himself. "But please God, keep my father safe." It came out in a whisper, and Adam's heart went out to him.

Prince Edward insisted that they return to the palace at speed, as Philippe de Valois had just ridden in.

"Louis says it has quite gone to his brother's head, his father dying and leaving him head of the Valois," the prince explained as they walked hastily in the direction of the royal castle. "He also says Philippe is praying the queen is delivered of a girl." He made a face. "He wants the crown for himself."

"Ah." Not, in Adam's opinion, an unlikely outcome. Philippe de Valois was the closest relative to the king – descended through the male line.

"I am closer to King Charles than he is," the prince continued. "After all, I am his nephew, not his cousin." He came to a halt and swirled on his toes, arms wide. "And to be king of all this…" He grinned. "Maman says it could happen."

"One thing at the time, my lord," Adam said, irritated with the queen for feeding her son's ambitious dreams. The French would no more countenance the heir of England as their king than they would accept a leprous whore as their queen.

"A magnificent entrance," William commented to Adam when they finally reached the palace. Adam could only agree. Given the number of retainers presently crowding the palace courtyard, the Count of Valois had left no one at home. Banners flew, dogs barked, horses snorted, and in the midst of all this chaos stood the count himself, a striking figure in blue.

Philippe de Valois was a long-limbed man, with eyes as sharp as flints and a prominent cleft chin, a feature he shared with his cousin, King Charles. He was also, or so rumour had it, a man obsessed with the French crown – a trait he had inherited from his father, that magnificent old warhorse Charles de Valois.

There was a disturbance by the hall, and people fell away, bowing deeply as King Charles made his way towards his cousin, arms extended to embrace him. Behind the king came his young wife, accompanied by Queen Isabella and Count Louis.

"He's here to attend the upcoming coronation," Prince Edward said as he made his way towards his mother.

"Him and everyone else," Adam muttered. Paris was heaving with people requested to be present at the coronation of Queen Jeanne – at present a radiant queen, swelling with child. The entire nation was praying that their young queen would present them with a son, and in the seedier parts of Paris a man could win – or lose – a fortune by wagering on the gender of the unborn child.

Once he'd ensured his young lord was safe and sound with his mother, Adam went to find Kit. She wasn't in their room, and neither Gavin nor Aline had seen her. Hmm. Adam pursed his mouth. At present, it made him itch all over if he didn't know where she was, so he did a thorough search of the palace, relaxing when he discovered her engrossed in a chess game with Richard.

"Who's winning?" Adam asked, studying the board. He smothered a chuckle at the irritated look the contestants threw him. They were remarkably alike at times, both of them favouring their father in looks.

"Lord Mortimer?" he asked, seeing as none of them seemed inclined to talk.

"In there." Richard gestured to Lord Mortimer's room. "Go right in – he won't mind."

Lord Mortimer was standing in the middle of his room, surrounded by a bevy of tailors. He was holding his arms out, attempting to hold still as the dark blue velvet was adjusted and tweaked – new clothes for his prominent role in the upcoming coronation. "I am to carry the prince's robes," he said with a wink. "An honour indeed."

"The prince is more than excited." At present, the only thing his lord talked about was the upcoming ceremony, and when he found Adam an unsympathetic audience, he turned to Kit instead.

"A coronation is always a coronation." Mortimer tugged a pleat into place. "King Edward will choke on bile when he hears of this."

"He will," Adam agreed, imagining just how King Edward would rage when he learnt that the French king had done Mortimer the honour of not only attending the coronation, but also by doing so in close proximity to Prince Edward. "I'm not sure—"

He was interrupted by the door banging open. With impressive speed, Lord Roger lunged for the shears on the nearby table, and coiled, ready to spring.

"Father?" The young man in the doorway stared at Lord Roger and the raised shears.

"God's truth, Geoffrey!" Three strides and Lord Roger had his son enfolded in a tight embrace – an uncomfortable exercise, to judge from the younger Mortimer's face. He met Adam's gaze over his father's shoulder and grinned. Adam grinned back, struggling to recognise the boy he had last seen as a combination of spindly limbs and intense, dark eyes. There was nothing spindly about this well-grown young man, but his eyes were as determined as ever.

"Adam." Geoffrey punched him lightly in greeting.

"My lord." Adam grinned. This was the laddie he'd taught to ride, to swim, and now look at him: a man – almost. "You rode in with Count Valois?"

"No." Geoffrey laughed. "We just happened to arrive together. Except that the count made an entrance, while we sneaked in." He nodded at his father. "New clothes?"

"For the coronation." Lord Roger waved away the tailor. "It's good to see you, son."

"Really?" Geoffrey sounded uninterested as he plucked a date from the bowl on the table and bit into it. "You've been back in France since December," he said through his full mouth. "And you haven't sent for me." He regarded Lord Roger. "As I hear it – as everyone hears it – you are busy elsewhere."

"Do they?" Lord Roger sounded unperturbed. "Busy with what?" His voice dropped to an icy whisper. "Well?" he barked, when Geoffrey swallowed, his cheeks a painful shade of red.

"They—"

"What?" Lord Roger loomed over his son.

"You have a wife, Father!" Geoffrey shoved at him.

"I have a queen!" Lord Roger hissed. "And that is all I have, y'hear? I have nothing – nothing! – unless my lady queen succeeds in her venture."

"Father," Geoffrey stuttered. "I heard—"

"Yes?" Lord Roger locked eyes with his son.

"Nothing." With a mumbled comment about seeing to his lodgings, Geoffrey escaped.

"Damn!" Lord Roger dragged his hand through his hair and collapsed into a chair.

"They're bound to find out, my lord," Adam said. "You have not been discreet."

"Why do I get the impression you're enjoying this, Adam?" Lord Roger poured himself some wine. His hand was shaking, and the haggard look on his face had Adam's gut clenching.

"I'm not," he replied. "But surely you must expect your children to side with your lady wife?"

"I expect everyone to side with my wife," Lord Roger said bitterly.

"Everyone but me," a soft voice said from the door. Lord Roger made as if to stand, but the queen shook her head. She approached, settled her hands on his shoulders and leaned over to kiss him on his forehead. His hand floated up, caressing her cheek. Adam chose to leave.

Philippe of Valois was not only in Paris to attend the coronation – that became very apparent when the count demanded a meeting with the queen and Mortimer. The prince was included as well – more out of politeness than any real regard for the lad – and so Adam was present when Philippe de Valois began by telling his sweet cousin that she'd overstayed her welcome in France.

"Really?" Queen Isabella murmured. "And is that your opinion or that of my dear brother?"

"It is the opinion of France," Philippe replied stiffly.

"So you speak for France while its king does not?" Queen Isabella laughed. "I don't think Charles will like to hear that."

De Valois went a bright red. "Charles is your brother and cares for you – as he should. He does not always set the interest of his kingdom before those of his family."

"Ah. And you do?" The queen picked up a honey wafer and nibbled at it.

Philippe poured himself some more wine, sat back in his armchair and studied her. "France is always foremost on my mind, dear cousin."

"I can imagine," Lord Roger said drily.

"It should be." Philippe gave Prince Edward a sly look. "Should Charles die without a male heir – and may God please bless my cousin with a son – then I am next in line to the throne."

"Or me," Edward said.

"Ambition is admirable indeed in one so young," Philippe said with a smile that did not reach his eyes. "Foolhardiness, however, is not a virtue."

Edward flushed, eyes narrowing into streaks of brilliant blue.

Philippe leaned forward. "And should you not be concentrating on setting your present kingdom in order before thinking of expanding it?"

"My kingdom?" Edward frowned. "It is my father's kingdom."

"For now," Philippe agreed. "But no one lives forever – and some die sooner than others."

The prince paled, hand dropping to the hilt of his dagger.

"Philippe!" Queen Isabella gave him a furious look. "What exactly are you insinuating?"

"Me?" Philippe smirked, drained his goblet and set it down on the table. "Nothing, dear cousin. But keep in mind that just as you will do anything for your son, so will I do anything for mine." He smiled. "In difference to dear Charles, I already have an heir – and isn't that marvellous news for France?"

"But of course you are on your knees daily, praying that Jeanne's baby will be a boy, aren't you?" Queen Isabella retorted.

"Ah, just like you, you mean?" Philippe said, and Adam couldn't quite stop himself from smiling. If the queen was spending any time praying for Queen Jeanne's safe delivery – and he found that unlikely – it was for a girl.

"Of course," the queen replied demurely.

Philippe left, and she turned to her son, but when she tried to approach him, he retreated.

"Leave me alone."

"Son," she tried. "He was just—"

"I know." He cut her off. "Just as I know that you are using me against my father." Edward glared at the queen. "And I don't like it that everyone seems to think that I have chosen you over him. But I didn't, not knowingly. You made that choice for me, Maman – you and your lover!" With that he stormed from the room.

Queen Isabella made to go after him, but Lord Roger stopped her.

"Not now," he said. "Let him cool his temper a bit." He shared a hasty look with Adam and grimaced, mouthing 'sons'.

The prince took his anger out on Adam. Not in so many words, but that afternoon during sword practice, Edward was an unstoppable whirlwind, coming at Adam over and over again. The lad was not much of a challenge for Adam as such – and the wooden staves they were using as swords ensured any injury was restricted to painful bruises – but when the prince succeeded in bringing his stave down on Adam's right foot, the odds were somewhat evened, with Adam unable to move quite as nimbly as required to sidestep the prince's hailstorm of blows.

Even then, Adam could easily have ended things. A few quick feints, a rap or two over his lord's hand, and their mock duel would have been over, but instead Adam concentrated on his defence, allowing the prince to come at him time after time, roaring in anger as he attacked, crashed his stave into Adam's, danced away and did it all again.

They were both drenched in sweat and had collected a number of interested spectators. Adam's foot was on fire, the prince lunged and swore, then retreated to draw a couple of breaths. A swift swipe from Adam had the prince overbalancing, and in retaliation he went after Adam's foot. Adam parried. The prince turned, darted to Adam's left, to his right, to his left, ducked and with a grunt struck Adam's foot, so hard Adam went down on his knee. At the last moment, he brought up his stave to parry his lord's vicious overhanded blow.

"My lord!" Sir Henry's voice cut like a whiplash through the air. "Stop that – now! Adam is hurt."

Prince Edward cursed, gripped the stave in both hands and brought it down with such force on the ground that it splintered. He threw the remnants down and stalked off.

"How could he do this to you?" Kit's voice was raw with anger as she carefully set Adam's foot to soak. The water turned a dirty brown as the dried blood dissolved. Adam carefully flexed his toes. He'd be limping badly for at least a week.

"He wasn't angry with me," Adam said. "He was just angry at the world in general." It hurt when she worked her way over his foot, and he gritted his teeth when she wrapped it in tight bandages.

"He knows your foot is damaged! Where is the honour in besting a man by striking at his weak point?"

"I was merely doing as Adam has taught me," the prince said from the doorway.

"Really?" Kit rose to her feet, bowl in hands. Without another word, she threw the contents at the prince and left the room.

Prince Edward wiped at his face. Adam just stared.

"One could almost believe I've displeased Lady Kit more than you," the prince said.

"Oh, you have, my prince. It will take time for her to forgive you for this – she is prickly when it comes to my foot and the humiliation it causes me."

The prince looked as if he wanted the floor to open below him. "I'm sorry," he muttered. "I didn't mean to—"

"Yes you did, my lord," Adam interrupted. "And just as you said, you were simply exploiting my weakness to win." He reached forward and ruffled his master's hair. "I have taught you well, it seems. You will make an excellent warrior king, my lord – a king who fights not for glory and honour but to win and survive."

To his surprise, the prince buried his face in Adam's tunic.

"My lord?" Adam hugged the lad to him. Edward just shook his head, and so all Adam did was hold him, saying nothing at all.

Chapter 28

In May, the court returned to Vincennes. This time the centre of attention was the newly crowned Queen Jeanne, who went happily into her confinement, assuring the king that she would soon present him with an heir. The king merely smiled and doubled the number of monks he had praying for the safe delivery of – please God – a son.

After months in Paris, Kit could not get enough of the sprawling gardens that surrounded the palace, preferring to spend as much of her time as she could outdoors. At present, Adam spent most of his days cloistered with Lord Mortimer and Prince Edward, long sessions in which Mortimer and the queen reviewed their plans for the coming weeks.

All Kit knew was that they were soon to ride for Valenciennes, and with every day she could see the prince becoming increasingly nervous. Once in Hainaut, he'd have no choice but to agree to the betrothal, thereby openly defying his father. Even if she hadn't quite forgiven Prince Edward for the incident with Adam's foot – this despite a most abject apology – Kit was sufficiently concerned to question the wisdom in having the poor boy involved in all these plans, but Adam had explained that it was for the best, ensuring the prince understood that the only objective behind the planned invasion was to reinstate order in the realm of England – and do away with the Despensers.

"And do you believe that is true?" she'd asked him. He'd given her a dark look.

"I don't know." He sighed and sat down beside her. "I don't think either the queen or Lord Roger have any notion of what to do with the king. Can one keep a king imprisoned, do you think?"

"Not for long," Kit had replied. "Sooner or later, someone will raise their banners and set out to free him."

"Exactly," Adam had said.

Well, Kit thought, shoving these dark ruminations away from her, at present they weren't in England, and there was no king with a fate to consider, so why expend energy on speculating on things that might never come to pass? Besides, she had other things on her mind, first and foremost that brief missive from William's friend at Tewkesbury, assuring them that both Tom and Meg were hale and hearty, the little girl now walking on her own.

It left her feeling bereft, somehow: her daughter's first steps, and she'd not been there to see them, just as she hadn't been there to dress Tom in his first tunic. To comfort herself, she took Aline with her and retired to a secluded spot in the garden, spending the afternoon in the dappled shade while working on Adam's new shirt.

They were on their way back to their rooms when Kit collided with someone in the dark passage separating the garden from the inner courtyard. A flurry of veils and kirtles, a lot of loud apologies and Kit straightened up, only to shrink back against the nearby wall. Lady Cecily! There was no woman on earth Kit feared as much as this particular lady, so to come upon her like this was the equivalent of meeting the Devil himself, complete with cleft hooves and horns. Kit sidled away, glad of the presence of Aline at her back.

"Ah, the impostor," Lady Cecily purred, one elongated hand brushing at her veil. Like talons, those long fingers, even more so when they crooked ever so slightly, each finger adorned by a long, immaculate nail. Widowhood had not improved Lady Cecily's looks. As narrow-faced as ever, she regarded the world from deeply hooded eyes that spat blue fire – and at present all that heat was directed at Kit, making her fear her kirtle would soon burst into flames.

"What are you doing here?" Last Kit heard, Lady Cecily remained on her vast estates just north of Bordeaux.

"Not, I think, any concern of yours, is it?" Lady Cecily said. "But if you must know, I am here to see my son." She approached Kit, dark skirts swirling. "I owe your husband for the life of my son," she said. "Had it not been for him,

Richard would have ended up dead in the Tower – together with Lord Mortimer." Her eyes glittered. "Dangerous information. What would Despenser say if I were to present him with a document naming Adam de Guirande as one of the men behind Lord Mortimer's escape?" She leaned closer. "And I can even provide a detailed account of events. My son shares everything with his mother."

"Your son would not forgive you if you betrayed the men who helped him." Kit breathed through her mouth. This close, Lady Cecily emitted a sour tang of unwashed linen and wet ashes, as if she'd been set alight by a bolt of lightning and had the resulting fires doused in urine.

"No, there is that." Lady Cecily tapped her finger to her mouth. "Some people would consider the slate wiped clean: you husband saved my son, and so I should forgive you the death of my daughter. But I don't, and you will pay!" She made as if to grab at Kit, but Kit evaded her hand and retreated several steps.

"I had nothing to do with your daughter's death," she said. "You poisoned your own child."

"I did?" Lady Cecily cackled. "And yet, who benefited? Me?" She shook her head from side to side. "Oh no, most certainly not I, bereft of my eldest daughter. But you…" She extended a claw-like finger in the direction of Kit. "You stole her name and her place. My dead husband's ambitious bastard daughter, out to feather her own nest, and what better way to do so than to murder her half-sister and pretend to be her?"

Aline gasped, and Kit swung to face her.

"That is not how it happened," Kit protested. Lady Cecily had threatened her into marrying Adam when her precious Katherine refused to marry a low-born knave like him. Kit licked her lips. "You coerced me into impersonating your daughter so as not to risk your position with Lord Mortimer."

Lady Cecily sniffed. "And who will believe you over me?" she asked with a malicious smile. She leaned forward. "I will have my revenge on you, little Kit. That, Lady de Guirande, is a promise." There was a rustle, and she was gone, hastening across the courtyard.

"A she-devil," Aline whispered, crossing herself.

"Who?" Kit gave her maid a long look. "She or I?"

"She, of course." Aline smiled shyly. "You would never poison anyone, my lady, it's not in your temperament." She gripped Kit by the elbow and hastened them across the worn tiles, making for the sunny courtyard beyond. "You must tell your husband, my lady."

Kit nodded and lengthened her stride, making for their room on the opposite side of the courtyard.

Adam listened in silence, cursed, and stalked out of their room, returning an hour later to tell her Lady Cecily had already left, having stopped by on her way to Paris.

"That was a brief visit," Kit said.

"Very." Adam grimaced. "It may have had something to do with Richard yelling at her, and telling her that he would not have her defaming your good name."

"Oh." A surge of warmth rushed through her.

"She left your sister," Adam added. "Alicia is to serve the queen."

"Isn't there a younger boy as well?" Kit asked, making Adam grin.

"It's your family, not mine," he teased, before confirming that yes, there was a young lad named Roger, but he remained in Bordeaux.

At sixteen, Alicia de Monmouth was as narrow-faced and sharp-nosed as her mother. Angular features combined with sharp eyes and long limbs to give the poor girl a general resemblance to a stork, already half a head taller than any other lady in the room.

"Poor child," Queen Isabella murmured. "She has her looks from her mother."

"And her temperament," Kit murmured back. "Alicia is as prickly as a hedgehog."

Despite her efforts to approach this unknown sister, Alicia consistently cold-shouldered her, making it very clear she knew exactly what Kit was — a fraud.

As Alicia found confidence in her new surroundings, she set to spreading rumours, and soon the entire court of Vincennes had heard Lady Cecily's version of events. Ladies sniffed and retracted their skirts when Kit passed, and behind her back she heard them murmur, "bastard" and "murderess".

"Ignore them," Adam said, looking preoccupied. His mind was elsewhere lately, their time together restricted to the odd moments before he fell asleep, exhausted after yet another day of military strategy with Mortimer.

"Ignore them?" She set her hands on her hips. "How can I?"

"She's a malicious little minx, sweeting. I'll talk to Richard and have him take her to task."

Adam was true to his word, and one day Alicia appeared at mass with red-rimmed, swollen eyes and mumbled an insincere apology to Kit. But the damage was done all the same.

A fortnight later, Lady Cecily came back, this time to visit her daughter, and suddenly it was no longer whispers – it was pointed fingers and demands that someone do something lest the murderess kill again.

"I haven't killed anyone!" Kit's voice rose. "And she, witch that she is, knows the truth." She gripped at her skirts. "I can't bear it anymore, Adam. I daren't even show my face, and today even the queen looked askance at me." She began to cry. "Why is she doing this to me? She started all of this, not me!" And it didn't help that Kit had been struggling with morning sickness these last few weeks, but that was something she chose not to tell him – not yet.

Adam didn't reply. He just took her by the hand and set off at speed.

"Where are we going?" Kit asked, having to run to keep up.

"This ends now. Unless that evil toad of a woman retracts everything she's said, I'll accuse her openly of murder."

He went to Mortimer first. "I have to," he explained. "He was just as fooled as I was."

Kit stood to the side and squirmed under Lord Mortimer's weighty stare, feeling soiled. After Mortimer, they went to the queen, and now Adam left it to Kit to tell her story. Once she was done, the queen raised her brows.

"You're Sir Thomas' bastard? The daughter he had with the salter's wench?" Her tone slashed Kit to pieces, and she retreated into the safety of her husband's arms.

"She is the woman who recently saved Lord Mortimer's life, my lady," Adam said stiffly, and the queen blushed and looked away.

"And are you content with her?" The queen asked, causing yet another wave of mortified heat to flood Kit's cheeks.

"Need you ask?" Adam raised Kit's hand to his lips. "My lady wife pleases me in all aspects."

The queen's lips quivered, a smile tugging at the corner of her mouth. "How gallant." She straightened up. "Have Richard fetch his mother and sister," she told Adam, "and have Lord Mortimer join us as well."

A heavy silence fell when Adam left the room. Kit retired to stand by the window, keeping her gaze stubbornly on the swaying branch of a lime tree. Behind her, she could hear the queen pacing back and forth.

"You should have told me before," Queen Isabella said.

Kit hitched her shoulders. It had not been her secret to tell. She leaned against the wall, wishing it were the whitewashed stone wall of Tresaints she had under her cheek, rather than the golden sandstone of Vincennes.

"I'm not sure I can allow you to remain among my ladies," the queen continued, sounding disapproving, and Kit was tempted to yell at her that at least she was not an adulteress, but she wisely held her tongue.

"You will do as it pleases you, my lady," she said instead.

Any further conversation was brought short by the arrival of Mortimer, closely followed by Richard, Lady Cecily and Alicia.

"What is this?" Richard asked, bowing to the queen and Mortimer.

"It is a matter of murder – and slander," Mortimer replied, pouring himself and the queen some wine. Adam entered the room and came over to where Kit was standing, placing himself as a bulwark between her and Lady Cecily.

"Slander?" Lady Cecily laughed shrilly. "How can it be slander when it is true?"

"Mother!" Richard shot her a furious look.

"Let us start with the basics," the queen said. "Is Kit your sister, yes or no?"

"Yes," said Richard.

"No," said Alicia.

Lady Cecily snickered. "That is not my daughter."

"No?" Mortimer looked at her. "And yet, I distinctly recall your presence at the wedding when Kit here was wed to Adam. And I do not recall you ever expressing that the bride was not your trueborn child."

Lady Cecily paled. "It…" she stuttered. "I…"

"It was Mother's idea," Richard cut her off. "When Katherine chose to run off, it was Mother who abducted Kit and—"

"Silence!" shrieked Lady Cecily, but Richard ignored her.

"Father didn't even know – not until the wedding day itself, and by then it was too late." Richard ducked his head. "It was wrong, my lord – wrong against you, against Adam, but also against Kit. It wasn't her fault she was an eerie double of her runaway sister."

"Hmm," said Mortimer, crossing his arms over his chest. "So what happened to little Kate?" His mouth softened into a little smile, his gaze darting over to Kit.

"She died." Richard looked away.

"She killed her!" Lady Cecily stabbed her finger at Kit. "She poisoned my precious daughter, and—"

"You poisoned her, Mother!" Richard interrupted. "Aye, though your intent was not to kill Kate, it was to kill Kit."

The queen inhaled, looking at Kit, then at Lady Cecily. "Kill Kit?"

"She stole my daughter's life," Lady Cecily said coldly. "My daughter needed it back."

"I never stole anything," Kit replied. "You forced me into this."

"So you say," Lady Cecily said, "but then you would,

would you not? What future did you have, the bastard daughter of a minor landowner? None!"

"Stop this, Mother – now." Richard gave his mother a shake. "My mother prepared a casket of her famous almond sweetmeats and ordered Kate to deliver them to me – together with a sealed letter. She laced the sugar paste with poison – deadly nightshade, my father believed – and instructed me to deliver them to Kit. Unfortunately, Mother did not inform my sister of what exactly was in the casket, and as Kate was ever an inquisitive person, she helped herself."

"Lies," Lady Cecily said. "The poor boy has developed a fondness for his half-sister and is lying to protect her."

"Developed a fondness?" Richard spluttered. "I owe her my life! Twice, I might add."

"What?" Lady Cecily blinked.

"You heard," Richard said, regarding his mother as if she were a lethal snake. "My saviour – my beloved sister – and you set out to ruin her reputation out of spite."

"Your beloved sister?" Lady Cecily advanced on her son. "Your sister is dead. Dead! And she…" Lady Cecily swung round to point at Kit. "She poisoned her."

"I still have your letter," Richard broke in. "Do you want me to get it?"

Lady Cecily licked her mouth, cleared her throat as if to say something, then licked her mouth again.

"Richard," Alicia gasped. "How can you? Your own mother!"

"Unfortunately," Richard replied. "Had my father lived, she would have been placed in a nunnery, there to pray until her dying day for absolution from her sins."

"A nunnery? Me?" Lady Cecily laughed out loud. "I'd have liked to see him try."

"Enough!" Mortimer strode forward. "You, Lady Cecily – and you, Alicia – have made some very grave accusations against Kit. But from what Richard says, it is you who is the murderess, not Kit."

Lady Cecily gave her son a look that should have reduced him to a heap of ashes on the spot.

"I—" she began, but Mortimer waved her quiet.

"Yet another poisoner," he muttered. "What is it with women and poison?" He gave Lady Cecily a disgusted look. "Now, either we take this whole matter to the law – and if we do, I will personally make sure you hang – or you stand up before the entire court tomorrow at mass and publicly admit to your horrendous slandering of an innocent woman."

"I will do nothing of the sort!" Lady Cecily straightened up to her considerable height.

"Oh, you will," Mortimer assured her. "If not, I dare say a stay at the Chateau Gaillard can be arranged – in the dungeons."

Lady Cecily paled, while Alicia emitted a series of high-pitched little squeaks. Kit could well understand them. It was said the dungeons were damp and dark, so deep underground there was no natural light at all.

"We will do it," Alicia said, gripping her mother's arm. "We will make public penance tomorrow – please don't throw us in the dungeons, my lord! Please don't hang my mother."

Mortimer raised his brows at Lady Cecily. "Well? Will you do as your daughter says?"

Lady Cecily's spine bowed. She nodded, once.

"Good," Mortimer said. "And after you've done your penance it is best you return home, or what say you, my lady queen?"

"I agree. There is no place for either of you at my court."

"But…" Alicia's bottom lip wobbled. "My lady queen, I—"

"I have no place for malicious gossips in my household," the queen said, and Alicia's features crumpled. Kit experienced a surge of pity for this unknown sister, forced to live under the thumb of Lady Cecily.

"My lady," she therefore said, "Alicia is not to blame – at least not entirely. Why not give her an opportunity to prove herself?"

Queen Isabella gave her a chilly look. "Very well," she replied. "Alicia can stay – she can take over your tasks."

Lady Cecily cackled gleefully, Richard looked mortified, and from the way Adam was holding his breath, Kit surmised he was furious. The queen waved her hand in dismissal and Kit followed Adam out of the door.

"Thank you," she said to Richard once they were outside. Lord Mortimer had arranged for an escort to take Lady Cecily and Alicia back to their room, where they would remain under lock and key until tomorrow's mass.

"What else could I do?" He made a face. "At present, the fact that we don't share the same mother is a point in your favour. I'm not sure I ever want to see her again."

"Do you have the letter?" Kit found it hard to believe Richard had held on to much private correspondence over the recent years.

"No – but she didn't know that, did she?"

"More to the point, would you have complied with your mother's instructions?" Adam asked.

Richard's brows came together in one fiery, bristling line. "Of course not," he snapped. "I may not have liked Kit much back then – and I recall demanding she should do the right thing and simply change places with Kate – but from there to killing her? No, that I would not have done, if nothing else for our father's sake." He scowled. "How can you even ask me that?"

Adam looked somewhat ashamed. "I just had to," he muttered. "At present I am not much taken with your family – or the queen." With that, he excused himself – and Kit.

Later that same afternoon, Mortimer came over to where Kit was sitting in the grass, busy with her embroidery. A soft breeze rustled through the trees, and the sun was agreeably warm, which was why the queen had decided that she and her ladies were to spend the afternoon outdoors. Not that Kit was sitting anywhere close to that particular circle, but at present she didn't mind, even if it irked her to see Alicia's distinctive height among the ladies.

"You were never my Kate, were you?" Lord Mortimer asked, sitting down on a bench. He was in green today, a colour that suited his dark colouring and served to show off the heavy gold chain round his neck. He held a walnut, tossing it from one hand to the other.

"No, my lord, I was not."

"Played the fool, was I?" Something dark moved in Lord Mortimer's eyes, and he threw a thoughtful look at Adam, fast asleep in the shade of a nearby oak.

"He didn't know – not at first. And once he did, you were already at war with the king. I dare say it slipped his mind."

"I think not." Lord Mortimer caught the walnut in mid-air and clenched his fist around it, crushing the shell. "He should have told me."

"How could he do that to me? To Sir Thomas?" She folded her work together. "He was as much a victim in all this as I was."

"A victim, Kit?" Mortimer's voice was edged with ice. "You ended up honourably wed to a man who now serves the future King of England." Strong fingers made quick work of the walnut, scattering pieces of shell on the ground below him.

"And none of it was of my making." She smiled in the direction of Adam. "But you are right: I am most fortunate in my husband."

Mortimer pursed his mouth and regarded her with a gleam in his eyes. "At the least, I should have a taste of those pleasures I paid so dearly for."

"What?" Kit croaked, her gaze flying to Adam, then to the queen.

Lord Mortimer burst out laughing. "I am jesting, Kit. To dally with you would be to risk dire death – by the hand of your affronted husband or my magnificently jealous lady queen." His features softened as his gaze settled on the queen. "It doesn't matter. All of that is in the past." He extended his walnut-filled hand to her. "Want some?"

Chapter 29

"I'm not sure I ever want to come back," Kit said to Adam the day they rode off from Vincennes. He made a concurring sound: this last week had been a trial for her – for them all. Lady Cecily's public apology had begun well enough, but halfway through the deranged woman had suddenly come to an abrupt halt. Her mouth had set; she'd extended her neck and glared at Kit, for all the world resembling a bird of carrion when she began to scream that this was a farce, a horrible miscarriage of justice, because why should she, a lady born and bred, be hauled to stand before them when the real culprit was Kit?

"She's the one who should be doing penance, not me!" she had screeched. "An impostor, a devil in disguise, a..." She gargled when Richard clapped a hand over her mouth, fighting like a demon when she was dragged out of the church. At one point, she succeeded in yelling a loud "Bastard! She's a low-born bastard!" and Kit had locked her gaze on the floor.

Since then, Adam's wife had lived in a bubble of isolation, shunned by everybody but a handful of the ladies. It didn't help that Lady Cecily had been locked up, her loud ravings such that the king's physicians were of the opinion she had lost her mind – Kit had been branded a fraud.

Adam glanced in the direction of the queen. She sat on her horse with her gaze fixed ahead, and had not as much as looked back once they'd ridden through the gate. Lately, Queen Isabella had been a quivering pillar of contained anger after her latest meeting with her brother, during which, as Adam heard it, she'd cursed him to Hell and back for abandoning his sister in her hour of need. King Charles shared more than looks with his sister, and a heated and loud argument had ensued, wherein the king had made it clear he would no longer countenance his sister living in sin with Mortimer – at least not under his roof.

In Adam's opinion, it was more a question of King Charles caving in to his counsellors. Not everyone in France found it politic to offer refuge to a condemned traitor, and even less so when the man in question had the temerity to seduce a married queen.

Whatever the case, the queen had decided to leave – no doubt influenced by the rumours that the Despensers were offering King Charles a minor fortune to ensure the safe return to England of the wayward queen, her errant son, and Earl Edmund. Sir Henry had expressed that he held it unlikely that King Charles would lower himself to such a heinous deed, but apparently the queen preferred not to put her royal brother to the test, and neither did Lord Roger, at present a smouldering presence Adam did his best to avoid. Some days on horseback would have Lord Roger regaining his equanimity, but for now those who were wise stayed well away.

"I don't think she wants to come back either," Kit said, recalling Adam to their conversation. She nodded discreetly in the direction of Alicia, astride a palfrey some yards in front of them. Adam grunted, eyeing his wife's half-sister with mild dislike. While Adam could feel some compassion for the girl, who had been more than distraught upon hearing that her mother was kept under lock and key, he was quickly reaching a point where he would no longer tolerate her rude behaviour towards his wife, that narrow mouth of hers setting in an expression of haughty disapproval whenever she was confronted with Kit.

"Who does?" Adam shifted in his saddle. "I long for home."

"So do I," Prince Edward said, holding in his horse to ride abreast with them. He was astride Louis' farewell gift to him, the magnificent horse Edward had eyed avariciously since last September. "I miss my father," he added as if to himself, and Adam did not know what to say. With every step they took on the road to Valenciennes, the prince was getting closer to that final breach with his father.

Sir Henry had recently received an enraged missive from King Edward, taking him to task for allowing his son to consort with traitors, and right at the bottom there'd been an oblique warning directed at Adam, with the king mentioning that de Guirande had best remember who had his children. Adam wet his lips. He had chosen not to share this with Kit, fearing it would cause her to despair, and so instead it was he who tossed and turned at night, trying futilely to convince himself that no one made war on children as young as his.

He studied his wife. Lately she'd looked tired, bruised around the eyes and with a tight set to her mouth, but today there was colour in her cheeks, and when he yet again caught her hand sliding down over her belly, he knew his suspicions were correct. His lady wife was carrying, and it made him want to shout with joy – were it not for the gnawing concern for Tom and Meg.

"Why haven't you told me?" he asked her that evening, watching her as she undressed. Aline had refused to leave the royal court, and so his wife had to do without a maid.

"Hmm?" She turned to face him, naked as the day she was born.

"About the babe." He patted the narrow bed, and the straw rustled when she sat down. He caressed the curve of her breast, smiling at how her nipple hardened in response.

"I thought you could find out for yourself."

"Find out? Well, that calls for a thorough inspection, doesn't it?"

She squealed with laughter when he tickled her flank.

"There's no need for any inspection now, my lord," she said, adopting a prim tone. "You already know."

"I like inspecting things."

"Things?"

"Yes, things such as these." He kissed her lips. For some moments, any attempt at conversation ground to a halt as he explored her mouth, kissing her so thoroughly she came away panting.

"What else do you want to inspect?" she asked in a husky voice. "And why are you still wearing your braies and hose?"

He threw himself down on his back. "Take them off."

Kit was in a playful mood: slowly she tugged at the points of his hose, one at the time. Her hands slid along his upper thigh and inch by inch, she pulled off his hose. Her hair tickled his belly when she leaned forward to undo his braies. She leaned close enough that he could feel her hot exhalation through the linen, and his cock swelled and hardened, tenting the thin material.

"Very promising," she murmured, before teasing him with yet another gust of hot air.

"Woman," he growled, his hands sliding into her thick hair.

"My lord?" She lifted her face to look at him, blue eyes burning into his as she kissed his member through the linen. He lifted his hips off the bed to help her relieve him of the braies, and his cock stood proud and erect. She kissed him, one hand fondling his balls. Her hair on his skin, her warm mouth, her soft grip on his privates…Adam inhaled.

Sometime later she was on her back, uttering a series of inarticulate sounds as he pleasured her, driving her right to the brink a couple of times before he entered her. He braced a foot against the bedpost and thrust – hard and deep. The bedpost creaked and shook. Adam slid a hand under her and lifted her, held her still as he thrust again. Again, and she dug her nails into his back. So close…so close…ah, yes! There was a loud crack, and the bedpost gave.

Kit couldn't stop laughing. Adam chuckled, pulled out and rolled off to study the now three-legged bed, tilting towards the left.

"It would have vexed me greatly had it broken earlier," he said, pouring them some ale. He brought the cup over to the bed, drank, and handed it to her. By the hearth, someone had stacked faggots, and he used some to replace the broken leg.

"Me too," she said with a little smile. She stretched, exposing her naked body. "So, what is your conclusion after all this inspecting?"

"That you are wanton," he grinned. "And with child."

He brushed a long strand of hair off her face. "And that it makes me very happy."

Kit just nodded and clasped his hand.

Riding through France in June was no hardship. For the first few days, they rode along the river Oise, a peaceful waterway dotted with stands of reeds, the odd boat, and here and there a bridge, often with an inn or two. At times, the queen would opt for a nearby monastery, but for the most part they moved from inn to inn, a leisurely ride through fields that were already ripening for the harvest.

A party as large as theirs required that riders be sent off well in advance of the main group to ensure adequate accommodation and food. Prince Edward would often volunteer to ride ahead, and as a matter of course Adam would be sent along with him, leaving Kit behind. Ever since he'd found out about her condition, Adam was solicitous to the extreme, but he was also quite adamant that there were some things she should not do, and this included galloping at full speed with the prince.

"Should you fall off…" he'd said, ignoring her heated objections along the lines that she was a competent horsewoman. And so Kit was obliged to plod along with the main party, maintaining an adequate distance from the queen, whom she hadn't forgiven for her hurtful comments.

"You should have confided in her," William said when Kit broached the subject – as she should have confided in him, Kit could hear from the tone of his voice. William had looked beyond astounded when Adam had told him the whole sorry tale, eyes darkening as he'd asked them over and over again why they hadn't told him before.

"My father swore us all to secrecy," Kit replied – as she replied every time. "I dare say he didn't want it shouted to the world that he had a bastard daughter."

"But now it has been." William gave her a concerned look. "Do you mind?"

"Of course I do! Not because it makes me any different, but because everyone treats me as if I'm different – starting with the queen."

"I don't."

"No." Kit reached over to clasp his hand. "You don't."

Some days on the road, and Kit was quite content to ride at a distance from the other ladies. Conversation was lively, whether it be with William or Sir Henry, the Earl of Kent or Richard.

"Better than sour-faced Alicia," she confided to Adam, making him laugh. Richard, in particular, was a cheerful companion, all of him bubbling with enthusiasm.

"Three months at the most and we'll be home," he said, offering Kit some cherries.

"Three months?" Earl Edmund asked. "Why so long?" He leaned over and helped himself to some of the cherries.

"Because Count Guillaume does not respond well to haste." Richard popped a cherry in his mouth. "In fact," he said once he'd spat the stone out, "he hates being hurried along." He laughed softly. "Like oil and vinegar, our lady the queen and the count."

"So why this alliance?" Kit asked.

"Why?" Richard eased his mount to a walk. "Beggars can't be choosers. France may have allowed the queen and Lord Roger refuge, but to place armed forces at their hands was out of the question. Spain has blood ties with King Edward and the Holy Roman Empire has no interest in these matters. The Hanseatic League would be willing to lend them money – at a hefty collateral – but offer no men. That leaves very few options, doesn't it?" He nodded in the direction of Mortimer. "He doesn't like it, to be beholden to someone like Count Guillaume."

"Beholden? They're trading the prince for an army," Kit said.

Earl Edmund shrugged. "The Hainaut alliance has been discussed since Edward was a boy. What does it matter if it is his mother rather than his father that finalises it?" He ran his fingers through his hair, as if to adjust golden locks already lying to perfection.

"It is not her right to do so, my lord," Kit replied. "Or

would you have your wife arranging marriages for your children against your will?"

"That is different," the earl blustered, his handsome features scrunched up in a scowl.

"It is? I don't think our king agrees." Kit said. "Or our prince," she added in an undertone.

Richard gave her a sharp look. "Edward will do as his mother bids him."

"Of course he will – he has no choice, does he?"

"No," the earl said. "He doesn't. The future of his kingdom depends on this marriage, this venture." He urged his horse to a trot. "And we'd all best pray things proceed as planned by the queen and Mortimer. Otherwise, we will all be destitute – or dead."

"The fact that he is here with us shows just how unlikely it is that we'll fail," Richard muttered to the earl's receding back. "Edmund would never have backed us if he wasn't quite convinced we'd carry the day. He has tested the winds long and hard before making his final choice."

"That's a relief," Kit said drily. "We have a weathervane among us."

That made Richard laugh. "Best not call him that to his face, dear sister."

Kit shrugged. The earl might be handsome and gallant, but she found him far less appealing than his brother. Interesting, how the old king could have fathered three such different sons. She threw Lord Mortimer a look; he also had several sons, and she wondered if they were as different from each other.

"Why isn't Geoffrey riding with us?" she asked. During the last few weeks, she'd seen Mortimer and his son together on several occasions, some seemingly awkward, others not. For all that Kit had been too preoccupied with Lady Cecily to properly get to know the young man, she had found him an attractive and serious younger copy of his father – if somewhat less forceful. "He was very upset when Lord Mortimer told him to return to his lands."

She'd been a reluctant witness to the loud altercation

between Mortimer and his son, and had been quite touched by how the two men had embraced afterwards, Mortimer clutching Geoffrey to his chest as if he never wanted to let him go.

"Why?" Something dark crossed Richard's face. "It would be foolish to put all your eggs in one basket, wouldn't it? Should this fail, there will be at least one Mortimer left alive."

"Oh." Kit focused on the mane of her horse. God help them all if this venture did not succeed.

That evening, they arrived in Noyon, and the innkeeper stood bowing and scraping as the queen descended from her litter, immediately surrounded by her ladies, among whom Alicia stuck out like a turret.

"Chicken, my lady queen," the innkeeper said. "I have nice fresh chicken for you tonight."

Kit smacked her lips. This early in the season, the chicken would be small and succulent, and at present she was hungry enough to devour two or three on her own. The child, she assumed – just as it was the child that had her waking to heaving nausea and a desire to remain forever in her bed.

"A good day?" Adam asked when he materialised beside her horse, holding his arms up to lift her off the mare.

"Good enough." She rubbed at his nose. "You're all covered in dust."

"I am?" He sounded distracted, his attention on a party of six men who had halted at the entrance to the yard. Their leader studied the crowded yard, muttered something to the man beside him, and they rode on.

"What is it?" Kit asked, not understanding what was so intriguing about a group of rich travellers. Her gaze snagged on a seventh rider – a person shrouded in black and astride a well-built little roan, its mane and tail a pure white. There was something familiar about the figure's angular shape, but further inspection was cut short by Adam's reply.

"They're too well-armed. And it is somewhat coincidental that I saw them last night as well."

"If so, they're rather inept spies," Kit laughed, noting how the little roan was harshly kicked to trot after the other six riders.

Adam shook his head. "Not spies, Kit. Fighting men – and I warrant there are more waiting for us further ahead. I must talk to Lord Roger – now."

Kit tailed Adam into the inn's main room, where Mortimer was in deep discussion with Earl Edmund. She stood to the side as Adam explained his concerns, and while the earl cursed, Mortimer merely nodded.

"Six, you say?"

"Seven," Kit piped up. "There was one more."

"I saw six," Adam interrupted. "Kit says there was a seventh person, shrouded from head to toe in black, but why would a nun ride with an armed escort?"

"A nun?" Kit looked at him. "I never said it was a nun – it didn't look like a nun."

"Six or seven, what does it matter?" Mortimer said. "Who?"

"My lord?" Adam gave him a bewildered look.

"Is it me they want to kill…" Mortimer broke off to cross himself, "or Edward they want to snatch?"

"Snatch the prince?" Adam grew before Kit's eyes. "Over my dead body."

"And if the lad goes with them willingly?" Mortimer asked.

"Well then, they wouldn't have to snatch him, would they?" Adam replied, thereby effectively sidestepping Mortimer's question. Lord Mortimer regarded him for some moments, dark eyes narrowed.

"Find them," he ordered, and Adam and the earl hastened from the room.

"Nothing," the earl reported later. "We've scoured this sorry little town and found not a trace of six armed men – or a nun."

Mortimer pursed his mouth. "We'll ride at the ready from now on." He strode over to the queen. "No more litter, my lady," he said, clasping her hand in his and bringing it to his mouth. "We must ride in haste until we reach the safety of Valenciennes."

"I saw one more," Kit insisted as she followed Adam to their allotted beds in a corner of the inn's main hall. She stepped over a sleeping man. "I think..." She broke off, shaking her head.

"What?" Adam gestured for her to lie closest to the wall.

"That it was Lady Cecily."

"Lady Cecily? Impossible! She's back in Paris."

Kit shrugged. "I saw what I saw."

Four days at most from Noyon to Valenciennes – that was the estimation Lord Roger and Adam agreed upon.

"We should be able to do somewhere around thirty miles a day," Lord Roger said. "Even the women can manage that." He drummed his finger on the tabletop. "It is unfortunate that we ride with so many to protect," he mumbled. "Four-and-twenty armed men don't count for much when spread so thin."

Adam nodded, frowning down at the collection of pebbles Mortimer had used to describe how he wanted to organise the men. A group of four to the front, four to the back, and the remaining sixteen eight to a side. Adam was to lead the front, the earl the rear, while Lord Roger intended to ride by the queen's side, with Sir Henry in charge of defending the prince. Kit, the six other women and William were to ride behind the queen, together with the queen's two chaplains and Lord Roger's new clerk.

"How many, do you think?" Adam asked.

Lord Roger shrugged. "Many more than six. I'd warrant they're at least as many as we are." He strapped on his greaves and looked about for his mail mittens, slapping his hands together a couple of times before fisting his right hand round the hilt of his sword. "Well, they will find us ready, I think." He flashed Adam a grin. "It is years since we rode together in battle. I am almost looking forward to it."

"Let us hope it doesn't come to that," Adam muttered, but he couldn't stop himself from grinning back. He adjusted his surcoat over his hauberk and followed Lord Roger outside.

Kit was looking fraught, as was the queen. Prince Edward

was still furious that he was not allowed to ride with the men, and kept on throwing his mother such hateful looks the poor woman should have been scalded. Queen Isabella ignored him, beyond pointing him to his place in the cavalcade.

One whole day riding at full alert was exhausting. But they made it safely to the little village at the foot of Chateau Guise, and upon the queen's loud demands that they be allowed entry, the mighty castle opened its gates to them.

"No one will attack us here," she said rather complacently, greeting the castellan politely.

"If they do, they die, m'lady," the garrison commander responded cheerfully, before escorting the queen to her room, the single solar available.

Adam bedded down with his male companions in the hall, while his wife and the other ladies slept with the queen. They rose before prime, attended the service in the castle's little chapel, and after breaking their fast with bread and ale, they were on their way again, finally leaving the Oise behind as they struck out due north, towards Valenciennes.

The surrounding terrain was flat, at times gently undulating. The narrow road cut through the open landscape, the surrounding fields of wheat dotted with poppies. No opportunities for an ambush, not here, and Adam's shoulders dropped an inch or two. Some hours on, and the fields were replaced by woodlands, herds of pigs scavenging for acorns under the trees. Now and then, they'd catch sight of the swineherd, but other than that the forest seemed deserted. Too deserted.

"I don't like this," Adam muttered to one of his companions.

The man spat to the side. "Me neither. I—" Whatever he'd intended to say was drowned in a gurgle. The shaft of an arrow protruded from his throat, and Adam yelled a warning, shield up to deflect the hailstorm of arrows that descended upon him. Kit. His wife!

"Dearest Virgin, keep her safe," he prayed out loud, struggling with the temptation to turn his horse and ride to protect her.

From a stand of oaks, a group of men appeared, spurring their mounts towards them. Fourteen men – no, wait; they were at least twice as many, the second group appearing from behind.

"The line – bring it together!" Mortimer yelled, and the women did their best to comply, sliding off their horses to huddle together, the prince visible beside his mother, sword drawn.

"Protect your mother!" Adam yelled to him – mainly to ensure the lad stayed where he was. Prince Edward nodded, lifting his sword. And then the men were upon them.

Adam had the advantage of height, further increased by the sheer size of Raven. Not much of an advantage, when the presence of the women behind him made him reluctant to charge the attackers and leave them unprotected. His sword sliced through the air, it connected with a jarring impact with a shield that shattered, and his next swipe struck his opponent full in his arm. Blood spurted, but Adam had no time to finish him off, because here came two more men, and out of the corner of his eye he saw Lord Roger fighting three at the time, an enraged Richard hastening to his aid.

A mace came swishing through the air. Adam brought up his shield, spurred Raven forward and the momentum of his horse was such that he drove his attacker off his mount. Two down. Adam's vision narrowed into a chute. Kill. His blood roared and sang, his arm rose and fell, and he screamed his rage as he cleaved a man's shoulder in two.

Swords clashing against swords, Raven pawing and neighing beneath him, and one man fell, then another. Blood. Death – aye, death to all of these accursed bastards! Vaguely, he heard Lord Roger calling his name. He turned Raven, and there were six men making for Lord Roger, riding at speed. Adam raised his sword.

"*À moi!*" he yelled, and then he was thundering towards the six, accompanied by Sir Henry and Gavin. Raven crashed into the nearest horse, unseating its rider. A touch of his heels, and the stallion pirouetted to his right. The man before him screamed, turned his horse and fled, his companions at his heels. Adam roared and plunged after them. They were on the run, the bastards, and it was but a matter of time before they were all cut down.

Over fallen trees, across a ditch, up a short incline, and Adam leaned forward over Raven's massive neck. Across a field, and he caught up with one of the men, bringing his sword down with such force the man was sent flying off his mount, blood spraying wildly. Adam's grip on his sword slipped. Everything was covered with blood – his surcoat, his mail, his sword, the hide of his horse.

"Four more!" he yelled, looking about for Gavin and Henry. What? Where were they? Adam rose in his stirrups, bringing Raven down to a canter. In the far distance, he could see his travelling companions, and riding towards him was Lord Roger and some of the men, the Mortimer banner flying behind him.

Adam waved and continued his pursuit. Raven snorted, powerful legs carrying them forward at speed. Adam yelled him on, and then suddenly he was no longer on the horse – he was flying through the air.

He landed with a thump, all the wind knocked out of him. His helmet was torn off, he lost his grip on his sword, and when he tried to regain his feet, three men swarmed around him, forcing him to his knees.

Someone prodded at his throat with a blade. Adam swallowed and tasted blood, blinking to rid himself of his blurred vision.

"And so we meet again, eh?" The voice came from somewhere to his right, and Adam's innards clenched.

"Despenser?" he croaked. A boot drove into his flank.

"Lord Despenser to you, de Guirande."

Adam was hoisted to his feet. He dragged in air through a constricted throat, leaning away from the blade that was digging at the side of his neck. He tried to wrest himself free, and something clapped him on the head. Pain made his knees sag, sent jagged spikes through his brain.

"I could kill you," Despenser said. "Maybe I should this time." He nodded, and one of the men beside him punched

Adam full in the gut, causing him to double over. "Or maybe I shouldn't," Despenser went on. A snap of his fingers, and Adam was released to fall on his knees. "Today we failed – again. Very much thanks to you and your prowess with a sword."

"In which case I die happy," Adam retorted, wiping at the blood on his face.

Despenser laughed. "Oh no, Adam. You won't die – just yet. But Mortimer will – by your hand."

"Never!" Adam said.

"Never?" Despenser laughed again. "May I remind you I hold your children, dear Adam? Little Tom looks just like you, by the way – a comely lad." He gripped Adam by the hair and twisted back his head, dark eyes boring into him. "If Mortimer reaches England alive, your children will die. Your choice, Adam dear."

Adam wanted to spit him in the face, but his mouth had dried up utterly, and his windpipe was painfully narrow, each inhalation an effort of will.

"You wouldn't," he said, hating the pleading note in his voice.

"No?" Despenser patted his cheek. "We both know I would – if I have to. And just so you know, should you tell Mortimer any of this…" He slid a finger over his throat. "I have spies everywhere, Adam."

"My lord," an unknown man said, hovering behind Despenser. "We must ride. Look, Mortimer is almost upon us." His voice rose to a whine. "Foolishness, my lord! You should not have come, what will our liege do if you—"

"Yes, yes. I'm coming!" Despenser looked down at Adam. "So what will it be, Adam? That beloved baron of yours, or your children?" A horse was brought forward. "What will your precious conscience have you do this time, I wonder?" With that he kicked Adam hard, and sat up.

Adam lay on his back and stared up at the sky, wishing all of this had been nothing but a figment of his imagination. But he knew it wasn't, and God help him, what was he to do?

Chapter 30

They reached Le Quesnoy by nightfall. With the exception of Adam and his badly bruised body and bleeding head, most of their men had escaped remarkably unscathed, even if Sir Henry's thigh sported a deep cut, and Richard could not use his left hand, all of it bruised blue after having been trod on by one of the frantic horses.

Three men died, unfortunately, and the queen's jennet had been severely wounded by a blade, giving Mortimer no option but to order the beast to be killed. The queen had wept more over her horse than over the poor men – but to her credit it had been she who'd seen to Sir Henry.

Kit's heart had stopped when Mortimer and his men had returned, with Raven on a leading rein and Adam slumped on top.

"He'll live," Mortimer snarled as they reached Kit. "I have a good mind to have him whipped for acting so irresponsibly. Damn you, Adam, what were you thinking?"

"I wasn't," Adam mumbled, clumsily sliding off Raven. He was covered in blood, and took a few careful steps towards Kit before collapsing to sit on a rock.

"You're a belted knight! Veteran of God knows how many campaigns and you set off like that without ensuring your company is safe?"

"I wanted to kill them," Adam growled. "All of them." He winced when Kit lifted off his chainmail coif and washed his face. The linen coif he wore beneath was dark with blood, and when she undid it, so was his hair. Gavin hurried over, and together they rid him of his coat of plates and hauberk. No blood on the gambeson. Kit's eyes blurred. He was not seriously harmed.

"Fool!" Mortimer beckoned Prince Edward over. "Learn this once and for all: an army has no need of men aspiring to be heroes. An army needs men who retain the capacity to think and obey orders – not men who allow the bloodlust to take over."

Adam flinched as if struck. "I've never failed you before, my lord." He inhaled loudly when Kit found the deep gash in his scalp.

"No." Mortimer relented. "Nor did you fail us today – except for almost getting yourself killed!"

"What happened?" Prince Edward asked.

"A rope," Adam said, now in only gambeson and chausses. "Sent me flying, and gave them the opportunity to get away."

"You were lucky they didn't have the time to kill you," Mortimer snapped, and yet again Adam flinched, averting his face.

Kit insisted on riding with Adam all the way from the ambush, sitting behind him with her arms round his waist. Any attempts at conversation had been consistently rebuffed, and she supposed he was angry with himself for having charged off as he did, thereby inviting near death.

Just thinking about this had Kit tightening her hold on him, and his hand came down to rest on hers.

"Unfortunately, Count Guillaume is not in residence," Mortimer said as they rode towards the count's palace. "But maybe they will offer us hospitality all the same."

Le Quesnoy was a thriving little town, and just as Mortimer had hoped, they were invited to stay at the palace, the count's castellan having met Mortimer on several occasions in the recent past.

Supper was a silent affair. Adam said nothing at all, staring at the trencher before him. Prince Edward was looking quite sick, and had done so ever since one of their attackers had fallen at his feet, his skull split in two. The queen sipped her wine and refused the food, large green eyes never leaving Lord Mortimer. Kit sat as close as she could to Adam, not quite understanding why he was so sullen – he'd not said a word while she saw to his head wound. Something was gnawing at him, but no matter how she tried, she couldn't understand what. Kit took his hand, and it lay warm but unresponsive in hers, his gaze locked on the opposite wall.

Things were not improved by the message waiting for them, informing Richard that his mother had fled her prison and was believed to be riding in their pursuit. Alicia was clearly heartened by this, her pale cheeks acquiring more colour than they'd had in days, but Kit's stomach twisted into a painful knot – there was no doubt in her mind that Lady Cecily was coming for her. To her chagrin, Adam seemed more distracted than distraught by the news, but given his continued silence, and the anguished set to his face, Kit supposed the events of the day were uppermost in his mind. She squeezed his hand. He could have died!

"We could all have died today," the queen said out loud, voicing Kit's thoughts.

"Not all, my precious lady," Mortimer replied. "They would never have killed you."

The queen gave him a flaming look. "And that is supposed to be a comfort?" she demanded. "What sort of life would be left to me, do you think, if King Edward should capture me? What would my life be without you?" She ducked her head, using her veil to dry her face.

Lord Mortimer leaned towards her and whispered something in her ear, his large hand settling softly over the queen's tight fist. She nodded and straightened up, and for a while she studied her trencher, using her eating knife to prod the meat this way and that.

"Maybe all of this is futile." Queen Isabella toyed with her bread. "Maybe it is time I return home and make my peace with my husband."

Mortimer's knife sank into the table, not a nail's breadth away from the queen's hand. She reared back.

"Never!" he growled. He took hold of her, lifted her to her feet and shook her like a ratter shakes a rat. "I will kill you rather than have you go back to him, you hear?" His voice cracked. "You are mine, goddamn it. Mine." He set her down. "If you leave me…" His chest heaved, his dark eyes glittered. "I would die," he finished simply.

He sat down heavily and hid his face in his hands. No one said anything; it was as if every person in the room was holding their breath. At long last, the queen set her hands to his head, smoothing his dark hair and murmuring his name. Lord Mortimer groaned, wrapped his arms round her waist and pulled her close, his face pressed to her stomach.

"Let's go," Kit murmured, tugging at Adam's sleeve. "This is not for us to see – this is just for them."

The moment they were in the room they were to share, she turned on him.

"Tell me."

"Tell you what?" He lay down on the bed, boots and all, and covered his face with his arm.

"Something is gnawing at you," she said, joining him.

"It is?" He snorted, but she was not convinced.

She forced his arm off his face. "Something happened to you today – well, beyond the sheer stupidity of riding off in pursuit all on your own."

"Stupidity?" Adam rose on his elbows. "How dare you call me a fool?!"

"Oh no you don't," she snapped back. "Don't you dare explode into rage so as to evade telling me what is weighing on you."

Adam collapsed like a punctured bladder. "I can't tell you." It came out with so much anguish Kit just had to take his hand. He squeezed, hard enough that she had to bite her lip so as not to gasp.

"Why not?"

"Because if I do…" He peeked at her from under his lashes. "If he finds out I have…" He choked.

"Who, Adam?"

He rolled over onto his side.

She shook him. "Who?"

In response, he leapt out of bed, cursed when he put most of his weight on his right foot, and made for the door. Kit reached it first.

"Get out of the way," he growled, eyes dark with something she couldn't quite interpret.

"Or you will hit me?" Kit raised her chin defiantly.

Adam sighed. "You know I would never do that." Yet again, he made as if to move her aside and open the door. Yet again, she refused to budge.

"You're frightening me," she told him. "Whatever it is you think you cannot tell me, it cannot be worse than not knowing."

"Oh, it is," he groaned. He drove his fist at the door, repeatedly, and then sank down to sit on the floor. "Despenser," was all he said.

"Despenser?" She kneeled down beside him. "He was here?" She cradled his scraped fist in her hands.

"He..." Adam stopped, cleared his throat. "I... Oh, God!" And then in a rush he told her, words tripping over his tongue at such speed that at first she didn't comprehend what he was saying. But once she did, she just stared at him.

"But you can't!" she whispered.

"And if I don't..."

"He is bluffing. He must be." Kit tightened her hold on his hand. Tom...little Meg.

"But how do we know that he is?" Eyes as dark as thunderclouds met hers, eyes in which she saw her own fear reflected and magnified. Somehow, it gave her resolve. She got off her knees and extended her hands to him.

"We have to think," she said. "And then we have to talk to Mortimer."

Mortimer was not pleased at being woken in the middle of the night. But at Kit's whispered explanation, he slipped out of bed, following her in only his shirt – and with his sword. Now he was standing in their room, leaning against the wall as Adam recounted his meeting with Despenser.

"Well," he said once Adam was done. "I take it you do not intend to assassinate me."

"My lord!" Adam's hands clenched into fists. Lord Mortimer grabbed at him and gave him a rough embrace.

"I'm sorry. But now let's concentrate on the matter at hand, shall we?" He frowned. "Pity you didn't tell me sooner. We could have given them chase. Now it's too late."

"I wasn't thinking, my lord." Adam looked away, shoulders bowing. Kit rushed to his defence.

"He was badly hurt!" She glared at Mortimer, who merely nodded before asking Adam to tell him everything again.

By a simple process of elimination, Lord Mortimer narrowed the potential spies down to two: his new clerk, or William.

"William?" Adam blinked.

"There's a number of months unaccounted for," Lord Mortimer said.

"He was in hiding," Kit protested.

"Or he was in one of Despenser's dungeons, negotiating for his life." Mortimer's mouth compressed into a tight little smile. "I suppose we'd better ask him."

"Now?" Adam stared out at the summer night.

"Most certainly now. It is difficult to lie convincingly when you're woken from sleep." Lord Mortimer was already halfway out the door. "Coming?"

Kit insisted on coming along. William was fast asleep in a corner of the hall, and woke up with a start when Mortimer covered his mouth and nose with a strong hand. Lord Mortimer held a finger to his lips, William nodded, and moments later they were all in the silent chapel – a stone structure so cold Kit had to clench her jaws to stop her teeth from chattering.

"Me?" William spluttered. "Are you accusing me, my lord?"

"I'm asking you," Mortimer said, which in Kit's opinion was not much of a distinction. William looked from Lord Mortimer to Adam as if he would gladly strangle them both. He crossed his arms over his chest.

"No."

"No what?" Lord Mortimer asked.

"No, I am not a spy. No, I do not serve Despenser. No, I would never betray you." William took a deep breath. "No, I have never been so insulted." He frowned. "And no, it isn't your new clerk. The man's shirt would be streaked with shit just at the thought."

Mortimer looked disappointed, two parallel creases

appearing on his brow. "Then who?" He shook himself. "No matter – we will find the spy, but you," he said, turning to William, "you must travel to Tewkesbury."

An hour or so later, and Kit was feeling much calmer. There was a plan, and already she could hear William moaning and wailing, complaining his guts were burning from within. By dawn, the entire company would believe that William had the bloody flux, and Mortimer was to throw a tantrum, demanding that they move on and leave the ailing man behind.

Once they were safely gone, William was to make haste to Brittany and find a ship to Wales, from there to make his way to Tewkesbury and the neighbouring Despenser manor.

"And then what?" Adam had asked.

"I don't think your children are kept under lock and key," Mortimer said, a shadow flitting over his face. His children were, Kit reflected, even the little girls were kept under close surveillance. "So William here just needs to find them and steal them away."

"It should be me," Adam said.

"It can't be you," Lord Mortimer replied. "You know that."

Come morning, everything proceeded as planned, and Lord Mortimer had the entire company out on the road just after prime. Adam maintained a constant distance from Mortimer, was surly with everyone – including his wife – and in general acted like a fox who'd stuck his inquisitive snout into a hornets' nest.

He noted with approval that Kit took the opportunity offered by his churlish behaviour to seek support from the women. One person, however, was not taken in, and just before noon the prince requested that Adam ride with him.

"What is going on?" he asked.

"My lord?" Adam gave him a blank look.

"Don't give me that! I have never seen you be so rude to your wife – ever. And she does not seem particularly surprised, does she?" He rode Thunder close enough that his leg brushed Adam's. "Something happened yesterday. You returned to us wounded, but also as pale and shivering as if you'd seen a ghost."

"Maybe I had," Adam said.

"Or maybe something else is afoot." Edward set his jaw. "I'll have you tell me the truth – right now."

Adam could not disobey him. The prince listened in silence, brows pulled together in a little frown. Once Adam was done, he shook his head.

"The clerk a spy?" He scoffed. "The man fears his own shadow. Besides, Despenser doesn't need a spy – he needs a man capable of wielding a knife and smiling while he does so. Someone with easy access to Mortimer – or my mother." Edward nodded discreetly in the direction of the queen's chaplains. "Like one of them."

"They're priests," Adam objected.

"So they say." Edward fingered his dagger. "But I find it strange that one of them always carries a Toledo blade."

"And have you told your mother this?" Adam asked.

"No." The boy gave him a surly look. "She never listens to me anyway."

"Mothers rarely do," Adam commiserated. "But this she wants to hear – trust me."

The prince nodded. "I'll talk to her." He made as if to turn his horse, but instead drew it to a halt. "You do realise there's a fundamental flaw to Mortimer's plan, don't you?"

"Go on," Adam said.

"You will still have to gamble. No matter his concern for your children, Mortimer – and my mother – will not wait to hear back from William. They will launch their invasion as soon as they're ready. They have to."

"I know." Adam tightened his hold on the reins. "But please don't tell my wife."

"Well done!" Lord Roger slapped the prince on the shoulder. Before them, the chaplain was on his knees, arms wrenched up high behind his back. Other than the dagger, they'd found a vial of something Adam suspected was arsenic, plus a root the man had admitted was hemlock when Lord Roger threatened to feed it to him.

Upon hearing of the prince's suspicions, Lord Roger had ridden for the closest inn and demanded food for his companions and a secluded room. With impressive alacrity the female innkeeper had set to, and after listening to Lord Roger's requirements had suggested they use her storage cellar for their interrogation. It was a cool but dry space, lit by a number of torches, and had the benefit of very thick walls and an equally stout door. What was said here could not be overheard.

"I had no choice!" the false chaplain said. He'd been repeating that for the last hour, no matter how much pain he was subjected to, in between bleating that he hadn't done anything. "The scarred man ordered me to do this," he wailed. "He said that otherwise he'd make sure my nephew ended up dead in the Garonne."

"The scarred man?" Lord Roger sat down on a stool, braced his elbows on his knees and leaned over the wretch. "How scarred?"

"Badly. As if someone once tried to cut his nose off." The man turned his bruised face towards Adam. "But you must know this – you've seen him too." He sounded triumphant.

"Me?" Adam was very confused.

"He told me you were the one who was going to murder Mortimer," the man said. "You're the assassin, not me!"

"And when did he tell you this?" Lord Roger asked.

"Last night," the man replied. "We met in the Chapel of St John."

"Apt," Lord Roger muttered. "To discuss assassinations in the house of God. Anyway," he continued, "in difference to you, Adam came to me immediately. Yes, the idea was to pressure him into killing me, but he won't." He cuffed their captive over the head. "You, on the other hand, would."

"No, my lord! Of course I wouldn't! But what was I to do when he—"

"...Threatened your nephew." Lord Roger kicked the man. "Take him away. Turn this priest-impersonator over to the bishop in Cambrai." He grinned wolfishly. "A very good friend of mine, as it happens."

Once the protesting man had been dragged off, Lord Roger stood. "Damn!" he said. "This is not good, not at all." He paced, moving swiftly back and forth. "Whoever that scarred man is, he'll know soon enough that his pet priest is gone, and then I fear it is but a matter of days before Despenser is informed." He sighed. "I'm sorry, Adam. Let us pray that William makes good time to Brittany and beyond."

Adam could not quite move – or think. His children! He licked his lips. Surely Despenser wouldn't…

He would, a little voice inside of him whispered, and Adam had to bend over with the resulting pain. Strong young arms helped him upright.

"We'll give out that the priest has the bloody flux as well," the prince said. "It will only delay things, but may buy us an extra day or two in which to find this scarred man."

"Any names spring to mind?" Richard asked.

Adam shook his head. He toyed with his dagger. Lord Roger's life or that of his children. He swallowed. How could he even consider… Tom, he moaned inside, throwing the dagger away from him to land with a clatter at Lord Roger's feet.

"Adam."

Adam kept on staring at the floor. What was he to say to Kit? That they'd caught the spy but there was another spy, and so in catching this one they'd increased the danger to their son and daughter? "Mother of God," he croaked, "not my children."

"Adam!" Lord Roger shook him, hard.

Adam turned unseeing eyes his way.

"We all have children held hostage," Lord Roger said gently. "We must all pray and hope that whatever their faults, Despenser and our king will not resort to harming the innocent among us."

Adam nodded, mutely. Pray. He could do that.

"And Adam?" Lord Roger smoothed at his hair, cupped his face. "You have to tell Kit."

No. Adam shook his head vehemently.

"You have to. Your woman deserves to know the truth –
she is strong enough to handle it."

Kit did not say a word. All she did was open her arms and hold
him to her, arms crushing him to her as he was crushing her
to him.

Chapter 31

Two days later, they rode into Valenciennes, supped in a daze and retired to their rooms just as dazed. But next morning Kit woke with one objective: to find the scarred man. She pestered Adam with questions as they navigated their way to the great hall, and so focused was she on the urgent need to neutralise this threat that she took in almost nothing of their surroundings, beyond concluding that the walls of the hall were hung with the most impressive tapestries she had ever seen.

"The Garonne runs through Bordeaux," she told her husband as she joined him at one of the trestles. There was bread and cheese, honey and ale, but Kit was too distressed to do more than tear her bread into crumbs.

"And?"

Kit shrugged. "I don't know. Maybe he is from Bordeaux?"

"Or maybe the priest is." Adam looked at her breadcrumbs. "You must eat, sweeting."

"Later." Kit studied the people in the hall. "Is he here, do you think?"

"No." Adam sounded definite. "If he's as badly scarred as the false priest said, it would be foolish to show himself."

That made some sort of sense, but at the same time this scarred person had to somehow gain access to the queen and Lord Mortimer. "If he's not here, will he not need a new accomplice?"

"That depends on what his objective is," Adam said.

"Well, to judge by what that priest–pretender said, he has been tasked with ensuring Lord Mortimer dies." Kit leaned forward. "Could the scarred man be that horrible Godfrey?"

Adam stopped chewing.

"It's just that I remembered you telling me you'd sliced his face open when he attacked you in the stables, and we know he's Despenser's man through and through." She cast a look over her shoulder, shuddering as she recalled the last time she'd seen Godfrey, that evening when Despenser had humiliated her before his men.

Adam nodded, slowly. "That makes sense."

Kit took a deep breath. "And what if Lady Cecily is working with him?"

"Working with him? Godfrey of Broseley has no time for deranged old hags." Adam sounded amused, and Kit slapped his arm.

"I saw her!" she hissed. "That night in Noyon, someone was riding with those six men. Godfrey might find her useful, and Lady Cecily will do anything to get even with Lord Mortimer."

Adam thought this through. "Maybe you're right. She'll never forgive Lord Roger for forcing her to stand in sackcloth in the Vincennes chapel while loudly confessing her sins."

"Not that she did," Kit muttered, glancing in the direction of Alicia. "Do you think her daughter knows where Lady Cecily is? Or her son?" She felt very disloyal to Richard in saying that.

"Only one way to find out. We must follow them." He gave Kit a stern look. "And by we, I do not mean you, sweeting."

"I am better placed than you to follow a woman," Kit protested.

"No." Adam took her hand. "I mean it, Kit."

Their conversation was brusquely interrupted by Gavin, who informed Adam that the prince required his presence, now. Adam groaned, but Gavin was insistent, and with a last look at Kit, Adam followed him through the crowded hall. Kit shoved the remnants of her uneaten meal away from her and made for the door. The noise of all those people was giving her a headache, and she needed to think, to find some solution to the dire threat Despenser had made.

Not that there was a solution, she sighed some while later, having turned the matter over and over in her head. If Despenser intended to make good on his threat, there was very little – nothing, in fact – Kit or Adam could do to stop him except hope that William would reach their children first. It made her itch to feel so helpless, and even if the queen had tried to reassure her yesterday by saying that she'd never heard of anyone – bar that king of old, John Lackland – who had actually killed children held as hostages, that was not much of a comfort.

Without really knowing how, Kit had made her way into the palace gardens. Enclosed by a high wall, substantially smaller than the sprawl in Vincennes, it was all the same a restful place, with ivy clambering up the wall of the keep and a number of large trees offering shade. Just beyond the wall, she could make out houses, scraggly lines of buildings of various sizes that offered a further bulwark between the peace of the garden and the noisy world outside. There was a well-tended herbal garden bordered by neatly trimmed privet hedges, a number of roses that dipped and swayed in the summer breeze, scattering white and pink peals on the ground below, and right at the bottom was a bower, thick vines growing over a trellis of sorts.

Kit picked a head or two of lavender and crushed them, inhaling their scent. Lavender to soothe an agitated mind, she thought, hearing in her mind her mother's voice as she patiently taught Kit everything she knew about herbs and their properties. But today, the lavender was not enough.

She was halfway to the bower when a flash of colour up a tree had her coming to a halt. A bird? A very big bird, and a bird that spoke in hushed tones. When Kit came closer she saw two girls, one of them trying to help the other down from a precarious perch on a branch.

"Sit still," the elder of the girls said. "I'll get you down."

"Mother will be so angry," the younger girl said. "Look at my new kirtle – and what will the prince think?"

"The prince? Who cares about him?" The older girl sounded annoyed. "Besides, it is me who has to marry him."

"That's not true." The younger girl kicked at her sister. "Father said he would be allowed to choose, and both Agnes and I are old enough to wed, and—"

The older girl released her hold. With a little yelp the other girl slid off her perch, landing on the damp ground below.

"Joanna!" The eldest girl jumped down. "Are you hurt?"

In reply, the younger girl bawled.

Kit hurried over. "Let me see."

The older of the girls backed away. "I didn't mean for her to fall."

"No damage done," Kit said with a smile. "Shush now," she admonished the younger girl, "you're only crying to frighten her."

"She let me go!"

"And you kicked her." Kit sat back on her heels to study the two girls – the count's daughters, she presumed, given their conversation about a prince. At present, they looked rather bedraggled, long, dark braids messy and their kirtles dirty. The oldest girl looked down at her skirts.

"I should have stayed with Agnes," she moaned. "Mother will have us belted for this."

"You had an accident," Kit said. "Tell her you slipped and fell."

Joanna laughed. "Philippa always has accidents." She grinned. "Mother says she's far too old to climb trees."

Kit smiled at Philippa. "One is never too old to climb trees. The secret is to know how to climb down." In response, she got a shy smile.

"I know how. She doesn't." Philippa gestured at her sister.

"I do too!"

"No you don't!" Philippa tossed her head, making her braids bounce. "But that's because you're so much smaller than me."

"I am not!" Joanna stood on her toes. "And you're only twelve anyway."

Philippa sniffed. "But you're a baby, only nine."

A voice rang out from the direction of the keep, and both girls started.

"Your mother?" Kit asked.

Philippa shook her head. "That's Mathilde, our nurse."

She shared a look with her sister. "We must go. Marie will have us reading Pater Nosters until vespers if we're late." She made a reverence, tugged her sister into one as well, and then they were gone, running towards the voice.

The incident with the two girls served as a distraction from her gnawing fears – until Kit returned to the bailey just as Alicia was handed a message by an unknown lad. Alicia read it and visibly staggered, a hand thrown out to steady herself against a nearby wall.

The message was torn to shreds and thrown to the muddied ground. Alicia turned, leaping up the stairs to the hall two treads at the time. Moments later, she was back and making for the main gate, the odd distinctive curl of bright red hair visible below the hood of her cloak. It was not a conscious decision. Kit just lengthened her stride and followed.

Valenciennes was a town dominated by water. Everywhere were small canals, crooked streets opening up into one marketplace after the other, more canals, and soon Kit was quite lost, jostling her way through the crowds in the fish market while attempting not to lose sight of Alicia. Now and then, Alicia stopped for directions, and from the fish market she crossed a bridge over one of the wider canals, took a left down a wide street bordered with the houses of the well-to-do, and moments later she came to a halt by a church.

Alicia threw a cautious look over her shoulder, and Kit shrank against a nearby wall. When next she looked, Alicia was gone, and Kit ran towards the church. The door was ajar, and she slipped through into the darkness within. Someone was droning a plaint, to her right three men were deep in a discussion that involved pouches changing hands, and just by the lady's chapel, Kit made out two familiar female shapes – tall and angular, the both of them. Except that one of them was held in an iron grip by a man, his face obscured by a hood.

Two men were loitering nearby, one seemingly sunk in prayer, while the other was openly staring at Alicia and her companions. A guard? No, Kit concluded when the man turned away and made for the door, where she lost sight of him in the shadows.

Kit edged closer. Most definitely Lady Cecily, she concluded some moments later, but the normally so formidable woman stared vacantly straight ahead, as if sedated. Alicia seemed agitated, at one point attempting to prise off the fingers holding her mother. The man slapped Alicia and said something that had her clasping her hands together and falling to her knees before him. The man laughed and gave Lady Cecily's arm a rough shake, causing her to totter.

He held something out to Alicia, who moaned and shook her head repeatedly. The man growled and threw Lady Cecily against the wall, miming a knife at her throat. Alicia cried out, rose to help her mother, and was pushed aside. The man held out the object again. A vial? The light from a nearby candle glimmered on its surface. Alicia was crying, thin shoulders heaving, and the man made as if to walk off, dragging Lady Cecily with him.

"No, wait!" Alicia's voice rang out. She clutched at his arm, lowering her voice while casting a cautious look at the people in the church. Kit pulled her veil closer and pretended great concentration on her prayers. Yet again, the man extended the object to Alicia, and this time she accepted it, tucking it away. The man said something else. Alicia nodded several times and then she was off. Kit lingered, reluctant to leave before the man with Lady Cecily. At last, the man made for the door.

Kit scrambled to her feet. Out of the corner of her eye, she noted that the praying man did the same, but she was in too much of a hurry to do more than register this. Out into the bright June sunlight, and for a moment Kit was blinded. There! Lady Cecily's distinctive shape had all but disappeared behind the church. Yet another canal, another bridge, and Lady Cecily was propelled forward at a brisk pace, away from the town's centre and the palace, towards the encircling wall.

Kit set off at speed. There was a convent on the other side of the bridge, and beyond that a cluster of houses she took for an inn. She never made it there. Something was thrown over her head, and when she made as if to yell there was a dull thwack. Kit's knees buckled, and she fell to the ground.

It only took a look at Gavin's face to know his news was dire.

"M'lord," Gavin gasped. "Lady Kit...a man." He gulped in air. "He took her!"

"Took her?" Adam was already rushing for the stable.

"Outside the church." Gavin's voice was strained. "She came out, and—"

"What church?"

"One of them," Gavin replied. "I can show you."

"And what was she doing there?" Adam had explicitly instructed his squire to stop Kit from leaving the castle, but now was not the time to discuss this. All the same, Gavin gulped at Adam's tone.

"Following her." Gavin pointed at Alicia, who was crossing the yard at a sedate pace. Richard's sister looked distraught, clutching at the pouch she carried on her belt in a way that made Adam frown. "She went into the church. Lady Kit followed, and then Alicia came out, and I waited and waited for Lady Kit to come out, but first came a man dragging Lady Cecily along, and—"

"Lady Cecily?" Adam interrupted. "She was there?"

"Aye – but she was not her normal self, meek like a cow in a halter, she was, stumbling in the direction she was led." Gavin gnawed at her lip. "Once Lady Kit came out, she hurried after the man with Lady Cecily, and I followed her. And then..." Gavin inhaled, a long, shaky breath. "I'm so sorry, m'lord," he added in a broken whisper.

"Not now," Adam said. "We will deal with your disobedience later."

Moments later, Adam was galloping through the streets, with Gavin shouting directions beside him. At his back rode four of the count's guards, and people fell away as they approached, yelling invectives.

"Here." Gavin pointed at the church. He led them round the back, to where a bridge led to a small alley. "And he took her there." He pointed at the convent. "I couldn't do anything. Not when his two companions appeared." They'd chased him off with a knife and an axe, he admitted.

"Did you see which way they were going?"

"No, m'lord. But Lady Cecily, she was led off in that direction." He made a vague gesture to the south.

"Towards Our Lady's Gate," one of the guards said. "But we've closed all the gates, so unless they were fast, they're stuck in here." He snapped his fingers at one of his younger companions. "Ride back to the palace and fetch more guards. We're going to search every inn inside the town."

The man nodded and turned his horse.

"We make for the gate," the guard said to Adam, introducing himself as Renard.

No one had passed through the gate. The guard waved a hand at the grumbling people standing beside it. "I can't keep it closed much longer."

"You'll keep it closed until the count says otherwise," Renard replied. "Hopefully, it will not be too much longer." He glanced at Adam. "He's right: we'll have to open them soon enough."

"But you can search whoever passes through, can't you?" Adam said.

"We can." Renard gave him an encouraging smile. "We'll not let your wife slip through."

Adam didn't reply. He stared at the carcass of a dog, bobbing in the nearby canal.

They tore through one inn after the other, they searched the nearby stables; they ran through bakeries and kitchens. Nothing. Adam suppressed a frustrated groan and glared at Gavin, who cowered under the weight of his stare.

"If we don't find her…" Adam began, and Gavin's freckled face mottled with splotches of bright red.

"I…m'lord, I…"

"You disobeyed me," Adam said.

"So did she," Gavin whispered.

"I love her," Adam retorted. "I don't love you." He turned his back on his squire. "Where next?" he barked.

Renard scratched at his beard. "There's an inn just behind St Magdalen – a scruffy place." He gestured to the right.

"Let's go. Now!" Adam didn't stop to ensure they followed. With every moment, the chances of finding his wife hale and alive diminished.

St Magdalen was a small convent standing on the opposite side of the wide canal that emptied into the town's moat. Just beyond was the southeastern gate to Valenciennes – at present as firmly shut as all the others – and by the gate was an inn with a sign proudly proclaiming it to be the Iron Dragon.

The innkeeper was uncooperative at first, but when Adam backed him into a wall and promised him he'd disembowel him there and then, he went the colour of curd and said that yes, he had a party of several people staying in the rooms above the stables.

"Men or women?"

"Men," the innkeeper said. "At least the ones I've talked to." He swallowed noisily, his gaze darting this way and that. "One of them I've just seen at a distance. A woman, I believe, ugly like sin."

"And have they been here all morning?" Adam asked.

The innkeeper started nodding, but the pressure of Adam's knife had him changing his mind, so he shook his head instead. "They went out together," he gargled, "and then they came back, one of them dragging the ugly old crone, the others lugging a sack between them."

"A sack? What sort of sack?"

"How would I know? But it was heavy enough to require two men to carry it." The innkeeper sniffed. "As to what was in it, I'm not in the habit of spying on my guests."

Adam released him to slide down onto the floor. "I need to know exactly how those rooms can be accessed."

Kit regained her wits when they carried her up the stairs, but found it wise to pretend she was still unconscious. The sacking they'd thrown over her had had been tied at her waist, and with some discreet wiggling she managed to get her arms free. Some more wiggling and her hand closed on the handle of her eating knife. Not entirely unarmed, she thought.

She had to bite her lip not to cry out when she was thrown to the floor. The men who'd carried her moved away, and she could hear the sound of liquid glugging from a pitcher. Nothing happened for a while. The men spoke silently, one of them laughing at something the other said. Now and then, she heard a stool scrape back, and moments later a toe would nudge at her. She remained inert. A door banged open.

"What's this?" A dark, commanding voice came from somewhere to Kit's right.

"She was in the church – slipped in after the daughter." One of the men nudged at Kit with the toe of his boot. "De Guirande's wife."

The dark voice laughed. "Well, well, well…fortune smiles on me today."

"De Guirande?" Lady Cecily's voice was unnaturally high. "Bitch, Kit de Guirande, bitch, bastard bitch."

There was a slap, Lady Cecily shrieked. "Hold your tongue," the dark voice said. In response, Lady Cecily giggled.

"She's insane," one of the men put in. "Why on earth you found it wise to bring her along is a right mystery. She belongs in a dark room chained to the wall."

Kit couldn't agree more, pressing her legs together to stop herself from trembling.

"She's proved useful, hasn't she?" the commanding voice said.

"Useful? We should have killed her when we caught her snooping around," the other man said. "She's a liability, Godfrey, you know that, don't you?"

Godfrey! Kit suppressed the urge to squeak. So she'd been right – not that she could find much comfort in that at present.

"Once her daughter has done what we've ordered her to, we don't need the old crone," Godfrey said. "So we'll clap her over the head and throw her in the moat – or we tie her to the gate of the old beguinage. Those do-gooders are fools enough to take her in."

The other men laughed. "Maybe she can become a beguine herself," one of them suggested.

"I doubt it," Godfrey said drily. "Whatever else one may think of the beguines, they're all good, God-fearing women. This one..." There was a pause, and Lady Cecily uttered a whimper, as if someone had kicked her. "...Is anything but kind."

"And this one?" A foot nudged at Kit.

"That one?" Godfrey laughed. "Well, her we will teach to be very kind, won't we, lads?"

Kit tightened her hold on her little knife.

Lady Cecily cackled. "Be good, be good, be good," she said in a singsong tone. "Be good or we will slit your throat." She giggled again. "Can I slit her throat? Please?"

"Maybe," Godfrey said. "If you promise to behave." There was yet another nudge – this one hard enough to make Kit groan. "Now let's see if our guest has recovered sufficiently to offer us some sport."

Adam had to bite his lip not to charge through the door when he heard Kit's voice.

"Leave me alone!" she yelled.

A man's voice cursed, and the sound was followed by a loud slap.

"Behave, bitch," someone snarled. "No king around to save you this time, is there?"

Alive, Adam reminded himself; we want her alive. Behind him, two men were standing with swords drawn, while Gavin had been sent up a ladder around the back, to burst in through the window. Renard and the youngest of his companions were standing by the back entrance, and were to come charging up the creaking stairs the moment they heard Adam's command.

From the room came the sounds of a scuffle. Kit's voice rose in protest. There was a dark laugh and then a male voice exclaiming in pain.

"You damned witch!"

Kit screamed, a sound that ended in a gasp.

Adam yelled and burst through the door. The three men

in the room whirled. Godfrey of Broseley launched himself towards the back door, one hand clutching at his groin from which protruded the handle of Kit's eating knife. The door crashed open, two more guards spilled in, and Godfrey drew his sword, cursing like a fishmonger's wife.

"Somewhat more even odds than last we met," Adam said coldly. "This time, I'll kill you."

Godfrey sneered. "I think not." With a strangled sound, he pulled the knife free from his privates and threw it to a shapeless shadow slumped against the wall. "Go on," he yelled, "cut her throat." He staggered backwards, one hand pressing his wound.

Lady Cecily uttered a wordless, piercing shriek and launched herself towards Kit, who had nothing with which to defend herself except her bloodied hands.

"Adam!" Kit went down in a flurry of skirts, and he rushed to help her. Godfrey made for the window.

"Stop him!" Adam ordered, gripping Lady Cecily's arm. When the crone tried to bite him, he shook her – hard.

Godfrey leapt onto the window ledge. Gavin stood no chance against the desperate man. With a muffled scream he dropped from sight.

None too gently, Adam heaved Lady Cecily to the side.

"All right?" he asked Kit, receiving a weak smile in return before he turned his attention to his hapless squire – and Godfrey's two men, standing back to back as they fended off the guards. Lady Cecily dragged herself up to sit, still clutching Kit's bloodied eating knife. A shaky Gavin appeared in the window, bleeding profusely from his nose – but Godfrey was gone.

"Damn!" Adam drove his fist into the wall. Moments later, Godfrey's two accomplices gave up, lowering their blades to the floor. Adam's shoulders relaxed, and the headache he'd felt building ever since he heard that Kit was missing bloomed into a nasty burst of pain, causing him to squint. From his left came a howl, and Adam spun around, just in time to see Lady Cecily leap at Kit from behind, knife aloft. She was dead before she landed, Adam's sword buried in her brain.

Chapter 32

They'd brought Kit back to the palace wrapped in Adam's cloak, her blood-spattered appearance hidden from prying eyes. Kit couldn't quite stop shaking, her hands knotted in Adam's tunic. So much blood! She hid her face against his chest, yet again seeing Lady Cecily leap at her like an avenging angel, and hiccupped with the effort not to cry.

When Adam brought Raven to a halt, Kit pressed even closer to him, but he disentangled her hands from his tunic, kissed her brow and lowered her into a pair of waiting arms. Lord Mortimer, she realised with some surprise.

"Almost like old times, eh?" Mortimer said, and she found the jest in bad taste, but was grateful that he'd tried to lighten the mood. "You're safe, Kit," he added far more seriously, relinquishing her into Adam's arms. Kit clung to her husband. Yes, she was safe, and Lady Cecily was dead, but Godfrey of Broseley was not.

"At present he has other matters on his hands than sending messages to Despenser," Adam said when she shared this with him. "Like keeping his head on his neck – and surviving the wound you've given him. Bleeding like a stuck pig, to go by the blood we found on the ladder and in the yard. Besides, the count has the countryside swarming with men looking for him."

He steadied her as she got into the tub. Kit sank down and submitted to his hands as he carefully washed her clean of blood and the rank odour of fear that clung to her skin.

"I told you not to follow her," Adam said, gently wiping at her face with a washcloth.

"I know, but—"

He placed his finger over her lips. "You disobeyed me, Kit – and it almost got you killed."

"I—"

Yet again that finger. "Never again, sweeting. You do as I tell you." His eyes met hers; angry, concerned eyes.

Kit exhaled. "I'm sorry."

"Not good enough. Promise me you'll never disobey me again."

She tried to look away, but his hand took hold of her chin. She licked her lips. "I promise," she said hoarsely.

She didn't like it when Adam explained their plans for Alicia. "She's been forced to do this by Godfrey," Kit protested, drawing a clean chemise over her head.

"There's always a choice," Adam replied. "Let's see what path Alicia chooses to follow."

"She's a young girl." And motherless – but so far no one had told Alicia her mother was dead.

"She's sixteen. Old enough to be a mother, old enough to wed – not that the poor girl will find all that many suitors, given her plain looks."

"She comes with dowry," Kit said drily. "Men seem to forgive their bride anything if she comes with sufficient land."

"Whether she weds or not will depend on her actions tonight." Adam tightened her laces and took a step back to look at her. "You look very nice."

"How fortunate," she muttered, "seeing as my dowry was nowhere close to Alicia's."

Adam chuckled. "I love you anyway, sweeting."

The count and countess presided over the high table, surrounded by Mortimer and the queen, the prince and the Hainaut daughters.

"The prospective brides to be," Adam muttered in Kit's ear.

"I know. I've already met them." Kit counted four girls at the table, but as she recalled the eldest was already a mother, the very young wife of Louis, King of the Romans. The girls she had met in the garden were the second and fourth, with a fair girl sitting between them Kit assumed to be Agnes.

The fare was excellent: chickens stuffed with mushrooms and lard and boiled slowly in a rich sauce, two small suckling pigs brought in standing on platters, fish pies, liver and onion set to simmer in burnt wine, veal cooked in milk and dill, small, spicy sausages made of lamb and garlic, dried fruit boiled in sweet wine and honey – Kit sat back and burped discreetly, eyeing the last remaining sausage on her trencher with regret.

Further down the same table, Alicia was sitting with her brother, and from what Kit could see, she had not done more than pick at her food, one hand clenched into a tight fist.

"She's scared," Kit muttered to Adam.

"Which merely indicates that she plans to go through with whatever it is she's been told to do."

"Which is?"

"I don't know. But I'd warrant it's something to do with poison – you saw him hand her a vial."

Kit shoved the trencher away from her.

Adam laughed. "She wouldn't do it here, Kit. Later, in the privacy of the queen's rooms."

After supper, the count and Lord Mortimer retired to discuss military matters with the men. Prince Edward scowled as the men left, but when Countess Jeanne invited him and the queen to her apartments, generously including most of Queen Isabella's retinue as well, he bowed politely and accepted, throwing smouldering looks at his mother.

Entertainment came in the shape of a troubadour, who sang them a selection of verses from the *Roman de la Rose*, which made Prince Edward shift on his seat while the three unwed Hainaut daughters blushed and tittered.

Fortunately, the troubadour had an ear not only for music, but also for his audience, and he changed to livelier tunes, accompanied by a man on a vielle and an old lady on a guimbarde, and Philippa rose to her feet and danced, graceful and lively. Her sisters followed suit, but it was Philippa the prince followed with his gaze, and when the young girl approached him, he took her hand and allowed her to lead him out to dance.

Afterwards, a flushed prince retired to sit on the window seat.

"Does she please you, my lord?" Kit joined him. The

potential future Queen of England was standing on the opposite side of the vaulted room, dark braids framing her face. The child had the most remarkable eyes: large and somewhat almond-shaped, they were the colour of ripe hazelnuts and seemed to glow from within when she looked at the prince.

"What does it matter what I think?" Prince Edward said morosely.

"Your mother is bartering your future for weapons and men," Kit said with asperity. "It seems only fair that you should end up with a bride you feel some affection for."

Edward shrugged. "I am a prince. Princes do not marry for love." He gave her a pained look. "My father never loved my mother. She was a child and he was a man."

"But you and Lady Philippa are of an age – a far better foundation for a good marriage, don't you think?" Kit nudged him in the ribs. "She's quite pretty."

Prince Edward went the colour of a boiled lobster, while muttering that aye, he thought she was. "She is so... uncomplicated, so sunny," he continued. "I could do with a sun in my life."

Kit was tempted to hug him. Poor lad; not quite fourteen and already so disillusioned.

"Well, we all need someone to brighten up our days, don't we? Tell your mother you want Philippa. Let her sort out the practicalities with the count."

Throughout this session of music and dance, Alicia had sat at the queen's feet, arms clutched round her bony shins. Pale blue eyes stared, unseeing, straight ahead, her teeth worried at her lower lip, and every now and then a shiver coursed through her angular frame. Kit might not like Alicia much, but this confused young woman elicited compassion, which was why she decided to warn her. The question was how.

She got her opportunity when the men returned to join the ladies. Voices rose and soared, more wine was brought out, and Kit sidled up to Alicia.

"Whoever the queen sends to fetch wine later tonight will be required to taste it first," was all she said, before throwing herself into a heated debate with the prince as to the existence of unicorns. When next she glanced in Alicia's direction, she was standing quite alone by a wall, hands gripping her skirts as if the only thing she wanted to do was bunch them up and flee.

At long last, the queen chose to retire. As a matter of course, her ladies and Lord Mortimer retired with her. The prince was sharing his mother's apartments and trailed along after her, followed by his men and Kit. As planned, the queen settled herself in an armchair and suggested Lord Mortimer do the same.

"Wine, I think," Queen Isabella said. "Alicia, will you be a good girl and fetch us some more of the count's excellent Cyprus wine?"

"Yes, my lady." Alicia looked paler than usual, her skin damp as if with a fever.

"And so we wait," the queen said quietly once she was out of the door.

"Wait?" Richard looked from the queen to Mortimer. "Wait for what, my lady?"

"Your sister," the queen replied dismissively, and Kit realised no one had chosen to inform Richard of this devious plan. She glared at Adam and received a lifted shoulder in response.

Alicia returned, carrying a heavy pitcher. Her hands were shaking, and Mortimer's dark eyes narrowed.

"What's the matter?" he asked, holding out his goblet. Alicia sloshed wine into his cup.

"Nothing, my lord," she mumbled, and went on to pour the queen a cup as well. The queen sniffed at the wine.

"I wonder what they do to it to make it so sweet?" she said to Mortimer. "Do you think they add honey?"

"Or poison?" Mortimer looked directly at Alicia. The pitcher slipped through her fingers to hit the floor.

"I'm so sorry, my lady." Alicia was on her knees, picking up the shards.

"I'm sure you are," the queen said drily. "Come here."

Alicia approached her like a doe might approach a ravenous lioness. The queen handed her the goblet.

"Drink."

"Me?" Alicia mewled.

"You."

"What is this all about?" Richard demanded.

"We shall see," Lord Mortimer replied. "Either your sister is just naturally clumsy, or she's a poisoner." He nodded at Alicia. "Drink."

Alicia lifted the cup to her lips and drank with no hesitation. And then she fell to her knees and began to weep.

Much later, the vial of poison was in the queen's hands. Alicia had stopped crying, and was nodding at everything the queen was saying. At least her brother had spoken up for her, saying he would accompany his sister back to Bordeaux.

"Besides," Richard had added with an edge. "She chose not to go through with it, didn't she?"

"Yes," Lord Mortimer said. "That counts in her favour – which is why she'll be allowed to return home rather than being forcibly cloistered with the Benedictines."

If at all possible, Alicia paled even further.

Alicia left the court in disgrace. Swathed head to toe in a dark grey cloak that gave her an eerie resemblance to a nun, veiled and wimpled, she sat on her horse with the grace of a barley sack, hands fiddling with the pommel of the saddle.

"Hurry back to us," Kit said to Richard, kissing him on the cheek.

"Oh, I will. I have not waited all these years to miss the invasion." He sat up and smiled down at Kit. "Thank you. Alicia told me what you did."

"She's my sister too." Kit looked at Alicia. "I hope she finds some happiness in her life."

"Not having Mother around will help," Richard said. "And she and Roger were always close. Maybe he can teach her how to smile again."

"Maybe." She patted his leg. "God's speed, brother."

Two days later, Edward and Philippa were formally betrothed. The two young people signed the contracts, with Edward gallantly helping Philippa manoeuvre the quill from the inkpot to the parchment. Two heads, one very dark, the other as bright as burnished bronze, leaned close together at the following dinner, and from the way little Philippa kept gazing at her prince, Adam supposed the girl was well on her way to falling in love with this gallant future husband of hers.

"A good start," he said to Kit. "They will suit each other, those two."

"Like Lord Mortimer and the queen do?" Kit grinned, but Adam did not find it amusing.

"They suit," Adam said. "Unfortunately, they are both married elsewhere, and therefore they sin. May God be lenient in his punishment of them."

For the following weeks, Edward was mostly to be found at the side of his future wife. Adam smiled, happy for his lord, who for once was acting like the lad he was, young enough to chase Lady Philippa through the grounds; male enough to show her just how agilely he could climb a tree, jump a wall.

Now and then, he stole a kiss — at least Adam surmised as much from the way Philippa would at times appear quite flushed and mussed up, the prince looking more than pleased with himself. And then came the day when a messenger rode in, and from the heavy seals affixed to the parchment, Adam knew this was yet another letter from the king.

Edward blanched, weighing the document in his hands. "He knows."

Adam inclined his head. Of course the king knew about the betrothal — it had been a thing done already back in December. But until the prince affixed his seal to the contracts, the king could still hope that his son would not disobey him in this matter — a futile hope, as Edward was in no position to disobey, not with his mother and Lord Roger monitoring his life. Now the king could righteously accuse his son of ignoring his royal command, and from the way the prince's cheek lost all colour as he read the missive, that was precisely what he was doing.

Finally, Edward was done. He dropped the parchment to

the floor and wandered over to a nearby window, bracing himself against the stone sill.

"I am lost," he said. "The king will never restore me in his favour." There was a loud inhalation, the boyish shoulders slumping somewhat. "He no longer loves me."

Adam picked up the document and rolled it together. The last line caught his eye: *you will be made an example to all other sons who disobey their lords and fathers.* No, Adam sighed: the son could no longer be restored to his father – it was far too late for that.

Chapter 33

Despite an extensive manhunt, Godfrey of Broseley was not found. This, combined with the fact that Despenser was still offering several barrels of silver for Mortimer's head, led to fraught nerves, and even more so for Kit and Adam, who had not heard anything from William. They submerged themselves in preparations: the queen rode off to Ponthieu to find gold and men, while Lord Mortimer scoured Brabant and Hainaut for experienced men willing to join the queen's army. With Mortimer went Adam and Richard, with the queen went Sir Henry, Earl Edmund and her son, and that left Kit in Valenciennes, together with the other stranded ladies.

As long as she distracted herself from thinking about her children, Kit found Valenciennes a pleasant enough place, and over the coming weeks she developed quite the attachment to Philippa, who for some reason had chosen Kit as her tutor in all things English. After some weeks, the queen returned with Edward in tow. The count took his future son-in-law to Le Quesnoy, where he arranged several days of hunting through the nearby woods. The prince and the queen participated with good grace, but while they hunted and dined, Lord Mortimer rode to Rotterdam to oversee the final preparations.

And then, in late August, Lord Mortimer sent word that they had the men they needed – or at least the ones who would fit in the ships provided by Count Guillaume. It was time.

Kit guided her horse down the lane, wrinkling her nose at the stench of mud and slime that rose from the nearby waters. For hours, they'd been riding through land as flat as a pancake, here and there dotted with trees and windmills. The closer they got to Rotterdam, the marshier the surroundings, and now she was facing a flat expanse of water surrounded by wharves and dotted with ships.

Wooden cranes swung back and forth, small boats bobbed between the ships and docks, and Kit had never before seen quite so many industrious people. Voices rose, men came strutting by, looking self-important in tunics of good broadcloth, hats and gaudy hose. Behind them came their servants – and their women – carrying baskets and bundles, snotty children and wineskins. Merchants, Kit concluded, men hastening to sell their goods to Lord Mortimer.

She rose in her stirrups, trying to find her husband. Kit shaded her eyes against the glare of the sun on the water, but no matter how she squinted, she couldn't see Adam anywhere. Lord Mortimer, however, was standing down by the wharves, his banner flying above him, side by side with a banner displaying the English royal arms.

"Why is Mortimer flying my father's colours?" Prince Edward asked of his mother, sounding gruff.

"Your banner as well, my son," the queen replied mildly.

Edward looked dismayed. "My arms?" He drew his horse to a halt. "I am not the one making war on my father."

"Now you are," the queen said. "Ever since you went against his wishes and contracted to marry little Philippa." She gave her son a cold look. "Your father has forfeited the right to rule – let us hope you are made of sterner stuff than he is."

That the prince had inherited many of his mother's traits was apparent in the look he gave her, his gaze sliding over to rest briefly on Mortimer. Kit shivered: with his jaw set, his eyes narrowed into piercing blue shards, her prince no longer looked like an untried youth – he looked like the future king he was destined to be. A king coerced into taking part in a venture he did not approve of, and someday those that forced him would pay. She crossed herself, praying that she would be nowhere close to either the queen or Lord Mortimer when that happened.

The mud squelched under the horses' hooves as they ambled towards the displayed banners. Prince Edward had retreated into a surly silence, riding several paces behind his lady mother. Not that Queen Isabella seemed to notice: all of her focus was on Lord Mortimer, who was standing with his arms crossed over his chest, regarding her as hungrily as she regarded him.

Whatever else one might think of those two, there was no doubt in Kit's mind that they were ideal mates – and irrevocably committed to each other. She shifted in her saddle. Adultery was a grave sin, and no matter the hours Queen Isabella spent on her knees begging for forgiveness, Kit feared it wouldn't help. They would be punished – whether in this life or the next.

Lord Mortimer lifted Queen Isabella off her mare and deposited her on the wooden boards of the wharf. The wind took hold of her mantle, lifting it to billow in the wind, the deep red silk matching the royal arms that flew above her. Isabella raised her chin and fixed the ships with a penetrating look.

"Will it be enough?" she asked.

"Would I take you with me if I thought otherwise?" Mortimer replied, bringing her hand to his mouth. The queen blushed, but made no move to retake her hand, even when Mortimer lingered over it.

Kit slid off her mount. Behind her, she heard a muttered curse, and she turned to see Edward swing his leg over the pommel before leaping off his horse. He glared at the queen as he adjusted his clothes, tugging his sleeves into place.

A length of pink silk ribbon fluttered to the ground, and Kit stooped to pick it up. The ribbon was embroidered in green, an *E* and a *P* carefully stitched into the fragile fabric.

"A token, my lord?" Kit handed the ribbon to the prince, who hastily stuffed it into his pouch.

"Aye." He peeked at her from under a heavy wave of hair. "She was sad to see me leave."

Kit inclined her head. "Lady Philippa is very fond of you, my lord." The young girl had appeared on the morning they left, red-eyed, and when Edward had taken her hand to bid her a formal farewell, she had clasped it between both of hers, whispering that she would pray for his safety every day until they were reunited.

The prince squirmed, but there was a light in his eyes and a softness to his mouth that made Kit suppress a smile: it would seem he was as fond of his intended bride as she was of him.

Someone called her name. There, at last, came Adam, moving at speed towards her. Tall and fair, long of leg and broad of shoulders, he drew appreciating looks from every female he passed, but his entire attention was focused on Kit. It made her tingle all over, to have him look at her like that, and when he came to a halt before her, she ducked her head, the intensity in his gaze making her want to throw her arms around his neck and kiss him, despite all the people around them.

He surprised her. His hands settled on her waist and he pulled her close, her belly resting against his.

"Sweeting," he said, before bending his head to kiss her passionately.

Kit pulled back, breathless and flustered. "I take it you have missed me, my lord husband," she mumbled, more than aware of the amused glances from the people around them.

"Always." He caressed the swell of her stomach. "How is the little one?"

"Safe," she replied. "Have you heard from William?" She'd been praying every step of the way from Valenciennes; she'd been begging God that there would be news for them, a message from William assuring her their children were safe.

"I have."

Any hope was extinguished by his tone. "And?"

"Sweeting, I…" Adam leaned his forehead against hers. "They were gone. When William arrived, neither Mabel nor our children were there, and he could find no one to tell him where they might be."

"Gone?" Kit's fingers tightened on his sleeves. "Gone where?"

"God knows." Adam cleared his throat. "William will continue looking for them – and he will start by going to Tresaints, hoping Mabel has fled with them."

"If she has, she would never go there. That's the first place Despenser would look." Kit took a deep breath. At least Mabel was with them, but her heart seemed to be breaking, so acute was the pain in her chest and her belly. Her babies!

"Kit, look at me." Adam's voice came from a distance, penetrating a fog of emotions.

Obediently, she raised her eyes to his, seeing in them a darkness matching her despair.

"I swear to you that I will find them," he said hoarsely. "I will bring our children home."

Kit nodded, incapable of uttering a word. He pressed her face to his tunic, and she rested her cheek against the scratchy wool, listening to the sound of his breathing, of his heart.

Kit knew better than to raise her concerns with the queen. At present, Isabella Capet had but one thing on her mind: the invasion of her husband's realm, there to end the Despensers once and for all. After some days in Rotterdam, the entire company relocated to the port in Brill – according to Adam, it would be easier to load the vessels there. While some went by ship, the queen and Mortimer opted for going by horseback, despite the resulting detour. A few days later, they were installed in yet another clean but rustic inn – except for the queen, who was lodging with Brill's harbourmaster in the little port's finest house.

What to do with the king remained an unsolved issue, but from snippets she overheard, Kit gathered the queen hoped to convince him to surrender the great seal to her, thereby making her the de facto ruler.

"We will give him the opportunity to retire from court," the queen said to Lord Mortimer, unaware of the fact that Kit was within earshot.

"How can a king retire from his own court?" Mortimer's brow creased. "I fear it will not be sufficient, my heart."

"Then what?" the queen whispered, and whatever else they said was lost to Kit as Lord Mortimer led Isabella away.

Yes, then what, Kit mused, staring down at the mud below her feet. And how would all of this affect her children's safety? Kit swayed on her feet, hands on her swelling belly. Her babies. A sob. One more sob, and the torrent of tears she'd worked so hard to keep at bay burst forth, causing her to bend over. A hand on her back, another on her face, and Kit was being held by the prince, who uttered low crooning sounds as he patted her on the back.

"My lord," Kit stepped back, wiping at her face with her veil. Edward gave her a crooked smile.

"It would seem, Lady Kit, that we share a common fear – that of not knowing what this venture will bring to those we love."

Kit wanted to yell at him that it did not compare: her children were innocents, while his father had repeatedly failed his people. But she didn't – there was no point, and he was being gallant and kind, an arm round her waist as he steadied her back to the inn at which they were all staying.

"Thank you," she said, once they were back at the creaking sign sporting a prancing unicorn. Not that the inn offered much in the way of magic, albeit that it was very clean and served good food.

"Your servant," the prince replied, bowing low.

Kit laughed – somewhat shakily. "I think you have that the wrong way round, my lord."

"Not today. Not when a lady I care for needed my help." He opened the door and escorted her inside.

After the brightness of the day outside, the interior of the inn was murky – and full of men. Kit spied Adam in a corner, his fair head distinctive among his dark-haired companions. All of them were regarding Lord Mortimer, who was pacing back and forth, his countenance stark and intimidating when a narrow sunbeam struck him full in the face.

"Dead!" he hissed, and swept the nearby table clean of earthenware mugs, bowls and baskets, scattering food all over the floor. For an instant, Kit thought he might mean her children, until she reminded herself that their deaths would never make Mortimer this upset. Lady Joan? She glanced at the queen, standing to the side, but could decipher nothing from her face.

"Why now?" Mortimer yelled, slamming his hand down on the table. "Why when we are this close?" He swirled, his mantle billowing round him. "Curse you to Hell and back for this! An old man, and you let him fester to death!"

Ah. Old Lord Mortimer of Chirk. Kit felt a twinge of pity for that bear of a man, forced to spend his last years locked away from the sun, slowly rotting. Mortimer came to a halt, bracing himself against one of the stout uprights.

"I loved him like a father," he said, his voice shaking. Beside Kit, the prince shifted on his feet. Mortimer bowed his head. The entire room seemed to be holding its breath. At long last Lord Mortimer straightened up.

"Well," he said, his voice gravelly, "what are we waiting for? We have a kingdom to free from cruel tyranny, and we have all lost loved ones who clamour for justice. It is time, my loyal companions. Tomorrow we sail for England, and God help me if I will not see myself – all of us – avenged!" Mortimer leapt up to stand on a bench. "To England, for England!" he roared, and the men erupted, rising to their feet and yelling their acclamation.

When Kit next looked, Prince Edward was no longer beside her.

The last horses were loaded at dawn, blindfolded before they were led up the narrow gangways. The men came after; some of them rowed out to clamber up rope ladders to the more distant vessels, others marching proudly up the gangways. Kit was among the last to board, following the queen, for the day dressed in English red, rampant lions decorating her cloak.

A flotilla of smaller boats surrounded their ships as they slowly turned into the wind. One by one the sails filled, bulging like the bellies of bloated cows. Pennants snapped, the boards creaked and from the waters rose wisps of summer fog.

"At last," Lord Mortimer said, standing like a figurehead in the prow, the queen beside him. The wind ruffled his dark hair, it lifted his cloak, and to Kit he looked like a bird of prey, as impervious and lacking in compassion as a royal eagle. To have Mortimer as your implacable enemy promised painful death, even more so when you considered his proud companion. The queen turned to her lover, and her face was as regal, as harsh, as his.

"Now begin our days of sun and glory," Mortimer said softly. "May they be blessed and many."

"Amen to that," the queen murmured, and from where she was standing, Kit saw their hands meet and braid.

The prince's gaze locked on their hands, an inscrutable look on his face. Behind him, Adam moved closer, close enough that Edward craned his head back to look at him.

"*Your* glory, my lord," Adam said in an undertone, but all the same Kit was happy that the wind threw his words backwards. "I'll not allow anyone to usurp what is rightfully yours. It will have to be over my dead body."

And just like that, Kit knew Adam had transferred his entire allegiance to the prince. She glanced at Lord Mortimer and prayed he would never put her husband in the unbearable position of having to choose between his new master and the man he loved like a father.

Chapter 34

They landed in Suffolk late in September, and the queen was first to step ashore, accompanied by her son. In a loud, ringing voice she informed the assembled people that she came only to set right all the ills that presently plagued the kingdom. She placed her hand on Prince Edward's shoulder and gently urged him to take a step forward, thereby presenting him to the people.

"My son," she said, "your future king!" Cheers and catcalls, loud clapping and stamping of feet, and from somewhere to the back several horns blared. The crowd parted, allowing a party of horsemen through, headed by Thomas of Norfolk.

One by one, the knights dismounted and knelt, and the queen smiled graciously, accepting Earl Thomas' offer to help her to mount the pretty little palfrey he had brought with him. Soon enough, Prince Edward was mounted as well, and they set off at a stately pace, slow enough that those unhorsed could easily keep up on foot. It was a royal progress. In the distance, the bells of Walton's church pealed their welcome and people sank to their knees, their hands extended towards the prince.

The closer they got to Walton, the denser the crowds. Voices welcomed their young lord home, women wept, girls threw posies and Prince Edward grinned and bowed, but from where Adam walked beside him, he could see just how tense the lad was. He shared a look with Sir Henry, who merely shook his head; just like that, the son had declared himself a rebel to his royal father, no matter how reluctantly. There was no going back.

As they approached the church, Adam came to a surprised halt. So many men! The Earl of Norfolk and his companions had brought a minor army, and together with the Flemish mercenaries presently at his back, this was a formidable force –

all the more so as every single one of the men knew that defeat would lead to a protracted and terrible death.

"Nothing like a wall behind your back to make you fight to the death, eh?" Sir Henry muttered, gesturing at the distant shore. "Our Flemish guests have nowhere to go should they fail."

"Aye." Neither do we, Adam thought, and fear puddled like green slime in his belly. Instinctively, he turned, searching for his wife. She was walking several yards behind him, and when their eyes met, she gave him a faint smile. Just seeing her willowy shape calmed him, a quiet determination settling inside of him. They would not lose – they could not lose.

After mass, a jubilant service during which the queen kept her son by her side, Earl Thomas invited them to partake of his hospitality at Walton Manor for as long as they should need it, but already Lord Roger was fretting – speed was of the essence, and there could be no celebrations until the king and the Despensers had been defeated.

The manor was an impressive collection of buildings and fortifications, the great hall easily holding several hundred men. In the absence of thick, high walls, the earl had encircled the manor with sentries, standing close enough to touch. Yet another show of strength, with every man in polished helmets, their hauberks spotless under tabards bearing the earl's arms, yellow lions on red.

The bailey was crowded with people, but soon enough the earl had installed the queen and her son in his own private chambers, opposite the hall that was thronged with men – and food.

Lord Roger fidgeted throughout the meal, dark eyes inscrutable as he watched the loving reunion between Earl Edmund and Earl Thomas. Loving was not the right word, Adam reflected, hiding an amused smile in his goblet when Earl Edmund stuck two fingers – held close together – in the air to illustrate how close he was to Lord Roger. In response, Earl Thomas slapped his younger brother on the back, so heartily Edmund nearly dipped his face in his trencher. There was some further posturing from Edmund while Thomas remained his normal unruffled self, seemingly more interested in everyone else than his brother. To Adam's chagrin, the earl's gaze returned repeatedly to Kit, something soft and vulnerable flitting over his face.

After the meal, Earl Thomas strode over to greet them, bowing to Kit before turning his attention to Adam.

"De Guirande," he said. "Welcome home." He grinned. "About time, eh?"

"Aye, my lord." Adam gave him a brief smile. As always, the earl was impeccably dressed, his mantle in dark blue contrasting nicely with the pale blue of his robes beneath. His dark hair fell in soft waves almost to his shoulders, and the beard was kept short and neat, highlighting the strong line of his jaw. Much more of a man than his flamboyant younger brother, even if Earl Edmund was beyond any doubt the most handsome man present – which he well knew, strutting about like an inflated pheasant.

"I hear you've had your fair shares of adventures," Thomas continued, this time directing himself to Kit. "And it is because of you that Mortimer still lives."

"Luck more than anything," Kit muttered.

"Luck?" Thomas laughed. "You downplay yourself, Lady Kit." He glanced at Adam. "Do you not agree?"

"I do." Adam gave Kit a tight smile. The earl was eating her with his eyes, all the way from her rounded bosom to the contours of her hips. Kit shared a quick look with Adam and excused herself.

"You're a lucky man, de Guirande," the earl commented, following Kit's hips and bottom out of sight.

"Very," Adam said drily. "And I don't take kindly to men gawking at my wife."

Earl Thomas laughed. "Surely by now you've grown accustomed to it?" He shrugged and fiddled with his belt, tugging a pleat in his robe to lie just so. "What man does not feel pride in a woman other men covet?" he asked, in a light tone that had Adam giving him a curious look. He'd never seen Thomas' wife, but from the slight frown marring the earl's features, he gathered the countess was not as comely as Kit.

"I am proud of my wife – but I will not have her drooled over," Adam replied. The earl gave him a mocking bow. "And some men take no pleasure whatsoever in having a beautiful wife," Adam added as an afterthought, nodding in the direction of the resplendent queen, all dark, glistening hair and glittering green eyes.

Thomas laughed. "You forget the queen is not a woman," he said in an undertone. "She is a she-wolf and the king a defenceless lamb."

Their conversation was interrupted by Lord Roger, his voice carrying easily over the din as he called together an impromptu war council. Within moments, messengers had been dispatched in all directions, and Adam was as engrossed as all the other selected participants, listening while Lord Roger detailed their strategy for the coming days.

"London?" Earl Edmund sounded surprised. "We ride for London immediately?"

"We do." Lord Roger gave him a wolfish grin. "Once we have the king, it is but a matter of time."

"But the king—" Edmund broke off, licking his lips. "He has an army too."

"He does." Lord Roger shrugged. "But he doesn't have me – he doesn't have any of you. And most importantly, he doesn't have the people – not anymore."

No sooner was the council concluded than Adam was waylaid by Kit. "Our children," was all she said. She looked pale, hands clasped tightly together.

"I know." He gently unclenched her hands and took them in his own. "I have already sent off two men, sweeting."

"Where to?"

"They're to ride for Tresaints first." He gave her a concerned look. "I wish I could send you there as well, but I don't dare to do so – it is too unsafe." And he couldn't bear the thought of having his wife whisked away from him as well. He caressed her face, and she softened into his touch. "We will find them," he said, hoping he was right. Dear God, he prayed, grant me this favour, that I will find my children.

Kit remained subdued over the coming days. Adam was torn with concern for her and for his lord, who was struggling with this new role thrust upon him – the future hope of the kingdom. It was the prince who rode by the queen; it was the royal colours of England that flew over their heads. Over and over again, the queen repeated her speech: she was here to safeguard the interests of the realm, to free them all from the yoke of the hated Despensers.

In all of this, Lord Roger remained almost invisible, riding several paces behind his queen. But it was Mortimer who was in charge, it was he who deployed their forces and planned their advance. It was Mortimer who controlled the men, threatening them with the most dire of deaths should they lower themselves to rape and rampage.

"They love him, don't they?" the prince said one evening, watching as their men cheered Mortimer.

"Love him? Some of them most certainly do. But command is not only about love. It is about trust and respect. There's not a man out there who doesn't know Mortimer will fight side by side with them if so required." Adam studied Lord Roger with pride. "He is a fine leader, my lord."

"As my father is not." Edward sighed.

Adam wasn't quite sure how to answer that. News had recently reached them that the king and Despenser had fled London, riding westward. Rumour had it the king was making for the safety of Ireland, something that made Adam chuckle, because the Irish has not forgotten Mortimer and held him in far higher regard than the king.

"The king flees for Despenser's sake, my lord," Adam said. "Without the king by his side, Despenser would not get very far." He gave the prince a little smile. "That takes courage."

Adam himself needed courage when the first of the men he'd sent out to find his children returned.

"Nothing," one of the men said. "They've not been to Tresaints, and John and William have scoured the nearby countryside looking for them."

Adam swallowed at the look Kit gave him. Without a

word, she turned on her heel and walked off. Adam made to go after her, but was detained by one of Lord Roger's men, and by the time he found her, she was standing on a hillock, staring to the west.

"I have these dreams," she whispered. "And Tom is crying, begging someone to let him out because he doesn't like the dark."

Tremors rushed up Adam's legs. His nightmare: even now that he was a man grown, he was still plagued by dreams in which his father threw him into the old well and left him there.

It was with utter relief that Adam saw his brother ride into their camp some days later. They were presently in Dunstable, the priory and the royal hunting lodge filled to bursting with their men, Lord Roger having decided that it was far more important to capture the king than enter London, no matter that three of his sons were held at the Tower. Besides, from what Adam had heard, it would require no battle to enter the capital city – the Londoners were jubilant at the return of their beloved prince and the much-respected baron.

However, all of this was inconsequential to Adam, whose entire attention was focused on his brother. His stomach knotted painfully when William met his eyes and gave an infinitesimal shake of the head. Dear Lord! Adam gripped the man closest to him, who happened to be Gavin, sinking his fingers into the lad's shoulder until he squawked with pain.

"Sorry," he muttered, his gaze on William who had dismounted, standing silent and dirty some yards away. From behind him came Kit's voice.

"William?" she called. "William, is that you?" She came running, skirts held high. "Have you found..." Her voice came to a halt.

"We've found Mabel – and Meg." William took a hesitant step towards her. "I'm so sorry, Kit, but—"

"And Tom?" Adam asked, even if he knew – he could see it in his brother's face, in the dejected curve to his back. Sweetest Virgin! This was his fault! Adam's vision tilted madly this way and that, and he was aware of a spinning sensation that made it near on impossible to walk, but walk he did, needing to close the distance between himself and his wife.

"He's dead," William said, and there were tears in his eyes, in his voice. "The laddie is—"

"No!" Kit voice rang out over the crowded courtyard. "No," she continued in a somewhat lower voice. "No, no, no." She turned to face Adam. Her eyes glazed over, and her mouth opened and closed a couple of times, the tip of her tongue coming out to wet her lips. "He can't be dead," she pleaded, looking at Adam. "Not my Tom."

"Sweeting…" Adam extended his hand to her, wanting to pull her close. She swung at him, her fist striking him full on his ear.

"Don't touch me!" she shrieked. "This is your fault. If you'd done what Despenser had asked you to—"

"How could I do that?" he asked. "How?"

"You killed our son!" she yelled, and Adam flinched at the look in her eyes, at how her hands slid down to protect their unborn child.

"Kit!" William stepped between them, and ignoring her flailing hands, he cradled her face and held her still. "This is none of Adam's doing, you hear? Tom died in late May."

Adam sank down in a crouch to hide his face and the hot tears that spilled from his eyes. His son – his firstborn, his Tom…He stuffed a fist in his mouth and counted slowly to twenty. He had to be strong; he had to be calm and supportive. Kit needed him, he could hear her weeping, hear her groan their son's name. He rose, and Gavin was there, silently offering his shoulder in support.

"How?" Adam asked, surprised to hear how normal his voice sounded.

"He was carried away in a fever," William sighed. "As was Amy, and three or four others. Mabel took the opportunity to flee with Meg and has since been staying in Worcester with a distant cousin."

"A fever?" Kit echoed. "So Despenser didn't—"

"Kill him?" William shook his head.

"But he threatened to. Even worse, he did so knowing our Tom was dead." Adam's fingers found the hilt of his dagger, tightening on the worn leather: please God, grant me the pleasure of killing him!

"Bastard! May he burn in Hell everlasting." Kit's eyes blazed, and for some moments she was all strength, all power. And then her face crumpled and her eyes overflowed. Adam threw his arms around her to hold her to him when she began to weep. With his cheek pressed to the top of her head, he shushed and crooned. At long last she quieted, a disconsolate weight that retreated into absolute silence.

At Lord Roger's suggestion, Adam spent the day with his wife. They retired to their little room, a dark space that essentially housed a bed and a stool, nothing more. A steady northern wind whistled through the slats in the shutters, and they huddled together under the pelts that covered the bed. They didn't speak. She lay on her side, staring at something on the wall, and Adam lay behind her, listening to her breathing. He slid an arm round her waist, and she reclined against him, her hand coming up to cover his. He nuzzled her neck, whispering her name as he pressed his lips to her skin.

Kit turned. Blue eyes met his, and her hands were soft on his cheek, on his mouth. Adam inhaled, trying to suppress the sob that was caught halfway up his throat. He rolled over onto his back and covered his face with his hands. His son...all the emotions he'd kept so strictly under control while comforting his wife boiled to the surface. Adam gulped air in an effort not to weep.

Tom...he closed his eyes in a vain attempt to bring forth an image of the boy he'd last seen more than a year ago, but apart from the colour of his hair, his general build and the sound of his laughter, he could not quite recollect the son who was now dead, already rotting in the ground. He inhaled and groaned his name.

"Shh." Kit rose above him. Soft lips pressed against his cheek, his mouth. "It's God's will," she said. "There's nothing we can do but bear it." Her voice wobbled. "He's safe now, our Tom." A tear slid down her cheek. "But he should have been here, with us."

"Aye," he whispered back, and gently pressed her down to lie beside him, her head pillowed on his chest. She gripped his hand. He kissed the top of her head. They lay like that until the daylight that seeped in through the shutters was replaced by night. At some point, she fell asleep. Only then did Adam allow himself to weep.

Chapter 35

A week later, the queen's army rode into Wallingford. She was cheered along the way, welcomed back to her castle, and Queen Isabella sat regally atop her horse, a cream-coloured mare as graceful and elegant as her mistress, smiling mildly at the people lining the road. Several horses behind, Kit sat in front of Adam, his heavy cloak drawn over them both. Since hearing of Tom's death, he seemed incapable of letting her out of his sight, and Kit alternated between irritation at his protectiveness and relief that he was constantly by her side, his mere presence sufficing to prop her up.

They'd had words some mornings back, Kit trying to convince him to allow her to go home, but Adam had flatly refused, saying there was far too much unrest abroad for him to even consider such a preposterous suggestion. Kit's temper had flared, until it struck her mid-sentence that there was more to his refusal than her safety: at present, Adam needed her as much as she needed him. So she'd backed down, all the while grumbling and protesting.

"That was wise," William had commented when she'd shared her insight with him. He gave her a sharp look. "I dare say you need him too, don't you?"

"I do." Kit had risen from her kneeling position, glad of William's help, and crossed herself. "The difference is that I can admit to it – he can't."

In response, William shook his head, before going on to say that Adam was right – it was far too dangerous for a woman in her condition to attempt to travel through a countryside torn in two by divided loyalties. "The Marches have their fair share of Despenser men too," he continued. "Not everyone west of Worcester loves Roger Mortimer."

No sooner was Kit off her horse than she set out to find the castle's chapel. She found it easily enough, and upon seeing Earl Thomas making his way towards her, she darted inside. Not that such evasive manoeuvres were of any use with the earl: moments later, she heard his boots on the stone flags behind her.

"I am sorry for your son," he said.

Kit nodded, not trusting herself to speak. She fumbled with her precious beeswax candle, and his hand closed round hers, steadying it.

"Let me help."

Together, they set the wick to the fluttering flame of a fat tallow candle, and soon Kit's candle was standing among the others, a little spark of brightness in remembrance of the child who was no more.

"He's with the angels now," Thomas said.

"Two," she whispered. "Two little angels." She couldn't contain the sob. "Two too many."

Without a word, Thomas swept her into an embrace. Kit was too heartsore to protest. Instead, she hid her face in the soft fabric of his robe.

"He died without me," she said at long last.

"It's not your fault." He leaned back to see her face.

"I know. But that doesn't help."

"No, I dare say it doesn't." Earl Thomas adjusted her veil. "Better?"

Kit shrugged. No, not better. It would never be better. "I—"

"Kit?"

She jumped at the sound of her husband's voice, retreating from the earl. Adam was standing in the doorway, his gaze leaping from the earl to her. "Sweeting?" He strode towards them, scowling at the earl. "And what are you doing here, Earl Thomas?"

"I was offering comfort, no more." Thomas bowed in Kit's direction. "Your wife is beyond doubt the most attractive woman present, but I would not stoop to paying court to a distressed and bereaved mother." He flashed Kit a smile. "But

I may be back to do just that once you are recovered, my lady."

"She's my wife!"

"And besotted with you, Adam." Thomas clapped him on the shoulder. "But you can't blame a man for trying, can you?" With a wink in Kit's direction, he left.

"Rogue," Adam muttered to his back.

"He was just being kind." Kit leaned into him. "Am I the most attractive woman present?"

Adam kissed her nose. "Seeing as there's only one woman present…"

"Adam!" But the bantering helped, and Kit emerged from the chapel in a far better mood than when she'd entered it.

The castle's kitchen staff outdid themselves that night. Ducks stuffed with chestnuts and simmered in sweet wine, venison served in a rich sauce in which juniper figured prominently, pork and cabbage, leek pies, beef braised with onions and ale – the great hall was alive with the sound of men eating and drinking, laughing and singing. At the high table, the queen presided, flanked by her son and the Earl of Norfolk, while Lord Mortimer sat some yards to her right, deep in conversation with the bishops of Hereford and Lincoln.

Kit nibbled at pork crackling and wondered if the two bishops knew that, come nighttime, Mortimer would join his lover in her chamber, only to emerge an hour or so before dawn. They probably did; neither of the men were fools, and from the look of things Mortimer considered both Bishop Orleton and Bishop Burghersh his friends.

It was well past compline by the time the queen retired, announcing she would see Mortimer, the bishops and the earls of Norfolk and Kent in her chamber for further discussion.

"And my son," she added, smiling at Prince Edward. Kit groaned inwardly; generally, where the prince went, there went Adam, and in his present mood Adam would insist on Kit accompanying him. Fortunately, this time Adam was not invited, and some moments later they were outside, making for their lodgings.

Wallingford had a sizeable garrison, with sufficient men to have held out against the queen and Lord Mortimer for some weeks had they so wished. Instead, they had opened the gates, and at present most of them were drunk, having been the recipients of the queen's grateful largesse. Walking across the inner bailey meant stepping over a number of sprawled men, and in one corner one of the guards was swiving a woman, only discernible by the pallor of her bared legs. Adam stroked Kit's inner wrist with one of his fingers.

No sooner were they alone in their room than Adam was on her. His lips left a trail of wet kisses down her neck, his hands slid over the swell of her belly to cup her breasts, and Kit exhaled, succumbing to his caresses. He was warm and he was strong, he was here and so was she, and Tom was dead, but they weren't, and... Kit's throat clogged, but instead of tears there were kisses – his kisses, soft and tender on her eyelids, on her mouth, and the grief receded somewhat, replaced by hot need, by skin that sizzled under his touch. She would have to confess for this later, but she had long ago decided that to take pleasure in her husband's body had to count as a minor sin. Why else would God have made Adam's touch so irresistible?

She stood on her toes to kiss him full on the mouth. He smiled under her lips and backed her towards the bed, deft fingers undoing her veil and laces as they went. The pelts tickled her naked skin, and she shivered in a sudden draught of air. His body atop hers, his weight on his arms, and her hips rose to meet his. A seamless joining, two halves made one as he gently entered her, moving slowly but steadily. She wanted this to last forever, this rhythmic rocking that suffused her with warmth, filling her with peace rather than passion.

Afterwards, she nestled close to him, pressing her naked body against his. A pleased rumble emanated from Adam, already sunk halfway to sleep. Kit yawned, pressed her ear to his chest and relaxed within the warmth of the coverlets.

The child in her womb turned and kicked. Kit rolled over onto her back; a healthy babe, but she couldn't quite rejoice in it, swamped by guilt. Tom was dead – she had failed in keeping him safe, had not even been there to hold him as he died. Kit blinked away a tear. At least little Meg was safe – as was her man, sleeping beside her. And then it struck her that this was not entirely true – not until the king and Despenser were destroyed. With a sigh, she turned onto her side. After some moments, she turned the other way instead, the entire bed swaying with her movements.

"Mmm?" Adam rose on his elbow, tousled hair standing messily around his head. "What is the matter, sweeting? You twist and turn like a sow in a beehive."

"What happens if the king and Despenser escape?" The messengers riding in earlier had said that the latest news had the king, Despenser and the royal treasure making for the Welsh coast, there to flee to Ireland.

"They won't." He sounded curt.

"But if they do? What then?"

Adam lay down, staring up at the ceiling. "Woe betide us if that happens," he muttered. "And especially Prince Edward."

"He's troubled," Kit said. "I heard him yelling at the queen today, saying that as far as he was concerned, the king was the king, fit to rule once free of the evil influence of the Despensers."

"Ah. And what did the queen say to that?"

"That he was a child, a fool if he believed the king capable of ruling this kingdom." Kit shifted on her bottom. "But he *is* the king. By what right can the queen and Mortimer relieve him of his crown?"

"What choice is there?" He sounded bleak. "The moment the king is back in power, he will destroy them."

"And Edward?"

"The prince?" Adam rolled over to face her and tugged at a lock of her hair. "He would pay the highest price of all. A rebellious son must be severely punished."

"And does he know this?"

Adam gave a mirthless little laugh. "Of course he does. The lad is far wiser than his mother gives him credit for." He tugged at her hair again, bringing her close enough that he could brush her nose with his. "Best pray that both the king and Despenser are speedily apprehended, Kit. For our sake, for the sake of our children, but also for the sake of our young lord."

They arrived in Gloucester some days later, and the queen gave yet another rousing speech, repeating that all she was doing was bringing an end to tyranny. The rabble cheered, and the same people who had hosted and feasted the king a week or so back now opened their larders and homes to the queen and her companions, an endless line of wealthy burghers and merchants hastening to assure the queen that they were her loyal men – as were all the nearby knights, the men-at-arms that guarded the gates, the apprentices and tradesmen, every single goodwife and all of the clerics presently in residence.

"Rats," Kit murmured to William. "The moment the ship starts to sink, they scurry for safety." She leaned against the window ledge behind her and studied the men, watching with wry amusement as they showered the queen – and her son – with gifts.

William grunted some sort of agreement, and Kit went back to watching the spectacle of the fawning men. Three dust-covered men were presently making their way towards the dais, one of them carrying a wrapped object.

"What now?" Adam said, having suddenly materialised beside her. "More merchants bearing gifts?"

"Travel-worn merchants," William said. "And in a hurry, as they've not even bothered to wash before presenting themselves to the queen."

"Hush!" Kit waved at them to be quiet.

"My lady!" The tallest of the men knelt before the queen. "We have come from London with a gift."

"From London?" The queen rose. "What is happening in London? And what of my son? Is he safe?"

"Prince John has been entrusted with the city," the man replied with a grin. "Your son rules us all in your name."

"God's truth!" William muttered. "The lad is what? Nine?"

"Something like that." Kit studied the smallest of the men, who was holding the wrapped object at some distance from him, his freckled nose wrinkled. "What have they brought her?"

"Not a posy, from the look of it," Adam said.

By the dais, the taller of the men signalled for the freckled man to unveil their gift. It took time, one layer after the other of cloth peeled away from something that was round and sticky – at least to judge from the stains on some of the rags that were dropped to the floor. One last length of cloth, a curse, and whatever the man was holding slipped from his hold to land on the floor with a sound like a lamb's carcass hitting a cutting board.

A head! Kit gagged, and the queen took three steps backwards, her elbow supported by Mortimer, who was staring down at the severed head with an expression of revulsion.

"What is the meaning of this?" he snapped.

"We bring you the head of Walter Stapledon, former Treasurer and Bishop of Exeter," the tall man pronounced. He proceeded to tell the story of the bishop's death, from when he rode out in armour, with his men-at-arms at his back to protect his London house from looting, to when he turned and fled, chased by the enraged mob. "He never made it to the sanctuary of St Paul," the tall man commented.

"No, I can see that," the queen said, wrinkling her brow when the tall man recounted how the mob had caught up with the hapless bishop and dragged him screaming all the way down Paternoster Row, before executing him on Cheapside.

"With a bread knife," the youngest of the Londoners piped up. "Took him a right long time to die, it did. Serve him right, bastard that he was." He looked at the queen expectantly, as a hound would look at its master when placing a hare at his feet. The queen gave him a weak smile, thanked them all for this precious gift, and then had her guards usher the people outside.

Only once they were alone did the queen turn to Mortimer, leaning heavily against him.

"Sweet Jesus, what have they done?" she groaned. "And on my behalf, no less." She glanced at the head, now covered by a cloak. "I may not have liked Stapledon, but he should not have died like that." She shook her head. "This is not right, Roger. That mob must be brought under control. We cannot condone this sort of behaviour – ever!"

"Of course not. But first things first, my lady. We must capture the king and Despenser before we turn our attention to London."

"And my son? He is nine! What will they expose him to?" The queen muttered something uncomplimentary about Londoners in general, making Mortimer frown.

"Some of our staunchest supporters are Londoners, my lady." He took her hands. "I will dispatch some of our best men to London today to keep watch over the prince. For now, that will have to do."

"I can go, Maman." Prince Edward skirted the covered head and came to stand by his mother. "With your leave, I can set out for London immediately."

Kit was not sure if it was only she who noticed the look that flashed between Lord Mortimer and the queen. A minimal headshake from Mortimer, and the queen's long lashes dipped in acquiescence.

"No, Edward, you cannot." She placed her hand on his arm. "I need you here, my son. Our men need you here – it is for you they fight."

"For me?" A mulish look settled on the prince's face. "I want to go, Maman!"

"And I say that you may not." With a wave of her hand, she dismissed her son before instructing one of the guards to take care of Stapledon's head. She said something to Lord Mortimer, and left the room without as much as a glance at her fuming son. In a matter of moments, the hall was empty except for the prince, Adam, William and Kit.

Prince Edward stood as if rooted to the spot, staring after his mother. "*Loupe*," he said, kicking at a nearby table. He turned to face them. "What am I lending myself to? As we progress through the country, the rabble rises in our wake, looting and burning as it pleases. In the name of freeing England from the Despenser yoke, we are allowing the mob to run wild – and all of this is done in my name. My name!" Edward slammed his hand down on the table. "I will not stand for lawlessness. And to see the head of a bishop roll on the floor…" He closed his eyes.

"These things are easily quenched, my lord," Adam said, moving close enough to place a hand on the prince's shoulder. "In time we will restore order – in your name."

"And meanwhile innocent men lose their lives," the prince said.

"The bishop was not innocent," Adam replied. "Walter Stapledon was not a good man, my lord."

"But he was a bishop, Sir Adam." The prince gave him a chilly look. "I will not condone the murder of prelates – not in my realm."

"Your lady mother was not pleased," Kit put in. "Nor was Lord Mortimer."

The prince grimaced. "No, they weren't," he conceded, throwing himself down in the armchair his mother had recently vacated. "But they won't punish the men who killed him."

"How can they?" Kit said. "Are they to execute the mob?"

"No, I suppose not." Edward hooked a long leg over the armrest. "But it is wrong all the same."

Chapter 36

A week before All Hallows', Bristol Castle fell to Mortimer and his men.

"At last," Adam muttered to William, watching as the Despenser banners were torn down and replaced by the royal arms. A short siege all in all, Adam reflected; eight days in which the beleaguered Earl of Winchester had attempted to negotiate terms of surrender which would guarantee him his life – to no avail. Lord Roger had every intention of avenging himself on the elder Despenser for his years in exile, for his lost lands and fortune.

"He's an old man," the queen had said that same morning. "Punish him, imprison him, but allow him to keep his life."

"Never." Lord Roger had slammed down his goblet. "The Despensers must die: for what they've done to me, to men I loved and respected." He rose, pulled on his gloves, and gestured for his new squire to fetch his cloak. "You can't expect me to forgive," he added in a calmer voice. "Had it been them capturing me, do you think they would have let me live?" He shook his head. "They'd have disembowelled me and hung me from the castle's walls, for everyone to see."

The queen blanched. Her hand closed on Lord Roger's sleeve, fingers tightening around the fine, blood-red velvet of his tunic. He covered her hand with his, and in one of his rare affectionate gestures, leaned forward to kiss her cheek. There'd been a soft rustling among the assembled men at his familiarity with the queen, a sound quickly suppressed when Lord Roger straightened up.

As he strode from the room, Lord Roger had beckoned for Adam to follow. On his lips hovered a shadow of a smile, and it was Adam's impression that Lord Roger was quite satisfied with the recent little scene. The prince, however, had smouldered like a thundercloud, trailing Lord Roger with his hand clenched tight around the pommel of his dagger.

A hoarse yell recalled Adam to the present. Hugh Despenser the elder was being dragged through the castle's main gate, so heaped in chains he could scarcely walk.

"He'll not live through the day." William jerked his head to where Lord Roger was astride his horse, watching Despenser as a spider might watch a trapped fly.

"He deserves to die," Adam said.

"Aye. And he deserves a trial." William frowned at the royal earls, who had dismounted and were now jeering at Despenser.

"He'll get one," Adam said.

"No he won't." William gave him an exasperated look. "The tribunal has already found him guilty."

Most likely. Lord Roger, the royal earls, Henry of Lancaster and his two retainers – all of them men with axes of their own to grind when it came to the Despensers. All the same, Adam could not dredge up any pity for the hitherto so proud Earl of Winchester.

The prisoner was marched into the hall, still in his hauberk and mail chausses. Lord Roger leapt off his horse and sauntered after him, accompanied by the royal earls. Some yards behind them came the prince and Sir Henry, who beckoned for Adam to come with them.

To his credit, Hugh Despenser senior did not break down and weep. He stood erect as his peers listed his crimes, and the single time he attempted to object he was waved to silence. Sentence was passed: Despenser was to be hanged and beheaded – immediately. Hugh the elder merely nodded, scratched at his scraggly beard and requested a barber and a priest. Lord Roger was so taken aback by the man's acceptance of his fate that he sent off one of his men for a chaplain, and another to find a barber.

"My son will avenge my death." Despenser the elder gave Lord Roger a mirthless smile.

"I think not." Lord Roger pared at a nail with his dagger, eyeing Despenser from under his brows. "In fact, I think dear Hugh will soon be adorning a gallows all of his own."

"You think?" Despenser rubbed at his stringy neck.

"Oh, yes." Lord Roger nodded slowly.

"He'll be back!" Despenser's voice rose. "He and the king will return, and then you will die like a dog."

"Return from where?" Earl Thomas asked, and Despenser snapped his mouth shut.

Lord Roger chuckled. "From what we've heard, the king and your son are still in Wales – blown back to Cardiff." His face hardened. "They will not get away. Not this time."

Despenser gasped. "He's your king! You owe him your allegiance."

"I owe him nothing, oath-breaker that he is," Lord Roger snapped. He swivelled, facing Prince Edward. "But I gladly pledge myself to his son." He bowed deeply.

"A boy!" Despenser glared at the prince. "Where is your loyalty, lad? How can you abandon your father in this, his moment of dire need?"

Prince Edward opened his mouth and swallowed a couple of times, making Despenser sneer.

"Abandon his father?" Queen Isabella entered the hall, followed by Kit, and approached the prisoner. A cloud, Adam reflected, watching the queen's garments billow round her – or rather the sky, seeing as his lady queen was dressed in various shades of blue, save her white veil, topped by a circlet of miniature golden flowers. "Is it not his father who has abandoned us? All of us?" She widened her arms, displaying her intricately embroidered sleeves. "The king has fled his kingdom, leaving the country rudderless." Isabella gave her son a dazzling smile. "Fortunately, his son is here, with us."

Kit was standing several feet behind the queen, demurely dressed in dark green, her vibrant hair covered by a matching veil. She gave Adam a brief smile before transferring her attention to the prince.

"Most fortunate," Lord Roger echoed, coming to stand beside the queen. Earl Thomas grinned and slapped Prince Edward on the shoulder, and suddenly Adam understood. So, apparently, did Kit, her eyes widening as she studied the prince.

"Maman?" Edward wet his lips. "What—"

"Not now," the queen interrupted. She clapped her hands together, and just like that, the hall emptied of people, while the Earl of Winchester was carried off to meet the barber and a priest, surrounded by a contingent of men. "It is time," she said softly, regarding her son.

"Time?" Edward shuffled on his feet, his gaze darting from his royal uncles to his mother. Earl Edmund was leaning against the wall, arms crossed over his broad chest. His brother lounged beside him, thumbs hooked in his sword belt.

"Your father has left the country," Lord Roger said. "The kingdom requires a regent."

"You?" Prince Edward demanded heatedly.

"Me?" Lord Roger laughed. "Of course not me." He knelt. "You, my lord."

"Me?" Edward stared at his mother. "Why me?"

"Why you?" The queen laughed softly. "Because you're the heir to the throne, Edward. Who else?" She strolled over to pat her son on the cheek. "But you need not concern yourself with all this – I will rule on your behalf. You're too young to be saddled with such responsibilities."

The prince's mouth set in a stubborn line, eyes narrowing. But he didn't say anything; he merely bowed and left the room.

It took Adam hours to find the prince. By the time he did, the Earl of Winchester was dead, his head adorning a spike, his body cut to pieces and the blood on the cobbles congealing. Edward was standing on the battlements, staring out towards the west, where the autumn sun was setting in a display of oranges and reds.

"They murdered him," the prince said when Adam joined him, leaning his elbows on the parapet.

"They executed him," Adam corrected.

"There was no real trial." Edward studied his hands, turning them this way and that. "A peer of the realm, and they just beheaded him."

"As your father did with his cousin, Thomas of Lancaster," Adam replied.

The prince shrugged. "Two wrongs do not make a right," he said softly. He dislodged some mortar from between the stones and crumbled it to grit. "She rules in my name, but what if I do not agree?" Without turning around, he jerked his head in the direction of Winchester's severed one. "I did not will that."

"He deserved it, my lord," Adam said.

"He did? And so says who? Mortimer?" Edward pushed off from the wall. "Maybe he did deserve it – but he should have had his day in court. In my kingdom, a man will always be allowed to speak in his defence. Always."

"Sometimes expediency is more important," Adam tried.

"Nothing is more important than honour," the prince said. "There is nothing honourable about dragging a defenceless man to the gallows."

Adam smiled somewhat sadly; soon enough, his lord would learn that sometimes honour came at a high price – too high, when considering the welfare of his realm.

Next morning, Adam was ordered to present himself before the regent, and found to his surprise that the prince was presiding over the meeting, Lord Roger standing to his right, Earl Thomas at his left. The earl was fuming, the prince looked discomfited, Lord Roger was his normal unflappable self, and Henry of Lancaster was beaming, his long hands twitching at the folds of his tunic – for the day in a shade of green that reminded Adam of summer peas.

"I can go!" Earl Thomas said.

"But you will not. Lancaster will," Prince Edward said, sounding tired. He glanced at his uncle and lowered his voice. "I can't send you off to capture the…" He cleared his throat. "…Our father. He's your brother!"

"Most wise, my lord," Lord Roger put in. "We have no desire to cause the king more anguish than necessary."

"Than necessary?" The prince kicked at the floor. "If we don't want to cause him anguish, we should invite him here and receive him as our lord and king."

"The people will not have him as their king, Ned," Earl Thomas said.

"The people?" Edward laughed. "The people do not care one way or the other – not really. The ones who care are the peers of the realm, Lord Mortimer and the princes of the church."

"As I said, the people – the ones that count," Thomas said, giving his angry nephew a patronising smile.

"I can leave within the hour," Henry of Lancaster broke in.

"Adam goes with you," Prince Edward said.

"My lord?" Adam was in two minds about this, one part as eager as an alaunt on the morning of a hunt, the other reluctant to leave his wife.

"You heard," Lord Roger said briskly. He gave Adam a fleeting smile. "I want Despenser alive – very alive." The tone of his voice made shivers walk up Adam's spine.

Kit listened, sighed deeply and said that she wished she'd gone home, but at Adam's stern reproof promised that she would do as he bid and remain with the queen while he set off with Lancaster to find the king – and Despenser.

"Will you catch them, do you think?" She folded an extra tunic and some hose, and rolled it all together before inserting the bundle into one of his saddlebags.

"We will – if they remain in Wales."

Kit followed Adam outside, standing to the side as he mounted. The cold wind had her crossing her arms in an effort to keep herself from shivering, her gaze never leaving her man, already so focused on the upcoming hunt. But at the last moment he turned Raven and rode over to where she was standing.

"Once I'm back, we'll go home," he said.

"Truly?" She stepped close enough to touch his leg, and his gloved hand came down to cover hers.

"Truly. When I'm back, it will all be over," he said softly. "Once the king and Despenser are taken captive, the queen has won."

"The queen and Lord Mortimer, you mean."

"The queen." He smiled wryly. "In this venture, Lord Roger remains in her shadow. Wise, if you ask me."

"Be careful." She squeezed his thigh, feeling his muscles harden under her hand.

"And you." Adam placed his hand over his heart and bowed slightly. Kit responded by blowing him a kiss, and then he was gone, galloping out of the bailey to catch up with his companions.

"God will keep him safe," William said, coming over to Kit.

She nodded distractedly. She did not fear for Adam's physical well-being on this mission – but she feared he might do something that would forever burden his conscience.

"Like killing that miserable creature Hugh Despenser?" William said when she shared this with him. He turned her slightly so that she could see Lord Mortimer, side by side with the queen. "They want Despenser alive."

"And the king?"

William threw a cautious look at their surroundings, and bent his head in her direction. "It would be fortunate if he died. Makes it simpler for everyone. But from wishing he meets with an accident to actually killing him…" William lowered his voice even further. "It would take a fool to do so – at least openly." He nodded in the direction of Prince Edward, standing very much on his own. "He would never forgive."

Kit shivered. William was right. "So then what?"

William gave her a helpless look. "It's in God's hands."

Her conversation with William stayed with Kit for most of the morning. After a frugal midday meal, the queen retired to her rooms – the only chambers in this huge castle that were moderately warm – and settled down to sew in the company of the few ladies present. On the opposite side of the room, the men settled down to play chess and drink wine, their voices low.

"Do you love Lord Mortimer, my lady?" Kit didn't look up from the yarn she was winding into a ball.

"Love him?" The queen laughed softly. "Do you need to ask?"

Kit glanced at her. The queen was sitting with her hands loosely clasped in her lap, gaze fixed on Mortimer, who was at present conducting an intense discussion with Earl Thomas, the chessboard forgotten.

"If you do, then you should let him go. You should encourage him to return to his wife, to leave all this." Kit made a vague gesture at the Flemish tapestries, the silk-embroidered cushions in the window bench.

"Let him go? I don't have Roger on a leash. The man is free to do as he pleases."

"You have him by his heart, my lady. He will never leave you unless you order him to."

"Do you truly believe so?" The queen's face softened, large eyes growing luminous.

"I do." Kit bent her head. "Unfortunately – for him."

"How unfortunate?"

Kit wondered how a woman as astute as Isabella could at times be so innocent – or maybe it was simply a matter of not wanting to confront certain aspects of reality.

"One day, your son will look for someone to blame for his father's fate. He won't blame you – how can he, you're his mother – and so he will blame him."

"Edward admires Roger," the queen protested.

"Sometimes – but not always." Kit regarded the queen steadily. "He didn't like it when Lord Mortimer threatened to kill you if you decided to return to your husband."

"Words spoken in passion," the queen scoffed, her mouth softening into a pleased curve.

"You know that, I know that. Prince Edward may choose not to know that." Kit shifted closer and lowered her voice. "A man who beds the queen commits high treason, my lady. And we all know how traitors die."

Queen Isabella's hand trembled violently. "How dare you speak to me like that?"

"I'm telling you the truth, my lady." Kit knelt before the queen. "Let him go – tell him you're tired of him, send him back to his beloved Welsh Marches, to his family. Clip his wings, my lady – for his sake."

"Clip his wings?" The queen looked at her lover. "How can you possibly suggest I do that? Look at him, look at how strong and noble he is. So much power, so much vitality... Besides, Roger Mortimer does not take kindly to people who tell him what to do."

"Unless it is you. He loves you, will do anything for you."

"You truly think so?" The queen sounded amused. "That man was destined for power, and now that it is within his grasp, he will not relinquish it. Besides, I can't give him up. Not now, when I have found him. He was meant for me." She shook out her skirts and rose. "And my son loves me. He would never harm my man."

Chapter 37

It was as cold and wet as Adam had expected it to be. Well over a fortnight since they had left Bristol, and they were deep into the Welsh countryside. So far, their party had met no resistance, and from what rumours they heard, it appeared the king had been abandoned by everyone but a small band of followers. Adam shifted in his saddle: it didn't sit right, to give the king chase as if he were a wounded hart. But Despenser was another matter. Adam tightened his hold on the reins.

That same evening they set up camp some miles east of Neath. Henry of Lancaster grumbled about the wind and the food, the lack of good wine and comely wenches. Some goblets of wine later, and he was staring blearily at the fire, muttering that it was not right if that upstart Mortimer was given more influence over the new king than he was. A sore point, Adam had gathered over the last few days, listening to Lancaster's aggrieved ranting. It wasn't only Lancaster: several of the knights held similar opinions, one of the more vociferous being William la Zouche, a man of Adam's age or thereabouts.

Adam was just about to retire to the tent he shared with la Zouche, Gavin and la Zouche's squire when the sentries called out. In a matter of moments, Adam had his sword in his hand, yelling his men-at-arms into order.

"An emissary," one of the sentries called. "From the king."

"Well, well," la Zouche said, returning his sword to his scabbard. He grinned at Adam. "We must be uncomfortably close, eh?"

"He has nowhere to go," Adam replied.

"No." La Zouche kicked at the ground. "Poor man: he had it all, and he's lost it all."

"He failed us – all of us," Adam said harshly.

"He did. But he didn't choose to be king, did he?" La

Zouche sauntered off to where Lancaster was standing.

The unknown man was riding a neat little palfrey, accompanied by four other men, unarmed and astride a motley collection of hill ponies. Monks, Adam concluded when he glimpsed their sandalled feet. The man in the lead slid off his horse.

"I come in peace," he said. He bowed, revealing a tonsured head. "I come on behalf of our liege, King Edward."

"And you are?" Lancaster asked.

"The abbot of Neath." The monk's eyes darted back and forth over the assembled men, his plump lower lip wobbling. "I come in peace," he repeated, sounding like a bleating sheep.

"I heard you the first time." Lancaster gestured for the abbot to sit, then snapped his fingers at one of the pages, who promptly pressed a goblet into the abbot's hand. "So, what does Edward want?" Lancaster studied the abbot from beneath bushy brows.

The churchman's hand shook as he raised the cup to his lips. "Our liege wishes to sue for peace."

"Oh, he does, does he?" Lancaster rocked back on his stool. "It's too late for that, I fear. My lady the queen has made it quite clear that they expect a complete surrender."

The abbot coughed, spraying his habit with wine. "A complete surrender? He's our king!"

"Not for much longer," Lancaster replied with a shrug.

"You aim to kill the king?" The abbot stood. "He's our anointed liege."

"No one has said anything about killing him," Adam interrupted. "But he must surrender – him and all his followers."

"That he will never do," the abbot said.

"No great matter." Lancaster beckoned for a refill of his goblet. "We will catch him soon enough." He studied the abbot over the rim of his cup. "Maybe you should tell him that."

Apparently, the abbot had done just that, Adam reflected the next morning. How else to explain the excited scout, who insisted he'd seen the king and his followers riding at speed away from Neath?

They caught up with the fugitives just after noon. Less than twenty men, riding Hell for leather over the moor.

"Outflank them!" Lancaster yelled, and Adam nodded, urging Raven into a gallop. His men followed his lead, thundering in formation over the undulating terrain. Before them, the fleeing men attempted to increase their speed, but their horses were flagging. A hat flew off, revealing the distinctive fair hair of the king. The king. Adam swallowed.

At some point, their quarry concluded it was pointless. They drew their horses to a halt and assembled in a tight knot, the king in the middle. Adam slowed Raven to a trot. Lancaster took the lead, followed by his knights. Adam did not need to see Lancaster's face to know that he was gloating. He could hear it in his voice as he addressed his king, curtly informing him he was now a captive and was to be taken to Kenilworth. There was an angry exclamation from one of the king's men, but the king raised his hand, silencing him.

"And my companions?" he asked.

"They go elsewhere," Lancaster replied. "The queen requests the presence of Despenser and Baldock in Hereford."

"Hereford? What awaits them there?" the king demanded.

"What do you think?" Lancaster hissed, and the king blanched.

"No," he said, sounding about to weep. "No." He turned to the man closest to him, still undistinguishable in a dark cloak. A gloved hand appeared from under the folds of heavy cloth, and the king gripped it, holding on as if he would never let go. Adam had to avert his gaze when the king was forcibly separated from his men, his fingers prised open. This was not right, for an anointed king to be dragged away like that.

"Hugh!" the king yelled, his voice breaking.

The cloaked man threw back his hood. "My dearest liege!" Despenser stood in his stirrups. "Edward, I—" Whatever he had intended to say was lost in a groan when Lancaster pulled him off his horse.

"Hugh!" The king tore free from the men holding him

and came running towards his chancellor. Lancaster blocked him, his sword hovering over Despenser's head.

"I have been charged with getting you to Kenilworth," Lancaster said. "Only you, my lord."

"I will not stand for it," the king snapped. "I insist on having my companions with me." He drew in a long, shaky breath. "Please, cousin, do not do this."

"I do as I must," Lancaster said. "You ride with us to Kenilworth. La Zouche, you come with me." He turned to Adam. "You are to take Despenser, Reading and Baldock to Hereford."

"Gladly," Adam said. He looked at Despenser, but the former royal chancellor did not even glance at him, all of him straining in the direction of the king.

"Ah, yes, I can imagine." Lancaster grinned. "He's to arrive in one piece, de Guirande."

"Of course, my lord."

Lancaster called his men together, the protesting king was transferred to a fresh mount, and with a wave in Adam's direction Lancaster set off.

"I will never see him again," Despenser said dully, raising a shaking hand to smooth his hair. Gone was the arrogant royal chancellor, the elegant grandee. No longer in silks and velvets, before Adam was a man in a simple worsted tunic, his hose stained and the once so elegant boots covered in mud. The dark hair was dirty and lank, the eyes lay like dark pools in hollows so bruised Adam surmised the man hadn't slept in days.

"Probably not – unless it is in Hell," Adam said, dismounting. His voice made Despenser jerk, a flash of fear across his face before he regained control over his features.

"Ah, Adam de Guirande," he drawled. "Imagine meeting here, dear Adam." He gave Adam a lopsided grin. "And how is your precious son?"

Adam's fist connected with Despenser's chin, hard enough to land him flat on the muddy ground.

"Dead," Adam said. "But you already know that, don't you? You knew he was dead when you threatened to kill him unless I murdered Lord Roger."

"I did? I think not – I do not concern myself with the well-being of hostage brats." Despenser got to his knees. "It was worth a try, dear Adam. I gambled – and it could have worked."

"And what if I had? What if I'd dishonoured myself for nothing?"

Despenser wiped at the blood that trickled from his burst lip. "I never held it to be particularly likely that you'd agree to assassinate that precious baron of yours. In fact," Despenser sneered, "I was quite convinced that you'd always set him before your wife and children – but it was entertaining to imagine you grappling with such a horrible choice. Predictably, you chose Mortimer." He feigned a yawn. "Does your wife not resent having to share you with him?"

"My wife shares me with no one," Adam said.

Despenser snickered. "No?" He licked his lips. "Ah yes, I forgot: it's the other way around, isn't it? You share her with him."

Then and there, Adam would gladly have gutted him, leaving him to die on the moor. He even pulled his dagger, but Gavin got hold of him, hanging like a weight on his arm.

"No, m'lord!" Gavin panted. "He's riling you on purpose. He wants you to kill him."

"So do I," Adam snarled, trying to shake Gavin off. His Kit had never been unfaithful to him, he knew that. It had been her lookalike sister who pandered to Lord Roger's lusts, and yet...

"But Mortimer doesn't, m'lord," Gavin said. "You know what Lord Mortimer wants."

So, apparently, did Despenser, who went a sickly white. With a curse, Adam sheathed his dagger.

Ten days later, Adam woke at dawn: a surly November day was in the making, an icy wind carrying the occasional shower of rain. Since that first heated exchange with Hugh Despenser, he had kept well away from his prisoners, ensuring from a distance that the three men were adequately restrained at night, were clothed and offered food.

Of the three, Baldock was holding up best, no doubt confident that his status as a clergyman would save him from the fate of the other two. Adam repeatedly told himself that they deserved what was coming, but today, mere miles from Hereford, he couldn't stomach the idea of food. Today, Hugh Despenser would die in the most gruesome way possible.

Gavin saddled up their horses. Adam sat up, and ordered the prisoners to be brought out. They led Hugh out in only his shirt, barelegged and goose-pimpled with cold. Someone tugged a surcoat over his head – backwards. Despenser did not seem to notice, his gaze fixed on a sliver of blue sky. Days of refusing food or drink had reduced him to a frail shadow of himself, and he stumbled when he was led towards the nag that was to convey him to Hereford and death.

Seeing him so stripped of all the apparels of power woke a most unwelcome sensation of pity in Adam, even more so when one of the other men pressed down a crown of nettles on Despenser's head – hard enough to cause the man to wince.

"Happy now?" Despenser asked once he was astride, and something of the old Despenser still lived in his voice, smooth and cultured. "Is this what you wanted to witness, dear Adam?"

"It is," Adam said.

"And when the time comes, will you witness Mortimer's humiliation as well?"

"That will not happen."

"You think not?" Despenser coughed, a loud, racking cough that left him out of breath. "Then you are a fool. That baron of yours is far more like me than you think."

Adam shook his head.

"Oh yes, he is. Have you not seen the signs already? A wish to rule, albeit from the shadows, a desire for gold and lands, restitution for what he lost at first, but soon it will be more than that – much more. Riches beget a hunger for more riches – trust me, I should know." He coughed again. "And what will he do when other men demand a say in how things are ordered? Will he welcome Lancaster, Norfolk and our dear, vain Edmund to the table?"

Adam looked away, and Despenser laughed. "He will overreach, dear Adam. Men like he and I always do – it is our curse, this unsated hunger for more of everything life can offer." He leaned closer. "Unfortunately for Mortimer, he has placed a pup on the throne that will grow into a magnificent hound, and God save whoever comes between him and his bone."

Once through the city gate, drums and horns greeted them. People surged around them, and Adam was ordered to not interfere as the mob threw themselves at the three hapless men. Despenser disappeared in a welter of arms and legs, and Adam caught himself hoping that maybe he would die, trampled underfoot. Surely a more merciful way to die than the one awaiting him.

A stark naked Despenser was hoisted back on his horse. His body was covered in what Adam at first assumed to be blood, but a closer look indicated it was ink, his entire back covered in scrawled writing. The crowd cheered, and Despenser and Reading were carried over to the market square, where the queen and Mortimer were waiting, together with the other members of the tribunal. Adam searched the people assembled around them, relaxing when he concluded that Kit was not there – nor was the prince.

It was a farce. There was no other word for it, and for all that Adam truly believed Hugh Despenser was a snake, a viper best stamped to death, it sat badly with him to witness this trial that was no trial. A long list of accusations was read out, atrocious acts, to be sure, each and every one deserving harsh punishment. Despenser did nothing, said nothing. All he did was stare at Roger Mortimer, who stared back, smirked and served himself some wine, sipping slowly as he listened to the detailed description of Despenser's heinous crimes.

When the expected sentence was read out, the crowd roared its approval. Adam turned away from the spectacle of tying Despenser to four horses, but the mob carried him with them as Despenser was dragged towards the castle. Christ our Saviour! Adam gaped. He had never seen a gallows so high: this one towered well over forty feet above the ground. On the ground, a fire was burning, and the executioner made a show of whetting his knife, slowly, in front of the condemned men.

A noose was placed round Despenser's neck. Up he went, dangling like a side of beef. Stark naked, his pale skin covered by welts and bruises, he was hoisted upwards, that ridiculous crown of nettles still clinging to his head. The people cheered. Adam had to look away, disturbed by the spectacle of the man twitching like a maggot.

Despenser was still alive when he was lowered to the ground. Of course he was; it was the executioner's responsibility to ensure he remained alive for as long as possible. The knife glinted in the sun. There was an inhuman shriek and the executioner held up something that had the crowd yet again erupting in cheers. With a grin, the executioner threw the bloodied genitals in the fire. They sizzled and spat like sausages, and a thin spiral of smoke lifted towards the skies.

When the executioner yet again turned to Despenser, by now a collection of bloodied limbs, Adam had had enough. He turned Raven and rode off, passing in front of the raised platform on which Mortimer and the queen were sitting, watching the spectacle while partaking of wine and food. Mortimer's dark eyes met Adam's, one brow raised. Adam made a disgusted face and spurred Raven into a trot, making for the castle's gate.

Kit was in the outer bailey, wrapped in her cloak. The heckling and cheering carried over the walls, there was a series of loud thumps, and Adam supposed that meant Despenser was well and truly dead – they wouldn't quarter him while still alive. The moment she saw him, Kit's face brightened, and she was half-running, half-waddling towards him. So ungainly and yet so graceful, he reflected, his gaze settling with pride on her rounded belly.

"Is it done?" she asked once she'd reached him. She gestured towards the lonely figure standing on the battlements. The prince. Adam dropped off Raven and drew her close enough to kiss her forehead.

"It is," he said with a little frown. "Has he been standing there for long?" From where he was standing, the prince had an excellent view of the proceedings.

"He has." Kit gnawed her lip. "And the king?"

"At Kenilworth." The king would never regain his freedom, of that he was sure. And as long as he was alive there was a chance someone would attempt to free him, and so... no, Adam refused to conclude the thought, but he couldn't stop himself from looking at the lad, standing like a lonely sentinel on the castle wall.

Kit leaned against him. "How are you feeling?"

Adam scrubbed at his face. "Tired. Confused. I thought I'd rejoice in his death – instead I feel...empty. And soiled, somehow."

"He deserved to die," Kit said. "For what he did to you, to me, to Lord Mortimer and the queen."

"But not like that, Kit." Adam crossed himself. "They were dining while they watched," he continued in a low voice. "A man was being torn apart, and Lord Roger poured our lady queen more wine, placing morsels of stuffed quail on her trencher."

"Mortimer has waited a long time for this." Kit slipped her arm into his. "It is done, Adam. And now we can go home."

Home. Adam smiled down at her.

"Home?" The prince's voice was gravelly – and very close. "And who, pray, has given you leave to go home?"

"My lord." Adam bowed. "I had hoped—"

"Well, you hoped wrong." The prince swayed where he stood, and belatedly Adam noted he was drunk. He waved his hand at Kit. "She..." He hiccupped. "She can g—"

"My wife will not travel alone," Adam said.

"If so, then she stays!" Prince Edward cursed, stumbled and fled.

Adam found him in the castle's chapel. The lad was as pale as a sheet, trembling hands on the floor as he kneeled before the altar.

Adam crossed himself, muttered a Hail Mary under his breath and joined Edward. "My lord? How are you faring?" Adam knelt beside him.

The prince shrugged. He chewed his lip, eyes sliding over in Adam's direction. "How will they execute my father?"

"Your father? My lord, why would they execute the king?"

"The king?" Edward laughed sadly. "He is no king anymore. And what does one do with a king nobody wants?" He dragged a finger over his throat, eyes brimming with tears.

"No," Adam said. "That will not happen, my lord."

"So then what? He remains under lock and key at Kenilworth?"

"I don't know," Adam admitted.

The prince was studying him avidly, eyes that startling shade of blue that seemed to drill holes through your body all the way to your soul. "He's my father, and I have unwittingly condemned him to death."

"Not you, my lord. Never you."

Edward shook his head. "Of course me. I should have done as he asked and returned to him. Instead, I chose to stay with my mother."

"Chose? Begging your pardon, m'lord, but you're a child with no voice in the matter."

"And now I am to be king – with as little a voice." Edward lurched to his feet, stumbling towards the exit.

"My lord." Adam hastened to the prince's side, a hand shooting out to steady him.

"Leave me alone." Edward gave him a bleary look. "Take your wife and go home, Adam."

"I can't leave you like this," Adam protested.

Prince Edward gave him a clumsy hug. "You can. I'm old enough to manage without my nursemaid for some weeks." His smile took the sting out of the words. "After all," he added with a hiccup, "I'm the soon-to-be king. Kings have to manage all the time." With that he collapsed against Adam and vomited.

Chapter 38

There was to be no return home – at least not in the immediate future. Kit was not about to tear her husband away from the prince, not when the lad was so disturbed.

"He's just fourteen," she told Adam as she helped him get Edward to bed. "Too young to be left alone in this pit of lions."

With a little grunt, the prince settled into the pillow, dead to the world.

"Lions?" Adam wiped at the lad's pale face. "Vipers, rather."

Kit nodded, ducking her head so as to hide the disappointment she was certain stood clear as the light of the day on her face.

"Sweeting?" Adam's large hand covered hers. "I know your heart is set on going home. If you want, I can arrange an escort." His lips brushed her cheek. "But I would prefer you to stay until we can go together."

"And when is that, do you think?" Kit stroked her belly. Meg – she yearned for her unknown daughter, for Mabel, for…Tom. She sighed inside.

"A week, two at the most?" Adam lifted his shoulders in a helpless gesture. "Now that the matter regarding the king has been resolved, I dare say the queen and Lord Roger intend to return at speed to London. And when they do, we ride home."

"Resolved?" Kit chewed her lip. A caged king, a young lad placed on the throne in his stead – it did not seem to her that this was a neat solution, rather the reverse.

"For now." Adam's mouth set in a grim line. Any further conversation on this subject was cut short by the arrival of Sir Henry, looking an unappetising shade of grey.

"That was one of the most gruesome spectacles I have

ever witnessed," he muttered, long fingers wiping fastidiously at his sleeves, for the day a sombre dark blue. He tugged his surcoat into place and adjusted his belt. "Drunk?" He nodded in the direction of the bed.

Adam got to his feet. "Aye – and heartsore."

"He is too young for all this," Kit said. "A pawn in a complex game for power."

"Best he grow up fast, then." Sir Henry sounded tired. "He's not destined to be the pawn forever." He ushered them towards the door. "I'll stay with him. Truth be told, I'm not sure I can face the victorious queen – or her lover." He shook his head. "First Arundel, the poor man hacked to death with a sword, then this."

"Arundel?" Adam asked.

"Oh, you haven't heard?" Sir Henry grimaced. "Captured and brought here, tried for treason and sentenced to be beheaded. Mortimer instructed the executioner to use a blunted blade."

"Say the rumours," Kit objected, with a concerned look at her husband, who'd gone quite white round the mouth.

"Yes," Sir Henry admitted. "So say the rumours. But rarely does an executioner arrive without his tools in order."

Upon exiting the prince's rooms, Adam turned to Kit. "Our chamber?"

"I haven't been accorded one," Kit replied. "I have been sleeping with the queen's ladies."

"Ah."

"It's a small castle, and daily the number of ladies and lords paying court to the queen increases." She gave him a small smile. "And now, I fear we will drown in an army of well-wishers, hastening to assure the queen they were ever her loyal followers."

"I need a bath." He cut her off. "I need time with you – alone."

"Alone?" She rested against him. "When are we ever alone here?" But she smiled at his chagrin, and assured him a bath could be arranged – and in a room all to themselves.

An hour later, and Adam was sitting in a tub, long legs pulled up. She'd scrubbed him all over, and was presently lathering his hair, her fingers massaging his scalp. He closed his eyes and made a series of humming sounds.

"He didn't know," he said abruptly.

"Who?" Kit had him lean forward and poured a pitcher of warm water over his head.

"Despenser. He didn't know Tom was dead."

Kit stilled her hand. "Oh. Does it matter?" She picked up a linen towel and began drying his hair.

"No. But..." He fell silent, scrubbing at his heel with the pumice stone.

"Yes?" she prompted.

"I find it strange that he didn't know." Adam stood, water sluicing off his body.

"It doesn't change anything," Kit said bitterly. She glanced at her husband, who was staring at the opposite wall, a distant look on his face. "Adam," she added gently, "do not build hopes on Despenser's words. He didn't know because he didn't care. Our son is dead."

Would their Tom have grown up to look like Adam, tall and broad with a fuzz of golden hair on his legs and chest? She extended her hand and touched his bare shoulder, sliding her hand down to his firm buttocks. Her man, strong and vibrant.

"But we are not," she ended in a whisper. In response, he gathered her to his chest, and under her ear she could hear the steady beating of his heart.

The prince was much recovered the next day, his face acquiring a truculent look when Adam suggested he postpone returning to Tresaints for a week or so.

"Why?"

"My lord, I..." Adam was lost for words. His lord had a prickly pride and would not appreciate being cosseted. "I—"

"You're concerned about me," Prince Edward interrupted, his face softening somewhat.

"I am," Adam admitted.

The prince settled himself deeper into the window seat. "Maman once told me that you'd prove yourself true to me – and you have, well beyond what she expected." He gave Adam a little smile. "But I can survive your absence for a couple of weeks, and that wife of yours needs to go home before she bursts apart like a seedpod." He grinned. "But if it's a lad, I expect you to name him after me."

"I hope for a lad," Adam said softly.

The prince's cheeks acquired a deep red hue. "Yes, of course you do," he muttered. "A lad to replace the son you've lost."

"Not replace, my lord, never replace."

The prince's cheeks burnt even brighter. "Of course not." He stood. "Take Lady Kit home, Adam. Leave as soon as you can."

"But—"

"That was an order." Edward whistled for his dog and made for the door. "And if it's a girl, I do think Philippa has a ring to it, don't you?"

"Philippa?" Kit laughed softly. "I think not." She hadn't stopped smiling since Adam had come to tell her they were leaving on the morrow. She returned her attention to her embroidery, a light-blue length of silk decorated with miniature daisies. "For Meg," she explained, stroking one of the little flowers. "A girdle."

"She's too young for such," Adam said.

"For now." She folded together her work. "I must finish packing." She threw him a look. "Best tell Gavin to start doing the same."

"I already have." He blew her a kiss before setting off to see to his horses – and find his brother.

William was predictably pleased with Adam's news, and promised to visit Tresaints over Christmas.

"And then what?" Adam asked.

William shrugged. "I don't know. But I am sure Bishop Burghersh will find adequate use for me." His tone was surprisingly caustic.

"I thought you liked him." Adam most certainly did, finding the Bishop of Lincoln an intelligent man who somehow combined genuine piety with a nose for worldly politics.

"I do, but these last few years…" William shook his head. "I've enjoyed them, being only at Lord Roger's beck and call. I did not expect to see myself so quickly transferred to another master."

Adam was about to reply when Lord Roger himself called his name, arm raised in a wave.

Beside him, William chuckled. "I do believe Lord Roger needs you, Adam."

"What now?" Adam muttered, not liking the determined look on Mortimer's face. He shuffled closer to his brother. "As long as he doesn't ask me if I enjoyed yesterday's spectacle."

"Hmm," William replied, giving him a long look. "Lord Roger did – as did the queen."

"Yes, I saw that." As they were within earshot from Lord Roger, Adam said no more, and with an affectionate slap on his back, William excused himself, leaving Adam alone with Lord Roger.

"You want me to do what?" Adam was so surprised he forgot to address Lord Roger with the customary 'my lord'.

"You heard." Lord Roger had the grace to look away. "I need…" He cleared his throat. "I would be grateful if you accompanied me. I'm not sure I can do this alone."

"And what about Kit? I've just promised to take her home."

"You do this and you are free to go – at least for some weeks," Lord Roger said.

"Begging your pardon, my lord, but that is not in your power to grant. It is Prince Edward I serve, not you." Lord Roger's request had Adam itching all over.

"I will talk to the prince." Lord Roger sounded dismissive.

"No, m'lord, that will not be necessary." Adam shifted on his feet. "Does his lady mother know about this…err…errand of yours?"

"Not as such." To Adam's dark amusement, Lord Roger looked flustered. "Best keep it that way," he added.

"Aye." To tell the queen Lord Roger was planning a visit to his wife was probably not wise. "When do we leave?"

"Tomorrow. Joan is at our manor in Pembridge, an easy enough ride from here." Lord Roger's eyes met his. "So, will you do it?"

Adam was tempted to say no, but he dearly loved Lady Joan, and in times to come there would be few opportunities to meet with her. "I must ask my lord's permission. And my wife's."

"Your wife's?" Lord Roger laughed softly. "So the hen rules the roost, does she?"

"No, but I gave her my word we'd set out for home tomorrow. She is entitled to hold me to it."

Lord Roger muttered an apology. "So, will you do me this favour? Please?"

Adam inclined his head. "I will."

They set off at dawn next morning, with Adam leaving behind a somewhat exasperated but forgiving Kit. Lord Roger, however, looked as if someone had fed him toadstools, and from his terse comments Adam was given to understand the queen had found out about his destination – and was less than pleased.

"Jealous – and green with it," Lord Roger muttered, and his mouth twitched into a proud smile.

"So then why, my lord?"

"Why? I have no choice," Lord Roger said. "I owe my lady wife a visit after everything she has suffered on my behalf."

"A visit?" Adam echoed. He rode Raven close enough that his leg brushed against Lord Roger's. "My lord, she deserves more than a visit. She deserves her husband back."

"Too late for that, I fear." Lord Roger gave a short bark of laughter. "Look at me: I am more fearful of braving my wife than of riding into battle."

"Lady Joan takes no prisoners, my lord," Adam said coldly.

"I know," Lord Roger replied. "And in this case, how can I possibly blame her?"

Some hours later they reached their destination, all of them chilled to the bone after the long ride through a fog so damp it left them soaked. A tired guardsman waved them through the half-open gate, and they were in a bailey, the sound of hooves echoing loudly in the enclosed space. Lord Roger dismounted and stood for some time, fiddling with his clothes. He looked magnificent, the cut of his robes accentuating the width of his shoulders, his winter cloak flung back to display its azure silk lining.

At the entrance to the manor, a threesome of young girls were standing, and it took Adam some time to understand who they were. Last time he'd seen them, Beatrice had been a toddler, while the girl he assumed to be Blanche had been a swaddled infant. And as to Agnes, the four-year-old he remembered was now a gangly nine-year-old, her previously glittering eyes shaded by years of confinement. He clenched his jaw: it was wrong, what had been done to the Mortimer daughters, incarcerated alone in various nunneries, separated from their mother and sisters.

Adam nudged Lord Roger. "My lord," he muttered. "Your daughters, I believe."

Lord Roger stilled. "Dearest Lord," he said in an undertone. "This I was not prepared for."

"My lord?" Adam smiled in the direction of Agnes.

"What do I say to them? How do I compensate them for years shut away from the world? How…" Lord Roger inhaled. "They had their childhood stolen from them. My girls, my precious daughters, were treated like minions by the nuns entrusted with their care. They've grown up hearing my name cursed, they—"

"Stop this," Adam interrupted. "It wasn't your fault."

"Of course it was my fault. I was fool enough to believe our king was honourable enough not to make war on defenceless children and women." He gave Adam an anguished look. "I risked them – and even worse, I would have done so again if I had to."

"Best not tell them that," Adam replied.

"No." Slowly, Lord Roger began moving in their

direction. The girls remained where they were, the two youngest openly gawking at this stranger who was their father. He came to a halt some yards from them. His mouth was working, he kept on blinking, and Adam placed a hand on his back, urging Lord Roger to close the distance.

"Agnes," Lord Roger breathed, widening his arms. "Come here, little squirrel."

At first, Agnes did not move. But then a shadow of a smile flew across her face, and moments later she was clinging to Lord Roger, weeping noisily. Adam looked away. Beside him, Lord Roger kneeled, arms wide as he enfolded all three of his daughters. Over their heads, Adam's gaze flew to the main door. There, a silent shape stood watching them. Lady Joan.

Had Adam been able to, he'd gladly have evaporated into thin air rather than witness this stilted and painful meeting between the two people he had loved the most during his youth. But once back on his feet, Lord Roger had taken a firm hold of him and together they entered the dark little hall, while Lady Joan sent the girls off elsewhere.

An ancient building, this hall still had a central hearth, the smoke spiralling upwards to the louvre. The stone flags were bare of any rush mats, and even through the thick soles of Adam's boots, the cold seeped through. The walls were adorned with heavy tapestries, there was a table and some chairs, and after having arranged for wine, Lady Joan retired to stand by the table, fingers tugging at the skirts of the cream kirtle that did little for her complexion.

Adam bowed deeply, grateful for this opportunity to compose his features. The lady before him bore little resemblance to the lady he conserved in his memories, her previously so womanly figure reduced to that of a stick-like waif, narrow wrists protruding from the embroidered cuffs of her heavy sleeves.

She was wearing a silk veil and wimple, but a heavy braid of grey hair hung in plain sight, and from the way Lord Roger winced, Adam suspected Lady Joan was taking the opportunity to show him what these last few years had cost her. While he had been safe and sound in France, his loyal lady wife had suffered years of deprivation, and her suffering must have been compounded by the rumours concerning her husband and the queen.

"My lady." Lord Roger approached her with his hands extended, as if to take hold of hers.

Lady Joan backed away. "My lord husband," she said stiffly, emphasising the last word. "Long have I awaited your visit."

Lord Roger looked away. "I'm sorry that I didn't come sooner, but I—"

She waved him quiet. "So now what?" she asked.

"I…" Lord Roger wet his lips. "I brought you a gift." He gestured, and Adam presented Lady Joan with the carefully wrapped bundle.

"A gift?" Lady Joan undid the cloth, revealing three books. Beautiful books, even Adam could see that, one of them reminiscent of Queen Jeanne's book of hours. For what seemed like an eternity, Lady Joan just stood there, studying the books.

"Thank you," she finally said. "And now what?" she repeated. "Will we return to Wigmore together, husband?" Yet again, she emphasised the last word. Yet again, Lord Roger looked away.

"Ah." Lady Joan nodded, and her hand closed on the uppermost book. "For close to five years, I have been held captive. Five years in which my life has shrunk to four walls and a constant fear – for you, for our children. Five years spent mostly on my knees, praying for your safe return, for the sanity of our daughters, locked away among the nuns, for the lives of our sons, held prisoners by the king. I have prayed and prayed, and what have you done? What?" The book flew through the air, hitting Lord Roger full in the face. "You, husband, have shamed me! Before the entire court in France, before our sniggering countrymen, you have paraded that whore of a queen as your mistress, while I – I, your loyal wife, mother to your children – have suffered on your behalf. And this…" She picked up the next book and hurled it at him. "This is how you see fit to repay me? By buying me books?"

"Joanie," Lord Roger said, "I—"

"You've dishonoured yourself," she interrupted coldly. "A man who sets such high store on his honour, and he makes himself the laughing stock of Europe by fawning on the she-wolf."

Lord Roger's eyes narrowed. "She is your queen, Joan. Best remember that."

"She is your queen too, Roger. Have you forgotten that bedding the queen is the equivalent of treason?"

"Treason?" Lord Roger made a dismissive gesture. "She loves me!"

"Oh, I am sure she does," Lady Joan replied, "but what about her son? What about the lad you have coerced into usurping his father's throne? Edward will not be a child forever, and God help you when he reaches his majority and starts looking for a scapegoat. What will he do to you when..." Lady Joan broke off, her narrow chest heaving.

"Am I to take it that you still care for me?" Lord Roger said with a little smile.

"Care for you?" The third book hit Lord Roger on his head. "I love you, Roger Mortimer, have loved you since the birth of our first son, but I swear on everything that is holy that I will never see you again – not unless you return to our marriage bed."

"I..." Lord Roger stuttered. "I can't, Joan. I am bound to her."

"Then go." Lady Joan pointed at the door. "Go, and never come back. You have broken my heart, and I cannot bear the sight of you."

"Joanie," Lord Roger said, "please. Surely we can find a compromise?"

"A compromise? You expect me to share my husband with that Whore of Babylon?"

"I expect you to be a dutiful wife," he snapped.

"A dutiful wife deserves a dutiful husband. I have none such." Lady Joan's voice quavered. "I would have you leave, my lord, because your presence causes me too much pain – and I have suffered enough on your behalf already."

Lord Roger strode towards her, but she held up her hand, arresting him. "Go," she repeated.

"Joan, it doesn't have to be like this," Lord Roger tried. "We could—"

"No." She gave him a tired look. "I cannot, Roger. I deserve more than the leftovers from the queen's trencher." Her tone made Adam wince.

"So is this goodbye?" Lord Roger said softly. "Will you shut me out of your life, Joanie?"

Lady Joan nodded, her mouth wobbling. Her eyes glittered with tears. "I have to. For my own sake."

"Ah, Joan!" The anguish in Lord Roger's voice had Adam wanting to comfort him – and her. "I never meant to hurt you so."

"Just go, Roger. Please."

"Joanie," he groaned.

"No." She crossed her arms over her chest, making her look even more abandoned. Their eyes met. Wordlessly, he held out his hand. Lady Joan remained where she was, a tear sliding down her cheek. With one last look at her, Lord Roger left. When Adam made as if to follow, Lady Joan called him back.

"Are you recovered?" she asked him, nodding in the direction of his foot.

"Well enough, my lady." He gave her a rueful smile. "But you, my lady, you've paid the heaviest price of us all."

Lady Joan shook her head. "The heaviest price will be paid by him – by my husband." She gripped Adam's hand. "Keep him safe, Adam. Like Icarus, he is flying far too close to the sun, and God help him if his wings begin to melt."

"I will do my best, my lady," Adam replied, feeling like a liar. What could he possibly do to protect Lord Roger from himself?

"You always do." Lady Joan released his hand. "God's speed, Adam – to you and him both."

Chapter 39

"She looked so…careworn." Adam wanted to say old, but it sounded too harsh, somehow.

"Lady Joan has suffered more than most," Kit said with a little sigh. "At least she is now reunited with her daughters."

"Yes." Adam nibbled at his lower lip, thinking that was not much comfort for Lady Joan. She deserved to have her husband back.

"Queen Isabella has been in a foul mood all day," Kit told him, folding together the last of her garments. "Over and over, she has repeated that men like Lord Mortimer are not served by having a jealous wife." She grimaced as she got to her feet, causing Adam to hurry over to steady her. "Nor, I would argue, by having a jealous mistress." She grinned.

Adam grinned back, but tapped his finger to her mouth in an admonishing gesture. "Shush, sweeting. In this case, it is the mistress who wields the power."

"Unfortunately." Kit shook her head. "It's not right, that he desert his wife like that. More than twenty years married, and he discards her like an old boot in favour of the queen."

"That's not fair. He loves the queen – he loves them both." Which was why Lord Roger had confided to Adam that he would do whatever it took to retain some sort of relationship with his wife – bar leaving the queen.

"But he is only married to one of them." Kit found her veil and arranged it over her hair, choosing an intricately woven circlet to hold it in place. "Ready?" She smiled again. "One last night, and tomorrow we ride home."

The hall was ablaze with candles, and at the high table sat the queen, with Lord Roger to her left and her son to the right. Prince Edward was scowling, his attention on his trencher and his eating knife rather than the company around him.

Fool, Adam thought; the lad was wearing his heart on his sleeve, those eyes of his dark with anger whenever they alighted on his mother or Lord Roger. It was too late to turn back the tide: King Edward was under lock and key and there was nothing his son could do to reverse this fact – not now. And by the time he was old enough to do so, he would not want to, Adam reflected, recognising in his young lord a hunger for power the lad himself was as yet unaware of.

"It will keep," Kit murmured beside him, and he turned to face his wife, who was smiling up at him.

"Are my thoughts so transparent?" he murmured.

"To me, yes. To Lord Mortimer as well, I believe." She nodded in the direction of Lord Roger, and Adam followed her eyes, only to meet Lord Roger's dark gaze. He bowed, and Lord Roger inclined his head before returning to his conversation with the Bishop of Lincoln.

Kit toyed with her food, listening with half an ear to Adam and Sir Henry, in deep discussion as to how to prepare their lord for kingship. From their hushed tones and the way they kept a cautious look on the people around them, she gathered what they were talking about was a sensitive issue, especially when Sir Henry muttered that once the prince had reached his majority, the best thing would be to exclude the queen from having any say in the actual ruling. Kit choked back a nervous laugh. Such talk was tantamount to treason – however much she agreed with Sir Henry. Adam's hand covered hers and gave it a reassuring little squeeze.

Once the tables had been cleared of food, the queen clapped her hands and presented the minstrels. Moments later, the high treble of a young boy filled the hall, joined by the lower voices of the two men who accompanied the singer on a small drum and a lute. A love song, Kit gathered, leaning back against a nearby pillar, but the words were unfamiliar to her.

"*Alas, I am left begging, for hope and relief,*" someone quoted in her ear, and Kit turned to meet the glittering eyes of Earl Thomas. "*Sweet, lovely lady, for God's sake do not think,*" he continued, singing along with the chorus, "*that any has sovereignty over my heart, but you alone.*"

"Are you wooing me, Earl Thomas?" Kit asked, trying to sound disapproving.

"If I was, would it avail me?" he asked in reply, smiling at her in a way that had his eyes crinkling at the corners. A very handsome man, dark where her Adam was fair, elegant and powerful.

"No," she replied. "But I don't mind you trying."

Earl Thomas burst out laughing. "Really, Lady Kit. What would your husband say?" He moved closer, the heavy skirts of his long robes brushing against hers. Kit inhaled, drawing in his scent. Mugwort and lavender, cedar and rosemary, and was that the tang of lemon?

"Having problems with moths, my lord?"

"Not me," he replied, just as low, "but my clothes…" He lifted his shoulders. Kit laughed. "You're leaving us," he added.

"I'm going home," she corrected.

"Ah yes, to that little manor you're so fond of." He smiled at her, and his eyes burnt into hers. "I have many manors, Lady Kit."

"You also have a wife, my lord – and I have a husband whom I love above all others."

"Do you now?" Adam said drily from behind her. "It gladdens my heart to hear it." He bowed in greeting to Earl Thomas. "My lord."

"Adam." The earl mumbled an excuse and moved off.

"He is too fond of you," Adam growled.

"I like him," Kit said. The earl made her feel attractive, and she enjoyed their mild flirtation.

"So do I," Adam admitted, "but I will not have him drooling over my wife."

"Adam!" Kit slapped his arm. "He never drools."

Adam didn't respond. But he spent the remainder of the evening at her side, ensuring no man had the opportunity to converse with her alone.

They left at dawn next morning. For a moment, Adam held in his horse, looking back at Hereford, the little town still fast asleep in the cold winter morning. The huge Cathedral seemed to soar several yards above the rest of the town buildings, its bells ringing for prime.

"A new dawn for England," he said, resting his chin on Kit's head. He studied the eastern horizon, streaked with bands of pink cloud. Yet another cold, bright winter day, and somewhere in the castle to the left of the cathedral, his young prince and master would soon wake to one more day in the shadow of his formidable mother – and Lord Roger. He shivered despite his thick winter cloak. The prince would not bide for long in the background, and both baron and queen could come to rue the day they used him as their unwitting pawn.

"Better for all," Kit said, leaning back against his chest.

"Better?" He buried his nose in her hair and inhaled her scent. "I am not so sure it will be better, sweeting. What have we done but replace Despenser with Mortimer?"

"Lord Mortimer is the better man – surely you believe in him?"

"Aye – for now." Adam tightened his hold on her. "But power corrupts, and what began as an honest intent to redress suffered wrongs and injuries may end in something else altogether."

She turned in his arms and cupped his cheeks. "And where does that leave you?"

"Me?" He laughed softly. "It leaves me torn in two, sweeting." He kissed her veiled head. "But for now, we leave all that behind. Now we make for home." He turned Raven due north, away from the sunrise. Beside them, their elongated shadows walked. Behind them, Lord Roger and his lady love still slept, safe in the knowledge that they had won. But none of that mattered now, Adam thought, tightening his hold on his wife. For now, all that mattered was that they were going home. At last.

They arrived at Tresaints just before vespers. The ride had been difficult for Kit, and Adam had insisted on a plodding pace, reprimanding himself for not having arranged a litter.

"I didn't want one," Kit had told him.

"No, but you have the sense of a hen at times. I should have insisted."

"I hate travelling by litter. It makes me feel as if I'm buried alive." Kit pulled the heavy cloak tighter round her shoulders and rested back against him.

"It does?" Adam's free hand slid down to rest on her belly. "And yet you're full of life."

It was a relief to slide off Raven's broad back, and a joy to see Mabel come trotting towards her, that old wrinkled face wreathed in a smile so broad Kit could see she'd lost yet another tooth. And behind Mabel came Meg, even if Kit would never have recognised her baby daughter in this delicate little girl, two huge blue eyes dominating a small face that ended in a pointed little chin.

"She looks just like you," Adam said, crouching down to greet his daughter. Meg hung back, gripping Mabel's skirts.

"Like me?" Kit tried to crouch as well, but ended up kneeling in the dirt, one hand extended to the child.

"Except for the hair." He smiled at her. "Fortunately. It suffices with one red-headed female in the house."

"Go on," Mabel said, nudging Meg. "That's your mama and papa."

"Papa?" Meg said, and her voice was surprisingly husky. She was still clutching at Mabel's skirts, peeking at them from under the wisps of dark hair that had escaped her coif.

Adam made as if to lift her, and Meg shrank back.

"She's shy," Mabel said, sounding apologetic. She stroked Meg's head and the child burrowed even closer.

"She doesn't know us." Kit tried to sound matter-of-fact, when all she wanted to do was grab her daughter and hold her close, whispering her name. With Adam's help, she got back on her feet. "We must give her time." Her gaze strayed to the bailey beyond, her gaze leaping from one building to the other. With a little start, she realised she was looking for Tom, hoping to see his distinctive fair head and sturdy little body running towards them. No Tom. Kit's throat itched with repressed sobs. No Tom. And there, in the midst of their bailey, it struck her that she would never see her Tom again. Never.

"Sweeting?" Adam's concerned voice penetrated the fog of loss that shrouded her. She turned towards him, and he held her to him, shushing as she pressed her face against his tunic. "I know," he whispered, "I miss him too." It helped. With an effort, Kit straightened up. She cleared her throat and managed to smile at John, who bowed deeply as he welcomed them home. After John came his grandsons, and there was Mall, as round and florid as ever, beaming when she greeted them.

"Stockfish," she said in reply to Adam's unspoken question. "With plenty of butter," she added at his crestfallen face. "And there's a kale pie as well."

"Ale?" he asked, and Mall nodded, promising to send one of the maids over to the hall as soon as possible.

"Coming?" Adam was already making for the hall. A gust of wind lifted his hair and made Kit shiver despite her heavy cloak. The December day carried a breath of snow and frost in the air, and the light that spilled from the open door promised warmth. Home. He held out his hand to her, and she took it, feeling the reassuring strength of his fingers as they closed around hers. They were home. For now, she added, throwing a look towards the east. Soon enough, they'd be recalled to court, but for now she shoved aside all thoughts of the prince and Lord Mortimer, the queen and the imprisoned king.

Historical Note

When Roger Mortimer escaped from the Tower in 1323, Edward II and Despenser went into a frenzy. It became paramount to cleanse the realm of England of any potential traitors, a.k.a. Mortimer supporters, and so a large number of men were hauled before the assizes, in many cases subjected to crippling fines, but just as often found guilty of treason and executed. Edward was taking no chances, and when he learnt that Mortimer had been welcomed by the French king, one can to some extent understand if this led to him being suspicious of his wife – who also happened to be the French king's sister.

Things weren't helped by the infected situation in Gascony. In principle, Edward found himself at war with France – yet again, his French wife was viewed with some suspicion. This may be one of the reasons behind Edward's decision to deprive Isabella of her income in 1324, but in retrospect all he managed to do was alienate his wife, even more so when he exiled her French retainers, some of whom had been with her since she first arrived in England in 1308.

The war in Gascony went from bad to worse. Charles de Valois crushed the English forces, and when faced with the possibility of losing his French lands, Edward had no option but to treat for peace. Suddenly, his French wife became an asset again, which was why she was sent to France in early 1325 to negotiate with her brother.

Whether or not Mortimer and Isabella were already in contact at the time is difficult to judge. I have taken the liberty of suggesting they were – I wanted there to be an element of cloak-and-dagger. Whatever the case, Mortimer was definitely in contact with other disgruntled Englishmen, and as the Despensers tightened their stranglehold on England, growing ever happier and fatter, the grumblings grew.

Having Isabella in France may have been an irritant to Edward, but in herself she posed little danger to him – the same goes for Mortimer, who would have found it difficult to raise an army to invade England on his own. It was only when Edward chose to send his son, Edward of Windsor, to France to do homage in his place that Isabella got her hands on the weapon required to bring down the hated Despensers – and her husband. The heir to the English throne arrived in France invested with the Duchy of Aquitaine, which in itself generated an important revenue stream. More importantly, the prince's hand in marriage could be bartered for men and ships. And finally, with the young prince at her side, Isabella could paint the invasion as a legitimate venture, intended to release the poor English from the triple yoke of king and two Despensers.

Obviously, Edward was fully aware of the fact that he took a risk when sending over his son. In fact, right up to the date of departure he dithered, one day deciding he would go himself, the other saying he would send his son. Hugh Despenser pleaded with him not to go – he was fearful for his own safety should the king leave him behind. Probably a correct assessment, and ultimately Hugh's fear convinced the king to stay home. Bad, bad decision, in retrospect.

Some of the portrayed events in *Days of Sun and Glory* are entirely fictitious, starting, of course, with Adam's and Kit's adventures. Likewise, I have never heard Prince Edward tried to scale a gatehouse, nor have I ever read he sickened in the autumn of 1324 – but I am thinking the poor boy suffered from the growing tension between his parents and maybe this would have led to physical symptoms. Also, Despenser did offer a substantial reward to whoever would bring him proof of Mortimer's death, but he was not, as far as I know, ever foolish enough to slip over to France to attempt to accomplish this himself. But then Despenser was not a coward, so maybe he did...

As to settings, I have taken some liberties: as an example, King Edward spent April (and Easter) 1325 in King's Langley, not Westminster.

While I hope I've managed to breathe life into Adam de Guirande, his wife Kit, his brother Will and all the rest of the Guirande household, these are invented characters as is Godfrey of Broseley. Richard de Monmouth, Kit's brother, did exist – but I have chosen to give him a family he would probably not have recognised. At all.

The King's Greatest Enemy continues in

Under the Approaching Dark

King Edward was standing by the window when Mortimer and Adam entered the room. It was freezing, the fire in the hearth a pitiful source of heat in a room where the shutters stood wide open, the northerly wind gusting snowflakes onto the floor closest to the window.

Henry of Lancaster had provided a sizeable chamber for his royal captive, but had not gone out of his way to furnish it beyond necessities. A large bed, covered by an assortment of blankets and pelts, one armchair facing the hearth, a table, a stool, on the table a goblet, a pitcher, a plate with a half-eaten roll of bread…The room reeked of loneliness, of hours spent in solitude – a most unfamiliar and uncomfortable sensation for their former king, Adam supposed, suppressing a twinge of pity.

"Mortimer." King Edward did not turn fully to face them.

"My lord." Mortimer bowed, and Adam followed suit before hastening over to fasten the shutters.

"What do you want?" The king sounded tired. "Come to complain about the she-wolf?"

Mortimer bristled, dark eyes narrowing. "Your son refuses to accept the crown unless you willingly abdicate."

"Good lad." Edward ambled over to the hearth, found a poker and dug into the embers. "So now what? Aim you to put a leash on me?"

"No." Lord Roger kept a cautious look on the poker, as did Adam. "You abdicate, of course."

"I do?" The king brought the poker down, hard. It made Adam jump, but Lord Roger didn't as much as flinch. "Why should I?"

"Why?" In a swift move, Lord Roger grabbed the poker

and threw it into the corner. "Because otherwise I will set myself up as king."

"You wouldn't dare! No one would accept it." Edward of Caernarvon drew himself up to his considerable height – he overtopped all but Adam – and glared.

"No? Do you wish to put it to the test? Of course, first I must rid myself of the other contestants, so both your sons must die, and your daughters I will force to take the veil." Mortimer grinned, and in the flickering light he looked akin to the Devil. Adam wiped his hand on his tunic: was Lord Roger serious?

"You wouldn't!" Their former liege shook his head, hands smoothing at the fine fabric of his robe. For all his bare surroundings, Lancaster was ensuring his prisoner was adequately dressed, his surcoat trimmed with fur, the robe beneath in velvet. Somewhat sombre, the black material caused the king to look wan and ailing.

"You think me less ambitious than your precious Despenser?" Lord Roger advanced on the king, who shuffled backwards, his gaze never leaving Mortimer's hands. "What would he have done, do you think?"

"He would never have threatened my children! Never!"

"No, he threatened other men's children instead," Lord Roger replied, and the king deflated, sitting down on the chest at the foot of the bed.

"I loved him," he murmured. "Loved him so much, and now he is dead, and I will never…" He bit off the rest of the sentence, raising a shaking hand to his hair – far more grey now than fair, but vigorous and curly.

"You loved him too much – more than you loved your children or your kingdom, and much more than you loved your honour. A king cannot allow himself such passion."

"Honour? Passion?" Edward's face hardened into a mask of royal displeasure. "And tell me, is it honour or passion that has you bedding my wife every night? What does Lady Joan think of your honour? What, pray, does my son think of it – and what does he think of his whore of a mother, that French—"

The slap resounded through the room. Adam moved forward, hand on his sword, not sure if his intention was to defend the king or save Lord Roger from himself, because from Mortimer's compressed mouth and the way his nostrils dilated, Adam feared the man was about to fly into one of his memorable – but uncharacteristic – rages. With a curse, Mortimer turned his back on them. Adam counted to six, and then Lord Roger turned to face them, his features fixed in a bland expression.

"So," he said. "Will you do it?"

"Do what?" Edward gave him a puzzled look, a hand to his flaming cheek.

"Safeguard the crown for your son by abdicating." Lord Roger sounded bored.

"Do I have a choice?" Edward's voice shook.

"There's always a choice – but one must abide by the consequences." Lord Roger stretched his lips into a wolfish grin. Silence stretched between them. The king and his baron glowered at each other. Finally, Lord Roger shrugged and made for the door. "Parliament has already made its decision." He threw it open and stood back, indicating Edward should precede him.

"Where are you taking me?" Edward retreated, the folds of his black robe merging with the shadows.

"To the hall – there is an entire delegation waiting for you there." Mortimer regarded his former king. "Sire," he added mockingly.

"No." Edward planted his feet wide and lowered his head.

"No?" Mortimer fingered the hilt of his sword. "And what makes you think you have a choice? Either you walk on your own, or I'll have you dragged there." Mortimer leaned his shoulders against the wall and waited. Edward looked from him to Adam before he succumbed.

"Very well. Lead the way."

"Oh, no. After you." Mortimer made a little bow.

The Author

When Anna is not stuck in the 14th century, chances are she'll be visiting in the 17th century, more specifically with Alex and Matthew Graham, the protagonists of the best-selling, multiple award winning, series The Graham Saga. This series is the story of two people who should never have met − not when she was born three centuries after him. A fast-paced blend of love, drama and adventure, The Graham Saga will carry you from Scotland to the New World and back again.

For more information about Anna and her books, please visit www.annabelfrage.com or pop by her blog https://annabelfrage.wordpress.com